The
Summ
Getaway

The Summer Getaway

TILLY TENNANT

Bookouture

Published by Bookouture in 2018

An imprint of StoryFire Ltd.

Carmelite House
50 Victoria Embankment
London EC4Y 0DZ

www.bookouture.com

ISBN: 978-1-78681-377-0
eBook ISBN: 978-1-78681-376-3

For Mrs Jackson, who taught me how a book can be so much more than words on a page.

Chapter One

'It's a hell of a lot of money.'

Ashley frowned at the letter. Addressed to her daughter Molly, there were deep creases where it had been opened out, read and refolded many times, though this was the first time Ashley had seen it. She looked up at Molly, who was perched anxiously on the edge of the sofa.

'But it's the best, most amazing music school!' Molly said. 'Seriously, Mum, how else am I going to get into a decent orchestra?'

'You can take music at A level at the sixth-form college. I thought we'd already agreed that.'

Molly folded her arms and pouted. Ashley knew that look well – she'd practised the art of interpreting it for around fifteen years now, ever since her daughter had been old enough to pull it.

'It's not as idiotic as it sounds,' Ashley insisted. 'Other kids do it, and it's good enough for them.'

'The course isn't the same… the conservatoire has teachers from all over the world. Proper teachers who've performed at huge concerts. They know everything.'

'Your music teacher says the course at the college is very good. The teachers are qualified, otherwise they wouldn't be there.'

'It's OK, but…'

Ashley let out a sigh. God she wanted to give her daughter this – of course she did. She wanted more than anything to give her daughter all the opportunities she herself had been denied. She didn't want Molly to end up like she had – pregnant at eighteen and going nowhere fast. Ashley had had dreams once, just like everyone else. And here she was, sixteen years later and not a scrap of them left to show they'd ever existed.

'It's just… of course you know I'd let you go in a heartbeat if I could find the money but…'

Molly stood up and took the letter from her, screwing it into her palm. 'I should never have gone to the audition.'

'You should have talked to me about it first.'

'But I wanted to surprise you; I thought you'd be so proud if I got in.'

'And I am! God, I can't put into words how proud you make me every day, and I would move heaven and earth—'

'It doesn't matter.' Molly shook her head, her shoulders slumping. 'I suppose I can check out the college music department. It's probably not that bad…'

Ashley turned to the window. She hated saying no so much. It wasn't like Molly was asking for overpriced clothes or an unnecessary new phone or permission to go to an inappropriate party – she was asking for a chance at an amazing future; Ashley wished that for her with all her heart and would sacrifice anything to give it to her. But they both had to accept that some things were out of her control.

'I'll see what I can do,' she said quietly. God knew what but there had to be a way, didn't there? For a chance this big she owed it to her daughter to try. 'Moll…?'

Getting no reply she turned to face the sofa. But Molly had slunk out, taking the letter with her.

In the end it had seemed sensible to give Molly a bit of space. Ashley had gone to make a coffee and was now sitting at the kitchen table, gripping the mug as it cooled in front of her. Staring at an invisible spot on the wall, she gazed into a past she'd reflected on so many times before, though never with such profound regret as she did today. She'd never wish undone what she'd done that night, because she would never have had Molly, the best and most incredible thing that had ever happened to her. But there were plenty of other things she would have done differently. Maybe she'd have found out the boy's surname for a start before she'd leapt into bed with him. *Slut* was what her mother had called her in a fit of temper when Ashley had revealed the news. *Stupid, stupid slut.* She hadn't meant it, of course, but it was only what plenty of other people were thinking. How could you not know his name? she'd asked. How could you not know where he lives? How could you not have his phone number? How drunk were you?

Even though not all the things she'd told her mum were entirely true, Ashley had no sensible answers for any of these questions. She'd asked plenty of her own too, long after her mum had stopped, when she'd lain in bed with a hand to her tummy as her baby kicked and wriggled inside her. Would the boy have stuck by her even had Ashley been able to track him down armed with only the scantest information? Perhaps not, but at least she'd have known where to go when her daughter needed exorbitant music-school fees to realise a dream she'd had since she could remember, a moment she'd been working hard towards since she'd first picked up a battered old violin in primary school. Her biggest chance to make the kind of life for herself that Ashley could only dream of was slipping away, and it all boiled down to money.

It would be easy to blame it on circumstances beyond their control – that the one and only scholarship had been snapped up by a girl from Japan who'd been playing practically since birth, that the school would have been beyond the reach of most working-class people, that maybe it was better to start small anyway – but Ashley couldn't shake the idea that, when all was said and done, her own mistakes were the bottom line. Molly would fail, and it was Ashley's fault.

She closed her eyes and it was 2001. She was sitting in a bar in Ibiza on her first and, as it turned out, only foreign holiday without parents. The air was sultry, heavy with a mass of synthetic perfumes and deodorants, of cocktails and hormones, pulsing with the rapid beat of dance music, lights low and hypnotic. Her best friend, Abigail, had gone to the toilet and that's when *he'd* come over. He'd seemed shy, sweet… not the sort of boy who'd leave you pregnant and disappear. He'd made her laugh, and he was good-looking – the kind of good-looking that at first was unassuming but got steadily better with every shot of vodka she downed as they chatted.

His friend came over and Abigail returned, and the four of them had a drinking contest. Who'd won? It didn't matter. They'd danced together, and he'd smelt so good. She recalled lifting his shirt and caressing his back – the skin smooth and taut. Those chocolate eyes that seemed so at odds with his sandy hair, though they'd pulled her in anyway. She'd thought she could see his soul in there, and she'd thought it was good. They'd kissed and it had been like a thousand volts, setting her on fire. They'd staggered back to her apartment and they'd kissed again on the porch. She'd asked him in for more drinks and in minutes they'd been naked in her bed. It had been strangely beautiful, and she'd been in love – of that she was certain. It was crazy to be in love with a man you'd just met, but it had happened. She'd wanted to see him again, and he'd written his phone number on a scrap of paper before rushing out at the crack of dawn for a flight he couldn't miss. He'd told her she was incredible, that he desperately wanted to see her again when she got back to England, and he'd left her with a fiery kiss.

But she never saw him again. The phone number he'd left led her to a haulage firm. She had only Molly's chocolate eyes, which showed her moods as plainly as if she'd opened them out as a book, a certain look, the odd turn of the head, to remember him by.

And a name. Haydon.

Chapter Two

Ella tucked a strawberry-blonde lock of hair behind an ear and grinned up at her dad. 'You want some?' she asked, offering him a spoonful of her ice-cream sundae.

Haydon leaned forward with his mouth open to swoop in and capture the prize, only for Ella to whip it out of his way, giggling. Haydon grinned. It was a well-rehearsed piece, something they'd done a thousand times before, but it never got boring no matter how much older Ella got. Perhaps they both saw it as a link, a connection back to the times when their family was together, when they were strong and happy and nothing could break them.

'You're such a tease,' he said.

Ella grinned through a mouthful of ice cream.

'So, what's the news?' he asked, lifting his coffee cup to his lips. 'Still madly in love with Jack in Miss Palmer's class?'

'Ugh!' Ella screwed up her face. 'Are you serious?'

'I saw you…' Haydon laughed. 'You were all goggly-eyed when I dropped you off at the school disco.'

'It's not a disco, and no I wasn't.'

'If it's not a disco, what is it?'

Ella shrugged. 'A party.'

'Isn't that the same thing?'

'Seriously?'

'Oh, OK. But you did look as if you liked him a smidgen.'

'No I didn't,' Ella fired back but this time Haydon detected a little blush. His baby was growing up, and it was too fast for his liking, but he couldn't say so, not unless he wanted the eye-rolling disapproval reserved for his full-on soppy dad moments. He seemed to have a lot of those lately too – at least, Ella kept telling him so. But he was missing so much. Every weekend Ella seemed to have leapt ahead in years; every weekend with her reminded him that soon this little girl would be gone and he'd have only known highlights, never the full picture, of how she became the wonderful adult he was sure she was going to be.

He'd been forced to respect her mother Janine's decision to divorce him, and he'd had to quietly accept her new partner Kevin's arrival. He'd even borne the news that Kevin was moving in with them after only six months of dating his ex-wife with a gritty silence that belied his urge to shake her and ask her what the hell she thought she was doing. She hardly knew this man, and yet he was going to be living with her and Ella, and there was nothing Haydon could do about it. He couldn't be there to protect them if things went wrong, and he wasn't allowed to offer an opinion unless he wanted to face Janine's rage. And even if he could have dealt with that, all it would make her do was clam up, so it would hardly be helpful in the end. All he could do was watch helplessly from the sidelines, glean as much information as he could from Ella's weekend visits and hope that all the reports continued to be good. So far, Ella seemed to get along with Kevin just fine, but somewhere deep inside, though Haydon knew he ought to be glad about this, he was also saddened beyond words.

'So I don't need to go round to his house and look intimidating while I give him the dad talk?'

'No!' Ella cried, looking mortified. But then she broke into a smile. 'Very funny, Dad.'

'So, what do you want to do for your birthday next month? Your mum's OK'd the weekend and fourteen is a pretty big deal. I thought we might go out to do something. Maybe bring your friends? How about I rent somewhere for a party?'

Ella shrugged. 'Kevin's renting out Pizza Express for my friends. We're going to have a pizza-making party. And then we're all sleeping over on his houseboat.'

'He has a houseboat?'

'Uh huh. He's just bought it.'

'He *just* bought a houseboat. Just like that? No big deal?'

'I guess. He just saw it and said he liked the look of it.'

'Where is it?'

'Somewhere in Norfolk.'

'Norfolk? Is your mother going to stay on it?'

Ella nodded. 'Says she can't wait to see it.'

'Funny. She always said she hated the idea of sleeping on a boat whenever I mentioned a boating holiday.'

'I suppose she changed her mind,' Ella said blithely, licking her spoon. 'They're looking at things all the time right now. He wants to buy a house too.'

Haydon swallowed hard. 'For you guys to live in together?'

'Yes.'

'Close to where you are now?' Haydon asked, dread of the reply bubbling up.

'In London.'

He paused, staring at Ella as she continued with her ice cream, seemingly unconcerned by the idea of moving to London. The one answer he hadn't wanted was the one he'd somehow known he'd get.

'And you're happy about that?'

'I don't know. It's not really up to me. Mum says I'll still be able to see my friends because the train journey is only an hour. And I suppose living in London would be cool.'

'But… how will I see you?'

'I'm sorry.' She looked up now, for the first time showing signs of awareness that the news she was relaying wasn't going down well.

Haydon ground his teeth. 'It's not your fault. Your mum should have talked to me about this.'

'She said she was going to when she knew for sure. I think she's still trying to decide.'

Haydon pondered this for a moment. Ella was backtracking now, he could tell. It sounded to him like Janine had already decided.

'On whether to move?' he asked. 'Or on other things?'

'About moving. But Kevin says the commute to London takes too long out of his day, and he wants to spend the extra time with Mum, but he doesn't want to lose his job in London because it pays a lot. He wants to show her some houses to help her make up her mind, and the photos had her excited, so I think it's going to happen.'

Ella's phone bleeped and she unlocked the screen, smiling as she recognised the sender of the text. Probably a schoolfriend, Haydon mused vaguely as he watched her. He sensed that chasm open again, that space between them that took her further and further from his life as she grew up without him. He wasn't around enough for her as it was, but if she moved to London, how much more difficult would it be? But he had never felt so powerless to stop it. What right did he have to ask Janine to live her life according to his own wishes? She was entitled to be happy and, as much as Haydon didn't like it, she had a right to fall in love again. Maybe Kevin would be able to get right what he'd clearly got so horribly wrong. Maybe Kevin would be the one to put the smile back on Janine's face, the one Haydon had never noticed was fading until it was too late. He'd thought they'd had a good marriage until the bombshell he'd never even suspected was coming. And then it had all been too late and too hard to fix – at least that was what Janine had kept telling him.

'You like Kevin?' he asked.

'Huh?' Ella looked up from her phone.

'You like Kevin? I mean, if you're going to be living in London with him then you should at least be happy about it.'

'He's nice,' Ella said.

'He treats you and Mum well?'

'He brings her a ton of flowers every week. Mum says she hasn't got the heart to tell him about her hay fever so she just takes an extra tablet. He got me a new iPad too.'

'But you're going to be living in his house far away from here… Ella, do you really understand how massive that is?'

Ella frowned. 'I'm not a baby. Mum says it's not that far away. She says the train is only an hour.'

'It's…' Haydon paused. How could he explain that distance was about more than physical space? It was about emotional and family connections being separated by more than miles. It was about the feeling of having someone close by who was on your side and would be there for you in an instant should you need them. It was about Haydon not losing his daughter to some slick banker who wanted to replace him in her life. When she needed a cuddle, or advice, or something as simple as extra pocket money, it would be Kevin, not Haydon, on hand to give it. And soon Kevin would slot into the Dad-shaped hole in her world, and Haydon would become obsolete, surplus to requirements, and she wouldn't need him any more.

And if Ella didn't need him, then who would?

Chapter Three

'What's that thing called?'

'Mum, I have no idea what you mean.' Ashley rubbed at her temples, phone clamped to her ear.

'You know… lots of people pay for the thing you need and you promise them something in return… Jane's daughter did it to make that short film…'

'Crowdfunding?'

'That's the one. Why can't you do that?'

'What on earth can we offer in return? It's not like Molly will have something to give people when they donate. At least, not for years.'

'Do you have to give something to them?'

'I'm pretty sure that's the way it works.'

There was a sigh from the other end of the line. 'Why won't you let Maurice help? You'd save all this worry and trouble if you'd just let him help, and he wants to.'

'I can't—'

'He thinks of you as family now and he's happy to give you the money; at least let him pay for the first year so you have more time to find the rest. When you can manage it, if you really feel terrible about it, you can pay him back, though he won't miss the money, so I'm quite sure he wouldn't nag about it.'

'Whether he misses the money is not the issue, Mum. I've never wanted handouts to bring Molly up and I'm not about to start taking them now.'

'It's not a handout – it's an investment in Molly's future. And you can't keep punishing yourself for a mistake you think you made all those years ago by refusing every scrap of help from everyone. If anyone was to blame for what happened it's that boy, the one you met on that stupid holiday… But that's all water under the bridge now. Molly is my granddaughter and don't you think I want to see her do well? She's got this wonderful talent – and I don't have a clue where she got her musical ability from because the rest of us are tone-deaf – and why shouldn't she have the best chance to show the world what she can do?'

'I'm not taking Maurice's money.'

'Would you take it if it were mine?'

'But I know it wouldn't be yours because you don't have that much cash.'

'How do you know?' Sue squeaked indignantly. Ashley, despite the nature of the conversation, had to hold in a laugh.

'Because I grew up with you, don't forget. We've never been rich enough to pay for things like music-school fees.'

'We never needed to before. Maybe we'd have found the money if we'd needed to.'

'Mum, I *know* it's Maurice's money you're offering, and that's why I'm saying no. And I'm going to say no every time you bring it up so you might as well stop. I understand why Molly phoned you with this, but I wish she hadn't because I haven't even had a chance to see if I can reach a solution yet without involving everyone else.'

'So what are you going to do? Last month you couldn't afford the new brakes on the car…'

'I'll think of something… Maybe I'll call the building society about remortgaging the house.'

'No!'

'Why not? It seems the simplest and cheapest way.'

'It's a one-way ticket to disaster!'

Ashley sniffed. 'Lots of people do it.'

'And lots of people get into trouble doing it. More debt is not the answer.'

'It's the only answer I have.'

'I've told you—'

'I know,' Ashley cut in. 'And I've told you that I just can't take Maurice's money.'

'Bloody stubborn. Proud and pig-headed…'

'I wonder where I get that from.'

There was a another sigh on the line, but Ashley could hear the exasperated smile in it.

'Don't be angry,' she said. 'I know you and Maurice mean well but I can't be indebted… not to anyone. Me and Moll, we'll make our own way in the world or not at all.'

'I'm not sure Molly agrees with you on that. And what's the point in being so noble about it when there's a simple solution that would give everyone the outcome they want? I wish you'd swallow this stupid, stubborn pride, just once, and let people help.'

Ashley paused, her gaze wandering to the ceiling. Upstairs, Molly was in her room, probably having to talk herself into a future that she didn't want, a plan B that she'd have to make the best of but one that was a million miles away from the plan A she'd dreamed of.

'I'll give it some thought,' she said finally.

'I'm not going to let it drop, so don't think you can say that and I'll conveniently forget about it.'

'I would never suggest such a thing,' Ashley replied with a wry smile.

'There was something else I wanted to talk to you about while I have you on the phone,' her mum added.

'Go on.'

'Now I don't want you to start telling me how you can't afford it…'

'Mum!'

'OK, Maurice's aunt Violette has a big birthday coming up and the whole family – I mean the *whole* family – are going to be there. That means he'd like us to go.'

'But we're not really family—'

'As far as Maurice is concerned we are. He couldn't have children with his first wife, and he's very fond of you and Molly; you're as close to a daughter and granddaughter as he has, you know that.'

'I know, but—'

'Please. I know you're absolutely fixated on this idea that you have to pay your own way, and I know you won't be able to afford this, but it's not fair to Maurice to turn us down flat. For once, put your pride to one side and think about the greater good. Yes, it will mean someone has to help you to pay for your travel down to the South of France, but it also means that you'll make Maurice, his aunt and the whole family very happy by being there.'

'Is it really such a big deal?'

'She's a hundred. I'd say that's a pretty big deal. Let's be honest, she may well never see another birthday beyond this, and that's why they're making such a big fuss. Besides, you've never seen Maurice's home in Saint-Raphaël… it's beautiful. And surely Molly deserves to see it even if you don't feel you do?'

Ashley stared at her slippered feet. She supposed it would go some way to making up to Molly for all the disappointment she'd had to endure of late. And it was certainly a lot less expensive than two years of fees for a prestigious music school. Neither could she argue with her mother's assertions that a centenary was a pretty big occasion in anyone's book. So when you looked at it that way it seemed only fair to make an effort to go.

'OK, Mum, but here's the deal – Molly and I are travelling separately and we're doing it on a budget. And when I get some money I'm paying you back for anything I might need to borrow. And no swanky hotels, so don't even think about trying to book one on the sly for us – we'll make do with a hostel somewhere.'

'I don't know where you get your stinginess from.'

'I'm not stingy, I'm frugal – I have to be.'

'You don't have to be anything…' Sue let out a sigh. 'We'll be staying with Maurice's aunt, anyway, and her house is huge. I expect she'll have room for two more small ones.'

'I'd feel bad about putting her out.'

'I don't think for a minute she'll be put out, and she does so want everyone there. Maurice can ask her, but I don't expect there'll be any problems.'

'As long as it's no bother and people aren't just pretending we're not under their feet.'

'That means you'll come?'

'When is it? I've got to check the holiday list at work and clear it with my boss.'

'Next month. I'll ping over the dates we're travelling when Maurice finalises them. As for travelling separately you might as well come with us as Maurice is planning to drive down to the South of France and there's room in the car. It will save all of us a lot of money.'

'A road trip? Through France?' Ashley stifled a grin. She'd told her mum that she was only going to this party to make Maurice happy but already she could feel the sun on her face, smell the lavender as they drove through a rolling purple landscape, taste the fresh croissants and seafood. She hadn't chosen this trip, and she hated the fact that it would set her back financially, but she couldn't deny that she was more ready for a holiday than she'd ever been. The last time she'd been away with Molly was a soggy week in a caravan in Bognor Regis where Molly had mostly sat messaging friends on her phone and Ashley had been forced to work her way through the extensive but very crappy library that the caravan owners had left in a cupboard for their guests. She'd hardly returned feeling rested, and since then, whenever a UK holiday was mentioned again, Molly had looked horrified at the prospect.

'We might as well make it one,' Sue said. 'Go on, tell me you're not a teensy bit excited…'

'Don't be daft. And remember that I can't say yes until I've checked with work.'

'But if it's OK with them then it's OK with you?'

'I suppose so.'

'Brilliant!' Sue squeaked. 'Maurice will be thrilled!'

*

Haydon gritted his teeth and swallowed the urge to swear. The last thing he needed was to send Ella home with reports of a foul-mouthed and impatient father when he really ought to be making the very best impression. He needed to keep Janine onside if he was going to persuade her that moving to London was a bad idea for the future of his relationship with Ella and for Ella's experience of a fractured household.

The van ahead inched forward and then the angry red of its brake lights pierced the rain on the windscreen.

'Seriously,' Haydon muttered, 'what's the bloody hold-up?'

'Will you be late, Dad?'

He forced a smile for Ella, sitting beside him with one earphone in, the other hanging down her chest. Not for the first time he marvelled that the volume of the music coming from the unoccupied earphone wasn't causing blood to come from her nose, though he knew better than to say so. He'd done that once before and the look she'd given him almost shrivelled him on the spot. It was classical music – Rachmaninoff, perhaps, though he couldn't quite place it – and he supposed that at least it was something cultured.

'You're learning to play that piece?' he asked.

Ella nodded.

'I could help.'

'Yeah, but you don't play piano.'

'I could help with the basics.'

'I don't think they'd be the same.'

Haydon turned his attention back to the road. The car inched forward again before juddering to another halt as the rain slammed into the windscreen. He turned up the heaters to combat the mist that was now joining it to seriously hamper his view of the road – or rather traffic – ahead.

'What time do you have to get to your student?' Ella asked.

'Are you worried I might not make it?'

'Worried for you, Dad. I know you get stressed about it.'

'You're too young to be worrying about my stress. You've plenty of years ahead to worry about things – enjoy the lack of a need to worry about things now while you can.'

'But what time?'

'I've got an hour,' he lied. 'Don't panic. Besides, the lad's so bloody bad if he had a lesson every day for the next fifty years he'd still make his cello sound like a wardrobe being scraped across a giant blackboard.'

Ella giggled. 'You must hate teaching him,' she said.

'A little. I wish you'd taken up the cello.'

'I prefer piano.'

'I know. But it would have been nice to teach you.'

'Sorry, Dad.'

'God, don't be sorry – I didn't mean anything by it. I love that you play the piano, and you're very talented. I only meant that you'd have made a fantastic cello student too.'

'Maybe one day I'll learn that too.'

'Maybe you will,' he said. 'And I'll be there for lessons if you ever decide to.' As the traffic crawled forward another inch he stifled a groan at the sight of the brake lights glowing in front again.

'You're going to be late, aren't you?' Ella raised her eyebrows.

'Perhaps a little.'

'Are you still going to talk to Mum when you drop me off?'

'I need to, but I don't know if I'll have time. Maybe you could tell her that I need a chat and she could call me later?'

'Yeah, I can do that.'

Haydon nodded. Janine wouldn't call him even if Ella asked; she was stubborn like that. She'd probably guess what it was about, and she wouldn't appreciate Haydon's desire to open up a debate on the possibility that they might move to London with Kevin, even if it did need to happen. She'd tell him it was none of his business, that he had no right to lecture, that he had no right to interfere in her life and perhaps, to a point, she'd be right. But he couldn't bear the thought of Ella being so far away.

His thoughts were interrupted by Ella's voice.

'Dad… the traffic…'

Haydon shook himself and saw that the van in front had moved forward to leave a gap of at least ten yards.

'Right…' He yanked off the handbrake to move the car along. Glancing at the clock on the dashboard, he held in another groan as he noted the time. He was almost certainly going to be late for his hopeless cello student, which meant he definitely couldn't talk to Janine until he'd finished up there. He might be desperate to sort this out, but in the face of having to earn his keep, it would just have to wait.

'Hey, I'm so sorry to keep you waiting… Danny in the study?'

Haydon stepped over the threshold. Ten minutes late wasn't as bad as he'd feared, and his pupil's dad, Bryn, wasn't the complaining type. Besides, he suspected that Danny, the teenage boy he was there to teach, dreaded the weekly cello lesson almost as much as Haydon dreaded having to listen to him scratch away at his old instrument, so he was probably hoping that his teacher wasn't going to turn up. Apparently it was Mum who was keen for her darling boy to play, though strangely, she never seemed to be around when it was practise time. Haydon hated that he was late, but there probably wouldn't be too much harm done.

'Aye, he's ready and waiting. If you call watching YouTube videos ready and waiting.'

'Are they videos about cello-playing?'

Bryn gave an easy grin. 'Somehow I think not.'

'I'll go through and get started. I can tag an extra bit of time on the end to make up for being late.'

'Aye, don't bother yourself. Traffic, was it?'

'Pig of a snarl-up on the dual carriageway into town.'

'The roadworks won't be helping. Or this rain.'

'God, don't I know it. It never seems to do anything but – and this is supposed to be summer. I can't remember what the sun looks like right now.'

'In need of a holiday, eh?'

Haydon hadn't really thought about it until this exact moment, but perhaps that was just what he did need? He certainly felt life's stresses more acutely these days. Impossible, though, with everything going on – bills to pay, an ex-wife to negotiate with and a daughter who might well need him more than ever before.

'You could say that but fat chance of one any time soon.'

'Well, that's a shame, because I happen to have a cancellation for my place in Saint-Raphaël.'

'Oh…' Haydon remarked vaguely as he followed Bryn to the study where Danny was waiting to start his lesson. 'Where's that?'

'South of France. Beautiful spot. It was booked out for the summer but the family due there at the end of the month have had to pull out. They paid their deposit and that's non-refundable, so I could afford to let it go cheap if you were interested.'

Haydon hesitated, his hand resting on the knob of the study door. But then he shook his head.

'Thanks, Bryn, but I don't have time for a holiday. It was good of you to think of me, though.'

Bryn nodded. 'If you change your mind, let me know. I'm putting it out to advert tomorrow, though, so be quick if you want it.'

Haydon smiled as he pushed open the door. Behind it slouched a gangly teen on an old sofa, staring into his phone, cello on its stand at the other end of the room. Haydon had to suppress a wry grin at the sight. Danny – as keen as always to get started.

The boy looked up at Haydon's entrance, and Haydon was convinced that if he could have leapt from the nearest window and run, he would have. Instead, he pushed himself wearily from the sofa and went to retrieve his instrument. And Haydon had to sympathise – he sort of felt like that himself today.

Chapter Four

Ashley locked the entrance door of Golden Meadows Retirement Home behind her and stepped into the tiny office directly next to it.

'Evening.' Rose looked up from a pile of rosters spread out on the table in front of her. 'How are you this fine evening, flower?'

'Fine? Which window have you been looking out of? It's cats and dogs out there.'

'I haven't been looking out of any windows – that's the problem. Haven't had bloody time. Two girls missing off shift today, a suspected heart attack – which turned out to be heartburn, though we had ambulances and all sorts – and a wanderer, so we've been run ragged.'

'Your wanderer...' Ashley smiled. 'Let me guess... Wilf?'

'Got it in one. He's determined he's going to get to that pub. How many times have we told him it was knocked down in 1980? I've even driven him past, but he's not having it. Insists the landlady has a pint waiting on the bar for him and a cuddle waiting in the back after closing time.'

'It must be lovely to disappear into your past like that.' Ashley shrugged off her raincoat and hung it on a peg. 'Leave all the troubles of the present behind.'

'Oh, and where would you go, flower?'

Ashley gave a small smile. 'I can think of a few places. Not that there's any point in wishing it, because wishing won't change the here and now no matter how many times I do it.'

'Someone sounds like they had a bad day. And then they had to come here and do the twilight shift. Poor bugger.'

Ashley laughed. 'I'm OK. Ignore me and my whining. People have it worse than I do. Like poor Wilf, who can't recall if he's in this world or the next.'

'Yeah, but he's happy enough in his little fantasy world, and if we can keep them happy that's about the best we can do for them, isn't it? I wish we could give them their lost years back, but we can't, and one day it's going to be us sitting in that day room waiting for death.'

'Oh, well that's a comforting thought – thanks. Now I feel so much better!'

'You're welcome. By the way, can you do an extra on Wednesday? Pat's got a funeral to go to.'

'I'll check with my mum if she can look after Molly for me, but it should be OK.'

Ashley hesitated, tussling with the request she'd been thinking about all the way to work. The holiday to Saint-Raphaël was very last minute and she knew Rose wasn't going to like her asking. She also knew Rose would struggle to say no, even if it did leave her in the lurch, and the thought made Ashley even more reluctant to ask the question. But she'd promised her mum she would for the sake of her stepdad, Maurice, who desperately wanted them to go. God knew both she and Molly would benefit from the time away from home – time to bond and relax without the worries of money and duty hanging over them.

'Thanks, flower. It would do me a huge favour. When you start will you just make sure Mavis hasn't hidden her meds under her mattress again? Petra found three days' worth under there last week when she was cleaning.'

'Sure. Rose…' Ashley began before clamping her mouth shut again. It wasn't fair to ask, and she realised it now as she watched her boss bend her head back to the rosters. Rose looked up.

'Yeah?'

'Nothing.'

Rose frowned. 'Nothing? Ashley, my love, we've known each other long enough now that I can tell when you have an awkward question and you know I'll give you a straight answer if you open your mouth and spit it out. What's ailing you?'

'I know. It's just… I don't want to ask because I know it's going to be really difficult. But my mum… well, my step-dad really… there's this huge family do for his aunt who turns a hundred at the end of the month and he wants me and Molly to go. It's really important to his family that everyone is there and, of course, my mum too.'

'So you need a day off? I'm sure I can jiggle the rota for you. Why didn't you just say – I'm doing them right now anyway.'

'Actually it's in France. Down south. So I'd need a week…'

Rose said nothing for a moment, but Ashley could tell by her expression what the answer was going to be.

'Flower,' she said finally. 'You know I'd let you go if I could, but it's such short notice, and I don't know if I have enough people to cover—'

Ashley shook her head. 'Don't worry. I knew it was a big ask and I know you'd let me if you could.'

'But—'

'Honestly, forget I mentioned it. It's putting everyone out massively and it's really not that important…'

Pulling a tunic from her locker, she buttoned it hastily and left the office to start her shift.

Ashley found the morning's dose of pills stuffed inside Mavis's pillowcase. After cajoling her to take them with a cup of tea, she set about making a huge urn of tea for the rest of the residents of Golden Meadows Retirement Home. She tried not to acknowledge the disappointment lodged in her throat as she dropped the bags in. And she tried not to dwell on how tired she was, how long it had been since her last decent holiday, or how wonderful the Riviera, which she'd never seen, though she'd often longed to, might look at this time of year. As she shoved Gladys's dentures back in she tried not to think about how nice it might be not to be shoving anyone's dentures anywhere for a week. Or breaking up arguments about which TV channel they were having on between a room full of people who really were all old enough to know better.

Instead, she smiled, offered gentle words and gestures, made sure everyone was as comfortable and as happy as they could be. She gave time and patience, a friendly ear and an understanding nod. And whatever any of the residents needed, she made sure they got it. Because what was the point in sulking over things she couldn't change, and it was hardly the fault of any of the pensioners in her charge. Disappointment was a fact of life these days, and perhaps after all these years, she ought to be used to it.

During her break in the tiny office she sat at the table with her sandwiches and opened a text from her mother.

What did Rose say?

Ashley let out a sigh and locked the phone again before putting it back in her pocket. Her mum would say that Ashley hadn't tried hard enough, that she needed to stand her ground, that she was the most faithful and reliable member of Rose's team and she ought to point that out and ask again. And she'd be right, but Ashley just didn't have the heart. She liked working here and she liked Rose, and she didn't see the point in rocking the boat. The holiday was a silly idea anyway, foolish daydreaming. Maybe her mum and Maurice would be able to take Molly with them and Ashley would man the fort at home? They wouldn't be pleased but at least that way Molly got a holiday and there was no doubt that Maurice and his family would spoil her rotten. She'd have the time of her life, and maybe it would take the sting out of her disappointment over the music school. She'd put it to her mum later.

As she was washing her cup ready to go on shift again, Rose came in.

'Sit down a minute, flower.'

'I'm due back, I—'

'Whoever wants a Horlicks can wait. You are my priority right now.'

'I don't understand—'

'If you want that week off you can have it.'

'But you said…'

'I know. But then I had a think about it. You're one of my best workers and I'd be lost without you. But you're no good to me burnt out, and it wasn't until I checked the records that I realised just how little of your allocated holidays you actually take. It's all very well me paying you extra to forfeit them and come in, but even you need a break from time to time. You rarely ask for time off and if you've asked me this time then it must be important to you. So I've called the nursing agency and they'll send someone to cover your week.'

Ashley blinked. 'You mean I can go to France?'

'Frankly you can go, stay at home… I don't care what you do with your week. So long as I don't see your face here while the agency nurse covers, I don't want to know what you're up to.'

Ashley broke into a broad smile and flung her arms around Rose. 'Thank you!'

'Don't be daft,' Rose said, pushing Ashley off. But she was smiling too. 'Now get back to work before I change my mind!'

∗

Haydon scanned the web page. The week Bryn had mentioned he had free at his villa in the South of France was at the end of July and so fell nicely into Ella's summer break from school. It was all too neat, and the more Haydon thought about it, the more he was wondering whether he should have snapped up the opportunity for a cut-price week away. Now, as he viewed a tourist guide to the area, taking in the glorious photos of palm-flanked beaches, breathtaking mountain passes overlooking glittering slices of ocean, quaint villages and vivid seas of lavender threaded by empty roads, he was regretting his immediate refusal more than ever. He could almost smell the garlic of a bowl of *escargot*, taste the crisp white wine, hear the relaxed chat of a roadside café. He and Ella could spend time on the beach – fishing, sandcastle-building, sunbathing – it didn't really matter what they did; what counted was the time spent together. They could bond, build their relationship to be stronger and more loving than ever, and even if she moved away in the future, they would always have this perfect week lodged in their memories, holding them together.

Closing the lid of the laptop, Haydon went through to the kitchen to wash up the single dinner plate he'd used to eat his microwave lasagne in front of the TV news. His eyes went to the window as he ran the tap. His flat was three floors up, and it was too dark to see much of the street below. Squally rain beat against his window and wind whistled through the cracks in the frame. It was meant to be summer, though there was little evidence of it out there tonight.

His phone bleeped in his pocket and he hurried to dry his hands before reading the message from Ella.

Are you OK? I didn't mean to make you sad.
Why on earth would you think I'm sad? he replied.
Because I told you about Kevin wanting to move us.
It's fine. Not your fault at all. Miss you already.
Miss you too. See you next week?
You bet. Goodnight. Love you.
Love you too, Dad.

Chapter Five

'If she makes lamb again I'm going to hurl.'

Molly folded her arms tight across her chest and stared resolutely at the front door of her grandmother's house. Ashley stood beside her, a bunch of flowers tucked into the crook of one arm and a bottle of wine in the other. She twisted to look at Molly, stifling a grin as they waited for the tinkle of the bell to be answered. Beyond the shelter of the porch the rain steadily pounded the garden, the skies heavy with the promise of much more.

'It's not funny, Mum!' Molly growled.

'I know it's not – I'm not laughing. I've told her you're off lamb so stop worrying. And even if I hadn't she wouldn't dare cook it again for you after last time.'

'It's gross – eating babies.'

'She didn't know you'd gone off it – you've always eaten it before.'

'That was before I knew what it was she was serving up – I thought it was beef or something.'

'I don't know how on earth you could have thought it was beef.'

'Nobody ever said it wasn't.'

'We didn't know we had to. You never used to ask – you just ate it.'

Molly aimed a withering look at her mother. 'Can you imagine what would happen if a restaurant just gave people mystery meat?'

'Well,' Ashley said, trying not to let Molly see her amusement, 'now you know and Grandma knows and we all know where we stand, don't we?'

'I suppose Maurice's family are going to be eating weird stuff too?'

'When we go to visit?'

Molly nodded.

'You don't have to eat it just because it's on the table. I'm sure there will be some things suitable for you.'

'Bread, I expect.'

Ashley smiled. 'More than bread.' She nudged Molly. 'Go on, admit that you're a little bit excited about the thought of going on holiday, even if we are staying with Maurice's family.'

Molly pursed her lips. But as Ashley nudged her again she broke into a grudging grin.

'That's more like it,' Ashley said. 'Grandma and Maurice will be thrilled when I tell them we can go and we might actually get to see a bit of summer, because we sure as heck aren't seeing any here in England this year.'

Right on cue, the front door opened and Ashley's mother, Sue, stood smiling before them.

'Hello, you're just in time!' She leaned to kiss Ashley and Molly in turn, ushering them in. Ashley handed over the flowers and wine. Sue pretended to frown but took them anyway. 'I've told you not to spend your money on us... we have plenty here.'

'I'm not going to turn up empty-handed,' Ashley said, taking her coat off and hanging it on a peg in the hallway as Molly did the same. 'We're eating your food so the least we can do is contribute a little something.'

'Well, you needn't have bothered. Maurice has a cellar full of wine – in fact, I'll let you take some back with you when you go home.'

'Honestly…'

'Don't argue – do what your mother tells you.'

Ashley laughed. 'I can hardly argue with that, can I?'

As they entered the kitchen, Maurice greeted them both with kisses on the cheek, as Sue had, but whereas her greeting had been rather tentative and reserved, his demonstrated full-on Gallic enthusiasm, as befitted his French heritage. His cheeks were ruddy – which could have been from the steam and heat from the stove, or it could have been down to the fact that he'd been taking full advantage of his wine cellar as he cooked. Knowing Maurice as Ashley had grown to during the last ten years he'd been married to her mum, it would be a combination of the two.

'Come, come!' He waved them over to take a seat, tightening his apron as he turned to stir a sauce on the hob. 'I hope you are hungry!'

'It smells amazing.' Ashley sat down next to Molly while Sue filled their glasses. From the direction of the open patio doors there came a sharp woof and the clatter of paws on laminate and Buddy the Labrador came skidding in, making a beeline for Molly. Her expression of delight quickly became one of disgust as she realised he was soaking wet from the rain outside.

'Ugh!' she squeaked, pushing him away. Which only made him jump and lick her all the more.

'Buddy!' Sue chided. 'Shooo! Off to your bed!'

Buddy's head went down and Ashley laughed. 'Poor fella, he only wants a fuss.'

'He can have one when he's dry.' Sue looked at Maurice with a frown. 'I don't know why you insisted on letting him out into the garden when it's pouring down.'

Maurice shrugged. 'He is an animal – he likes to be outside sometimes.'

'Not when it's raining and we have guests.' She shut the door to the conservatory, leaving Buddy watching forlornly through the glass.

'After dinner, Buddy,' Ashley said, smiling at him. He whimpered before deciding that experience had taught him he wasn't going to get a second chance to soak everyone and curling up to sleep in his basket instead.

'I will take him some chicken,' Maurice said. 'It is his favourite.'

'Garlic and rosemary?' Ashley asked.

Maurice grinned. 'But of course.'

'Mum is so lucky to have a Frenchman around the house. I could put up with any amount of disparaging remarks about the English if it meant eating your meals every day.'

Maurice put a hand to his chest and feigned the deepest offence. 'I would never disparage your wonderful countrymen.' He grinned. 'Some of my favourite people are English.'

'Maybe occasionally?'

'OK, maybe occasionally,' he said, laughing. 'But only when they deserve it.'

As Sue put plates out and Maurice began to bring the serving dishes filled with glistening veg, fragrant sauces and a plate of steaming chicken to the table, he turned his attention to Molly.

'So, I hear you have had great success at the conservatoire? They have offered you a place, yes?'

Molly glanced at Ashley, clearly trying to gauge whether she was allowed to discuss this openly or not.

'She has,' Ashley said, speaking up for her daughter. 'But not on a scholarship, sadly. There was only one she was eligible for, and it was won by another violinist.'

'This is what your mother tells me. So, we need to find money?'

'I don't think it's going to be that simple.'

'Why not?' Maurice sat down and waved his hands to indicate that everyone could help themselves to the food.

'The fees are huge, but it's not just about them. We'd have travelling costs because it's not easy to get to. There's the problem of getting Molly there when I might be on shift. And there's the extras like equipment, money for educational trips, travel to concerts and performances – and they do a lot of those. We'd love to accept the offer of a place, of course, but…'

Molly put a hand on Ashley's arm and gave a thin smile. 'It's alright, Mum. I've been thinking about it, and I've decided that I'm going to take the place on the music course at the local college. It'll be fun, and all my friends are going to be there, and there won't be the stress of trying to keep up with a load of posh kids.'

'This is what you want?' Sue asked.

Molly nodded, a bit too enthusiastically for Ashley's liking, and that needle of guilt for all the ways in which she felt she'd failed her daughter stabbed at her again.

'Yes,' Molly replied. 'I didn't realise just how posh it was going to be when I applied and I'll probably hate it if I go. I can learn just as much at the local college on their music A level as I can at the conservatoire, and I can do it all for free. I'll just do more violin work on my own to keep my skill level up.'

Sue and Maurice exchanged a look, and Ashley knew what they were thinking because she was thinking it too. Molly had no more changed her mind than Ashley's bank balance had suddenly gained a ton of zeros. But it looked as if Molly had seen the situation for what it was and decided to work with the hand life had dealt her.

Ashley should have been relieved but it made her feel worse. If Molly had been spoilt and unreasonable and angry about it, somehow it would have been easier to deal with than this quiet, deflated acceptance. Molly had packed her dreams away, and as she looked at her, Ashley realised she'd seen the look on her face before. It was the same one she'd worn sixteen years before as she'd watched the lines on the pregnancy test turn blue. The gap year travelling the world she'd planned, the university education at the red-brick institution, the exciting future in some high-flying career working in Barcelona or Paris or Lisbon or somewhere equally as glamorous – she'd parcelled all those hopes and wishes up and sealed the box shut, and she'd got on with the business of raising her child.

'If it's just about the money—' Sue began gently, but Molly shook her head.

'It's not, Grandma. It's not that at all. I'm happy with my decision. Honestly, I don't know what I was thinking of even auditioning for that stupid conservatoire.' She studied her plate as she piled vegetables onto it. 'Anyway,' she continued, not looking up to meet her grandmother's gaze, 'Mum has something she wants to tell you.'

'Oh?' Sue turned to Ashley now.

'It's nothing bad. Just that I managed to get the time off work next month. So we can go to France with you.'

Sue clapped her hands together in delight. It seemed all thoughts of money and conservatoires had been forgotten – or at least nudged aside for another time when emotions had cooled and they could discuss it properly.

'Although,' Ashley continued, glancing at the conservatory where Buddy lay in his bed. 'Who's going to look after Buddy if I'm away with you? Me and Moll always do it.'

'Tia across the road says she'll have him.'

'Oh, won't he be anxious with someone he doesn't know?'

'But he does know Tia. She's been taking him for walks all week.'

Ashley tried not to frown. It seemed her mum had assumed Ashley was going to say yes to this holiday regardless – to the point where she'd even been training the neighbours to look after her beloved dog.

'This is wonderful news!' Maurice said, beaming. 'My aunt Violette will be so happy to meet you!'

'It's probably about time,' Ashley said. 'As you've been married to Mum for ten years now and I've yet to meet any of your family in France.'

'You will love it, I am sure,' Maurice said. 'Let us toast,' he added, raising his glass and waiting for everyone to follow. 'To a week with my favourite people in the beautiful paradise of Saint-Raphaël!'

*

When Janine opened the front door the most glorious smell wafted out. Haydon was barrelled back to Sunday dinners around their table – him and Janine and Ella tucking into roast beef and potatoes, gentle banter and laughter carried on the aromas of cooked meat that filled the air. They were simple pleasures but the happiest times. He shook his head, chasing away the desperate melancholy that would swallow him whole if he let it. That life was gone, and pining for it was not going to bring it back. It certainly wouldn't endear him to Janine, and he wanted her onside more than ever.

'Haydon…' She opened the door to admit him. 'How are you?'

'Good,' he said, stepping in and wiping the rain from his feet on the doormat before following her down the hall. 'Something smells nice in here.'

'It's just beef – nothing special. We're just about finishing up, but there's a bit of everything left if you want some.'

He shook his head, and she turned to him with a questioning look.

'Sorry,' he said. 'I forgot those eyes in the back of your head aren't actually a real thing.'

She laughed. 'Even though you managed to convince Ella for about three years that it was.'

'She's never forgiven me for that...'

The kitchen was empty apart from a table full of leftovers and plates that needed stacking in the dishwasher.

'Where is everyone?' Haydon asked.

'It sounded like something big when you phoned me. I asked Kevin to take Ella out on the fields for an hour.'

'In this?' Haydon looked at the window, streaked with fat raindrops, the tension churning his gut threatening to show in a fit of pique. 'It's a bit wet for a walk.'

'She's got a raincoat and wellies, and she wouldn't be the first kid to get rained on. And I didn't want any external influences.'

'What does that mean?'

'I didn't want anyone else to influence any decision I might make about whatever it is you want to discuss with me. And I think I have a good idea what it is. I take it Ella has mentioned London to you?'

It looked as if the pleasantries were over. No offer of a plate of leftovers now, no making him a cup of tea and any potential ally safely out of the way. Janine had already made up her mind. She knew what the topic of discussion was likely to be and she'd already decided on her response – that much was clear.

'Well, yes, but—'

'And you're here to complain?'

'I don't think reminding you that she's my daughter too and that I should get a say in her life is being unreasonable.'

'I've never forgotten that.'

'So why wouldn't you consult me first before you decided you were moving her to London?'

'Because no decision has been made, so there didn't seem any point.'

'But you *are* thinking about it?'

'You know I am if Ella's been talking to you.'

'So when would you have seen fit to mention it? When you were packing? As you got in the car to leave? As you unpacked in the new house?'

'You're being melodramatic.'

'I'm asking for some respect. I'm Ella's father, for God's sake!'

'And I'm her mother, currently the woman doing most of the childrearing.'

'That's not my fault!'

'No, but it's still the reality.'

Haydon let out a sigh and rubbed a hand through his hair. 'Why does every discussion have to go around in circles?'

'You think I'm being deliberately obstructive?'

'Yes, I'm sorry, but I do.'

'I wouldn't march into your house and tell you what you could and couldn't do—'

'Whoa! This is not me telling you what you can do – this is about my daughter! I have as much right to decide her future as you do!'

'Not according to the courts…' Janine began to slam a stack of plates into the dishwasher.

'The courts awarded you custody, but if it means another court battle—'

Janine wheeled around. 'What the…?'

Haydon held his hands up in a gesture of surrender. 'Hey, I'm not trying to start a war, but you must know that I'll do whatever it takes to keep Ella near.'

'Even if that means dragging her through the courts again? Even if that means making her life a misery just when she's finally settled? Don't you think that's a little selfish?'

'Don't you think what you're doing is a little selfish?'

'You're saying I can never move from this house?'

'I'm saying you could have consulted me!'

'Argh!' Janine squealed. 'Just remind me how irritating you can be – that's going to change my mind about London!'

'You said you hadn't made up your mind!'

'Haydon!' Janine snapped. She drew in a breath and blew it out long. 'Haydon…' she repeated, her voice lower now. 'Please understand that I am not trying to take Ella from you. All we want—'

'All *Kevin* wants?'

'All *we* want,' Janine continued, 'is what's best for the family. *This* family. I know Ella is your daughter, but she's part of Kevin's life now too, and soon she'll be his stepdaughter, and despite what you think he's fond of her. He has her interests at heart – we both do – whenever we talk about the future. Think about it… think about the opportunities for her in London compared to here. For that reason alone a move to London makes sense in a thousand different ways. Would you deny her that?'

'There are opportunities here.'

'Not as many and tougher to make work, and you know it. London's where it's at.'

'Depends what *you* want for her. Doesn't she get a say? Didn't we always agree we wouldn't be pushy parents?'

'You're saying I'm a pushy parent?'

'You're starting to sound like one if I'm honest.'

Janine clamped her mouth shut and turned back to shoving plates into the dishwasher.

'I'm sorry,' Haydon said. 'That was uncalled for.'

'Damn right it was!' Janine spun to face him again. 'You can accuse me of many things, but that's not one of them. I'm just saying that, whatever Ella decides she wants to do, the opportunities will be twice as many in London as anywhere else.'

'And she wants to go?'

'She doesn't seem too flustered by the idea.'

'Maybe she's just trying to make you happy?'

'That's not fair. I've never put any pressure on her. There's no reason for her to think she has to do anything to make me happy.'

'Have you asked her if that's the case? She's been through a family break-up and we don't know how it really affected her. On the outside she's coped so well but…' He let out a sigh. 'Maybe she hasn't coped with it the way we think she has. Just because she's still smiling and not shoplifting or smashing up the school canteen doesn't mean she hasn't been affected by our divorce.'

'Is this a guilt trip?'

'No… maybe. But you know I'm right.'

'So what would you have me do about it? I can't tackle something I can't see and when I ask if she's OK she says yes. You're saying that's a reason not to make the move to London?'

'I'm asking you to think about it – *really* think about it. Don't rush into anything. If not for the sake of what we once had then for Ella's sake. I don't think that's a huge ask, is it?'

Janine nodded stiffly. 'I never intended to rush into anything, and I'm sorry if it seemed like that. One thing I would never do is jeopardise Ella's happiness. I'll talk to her properly before I make any big decisions, so if that's what you're most worried about you needn't be.'

'I suppose I'm scared of losing her.'

'We're both gradually losing her. It's what growing up is all about.'

Haydon forced a thin smile. 'I suppose you're right.'

Janine slammed the dishwasher shut and turned to him with her hands on her hips. But, despite the body language, it was clear from her expression that her mood had softened.

'Maybe you want to wait for Ella and Kevin to get back? Say hello?'

'You don't mind?'

'It would be pretty mean-spirited of me if I did. You *are* her dad.'

'And there was me thinking you meant saying hello to Kevin.'

A small smile tugged the corners of her lips. 'You're still not funny, you know that?'

'Yeah, I know.'

'You want a drink while we wait?'

'Coffee would be good.'

As Janine reached for two mugs from the cupboard, Haydon allowed his gaze to roam the kitchen that had once been his. Very little had changed apart from a lick of paint, and if Haydon closed his eyes he could almost imagine the same of his life. But then he'd open them again and, although his surroundings were familiar, they were about the only part of his life that looked like a landscape he knew. The one thing about Janine he'd always been able to count on was her wisdom, even when they'd been at each other's throats. Frustratingly, he had to admit that her take on life had always been infinitely wiser and more grounded than his. She'd blamed his musician's temperament, and he'd accused her of having no imagination, but none of that changed the fact that invariably she turned out to be right about most things, and that most decisions she made ended up being the right ones. Including dumping him, he concluded wryly. She'd landed on her feet with Kevin – there was no two ways about it. And Ella had a standard of life now that she could never have hoped for had their family still been together under the same roof – holidays to long-haul destinations, pony-riding, lavish sleepovers for friends, as many theme-park visits as she had the energy for...

'What's Ella got planned for the end of July?' he asked suddenly. Janine looked around from the kettle in mild surprise.

'Got planned?'

'I mean, are you guys planning to go on holiday or anything?'

'We haven't booked anything.'

'So she's free?'

'I suppose so. At the moment, yes. Why?'

'Can I take her on holiday?'

'Where to?'

'South of France. Just for a week.'

Janine gave a vague, uncertain shrug. 'I'd need to clear with Kevin that he isn't planning anything but... I guess it could be OK.'

'Brilliant!' Haydon said, and for the first time since he'd arrived a genuine smile lit his face. 'That would be brilliant!'

Chapter Six

It was hard not to be enchanted by the ancestral home of Maurice's ancient aunt. If someone had asked Ashley to list the features of what she imagined to be a typical Côte d'Azur farmhouse, Villa Marguerite would have ticked most of them. Wildflower garden – check. Olive trees – check. Vines hugging a gnarled old network of trellises – check. Extensive wine cellar – check. Sleepy cat on the veranda – check. Built from local stone and rendered in a warm salmon-pink plaster with chunky terracotta roof tiles, the air of its gardens humming with pollen-laden honeybees and the chirruping of crickets, the house was instantly welcoming. Maurice's extensive family had been even more so, and it hadn't taken Ashley and Molly long to disappear into the warm bosom of that very convivial collective.

Ashley was curled up now on an old wooden swing seat outside the back door as the balmy air of a coastal evening laid the tang of salt over the perfume of marguerites and lavender. She'd been a guest of Maurice's aunt, Madame Violette Dupont, for less than three hours but already, full of sausage casserole and red wine, she felt as if she'd always belonged here. Molly had gone off for a walk down to the harbour with Maurice and a young distant cousin of his from Paris who Ashley suspected Molly had developed an instant crush on. It was easy to see the appeal – he was good-looking, around Molly's age and infused with the instant veneer of glamour that living in France's vibrant capital would give anyone. Just so long as an innocent crush was as far as it went she was happy to indulge any whim Molly might have in that regard, and she had to be glad that there was someone Molly's age staying at Madame Dupont's house to keep her occupied for the week.

Sue appeared with two glasses of wine and kicked Ashley's legs out of the way with a grin so she could sit next to her.

'*More* wine?' Ashley said, taking one of the glasses from her mother.

'Well, we *are* in France. What else are we going to drink?'

'I don't know... when I took French lessons at school they all drank Orangina.'

'I think Violette would faint if you asked her for one of those.' Sue held her glass up to the evening light and gazed appreciatively into its claret depths. 'This wine's made by her family, and it's bloody good stuff too.'

'Oh, nobody is debating that point. It's wonderful stuff, but do you really want me singing filthy songs and throwing up over the poppies on my first night here?'

'Maybe save it for the second night,' Sue said with a solemn nod, and then looked at Ashley as they both burst out laughing. 'I'm so happy you decided to come,' Sue said. 'I love Maurice and his family, of course, but it's not the same as having your own around, and I'll have a lot more fun with you and Molly here.'

'If we ever see anything of her. I've a feeling she's got her week planned out already, and it might involve quite a lot of... whatever his name is.'

'Blimey, you've forgotten already? Perhaps you'd better cut back on the wine after all.'

'There are so many names to remember. What is it?'

'Bastien.'

'Bit of a mouthful.' Ashley took a sip of her wine and turned her gaze to the warm glow of a sun setting pink and gold over the burnished garden. 'We'll have to shorten it to Bazza or something.'

Sue giggled. 'I don't think that will go down too well with the uncle and aunt who've brought him down.'

'Perhaps not.' Ashley turned back to her with a grin. 'Why haven't his parents come with him again?'

Sue shrugged. 'Something to do with the company they run. It all sounds very glamorous and high-powered, but I haven't actually been able to work out what it does yet. But there was some boardroom crisis, and they had to stay behind at the last minute.'

'That's a shame. At least he seems sweet and polite, so that's something. With rich, powerful parents he could so easily have been a spoilt brat.'

'Molly wouldn't have cared if he was spoilt or not. She's too busy losing herself in those big dark eyes.'

'That's true.' Ashley took a sip of her wine. 'We'll have to keep an eye on her.'

'She's a sensible girl. And she's growing up so there'll come a point where she won't appreciate us keeping an eye on her in quite the same way.'

'I suppose you're right. I just worry…'

'You're bound to, but I don't think it's necessary. Maurice and I will intervene if we think there's a need, so I don't want you to stress about it. This week is a rest for you as well as anything else, and I'll be cross if you don't take advantage of that. God knows you deserve it.'

'Thanks, Mum.' Ashley smiled. 'I appreciate that.'

There was silence for a moment as both women contemplated the glorious evening. Swallows had begun to dip in and out of their home in the eaves of the house, and Ashley watched them race to and fro, swooping and soaring in the clear sky. The crickets seemed louder than ever, and yet all around was peace. The whisper of a breeze lifted the scent of night-flowering jasmine into the air and Ashley took a breath of absolute contentment. It had been a long time since she'd felt this relaxed.

'Isn't it just perfect here?' Sue said into the gap.

'Don't…'

'Don't what?'

'Remind me of how perfect this is. In a month it will be like a distant dream and everything will go back to rush and stress. I don't want to think about how perfect this is – I just want to empty my mind and live it.'

'You know you could come whenever Maurice and I visit.'

Ashley turned to her. 'You know I can't.'

'Well, the offer's always there…'

Sue took a sip of her wine and looked back towards the house. From within Ashley could hear the faint hum of lively conversation and laughter. Family reunions were in full swing involving relatives from all over France and one or two from further afield – like Maurice who had moved to England to be with Sue after meeting and falling in love with her at an art exhibition he'd organised.

Ashley had always loved her father most, of course, as all daughters are duty-bound to do, but she could understand why her mother had fallen so hard for Maurice that she'd left her husband for him. They had so much more in common – their love of art, theatre and good food, an almost telepathic understanding of each other, a harmony that was rarely matched in other relationships. He'd encouraged and nurtured Sue's creativity, whereas Ashley's dad had always treated it with a measure of suspicion. Maurice had encouraged her to start the pottery business that had raised her from housewife to entrepreneur and given her life the meaning she'd always craved. Molly adored him too because he showed real interest in her music, not the cursory and uninformed lip service her biological grandfather gave it whenever she visited. Maurice wasn't Ashley's father, and he could never be that, but he was a bloody good second.

As it sometimes did whenever the issue of family was raised, Ashley's thoughts went back to Molly's dad. These days she struggled even to recall his face, and yet he featured in her thoughts often – perhaps more than ever as she watched his daughter turn into a young woman. Would he be proud if he could see her now? Would he care? What was Molly missing out on by not knowing any of her paternal relatives? Was Ashley doing the right thing not seeking him out now? Even in sixteen years the world had changed, and it was easier to find someone than ever before. She'd questioned whether she ought to many times but every time had decided no. And Molly herself had stopped asking long ago, seemingly content that she had a mother and no father and that was just fine. But was it? Did Molly tussle with the question of his whereabouts at night, as Ashley did? Would it make Molly's life richer to know him, or would it simply complicate things?

'Ah… you are hiding!'

Both Ashley and Sue spun round to see Maurice's sister, Nanette, at the door to the house. She was smiling broadly.

'We are too noisy for you?' she added.

'Oh, of course not!' Sue laughed. 'We were just admiring the view and making the most of the sunshine. We've had precious little of that in England this summer so it's a novelty.'

'It is a beautiful place. I miss living here.'

'But Lille is beautiful?' Ashley put in. 'You do live in Lille, right?'

'You remember well,' Nanette said. 'Lille is wonderful but whenever I come back, Saint-Raphaël feels like home. You understand?'

'I do,' Ashley said with a smile.

'Maurice tells me York is beautiful. One day I must come to visit.'

'It's lovely,' Sue said. 'A lot greyer than this most days but we like it. As you say, it's home so that makes it feel special to us.'

'I understand,' Nanette said. 'We are about to eat – would you like to come in and join us?'

'Again!' Ashley squeaked. 'It feels like five minutes since we had dinner!'

Nanette laughed. 'And now we are having supper. It is only a few little treats. It's not every week your aunt becomes one hundred.'

'That's true, but if the feasting has started already I don't know how we can top this on the actual day – it'll be like watching a Henry the Eighth banquet.'

'Goodness!' Sue laughed. 'Even Violette isn't old enough to go back that far!'

'No,' Nanette agreed. 'You will join us?'

'Maybe we'll wait until Maurice is back with Molly and Bastien.' Sue glanced at Ashley who nodded agreement.

'Where have they gone?'

'To the harbour. I think Molly was itching to explore and Bastien… well… let's just say I think he'd rather like to be where Molly is.'

'I think the feeling is mutual,' Ashley said. 'We were just saying that we might have to keep an eye on them.'

'She is very pretty. I'm sure she must have so much attention from the boys in England,' Nanette said. 'Her papa must be looking all of the time—'

Nanette stopped, and colour flooded her face as she clapped a hand over her mouth. 'I am so sorry, I didn't remember…'

Ashley shook her head. 'Please… I'm used to it by now.'

'But I have caused offence?' Nanette asked, looking as if she might cry with the mortification of her mistake.

'Of course not.' Ashley smiled. 'It's old news now and I hardly even think of it.'

Nanette was silent for a moment, looking from Ashley to Sue.

'No, I don't know where he is, and no, I don't really want to know,' Ashley said, guessing at the questions that swirled around Nanette's head. 'No, I don't miss him, and no, I don't regret having Molly alone, not for one single day. Yes, I could use an extra income and pair of hands from time to time, and yes, sometimes I feel a little lonely in a romantic sense, but other than that I have my wonderful mum and your fantastic brother and Molly – why on earth would I need anything else?'

'You speak with wisdom,' Nanette said.

'I'm speaking with realistic expectations,' Ashley replied. 'I've managed for all these years, and if he walked into this garden right now I wouldn't give him the time of day. I certainly wouldn't extend an invitation for him to step back into my life. I'm happy as I am.'

Sue reached for Ashley's hand and gave it a quick squeeze, tears misting her eyes. 'I don't say it, but I'm proud of you. I'm proud of the way you rolled your sleeves up and got on with things and never complained or used your situation as an excuse to behave like an idiot and take things you hadn't earned. And Molly is a credit to you.'

She turned to Nanette. 'You know one day she's going to be a world-class violinist? Wants to play for the Vienna Philharmonic Orchestra and she'll do it too. She's determined and steadfast, just like her mother.'

'Oh, stop it.' Ashley gave a self-conscious little laugh and wiped away a tear of her own that seemed to have come from nowhere. 'Molly's got talent and determination, but I guess that's one thing she must get from her dad, because she certainly doesn't get it from me.'

'Don't talk like that,' Sue said. 'Give yourself some credit for raising her to be a fantastic young woman.'

'Absolutely,' Nanette said. 'For one so young to have such grand ambitions she must be a remarkable young woman. And you have been a good role model – no?'

Ashley shrugged. 'I try.'

'And you have done it all alone. That is commendable,' Nanette added.

'Yes,' Ashley said. 'I suppose it must be. But as I didn't have any choice in the matter it doesn't seem any great shakes to me that I did it alone. Alone was pretty much all I had.' She glanced at her mum. 'Not that you didn't offer plenty of support, I just mean…'

Sue smiled. 'I know what you mean.'

Nanette nodded. 'We will keep some food for you.'

Ashley watched as she went back inside. 'I love her already. She's so much like Maurice it's scary.'

'Absolutely two peas in a pod.'

'I sometimes wonder what it would have been like to have brothers or sisters.'

'I'm sorry you didn't,' Sue replied. 'It wasn't for lack of trying, but it just didn't happen. I often felt guilty about it.'

'Don't,' Ashley said. 'It wasn't your fault and it's not like I had a terrible childhood or anything. I just wonder sometimes, you know.' She paused. 'Do you think Molly has missed out not having a sibling?'

'I doubt it. But at least it's not too late for you to remedy that.'

'If I ever meet the right fella… you know what my track record is like. Not content with making one mistake with Molly's dad, the next bloke I gave space to ended up being a two-timing shit.'

'You've had an unfortunate sampling, but I'm sure Mr Right is out there. Not all men are the same.'

'If Mr Right is out there he's not making himself known to me.'

'You wouldn't give him a chance even if he did.'

'I would!' Ashley gave an indignant squeak, and Sue chuckled.

'I can count on one finger the number of successful dates you've been on since Ethan.'

'So that's one then?' Ashley said, unable to hold back a grin. 'Am I really that bad?'

'Picky.'

'Can you blame me? Getting in with an arse is one thing, but if I did that and he got introduced into Molly's life… well, that just wasn't going to happen. I had one lucky escape as it was – if I hadn't found out Ethan was also shagging the barmaid at his pub, the girl on the checkout at the corner shop, the one who worked in the betting shop… Best to keep men out of the equation.'

Sue raised her eyebrows. 'Do you think you might see your way to giving someone a chance now? That relationship was six years ago after all.'

'Does it matter?'

'I'd like to see you happy and settled, you know that.'

'I know.' Ashley turned her gaze to a pair of swallows chasing each other across the sky. 'If the right fella comes along, who knows? But it's not going to happen any time soon so what's the point of worrying about it?'

✳

'Dad…'

Haydon wafted a wasp away from the plate of crusty bread and soft cheese he'd just settled on the patio with. At the sound of Ella's voice he turned with a dopey smile. Since they'd arrived at Bryn's holiday home – La Bastide de la Mer – earlier that day he'd worn the same smile for just about everything that greeted him: the sight of the pristine white house with its cerise flowers frothing down the walls in fragrant swathes; the glittering blue swimming pool with its supply of fluffy fresh towels all ready and waiting for him and Ella; the emerald lawns edged with olive and almond trees; the welcome basket of fresh local goods that Bryn had ordered specially for Haydon and Ella's arrival and from which he was now indulging.

'What's up, snotface?'

Ella rested her hands on her hips and scowled.

'You look just like your mum when you do that,' Haydon remarked vaguely. Even memories of Janine couldn't ruin his current mood. What he'd seen of Saint-Raphaël so far had been heavenly, and he was now sitting in the evening sun where the light bronzed everything, shimmering on the horizon as it began its journey below it, perfumes of the night-time flowers starting to fill the air and swallows racing in circles (or were they bats? Too fast to tell but he liked to see them flit around anyway). It filled him with a greater sense of peace than he'd experienced for a long time. Perhaps the half carafe of local wine had done a little to help too, he mused dryly.

'Dad, there is a *lizard* in my room. An *actual* lizard!'

'That's cool.'

'It's not!' Ella squeaked.

'It won't stay for long. Want me to come and give it the death stare? I can make people feel very uncomfortable with my death stare, and they usually want to leave after a couple of minutes. Might work on lizards too – you never know.'

'Maybe you could just come and pick it up and carry it out?'

'They probably wander in all the time; I doubt it's the last one you'll see.'

'Not if I keep my windows closed the whole time we're here.'

Haydon pushed himself out of his rattan chair with a grin. 'Alright then, I'll come and sort it. As for keeping your windows closed, you might find it gets very hot in your room.'

'As long as I don't have any more lizards or bugs then I don't care about that.'

'Well, I expect the bugs can find other ways of getting in. Were you like this when you went to Mexico with your mum and Kevin? They have far more impressive bugs there, I would imagine.'

'Yes,' Ella said. 'Kevin checked round every night and made sure nothing got in.'

'I'll bet he did,' Haydon muttered as he followed her inside.

The lizard that had troubled Ella so much was barely a streak of green on the ceiling. If anything, it was rather cute, and Haydon was almost sorry to get rid of it.

After a minute of chasing it up and down the walls it was finally cradled in his hands, its little head poking out and regarding them dolefully with black eyes.

'Don't you want a good look at it before I put it out?' he asked. 'He won't hurt you.'

'How do you know?'

Haydon shrugged. 'I think if it was going to hurt either of us it would have done it by now. I've just lumbered around the room after it with my big sweaty hands and that would be enough to make most nasty creatures bite.'

'I suppose so,' Ella said doubtfully as she eyed it. She moved a millimetre closer but no more, peering at it. 'I suppose it's sort of cute. As long as it doesn't hurt me.'

'I expect there will be plenty more of these fellas in the grounds,' Haydon said. 'You might want to avoid the long grass for a start if you don't want to bump into anything like that.'

'I wasn't going to go poking in *there*!' Ella said, aghast. She glanced at the lizard again. 'Can you take it out now?'

'Are you sure? I was thinking it might be nice to keep him. Our holiday pet. Frank the lizard.'

'Have you been drinking wine?' Ella said, her hands going to her hips again, and this time Haydon couldn't help throwing his head back and laughing.

'As a matter of fact I might have had a glass or two. You were busy on your phone catching up with the world and his brother, so what else was I going to do?'

'I was just telling my friends about the house,' she replied, a defensive tone creeping into her voice.

'And what were you telling them?'

'That it's awesome. I told them about the pool, and the beach is nearby and a harbour too and that we're going to see it all tomorrow.'

Haydon smiled. 'I'm glad you were telling them good stuff.'

'Yah, of course! What did you think?'

'I don't know. It's hard to keep up with the cool-o-meter these days so I don't know what's considered awesome and what isn't.'

'This holiday will always definitely be awesome, no matter what,' Ella said.

'Well then, that's… *awesome*.'

Ella rolled her eyes theatrically. 'OK, so now can you put the lizard out please?'

'You hear that, Frank?' Haydon said, pushing his face close to the lizard's and putting on a silly voice. 'She wants you out. No way to treat our holiday pet, is it?'

'Dad!'

'OK.' Haydon laughed. 'I'm doing it now.'

Ella followed him as he went out onto the patio again.

'You're venturing into the sunlight?' he asked. 'Won't that turn you into dust or something?'

'Funny.'

'I thought so.'

'Where are you putting that?'

'I was going to set it free in the garden.'

'Can you put it outside the garden please?'

'We don't have a force field around the property, you know. I think it might be able to get back in if it wants to.'

'Yeah, but it might decide it's so far it's not worth the bother and go to...' She pointed to a salmon-pink villa across a field of wild-looking grassland. 'Why don't you take it over the other side of the field and it might go to that other house?'

'That's right, palm Frank off on another unsuspecting household.'

'Dad, stop it with the Frank jokes!'

'OK...' Haydon was laughing, even if Ella was trying very hard not to. 'I'll take him to the field, and then he's got free will to go where he wants. But if he comes back to our house we're keeping him.'

'You're impossible.'

'I know. And you sound just like your mother again.' Haydon made his way down the gravelled driveway of their villa and out through scrolled iron gates, before setting the little creature gently down in the long grass of the field. Ella watched from the relative safety of the villa garden.

'I wonder who lives in that house?' she asked, shielding her eyes from the sun and gazing out over the fields at the neighbouring property she'd just tried to banish Frank to.

'Someone very French, I expect,' Haydon said, making his way back.

'How can you tell? It might be someone else on holiday. They might have kids like me.'

'Oh, first night here and already you're making plans to ditch me for more interesting people.'

'No, of course not,' Ella said. Her gaze went to the ground as she scuffed her foot against the gatepost. 'I just meant it might be nice to meet them.'

'It might be nice to have someone your own age around, you mean? Well, I can hardly blame you for that, I suppose.' Haydon forced a smile. He didn't want to admit it, but was he feeling jealous and resentful towards a non-existent teenager who might or might not take Ella from him for the rest of the week? This trip was supposed to be about them spending quality time together, and he had no intention of anyone muscling in on it.

He pushed the notion to one side and made his smile bigger. It was ridiculous, and wasn't the most important thing for Ella to have a good time? If he could send her home with wonderful memories of this holiday then surely it was worth sacrificing a little of their together time to whatever new friendships she might make. And it was only natural that she'd seek out the company of her own age group.

'Maybe we'll go on a reconnaissance mission tomorrow,' he said, looping an arm around her and guiding her back to the house.

'A what?'

'We'll go and check the house out, but we won't make it too obvious. Looking at it, I reckon it's going to be a little old French couple – it's very rustic and not all gleaming and touristy like ours is.'

'I suppose,' Ella said, throwing a glance over her shoulder to look at the distant villa again.

'Maybe there'll be a hot French boy for you to ogle.'

Ella giggled. 'Maybe.'

'As long as ogling is all that happens,' Haydon added. 'If French boys are anything like English boys I'd better keep a close eye on you.'

'They wouldn't fancy me.'

'Of course they would – you're beautiful!'

'No I'm not.'

'Well, I think so, and I'm obviously right because I'm your dad, and dads know all.'

Chapter Seven

Breakfast had been every bit as lavish and glorious as Ashley had imagined it would be. By now she had realised that, despite her very advanced years, Madame Dupont was still a gregarious and welcoming host with plenty of family members willing to pitch in and help cater for the houseful she now had under her roof. The meal featured fresh bread and croissants with lashings of creamy butter and tart preserves; fruit and cheese and cured meats; hot, bitter coffee by the bucketload and juice squeezed straight from locally picked fruit. Ashley couldn't imagine a hotel where she'd have had better food or facilities and certainly not better company. By now the table in the kitchen had fourteen family members seated around it and more were expected to arrive during the next couple of days. The family house was big, but still Ashley had to wonder where all the extra people were going to sleep, until Maurice explained that friends in the area were going to put up the latecomers so they would probably only see them at odd mealtimes and on the day of the big party.

'So…' Ashley flopped onto the swing seat in the garden, full to bursting with breakfast as Molly settled beside her and began to push them into a gentle rock to and fro that was easily relaxing enough to make Ashley want to snooze. But she fought the silky, tempting veil of sleep stealing over her and forced herself to pay attention to Molly. There weren't going to be many opportunities to holiday like this, certainly not in the foreseeable future, so they were going to make the most of every second the day offered. She could sleep at home and if there was a way she could have staved off sleep for this whole week in France she probably would have done. 'What shall we do today? Explore? Beach or town? Or…' she said, waggling her eyebrows, 'do you have plans with a certain handsome boy named Bastien?'

'Shush, he'll hear you!' Molly hissed.

Ashley let out a lazy giggle. 'Don't be so paranoid. So you do like him?'

'I guess…' Molly said, glancing towards the open windows of the house. 'But, you know…'

'What?'

'He's French.'

'And?'

'Well there's no point because I'll never see him again after this week, will I?'

Ashley had to admit that Molly had a point there, and she was pleased to see that, despite the teasing, her daughter was being very mature. Certainly more mature than she herself had been when faced with the same temptation on her first trip abroad. But she tried not to think about that now. She had been a little older if no wiser, alcohol had been involved and Molly was a very different girl than she had been. Molly had grown up with the sorts of responsibilities that Ashley had never been exposed to at her age, and it had made her more measured, more level-headed. She'd learned the limits of their daily lives at an early age and Ashley had been careful to drill her in the importance of working hard to achieve her goals so that she might have a fighting chance of the life she'd missed out on. Sometimes she wondered, however, if she'd drilled those ethics in just a little too deep – often she felt that Molly worked too hard and wasn't a normal, carefree teenager as frequently as she ought to be.

'So if you don't have plans, how about we make some?' Ashley asked.

'I thought we might go to the old town. Maurice says Victor Hugo used to live there and I can see his house.'

'Victor Hugo?' Ashley shook her head.

'He wrote *Les Misérables*,' Molly said.

'And you've read that?'

'No, not exactly…' Molly gave a sheepish smile. 'But I have seen the musical on DVD about a million times.'

'Oh…' Ashley grinned. 'That's the film full of wailing with the really hot guy in it?'

'It's not wailing, it's singing!' Molly said, more than a touch of indignation in her tone, and Ashley had to laugh again.

'I'm just winding you up. Though give me a Take That album any day.'

'Honestly, Mum. Have I managed to teach you nothing about real music?'

'It *is* real music. Just not your sort of music.'

'Hmm…' Molly bit back a grin. Spirits were high, and Ashley was pretty sure nothing was going to dampen them if even her musical disagreements with Molly (and music was life or death as far as Molly was concerned) failed to irritate.

'So you want to go to the old town. We could do that. Your grandma says there's a market on daily and it might be nice to have a mooch around. I think there are some museums and stuff thereabouts—'

'An archaeology museum,' Molly cut in. 'Apparently Saint-Raphaël has been a holiday town as far back as the Romans.'

'Wow, you've been doing your research.'

'Bastien told me yesterday.'

'Ah…' Ashley nodded sagely and thought it best to leave ribbing about Bastien for now.

'He says there's a photography exhibition in the Jardin Bonaparte too and if you go to the top of the tower at the church you can see all of Saint-Raphaël.'

'Did he? He's very useful to know.'

'I suppose everyone else could have told us the same if we'd asked.'

'Lucky you thought to ask then. So you're happy with that plan?'

'Sure.'

'Maybe we can even grab lunch somewhere too.'

'Not here?' Molly asked.

Ashley gave a half-smile. Despite all protestations, there was probably a very good reason Molly wanted to get back for lunch, and his name began with B.

'We could come back to eat if you really want to.'

'I don't think it's that far to walk and the exercise will do us good. Maybe later we can go down to the beach. Bastien says there's windsurfing down there.'

'Well, Bastien can take you windsurfing, because there's no way I'll be doing that.'

'You might like it if you give it a try.'

'I might be in the sea more than I'm on it too. It'll be a total waste of money for someone as clumsy as me. But if you want to try it, don't let me stop you. I'm sure someone will take you.'

'What about something else? Scuba diving or something?'

'God, no! Are you trying to bump me off? I wouldn't last two seconds doing anything like that. Sorry, Moll, but you're going to have to get adventurous with someone else.'

Molly nodded, but Ashley couldn't help feeling she looked disappointed.

'I'll think about it,' Ashley said. 'But I can't promise that I'll suddenly develop a brave gene. Let's go to town first and see what this afternoon brings, OK?'

'OK.' Molly leapt up from the seat, setting it swinging madly. 'I'll get my shoes on.'

*

'I don't suppose we can get cornflakes anywhere?' Ella prodded the bread roll Haydon had put in front of her for breakfast. Buttermilk light flooded the warmly furnished kitchen and the terracotta floor was cool beneath Haydon's bare feet as he sipped a black coffee that chased away any last vestiges of tiredness. His hair was still sticking up from bed and he hadn't yet brushed his teeth but, from the looks of things, Ella had been up for ages and had quietly gone about her morning dress routine as he slept.

'I know it's not what you'd normally eat, but I clean forgot I'd have to shop for breakfast before we settled down last night. Can you manage for now with what Bryn has left for us and we'll try to find a shop or market to get supplies for later?'

'He only left wine and bread.'

'He left a little more than that. Besides, it's a continental breakfast… almost. Bread is what kids here eat for breakfast.'

'I bet they don't have it dry with some mouldy cheese.'

'I bet they do. They *love* mouldy cheese here. Eat it morning, noon and night. Decorate their houses with it, bathe in it, put it in their hair, drive around in hollowed-out mouldy cheeses with mouldy cheese wheels…'

Ella giggled. 'OK, I'll eat the bread but I don't want the cheese. The deal is you get me ice cream instead.'

'For breakfast?'

She nodded. 'As soon as you're dressed that's our first stop – the nearest ice-cream place.'

'I suppose we *are* on holiday. Don't tell your mother, though.'

'She had champagne for breakfast in Mexico. In bed. With strawberries and chocolate. Kevin ate it with her.'

Haydon swallowed hard. 'And what did you have?'

Ella shrugged. 'Cornflakes.'

Haydon gave her a small smile and smoothed a lock of hair from her face. It sounded like Janine and Kevin had treated their previous holiday like a honeymoon rather than a family trip. He wondered whether Ella had felt like a spare part at times. He was determined she wouldn't feel like that on their holiday.

'What do you want to do today? After we get food, that is.'

'I don't mind,' Ella said, nibbling the end of her bread roll. 'What is there?'

'I've been reading the guidebook. There's the beach, of course, the old town and market and the harbour. Or we could stay here and make the most of the pool. Maybe go hunting for Frank to say hello…'

Ella nibbled her thumbnail. 'Well, we have to go to the town to get food so we're ticking that off the list anyway. So maybe the beach. Is there stuff to do?'

Haydon rolled his eyes. 'There's sand and sea – what more do you want from the beach?'

'I don't know… maybe pedalos or something. Kevin went paragliding in Mexico. I was too scared so I stayed with Mum, but if you were with me maybe I wouldn't be so scared this time.'

'You want to go paragliding?' Haydon sat back and appraised his daughter. 'Well, didn't see that coming. I thought maybe we'd buy a bucket and go poking about in rock pools or something.'

'I didn't exactly say I wanted to go. I just meant that if you wanted to do something exciting I'd go with you.'

Haydon sighed to himself. Sometimes trying to understand Ella was like trying to make sense of quantum physics. He clapped his hands together decisively.

'So, town first, then I'm afraid we'll have to bring our bits and pieces straight back so they don't get ruined in the heat. Maybe, in that case, we should have a bit of lunch here and then head back down to the sea. It's not far to walk – at least, Bryn promised me it wouldn't be.'

'And check out the house across the fields, don't forget.'

'Oh, the mysterious pink house! I'd forgotten about that. We'll walk that way and try to look inconspicuous while we nosey. But if they chase us off it's every man for himself!'

'*Dad…*' Ella giggled.

'What? I'm being serious.'

Ella dumped half her roll onto the plate. 'I'm done.'

'You've barely touched it. I spent hours preparing this sumptuous breakfast feast and this is the thanks I get?'

'We can throw it out for the birds.'

'Throw it out for the birds?'

'OK,' Ella said, backtracking quickly, 'maybe save it for supper. I just want to leave room for my ice cream. You promised.'

He downed the rest of his coffee and pushed his chair from the table. Ella wouldn't have got away with demands like this at any other time, but he was feeling so relaxed and content that, just this once, she could get away with whatever she wanted. Perhaps she could sense as much and that was the reason she was trying.

'I'll get my shoes on and then ice cream it is.'

*

Ashley and Molly made their way through the streets of the old town. The bells of the stone church rang out, and Ashley checked her watch.

'Ten. Do you think it's too early for coffee and cake?'

Molly grinned. 'We've literally just eaten breakfast.'

'I know, but all these cafés look so lovely I want to try them all and we've only got a week.'

'Six days now,' Molly reminded her.

'Exactly.'

'Show some restraint, Mother.'

Ashley laughed. 'Yes, daughter. What's your plan then?'

'We go to the market and Place Victor Hugo first, and then maybe we can get something. But you don't want to ruin lunch, and it sounds like Madame Dupont has big plans for that. I heard her giving Nanette a huge list of stuff to go and buy.'

'We could have fetched it for her – we're in the market anyway,' Ashley said with a vague frown.

'She probably didn't want to ask us because we're on holiday and we're guests. Nanette is family so she can boss her around more.'

'I bet she gives them all a run for their money does Madame Dupont. She's a wily old bird.'

'I think she's cute.'

'Oh, she's lovely. But I bet there's an iron constitution beneath that wrinkled old-lady exterior. You don't get to a hundred without a little toughness.'

Molly checked a map on her phone and then pointed to a paved street on the left flanked by palm trees and shop fronts.

'I think it's this way.'

*

'Ten past ten.' Haydon looked at his watch. 'Didn't take us too long to walk down here in the end, did it?'

'It felt like hours,' Ella said.

Ignoring her, Haydon stopped and surveyed the road ahead. 'So this must be the old town. I was reading that loads of famous authors have lived here in the past. There's even a Place Victor Hugo.'

'Does it have an ice-cream parlour? Because unless it does I don't care who lived in it.'

'I don't know if he lived at Place Victor Hugo – it's just named after him.'

'Why?'

'I suppose because he wrote brilliant books.'

'Like what?'

'Like *The Hunchback of Notre Dame*.'

'The Disney film?'

'No.' Haydon smiled. 'I think his book came a little bit before the Disney film but that's where they took the story from. He wrote *Les Misérables* too.'

'I know that,' Ella said, perking up.

'Of course you do. I bet you've played stuff from the musical version at piano lessons.'

'Yeah.'

'So you want to go and check it out?'

'Can we get ice cream first?'

Haydon wrinkled his nose. 'Maybe, but I'm starving because breakfast was crap.'

'You said everyone eats bread for breakfast!'

'Yeah, I lied.' Haydon grinned. 'So how about breakfast in the market? There must be somewhere that serves pastries or croissants or something. Then we'll get the shopping, and then we'll get the ice cream.'

'But you said…'

'I know. Ice cream after, promise. I wouldn't dare deprive you.'

Ella let out a sigh. 'Alright. I suppose we could get breakfast first.'

'So we'll head for the market and if we see somewhere that looks nice we'll stop for a bite to eat.'

'Yes.'

Haydon scratched his head as he surveyed the streets. His attention turned to a street on his left. It was paved in slick grey stones, worn smooth by decades of footfall, and palm trees ran in neat rows along both sides.

'This looks promising.' He looked down at Ella. 'Let's go that way and see where it takes us.'

*

'These look gorgeous!' Ashley lifted a bunch of ruby grapes from a mound at the fruit stall and shook them at Molly. 'I could eat these in one go and I bet they're as fresh as it gets.'

'Very fresh,' the stallholder cut in, smiling. 'Grown very close by.'

Ashley blushed and placed the bunch back on the display. 'Sorry, I didn't mean…'

'No, no… you taste,' the man said, gesturing to the grapes. 'It's no problem.'

'I don't really need to buy them…'

'We could buy some for Madame Dupont,' Molly said, nudging Ashley. 'I bet she'd be chuffed to bits.'

'Violette Dupont?' the stallholder asked. 'At Villa Marguerite?'

'Well, yes,' Ashley replied. 'We're staying with her. She's my stepfather's aunt. You know her?'

'But of course!' The man bagged up a pile of grapes along with a pot of mixed olives and a handful of almonds as Ashley and Molly watched with vague frowns. 'You take these for her,' he said. 'No charge. She is very good and old friend; these are her favourites.'

'That's very kind.' Ashley took the carrier bag from him.

'And for you?' he asked.

'Us?'

'You like grapes? Here…' He pressed another paper bag containing a smaller bunch into her hand. 'No charge. You try them, you will come for more, I guarantee.'

'Wow, thank you!' Ashley smiled.

The man gave a little nod. 'You are welcome. Tell Violette I wish her well for her birthday.'

'We will,' Molly said.

The man waved them off as they left his stall and continued on their perusal of the market.

'Wow, he was lovely,' Ashley said.

'Perhaps him and Violette had a thing once. He looks about the right age,' Molly said with a wicked grin. She pointed to a stall loaded with glistening pastries. 'Fancy a nosey at the less healthy options?'

'What was that about spoiling our lunch?' Ashley asked with a sideways look.

*

'Right…' Haydon clapped his hands together as he surveyed the market square where canopied stalls stood on the gleaming cobbles, stocking everything from stuffed toys to locally made wine. 'Supplies. What shall we get first?'

A fruit stall caught his eye, where a trader was lazily wafting a wasp from a mound of juicy-looking nectarines. The movement almost looked too smooth and swift for a man who seemed to be way past retirement age, but it wasn't a great leap of the imagination to wonder if life in such a pleasant climate, minus traffic fumes and stress and all the other things that characterised Haydon's own life back in England, was a good prescription for a healthy old age.

'I suppose I'd better get you some of the good stuff. Just so we can say so to your mum when she asks what I've been feeding you on all week. I know she expects me to answer with Toblerones and hamburgers so let's impress her, eh?'

'I like fruit.'

'I know, but we're on holiday – I thought you might decide fruit was too boring on holiday.'

Ella shrugged. 'It looks nice.'

'I know what you mean. Everything somehow looks better and tastier when it's displayed out here in the sunshine rather than in a dingy supermarket back home.'

They began to make their way over. 'So what do you fancy?' he asked as they walked.

'*Bonjour,*' the stallholder greeted them. '*Ca va?*'

'*Bonjour, bien, merci,*' Haydon replied uncertainly, and clearly the vendor recognised the accent immediately as he made a smooth switch to perfect English.

'You are on holiday?'

'Yes,' Haydon replied with a degree of relief that he wouldn't have to continue in French. His command of the language wasn't too bad, but he'd had practically no cause to recall any of it for a great many years and he wasn't sure just how much he'd be able to remember under the pressure of having to. 'Just arrived yesterday.'

'You are staying at the hotel?'

'No, at a villa – hence the need to buy lots of food. I'm afraid we're not very well prepared.'

The man laughed. 'Plenty of food here and we will all be happy to take your euros!'

Haydon smiled. 'I'm sure.'

The old man looked at Ella. '*Bonjour, Mademoiselle.* What would you like?' He handed her a purple grape the size of her thumb. 'You like grapes? You try this and tell your papa if you want to buy.'

Ella took it and glanced at Haydon, who gave a tiny nod before she popped it into her mouth.

'It's lovely,' she said, but Haydon wondered if she was saying that just to please the old man or whether she really meant it. But the grapes looked pretty good and they'd doubtless eat them if he bought some.

'I'll take that bunch,' he said, pointing. 'And perhaps some apples?' he added, looking at Ella, who nodded.

'Peaches too,' Ella said. 'And strawberries…'

The stallholder chuckled. 'You like the fruit?'

'Yes,' Ella said, her smile suddenly shy as Haydon paid for their shopping.

The old man waved them off as they left his stall, and Haydon's attention turned to one piled with bread and pastries of all kinds. The vendor there was just bidding farewell in English to a woman and a girl who was already tucking into a croissant from a paper bag as Haydon and Ella arrived so it was another easy interaction if he shopped here for their bread. For a moment Haydon's attention was caught by them and he stared after the pair as they walked away. Did he know the woman from somewhere? He shook his head slightly. Perhaps it was one of his ex-pupils? Whoever it was, they were already disappearing into the crowds of the market, and to chase down someone that he may or may not know seemed a little crazy, so he let the notion drop and fixed a smile on Ella again.

'Look at all this cake,' he said, nodding at the stall as the woman who ran it greeted them with a warm smile. 'Now we can really spend some money!'

'*Bonjour, Monsieur,*' the stallholder said. 'Can I help you?' She pushed a strand of hair the colour of nutmeg away from her face and smiled as she smoothed it behind an ear. For the first time he was able to see her properly, and Haydon stopped and stared. And then he realised he was staring as he gave a hasty reply.

'Um… we're not sure what we want yet.'

'Take your time,' she said. And Haydon found himself staring again, despite trying so hard not to. Her long hair was tied back in a loose knot at the nape of her neck, her eyes were a startling green and her skin was the colour of warm caramel. Her limbs were slender and she wore her simple white T-shirt and capri pants with elegant ease. Haydon tore away his gaze and turned to see that even Ella was looking at the stallholder with awe.

'You are on vacation?' the woman asked.

'Yes, arrived yesterday.'

'You like Saint-Raphaël so far?'

'It's lovely,' Ella said. 'Though we haven't seen much of it yet.'

'Breakfast first,' Haydon said, sinking his hands into his pockets in a bid to look casual. 'You live here?'

She shook her head. 'In Fréjus – it's not too far away. I visit all of the local markets in the area.'

'That sounds like a nice life.'

'It is hard work.' She smiled. 'I must get up very early.'

'You don't look like it,' Haydon said and wished he hadn't as the heat travelled to his face. What a ridiculous thing to say. What a ridiculous reaction he was having to this woman, especially with Ella standing right next to him, but she was so impossibly beautiful that he couldn't help it. 'I mean, if I got up really early every day I'd look a mess… not great… if you see what I mean…'

'Are you married?' Ella asked the woman, and Haydon whipped round to stare at her. But the stallholder simply gave a musical laugh.

'No, I am not married.' And as she said it she shot a swift glance at Haydon. Was she *flirting* with him? He hardly dared imagine he'd be so lucky – she was way out of his league. In fact, she was way out of the league of any man alive.

'My mum and my dad aren't together any more,' Ella said, and this time Haydon widened his eyes in a silent warning.

'We'll get some pain au chocolat,' Haydon said, desperate to steer the conversation away from such mortifying territory. Had it been that obvious he fancied this woman like mad? And did he seem so desperate for a girlfriend that even Ella was trying to matchmake now? 'And perhaps half a dozen croissants to see us through tomorrow morning too, eh, Ella?'

'But of course,' the woman said smoothly, clearly aware that he was uncomfortable with the turn of the conversation, though at the corners of her mouth tugged a smile that spoke of amusement too. She began to pack the croissants into a bag.

'How many pain au chocolat?'

'Four?' Haydon asked, looking to Ella for approval. Ella, perhaps realising herself just how she'd overstepped the mark, simply gave a silent nod and then looked at her feet. The woman packed the pains au chocolat too, and then spoke to Ella directly.

'Mademoiselle…'

Ella looked up to see the woman was smiling sweetly, holding out a pink-iced cupcake. 'For you.'

Ella took it, breaking into a broad smile. 'Thank you!'

'You are welcome. Your papa is a lucky man to have such a beautiful and loving daughter.'

'I know it,' Haydon said, pride swelling in his breast as he looked at Ella now. She'd only wanted to see him dating, see him happy. He hadn't realised until this moment that she'd perhaps been hoping to see that for a long time, especially as her mum had moved on with Kevin. Perhaps she understood better than he gave her credit for that Haydon found it painful to see Kevin take his place in their household. But it was hard to understand at Ella's age that life or love wasn't so simple.

'Will you be here again?' Ella asked.

'In two days,' the woman said. 'But I will be at markets in Port Grimaud and Fréjus also.'

'We'll come back, won't we, Dad?'

'Absolutely,' Haydon said.

'*Bon.*' The woman gave Ella a warm smile. 'I am glad to have met you. And you also, *Monsieur*,' she added, turning to Haydon with a smile that was rather more coquettish.

'Haydon,' he said. 'My name's Haydon. And this is Ella.'

'My name is Audrey. I hope to see you again, Haydon and Ella.'

He gave her a dopey smile and picked up his bags. 'We should probably get going…'

'Of course. Goodbye.'

Ella whispered as they walked away, 'She was *so* pretty!'

'Yes,' Haydon said in a carefully neutral reply.

'And she's not married,' Ella said, licking the top of her cupcake. Haydon glanced down at her. She wore a wide-eyed look that he recognised well: her *you must believe I'm not up to anything* look.

'It doesn't mean she's not dating. And she's French.'

'So?'

'Ella…'

'Yes?'

Haydon shook his head. 'Never mind. Eat your cake, and if you still have room for ice cream after that I'll be amazed.'

*

'That's weird,' Ashley murmured as they walked towards the exit of the market and back into the streets of the old town where colourful doors in pale stone houses ran in higgledy-piggledy rows and every window box was stuffed with bright flowers. The sounds of the market were already fading to a murmur, but the sweet scent of the goods on offer still hung in the warm air.

'What is?'

'Huh?' Ashley shook her head and realised that the thought had also come out of her mouth.

'Oh… the pastry was cheaper than I was expecting, that's all.'

'I'd have thought it would be a good thing, not weird,' Molly said.

'Well, yes,' Ashley replied with a vague smile. 'It is, but I was just wondering how I'd got it wrong.'

'Because – and I say this with love – you can be a bit scatty.'

'Thank you.' Ashley looked askance at her daughter. 'I'm pleased to hear that I command such respect and awe in you. *Scatty?*'

'I did say it was said with love,' Molly replied.

'That makes it alright then.'

'If it makes you feel any better then I think I'm scatty too.'

'Not really, because that would make it my fault.'

'It might not. I do have more than one *biological* parent, you know.'

It was a flippant comment, and ordinarily Ashley would have attached no significance to it. For Molly, not knowing about her father had never really been an issue, and it was as natural a reality to her as it was for her friends to have a regular nuclear family. She'd never been bitter about it, though sometimes over the years she'd been curious. Ashley had told her as much as she knew – which wasn't actually very much at all – and that had been enough for Molly. She loved her mother and she didn't need anyone else. And sometimes, when schoolfriends came in with stories of embarrassing or overprotective fathers, Molly had even told Ashley that she was glad only to have a really cool mother.

Ashley tried not to connect what Molly had just said with the man she'd glimpsed in the market. He had looked so remarkably like a man she'd once known, one she had no wish to see again, that she'd felt the blood leave her face and her heart almost stop. He'd turned to chat to a teenage girl by his side and Ashley, shaken and confused, had ushered Molly away as quickly as she could while trying to pretend that all was normal.

But it couldn't be him. Here, in Saint-Raphaël, of all places? Now, of all times? That would be ridiculous. And he must have changed a lot in sixteen years – she was sure she had – so she'd probably barely recognise him if she did see him now. Ashley gave herself an internal prod and chased the thought away. It *was* ridiculous, and there was no point in worrying about it because it would only ruin her holiday. It was probably some random bloke with a passing resemblance and it wouldn't be the first time she'd seen someone who'd looked a little like him, though she'd never felt quite so shaken by it before.

'Mum?' Molly nudged her. 'Are you listening? Do you want me to save one of these pastries for you or not? Because I can totally eat them all.'

'What about lunch?'

'Don't worry.' She grinned. 'I've got a fast metabolism – lunch will be no problem.'

'You eat them,' Ashley said. 'I can wait now.'

As they walked past the church the clock bells struck the hour. Ashley counted eleven chimes. They hadn't been out for long, but for some reason she suddenly felt sapped of energy and she wanted nothing more than to sit in the shade of Violette Dupont's veranda and rock gently on the old swing seat. It would be lunch soon anyway, so perhaps Molly wouldn't mind if they headed back a little earlier than they'd planned. Ashley would make it up to her later, go to the beach or swimming or something.

'Maybe we should get some flowers for Violette and head back. It's going to take a little while to walk and we don't want to rush in this heat. After lunch, when things cool down, we can venture out again.'

'That's fine,' Molly said, licking her fingers as she finished off the second pastry. 'I can FaceTime Imogen anyway – it's her birthday and her parents are taking her out later.'

'I bet she can't wait for that,' Ashley said with a wry smile.

'I think they're getting on a lot better,' Molly said. 'At least her mum hasn't thrown a drink at her dad for the last few weeks, so they must be making progress.' She slipped her arm through Ashley's to walk with her. 'At least we don't have any of that crap to worry about when it's just me and you and we get on really well.'

Ashley forced a smile that felt as if it had no right to be on her face. Molly was right, but why couldn't she shake the unsettling and random idea that everything was about to change?

*

Haydon checked his watch. 'I think we're about done. It's eleven fifteen now and it's going to take us a while to walk back to the villa, so maybe we should start back?'

'We can get ice cream first?'

'You're not going to give up on this, are you?'

Ella grinned. 'Nope.'

'Well, if you can walk with it you can have it. I don't want to risk this food going off in the heat. But if you want to wait we can come straight back and spend the afternoon here and you can eat ice cream until you hurl.'

'Dad!' Ella groaned. 'Sometimes you're so gross.'

'Not funny?'

'Not as funny as you think.'

'Hmm…' Haydon said, pretending to be deep in thought. 'That's disappointing.'

'But you are quite funny. Sometimes.'

'When I'm not with you?'

'Usually,' Ella replied with a grin.

Haydon was quiet as they wandered the old town looking for an ice-cream parlour. He'd spent a great deal of the morning trying to work out whether Audrey's flirting had been flirting at all. Surely a woman that gorgeous couldn't be interested in someone like him? And yet the signs had been there. He wondered what she would say if he ran back there and asked her to dinner. But then he had Ella to think of too, and it didn't seem very responsible to get involved with a local. He supposed they could take Ella with them, though it would hardly be romantic. Perhaps that would be OK, though.

And then, for some strange reason, something else came back to him. The English woman he'd seen leaving Audrey's stall before he arrived. In the back of his mind, that had been bugging him too. She'd looked so familiar – and then all at once it came to him. She looked exactly like the girl he'd had a one-night stand with in Ibiza. He hadn't thought of her for a long time now, and he'd stopped wondering where she was and what had happened to her. It hadn't been his intention for it to be a one-night stand – in fact, he'd almost fancied he'd fallen for her that night. He'd left his number before rushing off for his early flight, but she'd never called him, and he'd taken that as a sign that she'd either been ashamed or appalled by their liaison, that she hadn't fancied him in the same way he'd fancied her, or that it was nothing new to her and she treated all her one-night stands as just that, with no desire to make them anything more lasting. He'd been a little hurt at first, but once he'd met Janine all that had faded.

The woman he'd seen in the market had a girl with her – perhaps a little older than Ella. Had his fling from all those years ago settled down? Maybe she'd found Mr Right, had kids, a successful career, the perfect family, the whole shebang. He hunted in his memory for a minute; what had she been called? Ashley – that was it! It was all he had. They'd been too drunk to exchange surnames, or if they had he didn't remember. He didn't even know where she was from; all he had was the memory of a sexy accent that sounded like something northern, though he couldn't even begin to say where. As for recalling her face, he wasn't sure he could until he'd seen the woman in the market just now; the more he thought about it, the more the details came back to him.

'Dad.' Ella pointed to a pink-and-pistachio-striped awning, interrupting his reverie. 'I think that's the ice-cream place there.'

'So it is,' he said, forcing himself back to the here and now. 'So, how about we get a cone as big as your head and fill it?'

Chapter Eight

'You want to walk past the pink villa on the way back to ours?' Haydon asked as they approached the fields on the outskirts of town that separated it from their own accommodation. 'You said yesterday you wanted to find out who lives there.'

'Don't we have to get our food back before it goes off?'

'It wouldn't take a minute. I'm sure the food could last that bit longer.'

Ella looked doubtful. 'What if they come out?'

'Then we'll just say hello and be on our way. It's no bother if you've changed your mind, though.'

Ella shook her head. 'It's fine – we can go.'

'You're sure?'

'Yeah, but we won't knock on the door or anything, will we?'

'I thought you wanted to find a new friend and ditch me?'

'Don't start that again,' Ella said, and for a startling moment Haydon could have closed his eyes and imagined that it was Janine chastising him. As Ella got older those moments happened more and more often.

'OK,' he said, his humour dampened, 'I won't.'

They veered off the path to their own villa and headed for the neighbouring house. It had seemed vivid from a distance but as they grew closer they could see the pink plaster was faded in places, even missing from some, and the wood of the veranda was sun-bleached and in need of fresh varnish. The garden was thick with wildflowers that almost obscured the path, and shrubs rambled and climbed every inch of available garden space the flowers had neglected. The air was thick with sweet floral scents and the drowsy hum of honeybees. Roof tiles had slipped here and there and a grey tabby lay stretched across a large swing seat strewn with cushions in the shade of the eaves. It was far from pristine and in need of some repair, but Haydon was struck by the perfect imperfection of it, by the overwhelming sense of contentment radiating from it. The place he shared with Ella was freshly and probably frequently painted and equipped with everything they needed, and it was a beautiful house, but this… this felt like someone's home. He couldn't help thinking that anyone who was welcomed into this house would immediately feel like they were home too.

He stood for a moment, perhaps ten feet away from the gates as he took the details in. And then he turned to Ella.

'Seems pretty quiet,' he said. 'Maybe there's nobody home.'

But then a long peal of laughter rolled out of an open window and voices followed – some speaking French and some English. Ella looked up at Haydon and seemed vaguely alarmed.

'Maybe we should go back to ours.'

'Maybe you're right,' Haydon agreed, and they turned to leave. But then a voice from behind them had them spinning around.

'*Bonjour!*'

A slender woman of around sixty stood on the porch, smiling patiently. '*Vous êtes perdu?*'

'Umm…' Haydon glanced at Ella, who returned it with a look of the utmost trust and faith. She was counting on him to be in control at all times, but being caught on the doorstep of the house had thrown him off guard. And his stubborn brain refused to translate the simple question that the woman had asked, even though he knew that if he thought about it quietly for a moment he'd figure it out.

'*Parlez vous anglais?*' he asked, annoyed at himself for having to resort to the most obvious cop-out.

'Yes,' the woman replied, making her way down the path to them. She was tall and elegant, dressed in a simple linen shift dress, dark-haired and caramel-eyed. She was a woman who would have turned heads in her youth. 'Can I help you?'

'My daughter and I are on holiday,' Haydon said as he walked back with Ella. 'In the house over the fields. We were just on our way back and were… admiring your garden. We didn't mean to disturb you.'

'You do not disturb,' the woman said. 'The garden is not mine – it belongs to my aunt. I'm afraid she's too old to keep it perfectly these days, but she tries.'

'She does a lovely job. Sometimes perfect isn't what's attractive.'

The woman inclined her head in agreement. 'So, you stay in Saint-Raphaël long?'

'Just a week. Arrived yesterday. It's beautiful – at least what we've seen so far is. Lovely people too.'

'Perhaps you would like to meet my family…' She looked at Ella. 'We have an English girl staying with us – Molly. I think you may be good friends if you met – she is perhaps the same age as you? They are here for a week only too. For my aunt's birthday celebrations. She is a hundred, you know.'

'Wow,' Haydon said.

Ella gave a shy smile but said nothing. It wasn't often that she was this quiet, but she suddenly seemed overwhelmed.

'Come…' The woman beckoned them. 'I will introduce you, and then you will have friends nearby.'

But Haydon hesitated and glanced at Ella, who seemed uncertain too. It wasn't that he had any issue with making friends, but he didn't want to intrude, and he felt he'd already done that to some extent.

'We have fresh food in the bags here,' he replied. 'And it's hot so we should probably get it back before it all spoils. Maybe another time?'

'Tonight?' the woman said. 'We will have a family meal and you are more than welcome to join us. It will be good for the young people to meet. I have a great nephew too – Bastien. He is sixteen.'

'Tonight?' Haydon repeated.

'You have another appointment?'

'No, it's not that, it's…'

'Well,' the woman said. 'It is there. If you wish to come, then come. If not, then that will be OK, and perhaps we will see you another time.'

Haydon nodded. 'Thank you.'

'Come at seven if you are going to,' the woman called as she turned to go back to the house. And then Haydon and Ella watched as she disappeared beyond the front door, both wondering just how they were meant to feel about their impromptu and very surprising invite.

*

Ashley sat at the huge kitchen table trying to follow a half-French and half-English conversation between four new arrivals and the family members that had arrived the day before. Molly was faring better, having taken GCSE French at school, but even she was struggling to keep up with the pace of the discussion. Every so often she'd whisper a rough translation in Ashley's ear, but some of it was so random that Ashley had to wonder if Molly was following it quite as well as she thought she was. At some point Nanette had decided to let a cricket that had found its way into the kitchen out into the garden and had disappeared, and although nobody else seemed concerned, Ashley couldn't help but notice she'd been gone rather a long time for someone who'd just nipped out to give freedom to a bug. She was just about to bring it to the attention of the table at large when Nanette returned. She spoke briefly to Violette in French for a moment, who broke into a broad grin and nodded enthusiastically. Then she turned to Molly, who sat with Ashley at one side of her and Sue on the other.

'You know the house across the field?'

Molly shook her head, but Nanette continued, unfazed by the negative response. 'There is a young English girl staying there this week. Perhaps you will be friends.'

Ashley thought this was unlikely – you couldn't just throw two teenagers together and assume they'd automatically become best friends simply because they were a similar age – but she thought better of saying so.

'I have invited them to dinner tonight,' Nanette added. 'And Aunt Violette will be happy to meet them.'

'Them?' Maurice asked.

'The girl and her father…' She aimed a most disconcerting wink in Ashley's direction. 'The father is very handsome, and I think he is alone with his daughter… no wife.'

Ashley's stomach dropped. The last thing she needed was matchmaking of any sort, but offending Maurice's gregarious and well-intentioned family hadn't featured on her to-do list either.

'So we have more guests?' Antoine, another of Maurice's cousins, asked. 'We have barely room for the family…' He twisted to look at Ashley and offered an apologetic look. 'I did not mean—'

'I know,' Ashley said.

'Aunt Violette is happy,' Nanette said defensively. 'She is almost a hundred and she wants the world to celebrate with her! Perhaps you will want the world to see when you are a hundred!'

Antoine's gaze flitted to Madame Dupont – also known as Aunt Violette or simply Violette, depending on where you featured in the family hierarchy – and it seemed she'd got the gist of the conversation because she nodded vehemently in agreement with Nanette. Antoine gave a vague shrug and turned back to his glass of lemonade.

'So, it is settled,' Nanette said. 'We will set two extra places at seven, and we will show them how kind and happy a French family can be.'

*

'Damn...' Haydon set the shopping bags on the kitchen counter. Ella turned to him with a silent question.

'We didn't get any eggs.'

'Can't we live without eggs?'

'I just thought we might have some in the morning.'

'But I thought you got extra croissants from Audrey for the morning.'

'Well, yes, but...' Haydon tried to play it cool, but Audrey was the reason he wanted to go back to town, and a lack of eggs had been the first excuse he could come up with. It was crazy, but he couldn't stop wondering how she might react to an invitation to join them for dinner. She'd almost certainly say no, but did it matter? It wasn't like he had to see her again if she turned him down. Maybe Ella had been right to give him a nudge; maybe he'd spent too long moping over Janine and maybe it wasn't healthy for any of them. The logistics of any kind of serious relationship with Audrey would be tricky, of course, but that didn't stop them spending a pleasant few hours together, did it? Perhaps there wasn't true love in it, but maybe there'd be enough fun there to rebuild his confidence and get him dating again once he got back home.

'I don't really care about having eggs.'

'Still, I think we should dash down before the market closes up.'

Ella flopped into a chair. 'But we just walked all the way up from town. And it's miles!'

'It's not miles – it honestly won't take more than half an hour. And then we can do whatever you want.'

'I can stay here.'

'You can't.'

'Why not?'

'Because your mum would kill me if she found out I'd left you home alone.'

'I'm old enough.'

'I know, but that's not the point. Please, Ella.'

'You must really want those eggs,' Ella muttered, pushing herself up.

'I do,' he said, already striding for the door. 'Thank you.'

Ella followed, and he let the door swing closed behind them as they began the journey back to town. The ground shimmered in the afternoon heat and a couple of minutes saw beads of sweat trickling down Haydon's back. He couldn't decide whether it was down to the sun or his nerves, but it was probably a combination of both. It had been a long time since he'd asked a woman out, especially one as beautiful as Audrey, and when he'd done it in the past he'd invariably been drunk.

'Slow down!' Ella panted.

'Sorry… just want to get there before the shops close.'

'Don't they close really late in the evening? Like, don't they have a siesta in the day?'

'I thought that was Spain.'

Ella shrugged. 'I don't think you have to worry, Dad. I saw some signs for a supermarket too – we could go there in the car.'

'I'd rather get farm eggs from town. I noticed a stall selling farm goods.'

'I didn't see it,' Ella said doubtfully.

'It was close to Audrey's stall.'

Ella didn't reply, and when Haydon looked again he could have sworn she was biting back a grin.

'What?'

'Nothing. I wonder if Audrey's still there.'

'I expect she's packed up and gone by now,' Haydon replied.

'I expect so. I expect all the market stalls have gone by now.'

'We can try anyway. If not then I'll have to head to the supermarket out of town after all.'

In record time they reached the old square. As Haydon had predicted, many of the stalls were already packed up and gone. He made his way to the place where he recalled Audrey's being and saw that hers had gone too.

'There's the stall with eggs,' Ella said, pointing to one nearby. 'But we'd better hurry because it looks as if they'll be gone soon.'

'Right,' Haydon said, disappointment visible in the slouch of his shoulders as they made their way over. He reached into his pocket for some money as Ella rushed ahead and placed the order. But then his attention was drawn to a lithe, elegant figure with caramel skin making her way across the square, nutmeg hair escaping a messy bun. Involuntarily, he gave a goofy smile as she set eyes on him and changed course.

'We meet again,' she said in sultry tones.

'I've come for—'

'Dad!' Ella shouted from the produce stall. 'Dad, I need some money!'

'Right…' Haydon looked helplessly from Ella, waiting to pay the man for eggs, and then at Audrey.

'Don't go anywhere for a second… please?' he asked. He beckoned Ella over and shoved a ten-euro note into her hand. Ella grinned up at Audrey and then shot a knowing look at her dad before racing off with the money.

'Yes,' Audrey said as Haydon turned back to her.

'What?'

'You were going to ask me to dinner?'

'I… How did you know?'

Audrey shrugged. 'You look nervous.'

'Oh.'

'You did not want to ask me to dinner?' Audrey said with a slight frown now.

'Yes… oh, God yes! Would you? I mean, we'd have to have Ella with us because I couldn't leave her, but I thought… well, it's just as friends, you know?'

'When?'

'I don't know… When is good for you?'

'In two days, when I am in town again. After the market has ended. Would that be agreeable to you?'

'Fantastic!' Haydon grinned. 'Two days, sounds brilliant. We should probably exchange numbers… you know.'

'*Bon.*' Audrey took out her phone. 'I will see you in two days.' She looked over to where Ella was making her way back and gave her a little wave. 'I will let your papa tell you the plans!' she said with a soft laugh as she walked away.

'What plans?' Ella asked, handing the eggs to Haydon. 'You're going on a date?'

'We're all going to dinner, that's all. Nothing to get excited about.'

'How are you supposed to have a date with me there?'

'It's not a date, and I'm not leaving you for a whole evening at the villa alone.'

'I'd be fine,' Ella pouted. 'She likes you and it'll be ruined if you turn up with me.'

'Nothing will be ruined,' Haydon said, gesturing for them to start walking. But Ella was right – having her there was hardly conducive to romance. Still, it couldn't be helped, and as he'd reminded himself a thousand times that day, perhaps he shouldn't be expecting romance in the form of Audrey, because circumstances were against it no matter how gorgeous she was.

*

Seven o'clock came and went. Ashley couldn't say why but she was relieved when no handsome English neighbour with his teenage daughter turned up at their family meal. Her mood had gone from vague dread to relaxed joviality, and as the wine had flowed and the sublime food kept coming, she had forgotten all about them. Aunt Violette, with the help of Maurice and Nanette, served up tapenade followed by traditional fish stew and fresh fruit and local cheeses. Antoine had called it peasant food, though he'd helped to polish it off just the same, and Molly, who'd viewed everything with the deepest suspicion, had been persuaded to try a little of each course and even announced, to Maurice's delight, that she'd always hated fish but his bouillabaisse wasn't half bad. It had turned out to be a very enjoyable night and Ashley had gone to bed more than a little tipsy.

But when Nanette announced at breakfast the following day that she was going to call at their neighbour's house to see if everything was OK and check if they needed anything, Ashley couldn't help but wish that she would stop being quite such a busybody. Things were made worse by Molly's agreement to go with her, along with Bastien, and then Ashley knew for sure that Nanette was trying to throw the kids together. Which would have been fine, if not for the fact that the kids getting to know each other would invariably mean that the adults would have to meet at some point too and Ashley had her hands full enough getting to know Maurice's huge clan without a handsome English neighbour to worry about.

It wasn't that she was against handsome neighbours per se, but she'd had her fingers burnt enough in the past to know that the handsome ones were usually trouble. In the end she couldn't really argue with Sue's agreement that if the little English girl at the neighbouring house of *Bastide de la Mer* was half as quiet and shy as Nanette said she was then Molly's friendship would probably do her a lot of good. When Molly herself backed this up, seemingly taken with the idea of being some poor lonely teenager's saviour, it looked as if the decision had been taken out of Ashley's hands entirely.

*

Feeling more than a bit chuffed with himself, Haydon had left the eggs in the kitchen and joined Ella in the pool for a splash about. They'd swam until long shadows crept across the garden and Ella's teeth had started to chatter, and it wasn't until they'd both decided that they were starving and had quite forgotten to eat that the discovery was made.

'Dad…' Ella called from the kitchen as Haydon towelled himself off. 'You know when you said earlier that you didn't want the food to go off…'

Haydon wrapped himself in the towel and went inside. Ella grinned at him, angling her head at the shopping bags on the kitchen counter, eggs next to them.

'Bugger,' he said. 'That's chicken off the menu,' he added, pulling a pack of breasts out and sniffing at them.

'Are they bad?' Ella asked.

'I have no idea, but I daren't cook them up now. How about we go and find a restaurant – and don't worry,' he added, seeing the look on her face, 'I can drive this time.'

'We could go to the house across the way – they did ask us.'

'I think we're a little bit late for a seven o'clock start,' he said. 'Did you really want to go?'

'I had a good time here,' Ella said. 'It was just a thought.'

'So you don't mind we missed it?'

'It might have been a bit weird I suppose, because we didn't know them at all.'

'My feelings exactly. So how about we find a pizza parlour or something? Sound good?'

Ella nodded. 'I'll go and get dressed!'

They'd found a cute little place on the coast road and they'd eaten to bursting, getting back late and falling into bed. In the morning, however, despite the lateness of their bedtime, Ella was up first and made so much noise clattering about that it was obvious she was keen for Haydon to get up too. But he was happy to oblige, in a great mood and enthusiastic for what the day might hold after their great start in Saint-Raphaël.

It was while they ate Audrey's buttery croissants with apricot jam for breakfast that the knock echoed through the house. Haydon looked at Ella and she returned his puzzled expression. Visitors? Here?

'It might be someone checking on the house,' Ella offered.

'Maybe,' Haydon agreed, silently chiding himself for the vague sense of alarm. What he didn't say to Ella was that maybe it was their over-familiar neighbour from the pink house across the fields. He was beginning to wish he'd never gone over to investigate and had stayed firmly on his own side of the grass. It had been enough of a trauma deciding whether to accept the invitation issued the night before and he'd tussled with the idea of not going long after he'd settled on it, certain that a huge room full of people they didn't know wasn't the most relaxing way to spend an evening, nice as Nanette seemed. So if it was her now then he faced the mortifying prospect of explaining to her why he hadn't turned up. What if she'd come to express her deepest disgust at his no-show? Offending the neighbours hadn't exactly been at the top of his to-do list this week. Then again, it would be a pretty weird thing to do if she had.

His thoughts were interrupted by another rap at the door. Glad that he'd decided to dress early, he got up from the breakfast table and went to get it, his worst suspicions confirmed as the woman they'd met the day before stood smiling at the doorway with two teenagers in tow.

'*Bonjour, Monsieur...*'

'Stokes,' Haydon replied, forgetting that usually he would dispense with formalities and get people to use his first name.

'*Monsieur Stokes, bon.* And here' – she gestured to the teenagers – 'Molly and Bastien. We are all here to celebrate my aunt's birthday for one week only – I think I told you this last evening. But perhaps a week is a long time for the children, yes? You have only one daughter?' Nanette asked, trying to see past him into the house.

'Yes, just me and Ella.'

'Ella – a beautiful name. We are going to the beach today. Would you like to come? Perhaps Ella would like to make new friends.'

Haydon wondered vaguely if this woman was some sort of self-appointed kids' entertainer for the area or whether she was trying to collect them for some sinister project. But she looked harmless enough – in fact, more than charming – and perhaps she was just trying to be friendly after all. He had to stop this silly notion that somehow all of Ella's time belonged to him alone. She'd have a much better holiday if she had some people her own age to socialise with and it didn't mean he had to give her up for the whole week.

He turned to call her to the door and she arrived within seconds – clearly she'd been listening.

She gave the visitors a shy smile.

'I am pleased to make your official acquaintance, Ella,' Nanette said. 'Here I have Molly and Bastien. We would love for you to come to the beach with us.'

Ella turned to Haydon as Molly and Bastien appeared to size her up. 'Are you coming, Dad?'

'But of course!' Nanette cut in. 'You are both invited!'

Haydon swallowed his doubts and nodded brightly. 'Sounds like a good plan to me. Nanette obviously knows the area well and she can show us all the best bits we might have missed by ourselves.'

'Then it is settled!' Nanette clapped her hands. 'What time shall we say to come back?'

'Give us an hour to finish breakfast and clean up?' Haydon said. 'Does that sound OK?'

'One hour and we will return,' Nanette replied. 'How wonderful,' Haydon heard her add as they skirted the pool on their way to the gates. 'You will have a charming new friend.'

Bloody hell, what had he got himself into now?

Chapter Nine

With some unexpected last minute faffing and the walk down to the beach, it was more like two hours later when they all arrived. The party had grown and included two other older relatives of Nanette's – a cousin and a second cousin, as far as Haydon could make out – who were all keen to make the most of the sun and sea. He learned that one of them – Blanche – was from Lille, up in the north as Nanette herself was, and the other was named Jacques and lived in Paris like Bastien.

During the walk he'd got to know them all a little better and they were all open and affable. Molly and Bastien seemed friendly enough. In fact, though Haydon had a natural dread of the teenage species – perhaps driven in part by his need to teach many of the less engaged ones how to play a musical instrument most of them had no interest in learning – he found them really quite likeable. Especially Molly. She seemed mature and thoughtful, and he quickly learned that she played violin; that point alone was enough to win him over.

Ella was sold too, despite Molly being two years her senior, or perhaps because of it. Younger teenagers were often beguiled by the glamour of an older one and Ella was no exception, keen to fit in and impress. Molly was sweet with her too, tolerant of Ella's excitable chatter, taking her under her wing like an older sister, and the fact that they shared a love of classical music certainly helped them find common ground.

'So your aunt is a hundred?' Haydon said as he helped lay a blanket out on the sand, slightly annoyed at himself that he hadn't thought to bring a blanket to sit on too. Now he and Ella would have to cram onto Nanette's. 'That's pretty amazing.'

'In our family it is not so amazing,' Blanche said.

'Many of our relatives have lived long lives,' Nanette agreed. 'We are blessed with years, it seems.'

'You must be,' Haydon said. 'I don't know anyone who's made it that far.'

Nanette smiled. But then her gaze went across the beach and she began to wave at two figures walking across the sand.

'Friends of yours?' Haydon asked.

'They are coming to join us, I think,' she replied. 'My brother Maurice and his stepdaughter. This morning they were too busy, but perhaps they changed their mind.'

Great, Haydon thought. Although a small part of him was now beginning to enjoy the company of his new friends, socialising wasn't really his natural territory and adding more people into the mix wasn't going to make him feel any more relaxed. At least the teens were faring better – Molly and Ella had already sprinted after Bastien as he beckoned them from the shoreline, and they were now leaping over the waves like kids half their ages. Haydon went back to searching for the sun cream he'd hastily stuffed into a bag.

He vaguely listened as he heard Nanette's greeting and his name mentioned and he looked up to offer a brief friendly smile. And then the world around him stopped, along with his heart, as he stared at the woman who'd come to join them.

It couldn't be. And yet some unnameable instinct told him that he'd already known she was here – the woman from the market he'd convinced himself was simply a trick of his memory was no trick after all. She was real, and she stood before him now. The name stuck in his throat and came out more like the squeak of a tuning bagpipe than a word.

'Ashley?'

She frowned. And then, it seemed, realisation for her too – the same disbelief and shock. But as he stepped forward with a million questions suddenly zipping around his head she turned ashen – and stumbled. His step turned into a lunge as he watched her sway, then wobble, and then crumple, and he raced to catch her. But Nanette's brother beat him to it and caught her nimbly in capable arms.

'Come,' he said. 'Sit here on the sand. You are too tired…'

'I'm fine,' she replied faintly, trying, but failing, to wave away his ministrations.

'I will phone Sue,' the man said.

'No.' Ashley shook her head, glancing across at Haydon again as if she was scared of him. 'Don't bother Mum. I'll be fine in just a minute… I moved too quickly, that's all – got a bit light-headed, but it will pass.'

She didn't look much as if it would pass, whatever it was. Was it shock at seeing him? The same shock he felt at seeing her after all these years, and here, of all places? He almost felt like fainting himself, but there would be nobody to catch him if he did, he was quite sure of that.

'What are you doing here?' he asked, the question, even as it came out, sounding ridiculous. Why shouldn't she be here? She had to be somewhere. But here?

'I could ask you the same thing,' she replied.

Haydon forced a smile, but it felt stiff and wrong.

'You know each other?' the man asked.

Ashley glanced uneasily at Haydon and then back at Nanette's brother again. 'Sort of. We met many years ago. But we haven't seen each other in…'

At this, the memory of their drunken encounter made Haydon's cheeks burn. He wasn't proud of the way he'd come on to Ashley that night, and he wasn't sure he wanted these nice, respectable people to judge him by the actions of one crazy evening. Not to mention that Ella was with him, and God only knew what she might make of it all. He'd really liked Ashley, and she'd promised to keep in touch, but she'd disappeared from his life the minute he'd left her apartment to catch his flight home. The rejection had stung, and had continued to do so sporadically until he met Janine a year later. It was beginning to look as if he had quite a talent for getting it wrong if his now-failed marriage was anything to go by. No wonder Ashley had chosen to steer clear in the end.

Nanette, seemingly oblivious to the tension suddenly choking the air between Ashley and Haydon, smiled brightly.

'You know each other – this is wonderful! So, Haydon, this is also my brother Maurice.'

Haydon forced his gaze away from Ashley, who still looked as bewildered and shell-shocked as he did, and gave Maurice a stiff nod of acknowledgement.

'Good to meet you. So you're Ashley's father?'

'Stepfather,' Maurice replied. Though the charged moment seemed to have escaped Nanette, Maurice was watching with a shrewd expression. Did he know who Haydon was? About their past? About what Haydon and Ashley had done that night? Had Ashley told him?

Haydon shook himself. Surely not. Surely it wasn't the sort of thing a girl shared with her parents – step or otherwise. Perhaps he was paying more attention because he recognised a weird reaction when he saw one, and Haydon had to admit that his reaction was probably about as weird as it got. He was only glad that Ella was somewhere down the beach and out of the way so she hadn't seen it, because it would doubtless have led to awkward questions later. He desperately needed to pull himself together. If Ashley was half as freaked out by events as he was then she was already a great steaming pile of freaked out, and she probably didn't need him adding to it.

'So, it's great to see you again,' he said to Ashley weakly. Even as he did he was struck by what a ridiculously inadequate sentiment it was. *Great to see you?* Like they'd once grabbed a coffee and promised to catch up next time he was in town? Like they'd once been at the same business meeting or been thrown together on an office team-building exercise?

'Yeah,' Ashley replied, staring at him as if he might disappear if she closed her eyes for a second. Which was also how he felt, though he tried hard not to let it show. What was going through her head as she looked at him? Loathing? Annoyance? Resentment? Or were there some stirrings of long-forgotten attraction now threading through the shock, as he felt now? She wasn't eighteen any more, but she was still gorgeous. The same soft grey eyes and that same golden hair that had rested on tanned shoulders that night. Even now, even at this most awkward and inappropriate moment, his gut groaned with desire, stronger with every new memory that assailed him.

His gaze went to the sand so he wouldn't have to look at her, so nobody might guess at the tumult of emotions beneath the surface that might give him away.

'Molly is Ashley's daughter,' Nanette said into the brief gap.

Haydon's head snapped up again. 'Molly's yours…?'

So she was with someone now? He should have realised that a woman like Ashley would be. She probably got attention wherever she went. How stupid of him to entertain for a single second the notion that they might somehow pick up where they'd left off, that she'd be remotely interested in him. After all, she hadn't wanted to see him again after Ibiza so why would now be any different?

'She seems a great girl,' he said stiffly. 'She and Ella have really hit it off.'

'Ella?'

'Ella's my daughter,' Haydon said. 'They're in the sea now with Bastien.'

His gaze turned to the shore, and when he turned back he could see Ashley watching them carefully as they splashed about.

'So…' Nanette clapped her hands together. 'We have food. Would you care to eat with us, Haydon?'

Haydon gave a vague nod. The last thing he needed was food, but what else was he going to say? What he really needed was a darkened room. Or perhaps a cold shower.

Nanette bade him take a seat on the blanket and Ashley did the same, sitting next to Maurice, who seemed to be glancing between them every so often as if to work them out. Haydon couldn't blame him because whatever history they had must have been written on his face at least. As for Ashley, he couldn't tell what she was thinking. The only thing he recognised was that same numb shock, disbelief that this could be happening. Of all the places she had to be right now, why did it have to be here?

Chapter Ten

Maybe she'd had weirder days, but she couldn't recall one. Ashley sat on the swing seat on the veranda of Villa Marguerite, lost in thought. The tabby who so often lay across the cushions when nobody was using it was now curled on her lap. Somehow, quietly and without ceremony, they'd become friends. One minute it was eyeing Ashley with the greatest suspicion, the next leaping onto her knee as she settled. It didn't have a name because Violette hadn't expected it to stick around when it had wandered into her garden and started to pilfer scraps of food. And if it did she hadn't expected to survive long enough to find out. That was ten years ago, but Violette had got so used to calling it *Le Chat* that it had become its official title. This was one amongst many stories Ashley had heard since her arrival – one of many lovely stories. If only the one she had to tell right now was quite as lovely.

After all these years, he wandered back into her life with a *great to see you*? Like nothing ever happened? They'd shared the most incredible night and, even though it was foolish and naïve, she'd thought he might have even cared for her. But he'd left her with broken promises, a dodgy phone number and a swelling belly, and today he showed up in her life *with another kid?* A bloody kid! It hadn't taken him long to move on and start getting other women knocked up. But she supposed she had to hand it to him that at least he'd stuck by this one, so lucky Ella. Or maybe it was lucky Molly, she told herself, because at least Molly knew where she stood and didn't have a letch and a liar for a dad. How many other kids bore his features? How many other women had he loved and left? He'd seemed so sweet and genuine all those years ago and even again today. If she hadn't known better, she'd almost fancy that those old feelings for him had rushed back to taunt her. He was a bloody good actor, she told herself. Nothing more than a conman. *So you can forget any sort of reconciliation because he will only break your heart again.*

Sue's voice came from the doorway. 'Mind if I join you?'

Ashley nodded and moved her feet to make room, dislodging Le Chat, who stalked off with a reproachful mew.

'So it sounds like Molly and Bastien had a good time at the beach with the girl from across the way. Molly says she wants to call for her again tomorrow. And Maurice tells me you bumped into an old friend…'

'Someone I knew a bit. A long time ago.'

'Maurice said he thought you both looked a bit shocked. That you both seemed embarrassed to see each other.'

'Did he now? And how would he come to that conclusion?'

'He has eyes, you know. He may be a man, but he's not completely ignorant of the little signs and signals of human emotion.'

'We were just shocked to see each other in such a random place, that's all. You know, the coincidence of the kids making friends first and then them being our kids all along.'

'Right. So how do you know him?'

Ashley hesitated. Her mum was on to her – at least she thought she was on to something. It would explain all the questions. Right now Ashley was glad she'd never revealed anything about Haydon to her mum. When she'd first got home and found she couldn't contact him, she'd simply felt foolish that she'd been used for sex by a guy who'd never intended to keep in touch, and so she hadn't said a word to her mum about the affair. And later, when she'd discovered she was pregnant, she hadn't wanted the manhunt that her mum, armed with any nugget of information, however small and insignificant, would inevitably begin. He hadn't wanted Ashley, and she didn't need the double humiliation of telling him she was pregnant with his child and being rejected again. Sue had asked, of course, and Ashley had pretended she didn't even know that much about him. It seemed easier. The dust would settle and Sue would get on with the business of supporting Ashley through those difficult first months, and then she would grow to love her granddaughter and it wouldn't matter where she had come from. Ashley had been proved right; all of that came to pass, and if this stupid coincidence hadn't cocked everything up today, that's how things would have stayed.

'He was one of Abigail's friends…' Ashley screwed up her nose. 'An ex, I think.'

'Abigail!' Sue huffed. 'I might have known – the friend who always managed to get you into trouble. Whatever happened to her anyway?'

Ashley shrugged, glad to have put her mum off the scent for now. 'I think she was running her own beauty consultancy last time I saw her.'

'Ditched you quick enough when you were expecting Molly. In your hour of need! I'd give her a piece of my mind if I ever saw her in town.'

'Then it's probably a good thing you don't often go to town. Anyway, it wasn't like that. We just drifted apart. She was never the maternal type so what would we have done together when I was always going to have a baby in tow? We could hardly go clubbing.'

'That's not what friendships are built on – clubbing!'

'I know, but I really don't blame her and you shouldn't either.'

'So they split up?' Sue said.

'Who?'

'The bloke you met today and Abigail?'

'Yes.'

'Why?'

'I don't remember. Does it matter?'

'Well, yes. We don't want Molly spending time with him and his daughter if he's a bad 'un.'

And then it struck Ashley like an icy slap in the face. Why hadn't she seen it before? She caught her breath and Sue threw her a sharp look.

Molly had been messing around on the beach that day with her sister!

'What's the matter now?' Sue asked.

'I... you're right,' Ashley replied. 'Maybe Molly shouldn't spend time with that girl.'

'Ella?'

'Yes, her.'

'So he's not nice?'

'No... I don't remember exactly. But we don't know anything about them, and we're being very friendly very quickly.'

'You don't like the girl? Molly's quite smitten – Bastien too. They had a great time together today.'

'I know, but...'

Oh, this was hopeless! What a hopeless, tangled mess! It was getting worse by the minute. If only she hadn't felt guilty letting Molly go to the beach without her. If only she hadn't offered to accompany Maurice down to join them instead of catching a sneaky hour in bed she'd have been oblivious to Haydon's presence in Saint-Raphaël and she wouldn't have had to worry about the girl who was currently Molly's holiday buddy. She wouldn't have to suffer this searing guilt that Molly was casually chatting to her father and had no idea, and that she was swimming with her half-sister and had no idea about that either.

If she put a stop to things now, Molly would want to know why she couldn't spend time with Ella, and everyone else would want to as well. How would Ashley be able to explain her decision? Unless she painted a very bad picture of Haydon – and as much as Molly and Ella being together without a clue of their real relationship was a dreadful situation, Ella didn't deserve that, even if he did. Today she'd seen that Ella enjoyed Molly's company as much as Molly enjoyed hers. Molly even seemed to have taken an instant shine to Haydon, especially when he announced that he was a cello teacher. A bloody cello teacher! At least it explained Molly's odd pull to play a string instrument herself. Talk about a cliché!

They'd done nothing but rattle on about orchestras and music schools for an hour as lunch was shared on the sand, and all the time Ashley sat wondering how he'd react if only he knew what she knew. Because, despite his shock at seeing Ashley – and it was obvious shock – he didn't seem to show any suspicion about Molly at all. Maths clearly wasn't his strong point, because he didn't even flinch when Molly told him her age. Typical bloke – it might have saved Ashley a lot of indecision if he'd worked it out. Molly had told him about the music school that she'd applied to and he'd gushed about how good it was, and how much she'd love it there, unaware of how much pain that dream had caused them, and how out of reach it was. Ashley had watched, her heart sinking further and further, as Molly's eyes shone with renewed hope for a dream they couldn't possibly afford. Would he have been quite so keen to sing its praises if Ashley had asked him to pay the fees? For a crazy second she'd thought about it, just to see his reaction.

She *could* tell Haydon the truth, of course, and she probably should. But then what? She wasn't sure she was strong enough for what the truth might begin. Would he demand to be a part of their lives? Would he want access, regular visits? Would he want to be a part of the decisions she made about Molly's upbringing? Worse still, would he want nothing to do with them at all?

No, Ashley decided, right now silence was the best policy. The status quo was far from ideal but it was the best option she had. So they would carry on as before, and Haydon didn't need to know about Molly. It was only a week, after all, and then Molly would be home and beginning the new term of her music course at college, and she'd soon forget about the kid she'd hung around with on holiday. Things would continue as they always had.

'Well, if Molly likes her then I don't suppose we can stand in the way of that,' she said lamely.

'Make up your mind,' Sue said. She stood up. 'I can't work you out today. Do you think you're coming down with something, because you're behaving very oddly.'

'I don't think so. I'm just tired – didn't sleep that well last night. I never do in strange places, do I?'

'Well, that's true,' Sue said, casting a critical eye over her. 'So there's nothing you need to share with me? Nothing I should know apart from you being tired?'

Ashley shook her head. 'Ignore me – I'll be OK tomorrow.'

'I'm going inside. Blanche and Nanette are going to teach me how to play some French board game. Want to join in?'

'Not just yet. Maybe later. Where's Moll?'

'Upstairs with Bastien.'

Ashley shot up in her seat. Sue chortled.

'Maurice is with them – Molly has found an old violin and she's showing off so you don't need to worry that there's hanky-panky.'

Sue's chuckle turned into a vague frown as she surveyed Ashley, and Ashley half expected her to remind her that Molly was nowhere near as stupid as Ashley had been as a teenager. But it never came.

'Right,' Ashley said. 'I'll be in soon.'

'And perhaps you'd like to leave your funny mood out here if there's nothing wrong as you keep saying.'

'I will.'

Ashley took a deep breath as Sue disappeared into the house. Leave her funny mood outside? How about leaving her funny life outside? If only.

*

A glorious morning streamed into the room through a gap in the curtains of one of Madame Dupont's many guestrooms. Outside a sweet symphony of birdsong harmonised with the drowsy buzz of a bee somewhere close to the window and the coarse yap of a dog in a distant garden. Ashley turned over to see that Molly was still fast asleep in the bed at the other side of the room. A little silver alarm clock – bells on the top and a tick loud enough to wake her workmates back in York – sat on the bedside cabinet and showed it had just gone six a.m. So much for getting some extra rest – this was earlier than she'd get up at home unless she was on morning shift at the care home. She'd blame her early waking on the noise outside, but it would be unfair, because if the room hadn't been so dark overnight she'd have seen the clock displaying every other hour of the night; she was pretty certain she'd been awake for all of them. But she'd come to a decision, and now there was just the agonising wait to act on it.

She had to tell Haydon about Molly. It was only fair and right. Before, when she'd had no idea where to find him, she owed him nothing. But now she couldn't let him leave here at the end of the week not knowing that he'd spent it with his daughter, not knowing that he even had another daughter at all. Already he'd missed sixteen years of her life and she owed it to him, regardless of how she felt personally about it, to give him the chance to be a part of it now if he wanted to. She had to tell Molly too at some point, but it was too difficult to think about that right now. One problem at a time was as much as she could deal with. She'd tell Haydon, and she'd see his reaction, and then she'd decide if Molly really needed to know or whether she'd be better off in blissful ignorance.

It was still so hard to believe that he was here, in the same town at the same time as her, after all these years. A figure from her past who had been absent from her life so long she'd almost fooled herself into thinking he'd never really existed. Why now? Why here? Was there some significance, some higher plan? Or was it really just the dumbest of luck? Bad luck, she'd argue. Certainly yesterday when the shock had been fresh and raw. But now? How did she feel about it now? Was it bad luck? Was there just a chance – the slimmest of all hopes – that seeing him again like this could become the start of something good? That maybe what went wrong all those years ago could be put right? Would him knowing about Molly change everything? Or anything at all?

After seeing him yesterday, the way he was with Ella, she couldn't believe that he was the villain she'd convinced herself he was. He'd been patient and understanding and full of such obvious pride. Ashley wanted him to look at Molly the way he looked at Ella; she wanted it for Molly with all her heart. And she wanted Molly to have a man who could guide her and protect her in the way he guided and protected Ella. Ashley had always been father and mother and she'd never resented it, certainly never felt the need for anything else, but that was before she'd had a choice. How about now? Now perhaps there was a choice. Perhaps. It all came down to Ashley's courage. She could do the right thing, however hard, and tell him. Or she could let him slip away again, and this time she was certain it would be for good.

Slipping a satin robe around her shoulders to stave off the early-morning chill, Ashley crept from the bedroom and downstairs. Violette had a heavy old kettle that had to be boiled on a gas hob, but Ashley reckoned she could cope with it. If she could only find a teabag lurking somewhere that would be perfect. Only three days without it and already she was missing her morning cup of tea. The kitchen was strangely silent and vast emptied of the crowds of relatives that Ashley had grown used to seeing in there since she'd arrived. Once this must have been a lovely family home, before they'd all moved away, and Violette must have felt she'd been transported back in time to see it full of relatives again. Ashley liked her very much. In fact, she liked them all. Her own family was very sparse in comparison. What sort of family did Haydon have? Were there lots of aunts and uncles, brothers and sisters?

Ashley filled the kettle, set it to boil after struggling with a strange flint contraption that lit the stove and found a caddy with a few odd-looking teabags in it. She wasn't sure what sort of tea it was, but it would have to do for now. Later she'd go to the market in the old town and get some proper tea if she could. Was that before or after she went to see Haydon and blew his world apart? Was that before or after they told Molly and Ella? She supposed he would want to tell Ella if they were telling Molly, but who knew how it would go? And how would the girls react? Talk about a bombshell.

'Is there enough water in that kettle for me?'

Ashley whipped around to see her mum at the kitchen door. 'Mum? What are you doing out of bed at this hour?'

'I could ask you the same thing.'

'I couldn't get back to sleep once I woke up.'

'Me neither. Maurice may have the voice of an angel but he has the snore of a haulage truck and wine only makes it worse.' She peered over at the caddy Ashley was holding. 'What's in there?'

Ashley opened it up and showed her the contents. Sue grimaced. 'You weren't going to drink those, were you?'

'I couldn't find anything else.'

Sue went to a large wooden larder set in the wall and stepped inside. After a moment or two of rifling she appeared with a box.

'This is more like it. God only knows what's in those you have there but I'd rather drink something I know.'

'They're proper teabags?'

'Of course. Usually they have this awful tinny stuff here but I fetched these over with me from England when we came to visit last year and they'll still be good to drink.'

'Mum, you're a lifesaver!'

'I know. So what woke you?'

'Don't know. Just woke up.'

'Because you were in a strange mood yesterday. After you came back from the beach. And Maurice said it too. He said… Never mind.'

Ashley took the box of teabags from her mum and dropped two into a little teapot. Violette didn't seem to be a mug fan so it was all delicate china cups and saucers. You couldn't get a decent vat of tea in a cup and saucer so the pot would have to do for a few refills. There was a brief lull while they listened to the kettle bubble on the stove, and then Sue spoke again.

'I'm worried about you.'

'There's no need,' Ashley replied, her gaze trained on the kettle. If she looked her mum in the eye she'd crumble.

'I'm your mother. I'm going to worry if I think something is wrong. And I'd like to think that you could tell me anything. If you can't then I've failed in my one most important task as a parent.'

'Of course I can tell you anything. Haven't I always?' Ashley almost looked for the lightning bolt to come through the ceiling and strike her down as she uttered the lie.

'So what's wrong?'

'Nothing.'

'Ashley…'

Ashley looked up now to see her mother's brow contracted into a frown. She let out a long sigh.

'Am I going to regret this?'

'Depends what it is.'

'See, Mum… how can I tell you?'

'Tell me what?'

'Maurice was right when he said I'd overreacted to Haydon's appearance yesterday. That's because…'

'He's Molly's dad,' Sue finished for her. 'I'm right, aren't I?'

Her mouth was a hard line as she stared at Ashley, willing the truth from her. Ashley hadn't even meant to let this out – not this soon and not in this way. But it had been so hard to keep a lid on things, and the truth had just sort of forced its way out, like it needed daylight and air before it became something gnarled and sinister that would choke Ashley if she kept it in. And when she thought about it, perhaps the best person she could tell first was her mum. She needed support now, someone on her side while she figured out what to do next, someone to share the burden. Who better than her mum?

She gave a weak nod and collapsed into a nearby chair. For the past twelve hours or more she'd been running on adrenaline, trying to keep it together, and now that her secret was out the adrenaline ebbed away, taking her strength with it.

'Does Molly know?'

'Of course not! Don't you think she'd be freaking out if she did? They spent the day together at the beach, for God's sake!'

'I know. Don't you think she's going to feel terribly duped when she finds out exactly that?'

'No more than everyone else,' Ashley said miserably.

'I take it *he* doesn't know.'

Ashley didn't need to ask who *he* was, especially when the word had been uttered with such venom.

'How could he? I never saw him again after that one night and he couldn't have known I was pregnant.'

'Bastard.'

'Mum... you're not going to do anything rash, are you?'

'It's not my place, but I would hope you are. You're going to tell him?'

'I think so.'

'*You think so?* What's wrong with you?'

'Keep your voice down!' Ashley pleaded. 'You'll wake the whole bloody house!'

'You're going to tell him! You can't let him get away from his responsibilities a second time. If you don't I'm going to march over there this morning and put things right.'

'I will... I just need to work out how to do it.'

'There's nothing to work out. You just come out with it – it's really quite simple.'

'It's delicate. There's more than just me and him to think about. How will Molly react? And his daughter?'

'I couldn't give a tinker's cuss about his daughter.'

'You don't mean that. All I'm saying is that there are more lives affected by this than just his. I don't want to cock this up, Mum. I've got one shot to get it right and I have to get it right. Please don't say anything to anyone else yet – not even Maurice. I will tell him, but I have to find the right moment.'

Sue let out a sigh. 'Well, it's a mess.'

'You could say that,' Ashley replied with a thin smile. 'I wish I'd never come to this bloody party. I might have known it would go to pot – story of my life. From now on there's no clubbing and no parties and no enjoyment of any kind.'

Sue turned the stove off and filled the teapot. 'When are you going to see him?'

'Later. When I've psyched myself up.'

'I can come with you if it helps.'

'No. Better if I go alone.' But then she was struck by an idea. 'Maybe if you could take Ella out of the way it would help.'

'Me? Take his daughter out?'

'There's no need to take a dislike to her just because she's his. It's hardly her fault her dad is a rat.'

'I suppose she does seem sweet.'

'And Molly really likes her. How much help that's going to be when they discover they're sisters is another matter entirely.'

'Half-sisters,' Sue reminded her stiffly.

'Still – it changes everything.'

'Where am I supposed to take her? What makes you think she'll be happy to wander off with me and that he'd be happy to let her?'

'Maybe get Maurice and Bastien to go with you.'

'What about Molly?'

'I'm not sure it's a good idea to throw them together again knowing what we know and what they don't know. It might make things worse when the truth comes out.'

'Won't Molly think it's odd that we're taking them and not her? They were like the Three Musketeers yesterday. If anything she'll be downright annoyed at being left out and she'll smell a rat anyway.'

'Probably,' Ashley said, staring into the depths of her teacup. 'I suppose you'll have to take them all out then.'

'I still don't think he's going to let us just turn up and take his daughter out.'

'OK. But that's where I come in. Somehow I'm going to have to explain to him, discreetly, that I need to talk to him in private.'

Sue rolled her eyes. 'Good luck with that.'

'Thanks.'

'But you *are* going to tell him? Because if you don't—'

'Yes. Please don't get involved. Not yet anyway. Let me see how the land lies. If I need someone to punch his lights out after the big reveal then you'll be my first port of call.'

'And you can get an explanation from him. How he thought it was OK to take advantage of a vulnerable young girl and then disappear into the night.'

'I was eighteen and I think the taking advantage might have been mutual.'

'You were left holding the baby.'

'True, but he didn't know there was a baby. We have to assume that he would have done the moral thing and stuck around if he had.'

Sue let out a strange growling tut that said she didn't agree with Ashley on that point. She'd probably read too many issues of *Prima* to think anything other than all men under the age of forty were absolute cads. Part of Ashley wondered whether she was right. She wasn't at all sure that Haydon would be putting out the bunting when he heard the news. He might well just hop into his car and head back to Britain quicker than you could say *child-support payment*. He might even be angry. He might accuse her of lying about Molly's paternity, and when she thought about it he'd only have her word for it. There was a lot to talk about, if he wanted to talk, and if he didn't… Well, Ashley didn't know what she'd do then. If she hadn't told her mum she could have skulked away and tried to forget about it, gone back to how their life was before, only this time there'd be no wondering about Haydon's absence from their lives, because she'd know for certain that he wanted the absence. But now Sue knew the truth it wouldn't be that simple.

She chewed the inside of her cheek as she watched her mum stir milk into her tea. Perhaps her haste to offload had been seriously misjudged after all. Sue wouldn't let this drop – not a chance. The way Ashley protected Molly like a mother tiger with her cub – that was just how Sue was with Ashley, even now at thirty-four. That would never change, and no amount of begging her to leave things alone would persuade Sue to keep her mouth shut on this.

'I'll have to tell Maurice,' Sue said.

'You can't. Not yet.'

'We can't tell the rest of the family, of course. I don't know that Violette could take the scandal – she might not see a hundred and one with the shock of it.'

'It's not her scandal – it's mine. And it's not even a scandal. It's not 1930, you know. There are single mothers everywhere – even in France.'

'But nobody in her family is in your… *situation*.'

'My situation is just bad luck. You make it sound like I'm some sort of brothel worker or something. I slipped up. Once.'

'You know I didn't mean that.' Sue reached across and squeezed Ashley's hand. 'I don't think that at all. I just wish…'

'That I'd shown a little self-control that night? That I'd stayed sober? That I'd never gone to Ibiza in the first place? I used to think that but now… I have Molly. How could you wish I'd done all those things when it would mean a world without Molly in it? Without making all those mistakes I wouldn't have her. If I could go back and do it again I wouldn't change a thing because she's amazing and my life would have been so much emptier, so much greyer and sadder without her. It's never been easy, but she's my daughter and, whatever Haydon says or does now, I'll always have her to make it OK.'

'I know all that too. Of course I don't wish her gone but it causes me such pain to see how you've struggled and missed out on all the things your friends had.'

'I was never in any pain, and I'm sorry if you are. I struggled, but it was a good struggle. I chose to miss out because I had a baby that I loved and wanted more than any stupid career opportunity. I don't care about any of that now because my daughter is amazing and worth more to me than all of those things my friends had. I was happy with my life and I still am, no matter how hard it sometimes gets.'

'You're right, of course. But I wonder if Molly will be quite so philosophical about it all when she finds out…'

*

'Can I see Molly and Bastien again today?'

'But you spent all day yesterday with them.' Haydon poured milk over a bowl of cornflakes and handed it to her before turning to his croissant. 'And don't forget that we're meeting Audrey for dinner later.'

Haydon winced inwardly as he recalled how he'd chased Audrey and how excited he'd been to meet up with her, his dreams of some kind of romance developing, because now he didn't know if having dinner with her was the right thing to do. There had been no explicit mention of romance but the hints had been there. She was beautiful and sweet but seeing Ashley yesterday… well, it had muddied the waters, and that was only the beginning of it.

Seeing Ashley had been like a punch to the gut. He didn't know how to feel about it, he only knew that where Audrey had filled his thoughts with soft-focus dreams of elegant romantic dinners, now his thoughts were filled with Ashley, but these were intense, messy, filled with the kind of longing that sucked the breath clean from your lungs. He'd always imagined he'd got over Ashley years before, but one afternoon in her company had shown that he'd never really gotten over her at all. Then again, despite this longing, perhaps getting involved with her wasn't the best idea. If she'd disappeared once from his life, who was to say she wouldn't do it again?

What to do about Audrey, however, he didn't know. He liked her, and he still wanted to meet up with her later, and perhaps that was the best plan after all – stick with his date and try to forget any kind of romantic involvement with Ashley.

'But that's later,' Ella said, breaking into his thoughts. 'She's got the market stall to look after all day.'

'I thought we might do something today while we wait for her. Something exciting.'

'What like?'

'Like windsurfing. Or kayaking. I've seen them both advertised on the beach.'

'Molly and Bastien could come with us. I bet they'd love it. I bet Bastien is brilliant at windsurfing and kayaking. I bet he can do everything. He looks like he'd be good at that sort of thing.'

Haydon tried not to think about how he wouldn't love humiliating himself in front of two teenagers who didn't belong to him as they watched him flail about in the sea and pretend it was water sports. The idea that one of those teenagers was the daughter of a woman who'd already confirmed once that she thought he was a big useless loser didn't make him any happier either. But there was no getting around the fact that Ella had had a brilliant time and she was quite besotted with both her teenage companions from the day before. She'd talked about little else when they'd got back to the villa that evening. But what if they brought Ashley along? Chances were they would.

'What if they're busy? Aren't they supposed to be in Saint-Raphaël for a big birthday party?'

Ella nodded. 'Oh yes. But Bastien says Madame Dupont's asleep half the day and cooking for the other half and wouldn't even notice if he was there or not. And Molly hardly knows her. She's only there because Violette is Maurice's aunt and Maurice wanted her and her mum to go to the party too.'

'And Maurice is Molly's granddad if I remember correctly,' Haydon said, vaguely surprised at the amount of information Ella had gleaned from her new friends. He had imagined that they might be swapping opinions on the latest social-media craze or comparing schools or something, not giving each other in-depth information on their family ties. He had to wonder just what Ella had told them about her own circumstances, but he didn't think he dared to ask. The last thing he needed was for Ashley to have it confirmed that he really was a major loser who couldn't keep a relationship going, even when he'd once persuaded the woman in question to actually marry him.

'Not really. He's just married to her grandma.'

'Right.'

'He's really nice. Molly doesn't mind that he's not really her grand-dad because he acts just like he is. Molly has two granddads and they both buy her presents.'

'You've got two granddads.'

'Oh well, then Molly must have three. But she doesn't know who her dad is so she can't count that granddad.'

Haydon spluttered, sending a spray of coffee across the table. 'She doesn't?'

'No.'

'So her mum isn't with her dad?'

'No. Molly doesn't care. She says he's probably a douche anyway.'

'Ella!'

'What? It's not a swear word – Kevin says it all the time. Anyway, Molly's mum isn't with anyone and Molly says she always says she likes it that way. Molly doesn't believe her, though. She says she went on a date with a man once but he smelt of onions so she never bothered again.'

Haydon fell silent for a moment as the new information sank in. Ella continued to chat between crunching on large mouthfuls of cornflakes, white noise in the background as he processed what he'd learned. But somehow it wouldn't compute, apart from one fact that kept swirling round and round in his consciousness. Ashley was single. It didn't mean that she would even look twice at him, of course, and perhaps going there again would only get his fingers burnt once more. And if it did it was probably no less than he deserved. Besides, these weren't thoughts he ought to be having when he'd got dinner with Audrey lined up. But he couldn't get the idea out of his head.

Something else nagged at him too, something half-formed and vague and potentially troubling but there all the same. How old was Molly again? Sixteen? And how many years was it since he'd last seen Ashley? A little more than that, but it was hard to pinpoint exactly how that fitted. Could Molly be…?

He shook his head. How stupid. Surely Ashley would have phoned him to tell him something that massive even if she hadn't phoned him to see him again. She'd have contacted him to discuss the formalities. He'd left his number for her before leaving Ibiza…

But what if she'd lost it? What if she'd thrown it away, not realising she might need it somewhere down the line?

But surely she'd have said something now – wouldn't she? They'd spent the day together and there had been opportunities for a quiet word.

'Dad!' Ella pouted. 'Are you even listening?'

'Sorry… what was that?'

'I said I'm going to get Molly's number today and am I allowed to text her because Mum said it costs more abroad and not to come back with a huge bill because Kevin won't be happy.'

'Well, if Kevin kicks up a stink then I'll pay your bill so you text who you want.'

Good old Kevin. Guaranteed to bring Haydon back to earth with a bump at the mere mention of his name.

'Thanks, Dad,' Ella grinned.

'You should probably phone your mum this morning anyway – she won't be happy if she doesn't get a phone call.'

'I've been busy.'

'Too busy for your mum? Shame on you!' Haydon threw her a conspiratorial smile. 'I don't want to get into trouble for not reminding you either.'

'That's the real reason you want me to phone her.'

'Got it in one. So when you've finished here you can call, nice and early so you wake her up.'

Ella shoved another spoonful of cornflakes into her mouth and chewed with a grin. 'After that I'm going to see if Molly and Bastien are up. Molly says I can go and stay with them in York when we go home, you know.'

'York? That's where they live?'

'Yeah. Have you been?'

'No. I've heard it's nice.'

'So we can ask them to go out with us today?'

Haydon paused. This really wasn't what he wanted. Things had been awkward on the beach with Ashley and her family and the thoughts he'd been having about her weren't exactly helping. There was a distinct danger he might do or say something mortifying.

'Please, Dad. I promise we'll spend the next day together but just today can we ask them to come?'

'You really want to?'

Ella nodded.

'Well, we can ask, but if they're busy we're not pushing it. Remember they're supposed to be having a family get-together and we're not family, so we can't keep butting in.'

'We won't. Anyway Molly says she can't understand half of what's going on when they're all there because most of them are speaking French.'

'I suppose you can't blame them for that, seeing as they are French.'

'Yes, but it's no fun listening to a conversation if you can't understand it.'

'Some of my most enjoyable conversations have been ones I couldn't understand, and there have been a great many that I wished I couldn't understand when I could.'

'I'm going to get ready.' Ella let her spoon drop with a clatter into her bowl and pushed her chair away from the table.

'Phone your mother first – or she'll string me up!'

'But what if Molly and Bastien go out before I've had a chance to go there?'

'They won't – don't panic. And even if they do I'm sure we'll run into them somewhere in town.'

'But what if they go out of town?'

'Then you'll just have to catch them another time.' He pretended to give her a stern frown. 'Phone. Your. Mother.'

Ella rolled her eyes. 'Alright.'

Haydon watched her leave the kitchen and turned back to squidging a blob of jam into the middle of his croissant. Bloody pink house across the fields – he was beginning to wish he'd steered well clear of it.

Haydon and Ella followed the path that skirted the fields between their villa and Villa Marguerite. He'd argued, vainly, to cut across them, but Ella wasn't taking any chances on the fact that if they did they might run into Frank the lizard or some of his less cuddly friends. The sun was high already, even though it had just gone ten. A small plane droned overhead and Haydon squinted up to see the vapour trail it left across the cornflower sky.

'What if they're not in?' Ella asked.

'Then there's not a lot we can do about it.'

'I should have asked Molly for her number yesterday.'

'I don't suppose you thought about it yesterday – too busy splashing each other.'

'That was Bastien. Molly lost it with him; he soaked everyone.'

'You were in the sea – wasn't that kind of the point?'

'But he kicked a load in her hair. She went mad.'

'I think maybe that's called flirting.'

'She said she was going to push him in if he did it again but Bastien just laughed at her.'

'Molly sounds a bit feisty.'

'She plays the violin.'

'She mentioned that.'

'She wants to be in an orchestra someday.'

'She mentioned that too.' Haydon looked across at Ella with a wry smile. 'Have we developed a bit of a girl-crush?'

'Shut up, Dad!' Ella squeaked, her cheeks flaming.

'I'm only teasing. She's cool and I'm glad you've found a friend.'

'Really? You don't mind calling for them? I thought…'

'I was tired this morning – of course I don't mind. Just as long as you don't forget to give your old dad a bit of attention from time to time. Half an hour here or there ought to do it, just so I don't forget who you are.'

'I could never do that.'

'Good. You might wish you could forget me when I embarrass you in the sea later.'

'You could never embarrass me.'

'I'll remind you of that when I fall off the surfboard for the fiftieth time.'

'I can't wait to go windsurfing. Do you think I'll be able to do it?'

'I think you can do anything you put your mind to.'

'Kevin says I've got no coordination.'

'Has he watched you play piano? When he can play better than you then he's allowed to say you've got no coordination.'

They arrived at the gates of Villa Marguerite to find an elderly lady in the garden trimming a shrub.

'*Bonjour!*' Haydon greeted. Was this the centenarian aunt? He could have hazarded a guess, but if he was wrong and whoever it was turned out to be much younger than a hundred they might have been very offended indeed. '*Ca va, Madame?*'

The old lady straightened up and regarded him carefully. '*Bien, Monsieur.*'

'Um… *Moi et ma fille…*' He paused, scratching his head for the connecting words. '*Amis* – Molly and Ashley…'

'Ah!' The old lady offered a scant-toothed smile. '*S'il vous plaît attendez.*'

With that she tottered into the house.

'I think she wants us to wait,' Haydon said in answer to Ella's questioning glance up at him.

'Here or at the door?'

'Maybe better to wait here. She didn't say anything about going with her.'

A minute later Ashley and Molly were walking down the path towards them. Ashley looked tired and tense, her hair pulled back into a simple ponytail and she was wearing barely any make-up, denim cut-offs and a plain white vest, but she still looked incredible. As they walked together Haydon could see now that Molly was actually a good couple of inches taller than her mum already and her colouring was darker – deep brown eyes and hair that was more caramel than golden.

'Wow, you're really tanned already!' Ella called to Molly, who returned the compliment with a grin. 'Was that just from yesterday at the beach?'

'I always tan easily. You and your dad haven't done too bad either.'

'Violette said you wanted us,' Ashley said, her gaze fixed on Haydon. It was so frank, so fierce and uncompromising that for a moment Haydon felt his courage shrivel in the face of it. She really bloody despised him and yet… what was this tight feeling in his chest every time he saw her? Why did he feel like a lovesick idiot when she showed no encouragement of this feeling whatsoever?

'We're going windsurfing,' Ella broke in. 'And we wondered if you wanted to come too? You and Bastien. If you wanted to.'

'Bastien's got to go to pick up some meat with his uncle.'

'Wow, how much meat is there?' Haydon asked. But his attempt at humour was met with nothing but a stony stare from Ashley and it seemed to go completely over Molly's head. Not that it had been all that funny, he supposed.

'It's for the party. Nanette is going to cure it or something,' Ashley said.

'Oh, the birthday party,' Ella said. 'Of course. But poor Bastien.'

'We could ask if you can come to the party,' Molly replied, but then clamped her mouth shut again as Ashley gave her a tiny, warning shake of her head.

'It's for family only, I expect,' Haydon said with forced brightness. He was beginning to think that coming here today had been a huge mistake. It was one thing Ella having fun with Molly, but it left him and Ashley together and she seemed far from chatty right now. What was he supposed to do with her all day in this mood?

'If you're busy,' he began slowly as the idea formed in his mind, 'I guess we could take Molly with us and it would leave the day free for you to do whatever you needed. I mean, if you wanted to stay home and relax or help with the party or whatever. I don't mind at all and Ella would be happy, wouldn't you?'

Ella nodded eagerly but Ashley dismissed the idea with a flick of her head.

'We'd love to come,' she said, though Haydon didn't think he'd ever seen the statement uttered with less sincerity. If this was something she'd love to do then he couldn't imagine her face when she was forced to do something she hated.

'Are you going now?' she added.

Haydon nodded. 'Might as well if we want to make the most of the day. Is that OK with you both?'

'We'll need to get some things together. Can you give us ten minutes?'

He nodded again, and Ashley ushered Molly back to the house. As he watched them go, his gaze was drawn to a window where a woman stared down at him. He sent an awkward smile her way but she didn't flinch – she just continued to weigh him up. But then he saw Ashley appear at the window and pull her away.

Weird. Everything about this was weird. Was there still time to run? Because he had a feeling today was going to be a huge mistake.

*

Ashley had been vaguely irritated that Haydon hadn't done a little more research into his whole windsurfing idea because they'd arrived at the little hut where the lessons went from only to be told they'd have to book in advance. Molly and Ella had been desperately disappointed until the owner of the school suggested that they might be able to buy bodyboards from the town and take themselves out into the shallows instead. Haydon had insisted on buying one for both of the girls as well as himself, which was lucky because Ashley didn't have spare cash to fritter on something they wouldn't be taking home with them and would probably never come back to Saint-Raphaël to use again anyway.

He'd offered to buy one for her too, but the last thing she needed was to be flailing around on the sea like a tit.

So she was left sitting on the sand alone as the others paddled about on their new boards. The sun burned through the straw hat she'd borrowed from Nanette, despite Molly telling her she looked like an old lady in it. Old lady or not, at least she wouldn't get sunstroke. With nothing else to do she applied another layer of lotion to her shoulders and wished that she'd packed a book. But she hadn't expected to be left alone for hours on end to read. Shrieks of laughter travelled up the beach, so at least someone was having fun. This wasn't how the day was supposed to go.

She and Sue had gone to great pains to get everyone discreetly out of the way so Ashley could get a moment during the day to talk to Haydon properly. In their original plan Sue had suggested that Bastien and his uncle go to the butcher's in a neighbouring town – something Bastien had sulked about but, being a dutiful nephew, had eventually had to agree to. Maurice was to take Nanette to the vineyard to stock up and Molly was meant to go with them, which then left Ashley free to see Haydon alone at his villa (assuming she could catch him in). What to do about Ella being there was something she'd decided she'd just have to deal with when she got there. But then Haydon had thrown them a lifeline by coming to call. It meant the four of them could be together, which was half the battle. She'd assumed that the girls would be out on windsurfing lessons and she'd be looking on with him, and that would be her chance to get things out in the open. She'd rushed indoors to find her mum giving Haydon a fair death stare out of the window, and when she'd told her about the new plan Sue had been in agreement that it was the best way. Simple enough? So you'd think, but so far she hadn't been able to get Haydon alone for a single second.

Shielding her eyes from the sun, she watched as Haydon emerged from the waves with his board under his arm and made his way up the beach. The girls were still splashing away in the surf, so perhaps this was her chance. Her stomach jolted, and she put it down to nerves, trying not to think about the multitude of reactions she might encounter from him. But perhaps it had more to do with the fact that he'd stayed in remarkably good shape since she'd spent that fateful night with him, as his dripping torso and sandy hair now curled from the sea attested. Surely she didn't still fancy him? After all that had happened? Where had this come from – now of all moments?

'Come and have a go!' he called.

She shook her head. 'Come over here!'

'Huh?'

'Come over here!' she shouted, gaining a reproachful stare from an elderly couple camped within the shelter of a beach umbrella a few feet away.

He shook the water from his hair, kicking sand up as he strode towards her with a broad smile, and suddenly she was filled with one overwhelming hope. That, somehow, hearing about Molly would bring them together. As in romantically. Which was ridiculous and probably the last place this was going.

Stop it, Ashley!

But he'd only got halfway up the beach when Ella began to chase after him, and then Molly followed.

Shit! Ten minutes – it wasn't much to ask, was it?

'Come in and have a go!' Molly called, racing towards her. 'It's brilliant!'

Ashley shook her head. 'What about all our belongings?'

'They're not going to go anywhere – there's hardly anyone here. We could ask that couple to keep an eye on things and we can see easily from the sea anyway so we could run back if someone tries to take them.'

'We wouldn't run back fast enough.'

'I would,' Molly insisted.

'I'm not a very good swimmer.'

'You don't need to be,' Haydon put in, joining them now with Ella. 'We'll keep you safe.'

'And who's keeping you safe?' Ashley asked.

His smile faded, but then he seemed to rally again. 'The sea's calm today. I think the guy at the windsurfing place would have said if he thought it wasn't safe.'

Ashley had no argument for that.

'Please…' Molly cajoled. 'Just give it a try.'

'I don't know…'

'We feel guilty that you've been left on the beach all on your own while we have fun,' Haydon said, and the girls both nodded. 'It'd be much better if you joined us.'

'And we'd have a better time if we felt less guilty,' Molly said.

Ashley sighed. 'I swear with arguments like that you'll be a solicitor one day, Moll.'

'Ugh, no chance. How boring.'

'Never say never.' Haydon laughed. 'I bet you'd earn a lot more as a solicitor than you would in an orchestra.'

'But I'd hate it, and you have to do what you love, don't you? Otherwise life is no fun at all.'

Ashley was tempted to ask who'd ever told her daughter life was meant to be fun but, as she had so many other times before, she stopped herself. It wasn't the type of wisdom she wanted to pass on. Why shouldn't Molly have bright expectations? Why couldn't she hold on to her dreams – just for a little while? Life would soon temper them without anyone's help, so why should Ashley speed that process up just because she might be feeling a little peevish?

'Come on, Mum. Just try it.'

Ashley looked from Haydon to Ella to Molly. 'You're not planning to sit this out at any point?' she asked Haydon.

He shook his head. 'I don't think I'd be allowed to! Maybe we'll stop for lunch a little later… if that would be OK with you?'

There didn't seem a lot of point waiting around for a moment alone with him then if he wasn't going to be able to lose the girls for a while, and it didn't seem like that was going to happen. Maybe it wouldn't be so bad to join them for an hour or two in the sea. It *was* hot, and the water did look *very* tempting… And then Ashley could work out a way to get him alone at lunchtime. She had no idea how yet, but she'd figure it out.

She stood up and stripped off her shorts and top to reveal a swimsuit beneath.

'Come on then. Last one in the sea has to buy dinner!'

*

Restaurants with a more relaxed dress code were hard to find, but they managed to get an outside table at one which overlooked the sea where their beachwear didn't cause too much of a stir. The menu was simple but both girls were happy to see chicken nuggets (as close as the French could manage to such basic fare) and chips on there while Ashley settled for a salad. Haydon, regardless of what kind of maturity he might want to show, joined the girls in their junk-food fix and, against her instincts, Ashley couldn't suppress a smile to see him dipping his chips into a huge pot of gloopy mayonnaise.

'I could eat this three times over,' he said.

'Me too,' Molly returned with a grin.

'I'm not surprised,' Ashley said. 'Imagine how many calories we've burned off in the last couple of hours.'

'So we can have pudding?'

'I would imagine so,' Ashley said, taking a quick glance at the menu to check the prices again.

'Absolutely,' Haydon said. 'We need to bulk up if we're going back into the sea later, so it's on me.'

'You're not supposed to eat too much just before you go swimming,' Ashley said.

'In that case, we'll have to make it a long and lazy lunch, won't we? There's nothing to race back for, is there?'

'Well, no, but—'

'So let's make the most of the day. I don't know about you lot, but I'm having a great time on these boards. I think it turned out better than windsurfing in the end.'

Ashley had to admit that she'd ended up having a great time too. Her balance had been terrible, of course, and a rogue wave had tipped her off more times than she could count. But Haydon had pressed a gentle hand to her back and helped her keep her weight steady, and eventually she was riding the waves like a natural. Well, perhaps not riding exactly, more like floating. And it was true that they weren't exactly going to be troubling any surfing competitions any time soon – they'd stayed in the shallows and really were messing around on the shore rather than proper impressive wave-riding – and they weren't professionally equipped. None of them really knew what they were doing either. They'd shared the three boards between the four of them and took it in turns to paddle around while the one left standing in the shallows offered words of encouragement and laughed out loud at every little disaster that sent the others flying off their ride. By the time they'd all decided they were starving Ashley's stomach muscles were aching. Mostly from trying to stay afloat but a little bit from laughing too.

As they'd emerged from the sea to get ready for lunch Haydon had thrown a towel around her shoulders and smiled down at her, and for a moment their eyes had locked. She'd been lurched into a confusing whirl of emotions that had been unexpected and not very helpful considering her main objective for the day.

She was surprisingly relaxed and content at that moment as they sat sipping drinks and gazing out to an azure sea, almost as if him being there with her was the most natural thing in the world – as if they'd never been parted since that first night together. But lurking in the background was the pressing need to tell him about Molly. It threatened to overwhelm everything else, and when Ashley really thought about it perhaps that was a good thing – her sensible self firing a well-needed warning shot. She'd become too relaxed that morning, too easy in his company, but as she'd spent more and more time with him it had become hard to do anything else. He was so sweet and considerate and funny and interesting. If only he hadn't given her that duff phone number in Ibiza, who knew what might have been?

'What do you want, Mum?' Molly said, interrupting Ashley's thoughts. Just as well because they were going to a place they had no right being in. He *had* given her a duff phone number all those years ago and that was that. Molly handed her the menu. 'I'm getting ice cream, but they have cheesecake and everything.'

'Oh, I don't know…'

'These are on me.'

She looked up to see Haydon smiling at her. The sea had tousled his sandy hair and the sun had bronzed his skin, and those eyes… those eyes of chocolate that seemed to smile even when he wasn't…

She gave herself a mental shake. If she could have slapped herself right now without looking like a nutter she probably would have done.

'What?'

'I'm buying dessert. And don't argue because I want to and I won't take no for an answer.'

'But—'

'Please…' he said gently. He reached across the table and settled a light touch on her hand. She looked down at it, and then back up at him, and suddenly he seemed to realise what he'd done as he drew it quickly away again, colour rushing to his cheeks.

Ashley glanced across at Molly to see her share a small conspiratorial grin with Ella. Could they see what was going on here? Or rather, what they *thought* was going on? Were they actually matchmaking? The idea snapped Ashley back to Planet Earth. They probably thought it was fun – a harmless game. This was getting out of hand, and Ashley needed to act before it all went too far; the last thing she needed was for Haydon or Molly to work things out before she'd had a chance to break it to them sensibly. She had to tell Haydon.

'Moll,' she said, glancing around and noting there was a queue at the bar. It would be a good ten minutes' wait for anyone wanting to get served. 'Go and get me another Coke?' She grabbed her purse from the table and handed her a twenty-euro note. 'Get Ella one too and Haydon…?'

He shook his head. 'I thought we were sorting out desserts.'

'I'm parched – I could do with a drink first. And you said we didn't need to rush.' She forced a bright smile and turned to Ella. 'Would you mind going with Molly to help carry them?'

Ella leapt up and followed Molly inside.

'They're getting on really well,' Haydon remarked as he watched them go.

'Yes,' Ashley said. She drew a deep breath. Time was short and there was no point in pussyfooting around with this. She could only hope that they could both hold it together when the girls got back, though she suspected that her next words might signal the end of their day together. Perhaps the end of their newly blossoming friendship too. But they needed to be said, and she had to trust that what she'd seen so far of him was the real Haydon and that he'd treat her news with the sensitivity it deserved.

'Haydon—'

'Look who we found, Mum!'

Ashley spun around to see Molly with Maurice and Sue. Her gut clenched at the realisation that the moment she'd built herself up to all day was going to have to wait – *again*.

'Ashley!' Maurice stepped forward and kissed her lightly while Sue tried to make what Ashley assumed was a covertly apologetic face. She'd probably guessed as soon as she'd seen Ashley and Haydon sitting at the table what was going on, though she couldn't have guessed at what stage the discussion was. Essentially nowhere now.

'Maurice saw you all from the beach road and insisted on coming to say hello,' Sue said.

'I thought you were getting wine at the vineyard,' Ashley replied.

'We did,' Maurice said. 'We got back an hour ago and Aunt Violette was sleeping. I wanted lunch, so I thought we would eat by the sea. How lucky for us now you are here. May we join you?'

'Of course,' Ashley said; she could hardly say anything else. She glanced at Haydon. 'That's OK, isn't it?'

'I'd love it,' he said. Ashley couldn't help but notice that he looked far from comfortable, however, and had to wonder whether it was something to do with the obvious scrutiny her mother now had him under. Ashley would have to have a word with her about that later too. It was understandable that she wanted to protect Ashley, but there was a line she was in severe danger of crossing.

'I will help Molly to get the extra drinks,' Maurice said, taking the twenty-euro note from Molly's hand and giving it back to Ashley. 'You keep this money for another day.'

Ashley would normally have argued, but she was so shell-shocked by the way events seemed to be slipping from her control that she simply nodded and put it back in her purse as Maurice took Molly back to the bar.

'So… you've had a good morning?' Sue asked, looking very pointedly at Ashley. At least Ashley thought so, but perhaps that was because she knew why. Haydon didn't seem to notice it, or if he did he certainly didn't react. She pulled a spare seat from a nearby table and sat down with them. 'You've had fun?'

'We've had a great time,' Haydon said. 'The girls get on so well… We were just saying that, weren't we, Ashley?'

'Yes.'

'So everyone's happy,' Sue said. 'Well, isn't that lovely? And what are your plans for later?'

'I don't know,' Ashley said. 'What are *yours*, Mum? Are you and Maurice planning to stay with us all afternoon?'

'I would have been happy sitting in the garden,' Sue said, continuing the subtext of their conversation. 'But Maurice insisted that we come to town and how were we to know we'd see you here when I expected you to be at the beach?'

'It is a coincidence,' Haydon said. 'There seem to be a lot of those this week.'

'Don't there?' Sue said, looking at him now as if she might want to cut some delicate bits of his anatomy off.

Ashley held in a groan. This was going from bad to worse. At this rate her mum would let the cat out of the bag before Ashley had a chance to do it properly. It was obvious Sue was dying to launch into a tirade and tell Haydon exactly what she thought of men like him and Ashley was beginning to regret telling her about it.

'Here we are…' Maurice returned with four glasses of wine. He placed one in front of each adult, despite the beginnings of an argument on Haydon's lips. 'You are in France – you must drink wine with your lunch!'

Molly and Ella settled back at the table with their Cokes while Maurice grabbed another chair and joined them.

'So… you are going to the beach again after you have finished eating?' he asked.

'I think so,' Ashley said.

'Yes!' Molly said. 'We're just getting the hang of bodyboarding now so we need more practice.'

'Bodyboarding?' Maurice said with a grin. 'That sounds wonderful! I will come with you!'

Ashley put the wine glass to her lips and gulped a mouthful back. *Great – that's all I need.*

*

'Dad…' Ella sat on his bed, watching as Haydon combed through his hair and spritzed himself in a woody cologne.

'Yes?'

'Do you like Ashley?'

Haydon paused, a hand to a shirt button he was doing up, and turned to her.

'She seems nice,' he said carefully. 'You like her and Molly, don't you?'

'Yes, but I mean *like*.'

'Why do you ask?'

'No reason.'

Haydon gave a tight smile. 'Is it because we're meeting Audrey tonight?'

'Maybe.'

'It's not a date – I told you that. We're just having dinner with her.'

'I know, but she's pretty.'

'She is.'

'And Ashley's pretty too. And nice and funny.'

'Yes…'

'So what if you liked them both? Who would you choose?'

'Ella… What is this? There's no reason for me to choose either. Audrey is just a new friend we've made, and Ashley is someone we've spent today with because you and Molly and Bastien have made friends. And to be honest,' he added, 'I must have been crazy to suggest that day on the beach because I'm knackered and the last thing I want to do is venture down to the town to meet anyone for dinner. My face will be in the soup as soon as I sit down.'

Ella giggled, her questions seemingly forgotten now. 'I'll keep kicking you awake.'

'You'll have to kick hard.'

'I can do that.'

'I know. I've still got the bruises from when we played football in the garden last year.'

'Dad!'

He smoothed a hand over her hair and kissed the top of her head. 'Go and get ready or we'll be late.'

'I *am* ready.'

Haydon stared at her. 'But… I thought you'd got your swimming costume on.'

'This is a bodysuit, Dad!'

'Oh. But you're going to put a skirt on?'

'I have got a skirt on.'

'Oh. I thought that was one of those little skirt things you wrap around your swimming costume when you're away from the pool.'

'Nope. I'm completely ready.'

'Oh…' Haydon wavered between the dad who insisted that his daughter dress appropriately for her age and the dad who didn't even know any more what age-appropriate was. Ella was growing up so fast he couldn't keep pace with her impending womanhood. But the fact was tonight she looked like a girl on the brink of womanhood as she sat in what he considered a skimpy outfit and he didn't know how he felt about it. Then he realised she was also wearing make-up and it made her look older still.

'Maybe you should take a jacket then,' he added lamely. 'You might get cold.'

'It's boiling, Dad.'

'Not at night on the seafront, it isn't.'

'I bet it will be.'

'Well… it's your problem if you get cold,' he said, not knowing what else to say. He heard Ella sigh as he hunted for his shoes. 'What?' he asked, looking up.

'Are you nervous?' she asked with a shrewd look.

'Nervous? About what?'

'Meeting Audrey?'

'Why on earth would I be nervous?'

Ella shrugged and hopped off the bed. 'I'm going to get my jacket,' she said. And Haydon smiled thinly as he watched her go. He wasn't so much nervous as torn. He wanted to meet Audrey and he still liked her very much, but after his day with Ashley he wasn't sure whether meeting Audrey was entirely fair to her.

He shook off the thought. Nobody had said it was a date, had they? And Ashley wasn't exactly returning his signals – as clumsy as they were – so it wasn't like anything was going to happen there anyway. Audrey was beautiful and she was sweet, and he could do a lot worse than getting to know her a bit better.

Pulling his shoes from underneath the bed he slipped them on and tied the laces. They were going to meet Audrey for dinner and they were going to have a great time and that was that.

*

The tiny restaurant Audrey had suggested was tucked away in a side street just away from the harbour and it had taken them a while to find. It wasn't glamorous and airy like the tourist traps along the front; it was intimate and rustic, with scrubbed wooden tables and terracotta tiles, the main floor of the restaurant sharing a space with the open kitchen, and the air was fragranced with fresh herbs and roasted garlic.

Audrey was waiting at a table, chatting easily to a man in a white apron and chef's hat, her lithe arms waving expressively and her eyes alive with humour. She was wearing a simple white linen dress that showed off her tanned skin and her nutmeg hair was loose around her shoulders, and Haydon had to stop and collect himself as he stood in the doorway, still unable to believe that such a woman had said yes to him. *It's not a date*, he kept reminding himself, just like he'd kept telling Ella, but they all knew that really it was. Audrey turned now and spotted them, and she rose gracefully from the table and strode across the restaurant to greet them.

'I am so glad to see you,' she said, kissing both Haydon and Ella on the cheeks. 'I thought perhaps you might come to the market today.'

'Oh, I'm sorry about that…' Haydon began, but Ella jumped in.

'We went bodyboarding,' she announced. 'With our new friends.'

'More new friends?' Audrey raised her eyebrows and smiled at Ella. 'Everywhere you go you make so many friends! It is because you are so charming.'

'No.' Ella laughed. 'They're our neighbours. They're English.'

'Not all of them,' Haydon said. 'They're staying with some French relatives at the villa near to ours. They have kids around Ella's age so naturally…'

'No need to explain,' Audrey said. 'Of course Ella would want to spend time with them. Come and sit. The fish has been caught this morning but it will not get any fresher if we do not hurry and tell our chef how we would like it cooked.'

'Do they have other things?' Ella asked as they followed her back to the table.

'You do not want to try the fish?' Audrey asked. 'But the restaurant we sit in is famous for the fish.'

'I don't really like fish all that much. Does it have heads on here?'

'I am sure they can take the head off,' Audrey said with a musical laugh. 'I think if you try it you will be surprised how much you like it.'

Haydon looked doubtful. 'Unless it's covered in breadcrumbs and shaped like a finger I don't think she will.'

'No,' Ella said, smiling brightly at Audrey and clearly in the mood to please her, 'I *will* try it. Maybe I'll find a new thing I like.'

'I don't think it's going to replace our McDonald's at a weekend even if you do like it,' he said. 'A bit far to come.'

'But perhaps you will have a reason to visit Saint-Raphaël again soon,' Audrey said, offering Haydon a coquettish smile that he couldn't fail to interpret as romantic interest. Suddenly, he wasn't quite as hungry as he had been when they'd arrived. *Don't blow it*, he thought. *Don't mess this up*. He didn't know quite how *this* – whatever it was – could turn into anything long-term, but he didn't want to think that far ahead, not tonight. He was in the company of a charming, beautiful woman who was actually interested in him, and why couldn't that be enough, just for now?

*

'Mum...' Ashley whispered. 'I don't suppose you have time for a chat?'

They were out on the veranda of Violette's house. Maurice was sitting on the steps sharing a home-rolled cigarette with Antoine that Sue had forbidden him to smoke, and it looked as if he'd imagined she hadn't noticed the sneaky puffs he was taking when he thought she wasn't looking. They conversed in rapid French, bursting into laughter every so often at some shared memory. Sue and Ashley were sharing the swinging seat, as had quickly become their habit. Violette was pruning her herbs – also a daily habit, it seemed – while Molly and Bastien splashed about in the swimming pool around the back that had only been cleaned that morning of years of grime, ready for the party later in the week. The sun was on its way down to the horizon and, although the evening was fragrant with flowers whose perfume grew in intensity with the dusk, it was still hot enough to have Ashley sitting out barefoot in shorts and a tiny vest.

'Chat away,' Sue said. 'Nobody's listening... I expect if I made a couple of very easy guesses I might know what you want to talk about?'

'I expect you could. Maybe we should go for a walk?'

'I wasn't planning to venture out tonight if I'm honest. Is what you want to talk about that complicated? Surely you're just waiting for another chance to give him the news. Unless you're going to go over now and do that, in which case you don't need me with you.'

'I wasn't...' Ashley sighed and tipped her head to the sky. 'It's just getting more complicated than that.'

'I don't see how.'

Ashley turned back to her. 'I really liked him, Mum. All those years ago I thought... He hurt me, that's all. He broke my heart and seeing him now... I thought I wouldn't care but I do.'

'You want to try again? After all he's done?' Sue's voice rose with her incredulity and Ashley shushed her, flicking a glance around to see if anyone had noticed.

'Of course not, that would be ridiculous! But today... he was so lovely. Can you blame me for feeling mixed up about it?'

'He's a good actor. He might seem lovely but believing that's the real man – isn't that what got you in trouble in the first place? I bet he seems lovely to every woman whose heart he breaks. Mark my words, the good-looking ones are always trouble.'

'So Maurice isn't good-looking?' Ashley raised her eyebrows.

'He's got what you'd call an interesting face. Anyway, I'm talking about the young good-looking ones. The older ones have already sown their oats and settled down.'

'Haydon's not that young, Mum.'

'Do you even know how old he is?'

Ashley coloured. The shameful fact was that despite him being the father of her child she knew very little about him.

'I know he's around my age.'

'A wild guess on your part?'

'An educated guess.'

'Still a guess. Hardly the basis for a serious relationship.'

'People on first dates don't know this stuff about each other.'

'People on first dates don't generally already have children together.' Ashley widened her eyes as Sue's voice rose again, and Sue grunted in acknowledgement. 'First things first,' she said, her voice lower now. 'Before you have any dreams of a happy ever after you should go and see him and tell him the thing he needs to know.'

'What if he doesn't believe me?'

'Then you'll have all the answers you need and we can happily ignore him and his daughter for the rest of the holiday.'

'Easier said than done,' Ashley replied, gnawing her lip as her pensive gaze went to Violette, who was now bent over a vast rosemary shrub, snipping away as she cut it into shape.

'But if I were you,' Sue added, her voice harder now, 'I'd steer well clear. It'll only end in tears, I guarantee it.'

'I appreciate your concern but I think you've got him wrong.'

Sue folded her hands in her lap, her gaze following Ashley's to Violette, who had now stepped back to appraise her work with a small, satisfied smile.

'We'll see.'

They fell to silence for a moment, and then Ashley stood up.

'I'm going to see him now.'

Sue merely gave a short nod.

'I'll know one way or another then,' Ashley added.

Sue only nodded again.

But then Ashley sat down next to her once more, elbows on her knees, chin resting on her hands.

'I thought you were going,' Sue said mildly, and Ashley turned to her helplessly.

'So did I. Saying it is easier than doing it. How do I have that conversation?'

'There's no easy way to have it but to come straight out with it. If he's as nice as you think he is then you'd expect him to be happy about it eventually.'

'Eventually. What about the beginning and in-between bits that come before eventually? Those are the bits that worry me.'

'I can't help you with that, I'm afraid. I'd offer to go across and tell him but I expect you'll want to do that yourself.'

'I don't think it's really appropriate for anyone else to do it.'

'Neither do I. But he's never going to know if you sit here staring at the lawn.'

Ashley nodded slowly. And then she got up and went to the house for her shoes.

Ashley closed the gate to Haydon's holiday villa behind her and set out on the path back to Villa Marguerite. Once again her plans to come clean had been thwarted and now, instead of nerves and apprehension, frustration was the emotion that seemed to be overwhelming everything else. How hard did this have to be? All she wanted was ten quiet minutes to say what she needed to say, for the load to be lifted from her shoulders, and she couldn't even get that. When they'd spent the day at the beach together Haydon hadn't mentioned any plans to be out that evening, but then, she supposed, just because they were spending time together it didn't mean he was obliged to. Still, she had expected him to be in and finding an empty house was beyond annoying.

There was no car outside, so did that mean he'd gone for a drive out? Perhaps to one of the more glamorous neighbouring towns like St Tropez? Or perhaps he'd simply gone to the supermarket? Ashley toyed with the idea of waiting around to see if he'd return any time soon but, after less than five minutes of watching the horizon for any signs of a car, she let out a long sigh and turned back to the path that would lead her to Violette's home. A lizard streaked across her path, so fast she could barely make out the eggshell markings on its back. The part of her that was still a big kid had longed to catch one of the many that hid amongst the rocks and shrubs of Violette's garden, just to know she could be fast enough, but as yet they'd all been too quick for her. Now, however, the event barely stirred any interest at all.

She'd left the occupants of Villa Marguerite preparing to stage some huge elaborate card game involving the entire family, and she supposed she'd be expected to join in with that when she got back, though she was hardly in the mood. It was going to be difficult to keep her current feelings hidden too, and if Sue didn't notice she was quite sure Molly would pick up on it. Maybe it would be a good idea to stay out a little longer, walk the fields until she'd managed to shake them off. With the decision made, she swung round and retraced her steps, taking the path to the coast.

*

Outside the restaurant the night air was still balmy but a brisk breeze that whipped in from the sea sent an intermittent chill across the harbour. The sun hadn't quite set and the sky was washed in pinks and lilacs over the horizon, giving way to deepest indigo as the first stars winked into life. Haydon and Ella followed Audrey out onto the patio area. His cheeks ached from laughing and it had been a long time since he'd felt so relaxed and content and so utterly charmed by a woman. He could see that Ella had fallen under her spell too, and she gazed up at Audrey now, smiling broadly, hanging on to every word that fell from her perfect lips. If Audrey had announced that the world was flat, at that moment, Haydon had no doubt that Ella would believe her completely.

'I have had a wonderful evening,' Audrey said. She smiled at Ella, but then threw a smouldering look Haydon's way and there was no mistaking the subtext. His response to this was caught somewhere between outright lust and mortification that Ella was present to witness their outrageous flirting. Well, at least Audrey had been flirting outrageously, while Haydon had tried but undoubtedly failed to keep his carnal desires under wraps. He glanced at Ella, but if she'd thought anything inappropriate had been going on under her nose then she didn't seem too distressed by it.

'Us too,' Haydon replied. He looked at Ella, who nodded in fervent agreement.

'You should come to our villa next time,' Ella said. 'We could cook for you.'

'I'm not sure Audrey would be impressed by my sausages and chips,' Haydon said.

'I would love to.' Audrey took Ella by the shoulders and kissed her lightly on both cheeks. 'I hope you will call me before you return home.'

'I will…' Haydon said, taken by a sudden dreamy stare. He shook himself. 'I mean, we will. Absolutely.'

'Don't make me wait,' Audrey said, that musical laugh of hers filling the night air. 'I don't like to wait – if I want something, I want to have it straight away.'

And then she gave Haydon another look filled with meaning and he almost gulped, cartoon-like. In the back of his mind there was a tiny voice telling him that he might just be the luckiest man on earth right now. Later, he would sit and wonder, still bemused by the idea that someone as impossibly glamorous as Audrey, who could have her pick of men, had deigned to even spend an hour with him, let alone show unmistakable signs of romantic interest. Everything about her was perfect, from the way she laughed to the way she smelt.

Audrey stepped forward, pressing her lips to his cheeks. '*Au revoir, Haydon*,' she whispered into his ear, her breath on his neck setting him ablaze. 'Do not forget about me.'

'No…' Haydon mumbled as she pulled away, feeling like an unready schoolboy being offered his first kiss. 'I won't forget.' He looked at Ella. 'Tomorrow?' he asked her. 'We could do tomorrow night, right?'

Ella nodded.

Audrey pouted. 'Tomorrow I cannot do. Perhaps the day after?'

'The day after… yes, we could do that,' Haydon said. 'The day after would be great.'

Audrey smiled, and then she reached to kiss him again, but this time she placed her lips firmly on his. She tasted sweet, like the figs they'd just eaten, and Haydon ached for more, but his mind kept warning him that Ella was right there and he had to be content with a goofy grin as she pulled away.

'Let me know the time,' Audrey said. 'I will be there.'

'We should walk you to your car…' Haydon began, but Audrey waved an airy hand.

'It is not necessary – I am quite safe.'

'But—'

'You must take Ella home,' Audrey said, nodding at Ella, whose mouth was wide in a huge yawn. 'I think she will be asleep walking if you do not.'

Ella grinned, and without any further reply, Audrey gave one last impossibly dazzling smile and turned to leave. Haydon watched her walk into the night, her skirts swishing around her, her steps light and elegant, and he still couldn't quite believe his luck.

*

Walking beneath the twinkling lights, it was hard not to be utterly enchanted by the easy atmosphere of Saint-Raphaël. Ashley strolled past the colourful awnings of shops still open, their bright displays beckoning her in, and the lively chatter underneath the umbrellas of restaurant patios as they fluttered in the breeze whipping in from the sea, and her overwhelming sense of frustration lifted from her, minute by minute. By the time she reached the harbour where the shadows of boats jostled for space on the glittering night-time swells, where distant bells clanged out at sea and gentle waves kissed the harbour wall and people greeted her with open, friendly faces and warm words, she was relaxed and optimistic.

She hadn't managed to catch Haydon tonight, but she had days yet and surely she could find a moment. It was such a small sentence to utter that she only needed a second to say it. And yet, such a small sentence had such huge implications, but she didn't want to think that far ahead just yet. For now, telling him was the important bit, and there was a secret hope too that she dare not acknowledge, but one that nested in her heart just the same: that perhaps the knowledge that they shared more than a brief past together might be enough to start something new between them, something real and solid this time, something that he wouldn't want to run away from as he had done once before. They'd both been young in Ibiza, and perhaps he'd simply felt too young to get tied down to one girl. Blokes liked to sow their oats, didn't they? But now, with a daughter and a divorce, perhaps the sowing-oats years were well behind him, and perhaps he was ready to commit again. And perhaps that could be with Ashley.

She turned away from the sea now, taking a winding alleyway lit by the golden glow of lamps hanging from stone-walled houses and candles on tables from various eateries. One particularly quaint place drew her attention, a large chalkboard standing outside and announcing fish dishes and house specialities in colourful looped handwriting. Inside she could see that the kitchen was entirely open so that patrons sitting at scrubbed wooden tables could see their food being cooked and the smell on the air was of fragrant herbs and sweet roasted garlic. If Molly had been a more adventurous eater she might have suggested they come down one evening, but she was quite sure no amount of cajoling would persuade her. Perhaps her mum and Maurice would come with her. In fact, she'd probably find Maurice was related to the owners – he seemed to be connected to just about everyone in Saint-Raphaël in one way or another.

With the decision made to walk back and ask them – Ashley had decided right there and then that she would be missing out on something very special if she didn't try this place out – she turned to continue down the lane, but a voice stopped her. She turned again to see Haydon emerge from the restaurant with Ella and a woman.

Without really knowing why, she slunk back into the shadows of a nearby house and watched. They were all laughing, relaxed, and the woman sounded like a local. Ashley vaguely recognised her and frowned as she tried to place her. Wasn't she the vendor from the patisserie stall at the market? And then the weight of all Ashley's newly built hopes and dreams crashed down onto her as the woman pulled Haydon into a kiss, one that he seemed to be enjoying immensely. This was no friendly Gallic greeting – this was a kiss with unmistakable lust in it.

Ashley's stomach clenched, her throat tightening. She'd been so stupid to fall for his charm and lies once again. All that day on the beach she'd thought him interested, imagined that she'd sensed genuine regret for the way he'd left her that morning in Ibiza. In her foolish daydreams she'd even thought there might be a chance for them to pick up where they'd left off.

Her expression hardened, along with her resolve. There was no way she was letting a man like this be part of her life and even less chance that he could be anything but bad for Molly. Her secret was going to stay secret, and once they were home she'd never have to think about Haydon whatever-his-name-was ever again.

Chapter Eleven

Ella had been thrilled with the suggestion, of course, but, though Haydon was determined to devote all his attention to giving her an amazing day out at a theme park in neighbouring St Tropez, he was finding it hard to concentrate as they prepared for the day.

Dinner with Audrey had been incredible and he couldn't help the stirrings of excitement for the start of something new. It wasn't a relationship that was at all practical, and he had to keep reminding himself of that, but he'd make the most of it in any way he could. He'd been so beaten by Janine leaving him, so lonely and insecure for so long since the divorce, that he'd hardly been able to pluck up the courage to get himself back out and dating again. And even if all meeting Audrey this week led to was one or two lovely dinners, then it was a start. It was the new confidence it had given him that was buoying him up this morning, and he couldn't deny that he was looking forward to seeing her again more than perhaps he ought to for a romance that could only be a holiday one at best.

And then thoughts of holiday romances suddenly took him back to Ashley again. The previous morning on the beach with her and Molly had been fantastic – not only for Ella, who was seriously in awe of her new friend – but for him too. And even though his thoughts this morning were filled with Audrey, there were moments when Ashley would pop in there too. But it was strange, because he couldn't read her at all and he couldn't understand why he'd be thinking of her that way. He'd gone to bed thinking about Audrey but his first thought on waking was of Ashley, in spite of all this. And all through breakfast he thought of Audrey, but every so often Ashley's face would appear behind his eyes and his feelings would become confused and muddy, and he didn't know what to think about any of it. More than once Ella had clicked her fingers in front of his face to gain his attention, and more than once he'd recognised a knowing smile. He supposed it wouldn't have escaped her attention that he and Audrey had shared a pretty steamy kiss; it was just lucky that she couldn't see into his head right now or she might want to disown him.

Trying hard to put his conflicted thoughts to one side, Haydon decided that his real focus for today needed to be Ella. He'd promised her a jam-packed day out and that was what he was going to give her. So they finished breakfast and hopped in the car with a bag of supplies and wound their way around precarious mountain roads with drops that made Haydon's stomach churn, overlooking the glittering swells of a calm ocean, past fields of wildflowers, past orchards and vineyards and tiny farmhouses, past marinas full of pristine white boats and sleepy roadside cafés where old men in cloth caps played card games in the shade of trellises covered in vines. Haydon would have suggested stopping the car to get a closer look at any one of these marvels but Ella was too excited to get to their destination, and, besides, he probably wouldn't have been able to keep his mind on any of it anyway.

'Dad… are we lost?' Ella asked finally, breaking into his thoughts. 'Only I'm sure we've seen that café before.'

Haydon blinked as Ella pointed to a little building with a striped awning throwing shade over a collection of mismatched tables and chairs.

'Oh…'

Pulling over, he flicked on the satnav that he'd convinced himself he didn't need. Normally, he'd cast a glance at a map and do a pretty good job of getting where he needed to be. Perhaps if his concentration had been better his usual method would have done just as well for him this time too, but his concentration was shot and it seemed there was no way to deny it now as the screen showed him just how far they'd driven off their route.

'Sorry. Perhaps we'll leave this switched on,' he said.

Giving himself a mental slap, he started the engine again. *Focus, idiot!* There was a time and place to daydream about what might be with a woman who was way out of his league, but this wasn't it.

*

'I'd say you didn't want to tell him.' Sue handed Ashley the lettuce she'd just broken up to wash.

'Of course I want to tell him,' Ashley hissed as she ran the tap. 'Do we have to talk about this now?'

'Nobody's listening,' Sue said. 'And if they were it might do you a favour because it looks as if someone else is going to have to tell him if you won't.'

'It's not a case of won't; it's a case of can't. It was hardly my fault you turned up with Maurice yesterday and decided to stick around. And I told you, when I went over last night he wasn't in.'

'Considering he wasn't in you were gone for a long time.'

'I told you I went for a walk to clear my head. There's no law against that, is there?'

'No, of course not. As for me turning up with Maurice yesterday, that was hardly my fault either. Perhaps if you'd allowed me to be open with my husband about all this then—'

'I was about to say something to Haydon when you turned up, actually,' Ashley said, her voice rising. She checked herself and glanced at the kitchen table to where Nanette and Violette were chatting as they sliced up tomatoes from a huge bowl. 'You know this.'

'I'm not so sure you would have done. And you could have asked me at any time to take the girls off somewhere and we would have left you alone with Haydon to tell him.'

'It was just all wrong after lunch,' Ashley said huffily. 'I'd planned it and then my plans were ruined, and if I'd done it after that it would have come out wrong.'

'I'm not sure there's any way for that news to come out that isn't wrong,' Sue shot back. 'He's not going to take it calmly and the longer you leave it the worse it will be.'

'I know,' Ashley snapped. 'You don't need to keep telling me that leaving it will make it worse because I know.'

Her phone bleeped the arrival of a message and she fished it from the pocket of her shorts.

'Molly,' she said, reading it. 'Says she and Maurice are going to get some fish from the market. Haydon and Ella were out this morning when they called at the house and apparently they're on their way to the theme park at St Tropez.' She looked up at Sue. 'That's put paid to me going to see him today as well.'

'I would imagine he'll be back this evening,' Sue said. She gave Ashley a pointed look.

'Yes,' Ashley sighed. Right now she knew she ought to come clean with her mum and tell her that she'd changed her mind and had no intention of getting Haydon involved in their lives, and that she just wanted to forget about him. But she couldn't bring herself to say it, to acknowledge the betrayal she felt after seeing him with another woman, to admit just how stupid she felt for ever thinking she could trust him, not even to Sue.

Worse still, there was a part of her that she didn't want to acknowledge, a part that was still attracted to him. She'd never thought of herself as the sort of woman who went for bad boys but right now her track record wasn't doing much to dispel that notion. First Haydon in Ibiza, then her three-timing ex, Ethan, and now unreliable Haydon again. If things carried on this way she might need to book some therapy just to meet a decent man.

'I know,' she continued. 'I should go and see him later. It's just… how am I supposed to have this conversation if Ella is around? Besides, if I'm going over there then Molly will want to come and I have no excuse not to take her.'

'Leave that to me,' Sue said. 'I'll think of something to get the girls out of the way, but then you'd better sort this before it really gets out of hand.'

*

He'd tried most of the rides, even the ones that had spun him into a state of intense queasiness, but he'd had to concede defeat when it came to the huge rollercoaster that he was currently standing staring at. Ella was on there, screaming her head off, having decided that even the awkwardness of the single rider queue wasn't going to put her off giving it a try. As she'd reminded him, once they'd returned home it wasn't likely they would be coming back to the South of France for a long time, if at all, and she'd regret missing out if she didn't ride the rollercoaster when she had the chance. So Haydon had watched with a small degree of awe as she'd gone off to join the special queue for those wishing to ride without their companions and almost instantly had begun a conversation in broken French and hesitant English with a girl who looked about her age. It was just another sign of how fast and how confidently she was growing up, and how, before very long, she wouldn't need him at all.

He watched now as the cars went past with a dull rumble and a wave of screams, so fast that he had no hope of spotting Ella.

'It looks awful, doesn't it?'

He turned to see a woman about his age talking to him. She was watching the rollercoaster with a baby clamped to her hip and, as seemed to be the theme for today, his thoughts, momentarily, wandered to Ashley. The woman was blonde, attractive, perhaps in her mid to late twenties. It could have been her, a few years ago, with Molly in her arms. He tried to banish the image and replace it with one of a very sexy Audrey instead, suddenly feeling duplicitous and guilty without really knowing why.

'More than a match for me.' He smiled. 'You didn't fancy it either?'

'Someone's got to stay on the ground with the baby. It was a hard-fought competition but my husband lost and is currently on there with my son. I'll bet he's having the time of his life,' she added dryly. 'Your other half on there?'

'Just my daughter. No other half, I'm afraid. Not now.'

'Oh,' the woman replied, and Haydon supposed there wasn't much else she could say to it. With a vague smile she turned her gaze back to the coaster but Haydon could see her move ever so slightly out of range. Did she think he was going to pour all his troubles out? Did he look like a man who had a lot of trouble that needed pouring out? Oh God, what a notion, that he might look a little bit desperate!

He was spared further torment by the shrill ring of his phone. He pulled it out of his pocket to see Janine's name on the screen.

'Hey,' he said, taking the call with a frown of vague surprise. 'Everything OK?'

'I was going to ask you that,' Janine said. 'Ella phoned me last night.'

'Did she? She never mentioned it.'

'I think you were in the shower or something at the time or I would have had a word with you then.'

'About what?'

'This woman you've met.'

Haydon blinked. 'What?'

'Ella says you've met someone.'

'We've met a lot of people,' he replied carefully, his mind racing. Of course, he'd had an inkling that Ella had been watching him and Audrey carefully, but he hadn't expected her to report back to Janine quite so immediately.

'Don't be evasive,' Janine said. 'She says you went out for dinner together.'

'Well, Ella was there too so it was hardly romantic.'

'But you like her?'

'Janine...' He frowned. 'Where is this going? Are you saying you don't want me to meet up with other women because—'

'I'm saying exactly the opposite,' Janine interrupted. 'I wanted to know how serious it might be.'

'We're on holiday so it's not really serious at all.'

'But if it was then I just wanted to say that would be good, and I'm happy for you.'

'But it isn't.'

'No, but if it was. It's about time you started dating.'

'You're feeling especially guilty about dumping me today?' Haydon cocked an eyebrow but immediately wished his tone hadn't been so confrontational. Often, he was thankful that he still had a good relationship with Janine when so many other divorced couples didn't, and he was aware of how unwise it was to jeopardise that.

She laughed. 'I'm always feeling guilty about it. Nothing new there. But I hate the thought of you being on your own.'

'Perhaps Kevin will build me a granny flat in your garden.'

'Haydon… Please be serious for one minute.'

'Is that all you've phoned me for?'

'Does there need to be another reason? I just wanted to offer my support, that's all.'

'It's just… phoning me for that. You're sure there's nothing else?'

There was another pause at Janine's end and Haydon felt that kick of vague dread that the next thing out of her mouth was going to be something he wouldn't like. She'd have been in regular contact with Ella during their time apart, but phoning Haydon… well, it wasn't something she'd ordinarily feel the need to do. Was she really that happy about the prospect of him finding a girlfriend?

He looked up and realised that the rollercoaster had come to a halt. Ella climbed out of a car and dashed towards him.

'Listen, much as I don't want to cut you off I'm at a theme park with Ella right now. I'm not sure this is the best place to be having deep and meaningful conversations about my existential crises or anything else. Maybe you want to call me later with anything else you need to discuss?'

'It's OK,' Janine said. 'That was all I wanted really, to say that I want you to be happy, and if you meet a woman you don't need to feel guilty about it. Ella seems to think there's a spark of something between you and this girl you've met. If you like her you should do something about it because I don't think you would if you thought it might affect me or Ella. And it wouldn't affect either of us, except to make us worry about you less because you'd find a little bit of happiness.' Janine sighed. 'I don't know that I'm getting this across very well, but do you see what I mean?'

'I see what you mean.'

'Right. That's it. Tell Ella that I'll call her later to hear all about the theme park.'

'I will. And Janine…'

'Yeah?'

'Thanks.'

'No need. Good luck, whatever you decide to do.'

'That was amazing!' Ella squeaked as Haydon ended the call and put his phone away. 'You should try it with me!'

'You have got to be kidding,' he said with a warm smile. Little Ella, taking everything in. She really was growing up faster than even he'd given her credit for. 'How about we get a hot dog or something instead – I'm starving.'

She nodded. 'Who was on the phone?' she asked as they began to walk in the direction of a cluster of fast-food huts.

'Your mother.'

'Oh,' Ella said, colouring. 'What did she want?'

Haydon could have used the opportunity to quiz Ella and ask why she'd felt compelled to tell Janine about Audrey, but he wasn't annoyed. Far from it, he was touched that Ella had felt the need to share her hopes for his happiness with her mum.

'She just wanted to know if we were having a good time,' he said.

'Oh, OK. And you told her we were?'

'Of course – what else was I going to say? I'm having an amazing time.'

'Me too.' Ella smiled. 'The best.'

'Right then, so there's nothing to worry about, is there?'

'No.'

Ella slipped her arm through his and yanked him playfully towards a burger bar. 'Can we have burgers instead of hot dogs?'

He smiled down at her. What she'd told Janine led him to believe she wanted him and Audrey to get together, but it wasn't that simple. Ella wasn't yet fourteen. She was still full of faith, full of belief in the magic of dreams and wishes, still thought that if you wanted something it would be enough to make it happen, and to learn life wasn't like that was no lesson he wanted to teach her at such a tender age.

'Right,' he said, putting the matter firmly out of his mind. 'Burgers all round and then maybe, just maybe, you might persuade me to try that rollercoaster after all.'

*

Sue's best-laid plans had come to nothing. At her behest Molly had sent Ella a text that evening inviting her out for a game of boules in a local park only to be told that Ella was so exhausted from her day at the theme park she'd developed a headache and couldn't bring herself to go anywhere at all, not even with Molly. So while Molly sulked about Ella's no-show, Sue and Maurice had decided to take her and Bastien out for supper at the harbour (the prospect of a dinner with Bastien going some way to soothing her disappointment), leaving Ashley at a loose end.

She'd tried reading a book, and she'd tried sitting quietly on the swing seat in the garden as the sun set, and she'd even tried chatting to Nanette and Violette, but she couldn't settle. Her mum was right – she needed to see Haydon. Perhaps it was unfair to take the decision away from Molly and him about whether they got to know each other by telling neither of them the truth of their relationship. Nonetheless, knowing what she knew now about Haydon's fickleness, she just couldn't bring herself to do it.

But there was no denying that she'd never be able to settle with the secret hanging over her. If Ella was tired and unwell, perhaps she'd be out of the way, leaving Haydon free at least long enough for Ashley to say what she needed to say and then leave. After that it didn't really matter, she supposed, because it was the telling that was the important thing now. Once he knew the truth it was his call.

Pulling a cardigan around her, she slipped out of the house before anyone could ask where she was going. Easier that way, and certainly less complicated than trying to make up some convoluted lie or, worse still, having to put Nanette off when she decided she wanted to go for Ashley's 'walk for some air' with her.

The sun sat on the horizon, orange and plump, bronzing the field as she crossed it. Amongst the grasses she could hear the crickets getting louder and the odd rustle that reminded her she needed to keep an eye on what was sharing the grass with her. But now that she was on her way she just wanted to get there before she lost her nerve and the paths around the field would take too long.

But how did you begin a conversation like the one she was planning to have? *Hi, Haydon, remember that night we shagged like absolute idiots with no protection? Well, ta da!* Or, *You seem to like kids, which is lucky because here's one you didn't know about!*

Before she'd worked out that crucial first sentence, Haydon's holiday villa was in front of her. Ashley took a deep breath and pushed open the iron gates. The garden smelt of honeysuckle and jasmine. The house seemed quiet and still, and if Molly hadn't already checked Ashley would have sworn nobody was at home. She was about to knock on the door when it swung open.

'Ashley?' Haydon looked confused to see her. He probably was, Ashley reflected, but it was nothing compared to how he was going to feel in a few minutes.

'Are you psychic?' she asked.

'What? Oh, no.' He smiled. 'I was just taking Ella some paracetamol and a drink and I noticed you from her bedroom window. I'm a bit surprised to see you here, though. Is there anything I can do for you?' he asked, glancing up the path behind her. 'You're not with Molly?'

'No. She's gone into town with my mum. Is Ella OK?'

'Oh she's fine. A bit headachy and exhausted but we had a pretty packed day out so she probably just needs a nap. She's in bed now trying to get forty winks.'

'She won't sleep tonight,' Ashley said with a frown. God, she sounded just like a mum. 'Sorry, not my place to lecture – ignore me.'

'It's only what my ex would say if she was here,' he said.

'Mums always think of stuff like that.'

'I know. So… you want to come in? I mean, I'm guessing you haven't come all this way to stand on the doorstep?'

Ashley nodded and stepped in as he moved out of the way to admit her.

'You want a cold drink?' he asked. 'Or I've just opened some wine?'

'Wine sounds nice.'

'I'm camped out in the back garden; it'd be a crying shame to waste this sunset.'

'Yes,' Ashley said, following him out to the garden. This villa was so different to the one she was sharing with Maurice's family – neat and precise and organised, apart from Haydon and Ella's belongings, which were scattered everywhere – but though she noticed this it was a vague, half-formed observation that floated across her thoughts. The garden was the same – well-ordered shrubberies and straight paths lined by immaculate borders and actual gardens as opposed to Violette's rambling tangles of herbs and wildflowers. She liked Violette's chaos better, though – it made her feel comfortable.

She sat at the table on the patio while he went to get another glass. Rivulets ran down the side of the wine bottle he must have just fetched out of the fridge, forming a little puddle on the mosaic tiles of the table. A moment later he emerged from the house again and poured two drinks, handing one to her. She took it and wondered why she was bothering. Why not just get it over with? What good was drinking wine with him when she had something so huge to get off her chest? She was only delaying the inevitable – that he would want nothing more to do with her when he learned the truth. He might not even believe her, and she couldn't say she'd blame him. She had no proof to offer except for Molly's existence – at least not here and now. What if he thought she was somehow trying to trap him? That she'd spotted an opportunity to improve her situation at his expense? What if he thought she fancied him gullible? Vulnerable after his divorce? What if he lost his temper?

Now that she was here Ashley wasn't sure she could go through with this at all. And yet if she didn't her mother would do the job for her and that would only make it a hundred times worse. Sue wasn't exactly famed for her tact and she had no love for Haydon or his feelings right now. It was lucky Ashley hadn't told Sue about seeing him kiss another woman, and even as this thought occurred to her the memory of the event made her face burn with the shame of her trusting stupidity.

Taking a sip, she watched him as he watched her, trying to gauge his mood, trying to see how this might go. But then he spoke, and it threw her thoughts into complete disarray.

'Ashley…' he began. And he suddenly seemed nervous, desperate almost. 'I'm actually really glad you've come because… Well, there's something I need to tell you. I'll admit that when I first saw you after all these years I didn't know how to feel. I probably reacted badly and said the wrong things, but, you see, I was in shock. I'm sure you were too…'

'Yes, but—' she cut in, and he held up a hand.

'Please, I need to say this before I bottle it.'

Ashley blinked. Hadn't she come to say the awkward thing? Wasn't she the one who should need to talk, who ought to be afraid of losing her nerve? What reason did he have to be anxious?

'I can't stop thinking about you,' he said, the words rushing out like air from a balloon. 'I've tried – God knows I've tried – but I can't. And I'm sure it's not what you want to hear but I think… I thought… that night we spent together was incredible and afterwards… and then seeing you again, well…' He brushed a shaking hand through his hair and then took a gulp of his drink. 'I'm sorry. You don't want to hear this and I shouldn't be saying it.'

'What?' Ashley stared at him.

'It's crazy, isn't it?'

'It's more than crazy!' Ashley hissed. 'I don't believe I'm hearing this! Do you honestly think I'm that stupid?'

It was Haydon's turn to stare. 'I don't understand…'

'I saw you! I saw you with that woman last night – and that's completely fine, none of my business – but now you tell me this! You tell me this after I saw you in full view of the world kissing another woman and you tell me you can't stop thinking about me? What's wrong with you?'

'Ashley…' he began, but shrank back at the fury in her expression. 'Audrey… it was just a friendly dinner… I didn't know when I asked her that I'd feel this way. We went out last night because it had already been organised but today when I should have been thinking of her, I kept thinking of you. I'm going to tell her later—'

'You're going to tell her later? You really do think I'm a mug, don't you? I wonder if you would have bothered telling her if I hadn't seen you? Or would you have strung both of us along for the week and then never phoned again once you went back to England?'

'No, of course not! Why would you think that?'

Ashley stared at him. And then she threw her hands in the air.

'What's the point?'

With that, she got up and marched for the gates.

Chapter Twelve

You were wrong. My love life will forever be complicated and it's probably my fault.

Haydon pressed send on his text to Janine and then turned his attention to pouring a strong coffee. He was going to need it if he was going to get through today without falling asleep, because sleeping was the one thing he hadn't done very much of overnight. He hadn't planned to come clean with Ashley the previous evening but, somehow, just seeing her there had unleashed this whole other spontaneous person he had no idea existed inside him. But the fact was, he could understand why she'd reacted the way she had, having seen him with Audrey, and now that he really thought about it, he realised he'd probably been behaving like a total shit.

Taking his coffee out to the patio, he sat next to Ella, who was already tucking into a pile of croissants and jam. When they'd first arrived in Saint-Raphaël she'd been determined to eat cornflakes, just as she always did for breakfast, but today, perhaps influenced by Bastien, she seemed more amenable to local food. Although, Haydon reflected wryly as he watched her eat, if she ever put a squid ring in her mouth he might just faint from the shock.

The phone he'd placed on the garden table bleeped and he unlocked it to see Janine's reply.

What happened?
I screwed it up.
How?
You don't want to know.

'Where's your breakfast?' Ella asked, glancing across at the solitary cup in front of him.

'Not hungry.'

'It's the most important meal of the day! You need to eat it whether you're hungry or not!'

'Hey, that's my line!' Haydon said, forcing a cheery tone. 'I say it to you but it doesn't mean I have to follow that rule too.'

'What if you go all faint when we're out?'

'I won't, and if I do then I'll get some food.'

'But you always have a huge breakfast,' Ella said, looking vaguely confused. How could he tell her that he couldn't think about food because there was no room for anything but thoughts of Ashley? He needed to see her, like an ache in his heart that was so extreme it was almost physical. If he closed his eyes he could hear her voice. Last night she'd called him out and he felt ashamed, but that didn't change the fact that, despite Audrey's perfection, her warm openness, it was cold, disapproving Ashley who kept creeping into his thoughts.

It was crazy, but the previous night had only made it worse. Audrey was like a dream that was almost too perfect to hold onto, a promise too impossible to keep. But Ashley could be his reality – a messy, imperfect, confusing reality that made him feel alive. She was someone who lived in his world, someone who made his heart beat faster, someone who would challenge him and keep him anchored and force him to be the best of himself. Audrey was beautiful and charming, and he would be a fool to let her go, but maybe he was, because the more he thought about it, the more strongly he felt about Ashley. But he'd messed it up and perhaps there was no going back now. Did that make it right to continue to see Audrey, even if all it would ever be was a holiday romance, as he'd kept telling himself?

'It's hot today,' he said vaguely in answer to Ella's statement, trying his best to keep things with her as normal as possible despite the turmoil in his head. 'I don't eat well when I'm hot.'

Ella shrugged, seeming to decide that the conversation wasn't worth pursuing. 'What are we doing today? Can we see Molly?'

'If they want to do something I don't see why not,' he replied, trying to sound as casual as he could.

'Shall I text her? What shall I say?'

He stood up. 'Ella... I need to do something first. I won't be a minute.'

Ella stared at him. 'Now? I thought we were planning our day? And we have to be back in plenty of time for Audrey—'

'About that,' Haydon cut in. 'It's the thing I need to sort out.'

'What do you mean?'

'We can't have her over tonight. It wouldn't be fair.'

'But I thought...'

'I know. I like her. I mean, she's lovely. But she lives here and we don't and I just think... well, you're not daft, are you? You could see that we liked each other as more than friends and I don't think it's right to let it go further than it has already.'

'You're dumping her?'

'No, because we weren't going out in the first place. But I am going to cancel tonight.'

Ella looked solemn but then she nodded. 'I suppose so. You don't want to break her heart.'

Haydon gave a wry smile. He didn't think there was much danger of that when in reality Audrey had been the one pulling all the strings. He'd basked in her glory for a brief moment, but he was certain she wouldn't waste any tears on him. For her, flirting with Haydon had been fun, and perhaps there was a certain amount of lust on both their parts, but now that he really thought about it, there had never been anything deeper than that.

'I won't be long,' he said. 'Then we can figure out what we're going to do with our day.'

'So, does that mean you don't want me to text Molly?'

'I guess you could just to see if they're free.'

'You think we'll see them after we get back to England? Maybe we can visit them in York? That would be amazing!'

'If they want to then I'd drive you up there,' he said carefully. He was still hopeful that when he'd done what he needed to do this morning he could smooth things over with Ashley, but he couldn't be sure, and he didn't want to promise something to Ella that he couldn't deliver. He wasn't even sure they'd be allowed to see Molly today. 'I've never been to York,' he added.

'Me neither! It'd be like another holiday!'

'It would. We'd have to check with them and with your mum but I'd love to take you.'

Ella flung her arms around him. 'I can't wait!'

'Steady on!' Haydon said, laughing. 'We haven't even asked them yet.'

'But they'll say yes…' Ella folded the last of her croissant into her mouth. 'I'm going to text Molly now,' she added through a mouthful of pastry. 'I'll ask her if she wants to go out today. Where shall I tell her we're going?'

Haydon was thoughtful for a moment. 'How about a boat trip?' he asked. 'Maybe we could hire one if we pop down to the marina?'

Ella's eyes widened. 'Brilliant! I'll tell her we're going to get a boat!'

'I only said we'll see about it,' Haydon reminded her. 'I can't promise anything.'

'OK, well I'll tell her that.'

Haydon watched as she raced indoors to get her phone. Once life had been that simple for him too, though it was hard to recall those days right now. But he had a difficult phone call to make and no promise at the end of it that Ashley would be willing to give him another chance. He could only hope that she didn't take her anger out on Ella by preventing her from spending time with Molly and Bastien, because Ella really liked them both and he didn't know if he could deal with trying to explain that turn of events to her. Rejecting him was one thing, and perhaps something he deserved, but rejection of Ella, that was quite another matter entirely.

*

'I don't believe this!' Sue hissed.

'I couldn't tell him because Ella appeared.' Ashley hated lying to her mum but what else could she do? If she told Sue the real reason – that she hadn't been able to tell Haydon because she'd stumbled upon him being rather preoccupied with another woman, and that she was now never going to tell him for the same reasons, it might open up a whole new can of worms that Ashley could really do without.

'I know, but you can't keep socialising with them as if nothing has happened. The longer you leave it the worse it will be.'

'I know, I know…' Ashley snapped. 'I'm doing my best here. I'll tell him today.'

'While he's piloting a boat with you all on it? He's likely to throw you overboard if you tell him then!'

'Before we get on the boat then!' Ashley wafted a fly away from her face and scowled. Sue wasn't annoying her as much as it seemed; rather she was irritated because she knew full well her mother was right. And after the way they'd parted last night, Ashley couldn't quite believe she'd agreed to give Haydon the time of day again, let alone spend it on a boat with him. She must want her head examining. There was no way she could tell her mum any of what had happened between her and Haydon and his mystery woman now.

Sue handed her a bottle of sun cream, which Ashley shoved into a cloth bag.

'Be sure you do,' her mother said tartly. 'It's not fair to anyone, dragging it on like this. Especially not to him, even though he doesn't deserve the courtesy of any consideration in the matter.'

'He's not the monster you think he is, Mum. We both decided to sleep together in Ibiza and it's not like I didn't know how babies are made.'

'And then he disappeared for the next sixteen years.' Sue gave a loud sniff. 'You'd think he'd have worked it out by now, knowing how old Molly is.'

'I don't think men take that sort of stuff in the way we do,' Ashley said with a weak smile. 'I was sort of hoping it might occur to him too – it would save me the job of having to break it to him. But he doesn't seem to have thought of it at all.'

Both women spun round at the sound of the door opening, and Maurice wandered out onto the veranda.

'Thought of what?' he asked carelessly.

'Sun cream,' Sue fired back and Ashley, for once, was glad of her mum's quick wits. 'We're making sure Haydon remembers to take some for the girls. If they're going to be on the water they'll burn quick as a wink without it.'

'Oh,' Maurice said. 'Are you sure we need to go into Fréjus? I'd much rather go on the boat with Ashley and Haydon.'

'Yes, we need to go into Fréjus. There's something in a shop there I want to get for your aunt.'

'We have a gift for her.'

'I know, but I want to get this too – I think she'll love it.'

Maurice pouted and it was hard not to laugh. Ashley knew the real reason her mum was determined to get him out to the neighbouring town and it had nothing to do with extra gifts.

'Have you asked Bastien and his uncle if they want to come?' Sue continued.

'I think he'd rather go on the boat too.'

'He's not invited.'

'Molly has invited him.'

Sue rolled her eyes. 'She can't just ask who she wants.'

'Tell her that, because she just has.'

'It's fine, Mum,' Ashley put in. 'I'm sure Haydon will be fine with one extra and the girls get on well with Bastien so they'll enjoy having him along.'

'But—' Sue began, but Ashley cut across her.

'Bastien will keep the girls entertained.'

What she meant was that the more kids were on board, the more noise they'd make and the less notice they'd take of anything that was being discussed between Ashley and Haydon. Whatever that might be. Sue seemed to understand this because after a short pause she nodded agreement.

'Looks like it's just you and me in Fréjus then. Unless anyone else wants to squash in the car?'

'I will go and ask,' Maurice said. Sticking his hands in his pockets he sauntered back indoors again. Sue turned to Ashley.

'Please get this sorted.'

'I'll try, though I can't promise anything with a boatful of kids.'

'I'm sure you can find a second and that's all it takes.'

'It's the fallout I'm worried about. Yes, it only takes a second to say the words but what about the stuff that comes after? He's going to want to talk about it and how do we do that in private? Every time we try to get everyone out of the way so I can talk to him properly it backfires.'

Sue threw her hands in the air. 'Damned if I know, but you're going to have to figure that out.' She glanced at her watch. 'He'll be here soon. You know, *I* could just tell him and it would be done with.'

'And I can just imagine what you'd say. Absolutely not – I'll handle this.'

Sue narrowed her eyes. 'You're not seriously developing feelings for him, are you? I know you said the other night, but I thought it was just silly talk.'

'Don't be ridiculous!' Ashley squeaked, but she couldn't help wondering whether her denial had been just a little too forceful. It seemed Sue thought the same thing, because she paused for a moment before pursing her lips.

'For God's sake, Ashley—'

'I'm not! He's good-looking and everything, but do you really think I'm that stupid?'

'Do you really want me to answer that?'

Ashley frowned. But then, from the corner of her eye, she saw Haydon and Ella on the path that skirted the field, making their way to the house.

'We're going to have to continue this later,' she said.

'Later I want to hear that you've sorted it,' Sue replied.

*

Ashley watched Haydon and Ella arrive at Villa Marguerite from her bedroom window, her stomach churning. Why had she agreed to this? A moment later Molly yelled from the floor below to alert her to the same.

'Coming!' she shouted and stopped for a last check in the mirror before grabbing her bag and racing down the stairs.

When she got outside, Molly and Bastien were already there, chatting to Ella. Haydon gave her a tentative smile, and Ashley returned it with something more restrained and courteous. But behind the mask her stomach still flipped and she still felt that jolt of desire seeing him standing there, the way those chocolate eyes made her feel, the sense of longing for those arms to wrap around her, even after everything he'd done and everything she knew he was.

He glanced across at where the teenagers were still talking and beckoned her to one side, his voice low.

'I called Audrey this morning and told her.'

'Told her what?'

'That it's over. You're right, I never should have let things go so far with her.'

'It had nothing to do with me – you can date who you like.'

'Not when I'm thinking about someone else I can't – it's not fair.'

Ashley frowned. 'Don't…'

'I can't help it. Please… just tell me there's a chance and I won't say another word until you're ready to talk about it.'

'How can I trust you?'

'I don't know how to prove it, but you can. Just let me show you. Let's pretend yesterday never happened and try to enjoy today in each other's company, and if you still feel the same way by the end of it then I'll know that there's no hope.'

'We don't have a choice but to get on today as the kids are with us.'

'But if they weren't? Would you still be willing to do that?'

'They *are*, so it makes no difference whether I would or wouldn't.'

'We had something, right? You're telling me that night in Ibiza meant nothing? Because it meant something to me and I can't stop thinking about it now that I've found you again. I feel like it could be the start of something special. Tell me you haven't thought about it a little too…'

'That was a long time ago.'

'But you're not denying it,' he replied with a small smile. Ashley tried not to smile back, but it was hard. Even now, a part of her wanted to trust him but how could she? She'd been down this road before with another man who hadn't been worth her trust either, and, right now, her faith in men was pretty much shot. One more betrayal might just shatter it forever. A life lived with no trust at all promised to be a lonely one, and it wasn't a possibility she wanted to think about.

'I don't know,' she said. 'I need time.'

'I can give you time, as much as you need. As long as there's hope.'

'There's nothing until you can prove yourself.'

'I will. You'll see.'

His small smile had turned into a broad, dazzling one now. He looked like a man who thought he'd already won. Well, she'd show him it wasn't going to be that easy and she wasn't going to forget all the wrongs he'd done her before so quickly either. If he wanted her then he was going to have to work to convince her he was worth the risk.

The sun was already high, the old road to town shimmering in the heat, spiny roadside shrubs heavy with vibrant flowers as the group walked together in the direction of the marina, the teenagers a few paces ahead of the adults.

'I hope you've got your sea legs with you,' he said.

'I hope you've got your captain's hat.'

'Do you think they'll still let me hire the boat if I don't have one of those?'

Ashley nudged him and laughed, despite her reservations about giving him too much encouragement. It was strange and lovely, this banter, a side of him she'd never really had a chance to see before. They'd joked and flirted, of course, that night in Ibiza, but they'd both been so drunk that it had somehow got lost in the haze of their alcohol-fogged memories. The main thing she'd taken away from that fateful night was the pure sexual chemistry, and then the stinging disappointment of never seeing him again when she realised that what she'd actually felt had been so much more than lust.

'If they don't we can always go bodyboarding again.'

'Oh,' he said, looking perplexed. 'Would you rather do that? I didn't think to ask…'

'I don't mind what we do. But this sounds lovely and probably a lot more sedate.'

'So you like sedate?'

'Not always…'

He grinned and his hand brushed hers, fingers reaching to lock, when he suddenly seemed to realise what he was doing and pulled away with a quick, guilty glance.

'Sorry,' he whispered. 'I didn't mean to…'

'Not yet,' Ashley said. 'Give it some time – please.'

'Of course, whatever you want. It's just…'

They were silent for a moment, the awkwardness of the moment hanging in the air between them. But then Haydon spoke again.

'I was thinking,' he said. 'About Molly's music school.'

'Oh?'

'I don't know anyone who could help her get into the one she originally wanted but I might be able to help with another one in Oxford. I know someone who knows someone… you know?'

'Oxford? But it's nowhere near us.'

'I know, but I just thought… well, if she really did have her heart set on a conservatoire then perhaps it might be worth considering?'

'I can hardly afford the one in York, let alone a move to Oxford.'

'But you wouldn't have to pay the fees in Oxford. If she could get the scholarship, of course. But that's where my friend comes in handy.'

'Are you suggesting a bit of jiggery-pokery?'

'No, but he'll be keen to do all he can to help a talented girl. It's his passion and he wouldn't let any talent go unnurtured if he could do something about it. I'm pretty sure he'd help to arrange accommodation nearby too.'

'It's kind of you but there's no way I could let her live in Oxford alone and I can't afford the move.'

'Well, I just wanted to say that the offer is there. No promises that it would happen anyway, of course, but I'd be happy to put a word in if you change your mind.'

'Thanks; that's really sweet of you.'

'I'd love to hear her play,' he said after a brief lull.

'I'm sure she'd love to play for you – she's such a show-off when it comes to her violin.'

'That's actually another thing I was thinking about… well, both me and Ella actually. We thought… never mind. It's probably too soon.'

'What?'

'It doesn't matter. Ashley… why didn't you ever phone me?'

She halted on the road and stared at him. 'I did. The phone number you left me didn't work.'

'What?' He stopped too. 'What do you mean?'

'I mean I phoned the number you gave me and it was wrong. I thought you'd deliberately left me a number that wouldn't work to get out of seeing me again.'

'I would never do that! And I thought... Oh God! All these years I thought *you* didn't want to see *me* again! I really liked you, I mean I...' He gave a shaky laugh and ran a hand through his hair. For a moment he looked so genuinely distressed by this revelation that Ashley wondered whether he might burst into tears. 'Things could have been so different!'

'They could,' Ashley said quietly. She wasn't just thinking about how different their own lives could have been but about how Molly might have grown up with a father. One tiny, stupid mistake was responsible for all this heartache? It seemed so inconceivable, and yet there it was.

From the corner of her eye, Ashley saw Molly turn to look behind her.

'What's going on back there?' she shouted with a grin. 'I thought the adults were supposed to keep an eye on what we were up to, not the other way around!'

Bastien and Ella laughed at Molly's quip as they stopped to see where Ashley and Haydon were too. Ashley's face grew hot and she wished she could say it was just from the sun.

'We were just discussing where to take the boat,' Haydon said, firing a guilty glance at Ashley as they started to walk again.

'Well, I hope you've got a map,' Molly said. The three waited for Ashley and Haydon to catch up before they started off. What Haydon had just told her changed everything but it looked as if this conversation was going to have to wait. Ashley's head was buzzing with a million more questions, a million alternative scenarios to the way her life had played out now running like movies in her mind. Now was not the time or place, but it was going to kill her to hold all this in for the next few hours.

Chapter Thirteen

Maurice had recommended a boat-hire company owned by a childhood friend, Pierre. At the marina, Haydon pointed to the shack at the end of a jetty where the sign hung: *Paradis Sur La Mer.* Underneath it read in English: *Boats for hire.*

'Paradise on the sea,' Molly translated, shooting Bastien a coquettish look that begged for his approval of her French. 'Sounds swanky.'

Haydon nodded, reflecting, as he regarded a small collection of half a dozen vessels moored nearby, that it *looked* swanky too.

'You know, we don't have to hire a boat,' Ashley began. 'We'd be quite happy on the beach if—'

'I promised everyone a boat, and a boat is what we'll get,' Haydon cut in. 'I don't know about you, but I suspect it's going to be a long time before we get the opportunity to do something like this again so to hell with the expense – let's just do it and make the most of our holiday.'

'But—'

'Before you go on about money again, I've told you that I was going to hire something for me and Ella anyway. It won't cost any extra for you guys to come along, so I don't need anything from you. Please don't worry about it.' He was about to beckon everyone to follow him, but Bastien and Molly beat him to it, tearing down the jetty together, leaving Ella to give chase and Haydon and Ashley bringing up the rear.

'Ooooh, that one's gorgeous,' Molly said, pointing to a long, sleek-looking yacht. 'And that one too,' she added, switching to a motorboat with a honeyed wood hull.

Haydon dug his hands in his pockets, eyeing up the tiny fleet bobbing on a gentle swell, the sun bouncing off chrome guardrails and glossy bows. One stood out to him – a roomy-looking motorboat with a canopy and a large deck for sunbathing. It looked like something out of a James Bond movie, and for a moment he allowed himself the crazy fantasy of how cool and sexy he might look grasping the wheel and directing it out to sea. It was gorgeous, and spending time on it was bound to make it a day, not only for the kids but for Ashley to remember.

Trying hard to suppress a boyish grin, he wandered up for a closer look. 'How about this one?' he called over his shoulder to the others.

'You would like to hire?' a voice came from behind them and Haydon swung round to see a man standing at the doorway to the tiny hut that he assumed served as the boat company's office.

'How much is it?' Haydon asked.

'Three thousand,' he replied, stubbing out the remnant of a rolled-up cigarette on the side of his hut.

Haydon gulped, his James Bond fantasy floating off with the currents that trailed away from the marina.

'A week?' he asked hopefully, though he already knew the answer that was coming.

'For one day, *Monsieur*.'

'Right…' Haydon fiddled with the change in his pocket. Fat lot of good that was going to do him, though. But then Ashley let out a giggle.

'Maybe you have one just as sexy but a little cheaper?' she asked the man.

He inclined his head. 'Perhaps. How much do you want to spend?'

'About ten euros, I'd say,' Ashley replied, giving Haydon a wry glance.

'I have this one,' the man said, pointing to the wooden-hulled boat. 'This is fifteen hundred euros a day. Plenty of room for you all.'

'Do you have anything around five hundred?' Haydon asked. Even that would have to go on his credit card, but anything less was just going to be embarrassing.

'This one is three fifty,' the man replied, pointing to something that looked barely more than a rowing boat. 'It is not so fast, but you will find it comfortable.'

'It really is only for a bit of fun – a few hours to see the coast. Will it be suitable for that?'

'Certainly,' the man said.

Haydon stepped forward to get a closer look.

'I have sailed one like this,' Bastien said, joining him. 'With my uncle. It will be strong enough.'

Haydon smiled at him. At least they had one competent sailor amongst them if it turned out he was completely hopeless. Which it probably would.

'Are you Pierre?' Ashley asked the boat-hire attendant.

'Yes.'

'Only, Maurice Dupont said to say hello.'

'Ah Maurice!' Pierre cried. 'I know him well – a good friend from my childhood! He is here, in Saint-Raphaël?'

'Yes. He says he's sorry he hasn't been to see you yet, but he's been busy with Violette's birthday-party preparations. But he asked me to let you know about that too – it's on Friday night and they'd like to invite you.'

'I would love to come to her party!' Pierre beamed. 'Please tell him I accept!'

'I will,' Ashley said.

'So, you are family?'

'He's my stepfather.'

'You should have told me this!' Taking Haydon's arm, he led him away from the boat he was mulling over to a bigger one. It wasn't as playboy as the one Haydon had drooled over, but it was more like he'd envisaged when he'd first hatched the plan for the day's adventure. 'You like this one?' Pierre asked. 'This is better, and I will charge you only five hundred euros.'

'Really?' Haydon asked.

'Of course! This is why I show it to you.'

Haydon looked at the others. Ashley nodded her approval. 'It's lovely.'

'OK.' Haydon turned to Pierre. 'We'll take that one – thank you!'

'Please follow me,' Pierre said, starting towards his little office. 'We must complete the papers first.'

*

After a brief (far too brief, Haydon felt) safety demonstration and a run-through of what was where on the boat, everyone climbed aboard and Pierre waved them off. This was madness, Haydon reflected as he watched the gap between them and the land widen. He didn't even know what the front and the back end of a boat were called, and yet now he was in charge of one. What had he been thinking? He'd put the whole party in danger because he wanted to impress a woman, like a sad teenage boy. Come to think of it, Bastien – the real teenage boy on board – had more sense than he did and would probably end up taking on most of the sailing anyway.

'This is amazing!' Ella squeaked as the wind picked up her hair.

'It is!' Molly agreed. 'The best!'

At least that made Haydon feel a bit better. He tried to relax and focus on calming the nerves that were making his hands shake as he gripped the wheel awkwardly. Maybe it wouldn't be so bad after all, and if everyone enjoyed themselves it would be worth the stress.

'It *is* pretty cool,' Ashley said. 'I've never actually been in charge of a boat before. Not that I'm in charge, of course.'

'Right now, I'm not sure I am,' Haydon said. 'I think the boat is actually in charge.'

'Follow the headland,' Bastien said. 'Stay clear of the rocks. We will be OK.'

Useful advice, Haydon thought wryly. Stay clear of the rocks – it wasn't like he'd planned to do anything else.

'Would you like to navigate?' Haydon asked him, realising that now was perhaps the time to swallow his manly pride and bow to Bastien's superior knowledge. 'I'd appreciate your help with the instruments because they all look very confusing to me.'

'The boat guy explained them,' Ella said.

'Yes, he explained them to a moron,' Haydon replied, and Ella let out a giggle.

'No, you're not,' Ashley said kindly.

'I'm very happy to help,' Bastien said. He climbed over a seat and peered at the compass on the dashboard.

'You're doing fine,' Ashley said quietly as the girls joined Bastien to watch in awe as he became the man of the hour.

'Ignore my fussing,' Haydon said. 'I just want everything to be perfect today.'

Their eyes met, and he wanted nothing more than to take her face in his hands and kiss her. But her earlier request to take things slow came back to him – she needed time to see that she could trust him and he had to respect that.

'Thank you,' he said.

'No, thank *you*!'

'No, thank *you*!'

'Oi!'

Haydon grinned. He had words, words of devotion, hours of explanations fighting their way out, but he had to swallow them back. Instead, he turned his attention to steering the boat and savoured the closeness of her beside him, the skin of her bare arm touching his as she scanned a sea that was crystal blue and calm for miles.

'When you're at home and it's all grey and drizzly you can't imagine anything like this,' she said. 'And when you're here you can't imagine there's a place all grey and drizzly.'

'Which would you prefer?'

'It's gorgeous here, but home's home, isn't it?'

'I've never been to York.'

'You should come and visit us. You and Ella would always be welcome.'

Haydon smiled, his heart soaring. Things were going so well so fast that it was almost frightening. He was only glad he hadn't ignored whatever impulse had forced him to confess his feelings for Ashley, because whatever happened from here, even if it didn't work out, he would never regret this day spent with her.

'Ella was only saying this morning how she'd love to visit,' he said. 'I suspect the kids are already sneakily organising it. Don't forget to give me your details before you go home and we'll fix something up.'

'And maybe you could give me the right phone number this time,' Ashley replied, and when he looked at her now he couldn't tell if it was humour or pain in her smile. Perhaps it was a bit of both, because if she felt half the regret he did for all those lost years, then pain was inevitable. But they'd found each other now, and if life had taken the path they'd hoped for all those years ago, he wouldn't have Ella. Things happened for a reason, or so Janine had always said and, for once, he had to agree with her.

'I'm not losing you a second time,' he said. 'You can have my phone number, address, National Insurance number... just so long as you know how to find me.'

She leaned in closer, her arm pressing gently against his. It was slight, just enough to tell him that she wanted him as much as he wanted her. At least, that was what he was hoping.

'There is a cove just around the headland,' Bastien called. 'I remember it now from when I came to visit before. It's quiet and good for swimming.'

'Aye aye, Captain,' Haydon called back. 'So we'll set a course for it...'

Out at sea the heat was tempered by a stiff breeze, but it was still glorious, the sun bouncing off glittering waves as they cleaved a path through them. The sky was blue and endless, meeting the sea in a smoky line marking the distant horizon. Ashley's hair whipped around her face and she dug into her bag and produced a hairband to tie it back, revealing the curve of a neck that Haydon just ached to kiss. He shook the thought and tried to concentrate on steering the boat again, though every so often his gaze would wander back to her as she contemplated the sea ahead, every detail almost too perfect to be real.

'You look amazing,' he said finally, as quietly as the roar of the boat engine would allow and unable to help himself any longer. 'I can't stop staring at you.'

'Please try,' she said with a soft laugh. 'Remember that you're in charge of a boat here.'

'I'm doing my best, believe me. But you're making it so damn hard.'

'Easy, tiger…'

'Oh, God, I didn't mean that!'

'I know you didn't.' Ashley giggled. 'But you missed a trick!'

Haydon blushed. He wasn't usually the blushing kind, and yet every time he saw her he felt like a blushing, bumbling teenager, all hormones and longing.

'Haydon,' she began, 'there's something…'

'Dad!' Ella shouted across them. He looked to see her leaning over the side of the boat, peering intently into the waves. 'Dad, you need to see this!'

'What?'

'The biggest fish I've ever seen!'

Haydon grinned. 'I can hardly come and look while I'm steering the boat.'

'Let me take it,' Ashley said.

'You're sure?'

'Are you saying I can't drive a boat because I'm a woman?'

'No, I'm saying neither of us has driven a boat before, and I don't know about you, but I was crapping myself at the thought.'

'I'm not.' She smiled. 'Go and see what Ella wants.'

'Thanks.' He nodded. 'What was that you wanted to say before we were interrupted?'

She shook her head. 'It's nothing.'

Haydon smiled, but the idea of not getting to hear what she'd begun troubled him, though he couldn't say why. But Ashley took the wheel from him and looked about as natural as anyone who'd never done it could look, and he decided that perhaps it was better to put his worries out of his mind for now and concentrate on enjoying the day.

✳

They were anchored in a quiet cove that they'd found exactly where Bastien had said it would be. It was hard to imagine anywhere more beautiful than what they'd already seen so far in the Côte d'Azur but this place managed it – a sweeping shoreline, cliffs dotted with cypress and juniper tumbling into a sapphire sea, gentle waves breaking on their jagged outcrops. Ashley didn't think a more perfect spot for their day out could possibly exist.

'I wasn't expecting your lunch to be quite so amazing,' Ashley said as Haydon unpacked the bag he'd brought. 'I feel guilty that I never thought to bring anything.'

'I'm always thinking about my stomach so that's probably why I packed lunch.'

'That's true,' Ella agreed. 'He thinks everyone else wants to eat constantly too. And he didn't eat any breakfast today.'

'You don't eat enough,' Haydon said, raising his eyebrows at her. 'If someone isn't nagging you you'd skip meals every day.'

'Yeah, but Kevin says if I needed it I'd eat it so not to worry.'

'Kevin?' Ashley asked.

'Mum's boyfriend,' Ella replied carelessly. Ashley glanced across at Haydon to catch him bristle at the mention of the man who must have taken his place in Ella's home. She'd heard something of him, second-hand from Molly, but it was the first time Haydon and Ella had talked about him in her company. She supposed it was a sign of how comfortable they were all becoming with each other already, and she didn't know how she felt about that. The attraction to Haydon was all too real, but the force of it scared her, and she could have no idea how it would all end. Could she trust him? Was anything he'd said to her true? But then she glanced at Molly and was reminded that she was keeping secrets too, and perhaps trust had to work both ways.

'Haydon, did you pack any cutlery? Or plates?' Molly peered into the bag he'd just emptied. Displayed proudly on the picnic blanket on deck were loaves of crusty bread, butter and cheese, ham and chicken, bottles of wine and juice, fresh fruit, pastries and assorted canapés.

Haydon's smile faded and Ella giggled. 'Always thinking about food, just not how to eat it.'

'We'll manage somehow,' Ashley said. 'It might get a bit messy, but if the cavemen managed to eat without knives and forks I'm sure we can.'

'The cavemen didn't have bottles of wine to uncork,' Haydon said with a doleful glance back at the picnic he'd unpacked with such pride before the flaw in his planning had been revealed.

'Perhaps it's better if we don't drink the wine anyway,' Ashley said. 'We've got to get this boat back in one piece.'

Bastien stood up and pulled off his T-shirt to reveal a still hairless chest and lithe, golden limbs. Ashley wondered which girl's mouth she ought to tap shut first as they both watched with obvious longing.

'I am going to swim,' he announced. 'It is better to eat afterwards.'

'Can I swim here, Dad?' Ella asked.

Haydon looked doubtfully at the rocks surrounding the cove.

'It is safe,' Bastien said. 'I have been here before.'

'You'll be careful?' Haydon asked, turning back to Ella.

'Of course. Bastien will be in the water with me and he's a brilliant swimmer.'

'I'm sure he is,' Ashley put in. She was quite sure that if anyone had questioned Bastien's ability to split the atom Ella and Molly would both have agreed he was brilliant at that too. 'But the sea can be unpredictable and we're miles away from help here.'

'I'm going in too,' Molly said, stripping down to her swimsuit. 'Ella will be fine with both of us there.'

For a moment Ella looked vexed at being treated as the baby, but then her expression softened again as she clearly calculated that if the others were going in Haydon could hardly stop her without looking like a killjoy.

Ashley went to open her mouth. But then closed it again.

'I'll be careful, Mum,' Molly said.

'You'd better,' Ashley said.

Bastien balanced on the edge of the boat. For a second he was poised, with the impossible grace of a ballet dancer, before he tensed and flexed and then dived effortlessly into the sea with barely a splash. Molly, with rather less grace, threw herself off the boat in such a violent manner that Ashley suddenly felt sick with worry. Then Ella followed, clambering down the steps at the side of the boat to ease herself gently in. Haydon went over to check the situation.

'They're OK?' Ashley asked.

'Yes,' he called from the side of the boat. 'It actually looks nice – do you fancy it?'

Ashley shook her head and lay back on the pile of cushions they'd spread on the deck. 'I'd rather work on my tan right now.' She closed her eyes, and listened to Haydon's footsteps as he came over to join her.

'I could get used to this,' she said.

'Me too.'

'Do we have to go home?'

'I'll stay if you do.'

She opened her eyes and smiled at him. 'If I didn't know better I'd think you actually meant that.'

'How do you know I don't?'

From the sea they could hear shrieks of laughter and enthusiastic splashing. Ella was chastising and the others were laughing.

'I hope they're not too mean to her,' Haydon said. Ashley frowned.

'Oh, I didn't mean that the way it came out. I worry about her, that's all. She's not as tough as some kids.'

'She seems to hold her own as far as I can see,' Ashley replied, relaxing again.

'She's good at making it look as if she's OK. All through the break-up with Janine, Ella didn't once complain. But you could tell she was hurting, underneath. I think sometimes she still does. She hides it because she doesn't want to make us feel guilty.' He rallied a smile. 'I don't suppose you want to hear about that now.'

'I don't mind if you want to talk about it.'

He shook his head. 'What would you say if I kissed you?' he whispered.

'Haydon…'

'The kids can't see us from down there.'

'That's not what I meant.'

'I know.'

He hovered, his face now framed by the sky above her. Somewhere in her head, the voice of reason screamed for her to stop him, but she didn't want to and she shut it out. She gave a faint nod. Taking her silence as permission, he dipped his head and pressed his lips gently to hers. They were salty, warm and responsive. She fell into it, all thoughts of earning trust forgotten, driven by a need that defied reason and logic and the recognition of consequences.

'You're OK?' he asked, breaking off. 'This is OK?'

'I don't know,' she said. 'It doesn't seem to matter right now if it's OK or not.'

'I'm not asking for anything you don't want to give.'

'I know.'

'And we can take this as slow as you like.'

'I know that too.'

'But this is OK now?'

She nodded. 'Don't ask me to make promises, but this is OK right now.'

He kissed her again, gentle at first, but then urgency building as he slid on top of her. The sun burned down and the waves lapped against the boat and the sounds of squealing and splashing came from the sea, but it was all lost as her need built too and she pulled him in, deeper, harder, barely taking air.

Then he broke off, panting as he held her gaze. 'I can't tell you how hard this is. I feel like I'm going to explode.'

'I know,' she said. 'But I need time, and you said—'

'Come to my place later?' he asked. 'When Ella's gone to bed. I mean...' he added, 'if you want to. Obviously there's no pressure, and I understand if it's all a bit too soon—'

'What happened to giving me more time? Maybe you'd better take a dip in the sea to cool off.'

'Yeah... probably.'

Ashley's resolve crumbled as she saw the look of disappointment on his face. 'I'll think about it.'

'About what?'

'Later. Maybe I'll come, but I don't know yet.'

He smiled. 'I'd like that.'

'I bet you would,' Ashley replied, unable to stop a grin spreading across her face now.

Haydon's smile widened too, clearly encouraged by her response. 'If I'm swimming then you're coming with me.'

'Nope, I'm staying here. I'm going to get the corks out of the wine bottles with my teeth and drink the lot.'

'Yeah?'

'Yeah.'

'We'll see about that,' he said, sweeping her up before she'd had time to react. She squealed as he carried her to the edge of the boat, and seconds later she crashed beneath the waves.

She came up for air to see Haydon treading water next to her, laughing.

'You bastard!' she cried, but he only laughed harder, and how could she be angry when he looked so handsome and happy? So instead, she splashed him. And then he splashed her back. Then the kids noticed and joined in, and before long her stomach was aching from laughing as they all indulged in a huge water fight. Ashley couldn't remember when she'd had a better time, and whatever else happened, she'd have this memory to carry with her, always.

If only the old folks back at Golden Meadows Retirement Home could see her now. Ashley smiled to herself as she lay against a pile of cushions, the sun beating down on her, the remains of their lazy lunch littered across the deck. In the end, Molly had been resourceful enough to go hunting below deck and had found a cupboard with a small stock of crockery, cutlery and – most importantly – a corkscrew for all that lovely wine.

'I suppose we'll have to clear this lot up before we head back,' Haydon said. Ashley opened one eye and threw him a lazy grin. He sat across from her, nursing a glass that contained the last of their Merlot while the teenagers had taken themselves back to the sea. She could hear them splashing and shrieking and vaguely wondered where they were finding the energy.

'I'm having a nap first. What I'm actually hoping is that when I wake up the fairies will have come and magicked it all away.' Closing her eyes again, she snuggled into her nest of cushions and let the sun warm her. But then a shadow fell across her and lips touched hers.

'You're incorrigible,' she said with a soft chuckle.

'Sorry. What's a man to do when you're lying there looking all magnificent?'

She opened her eyes and smiled up at him. 'If you keep saying that I might start to believe it.'

'It's true. Not only do you look magnificent, but you *are* magnificent.'

She giggled. 'Shut up.'

'I think you're amazing.'

'Haydon…' Now was the moment. It was all very well drinking wine and sunbathing and flirting, but none of this meant a thing unless he knew the truth, the real basis of their relationship. It was time to come clean. 'Before we go any further there's something—'

A whistle split the air and they both whipped round to see Bastien, dripping wet on the deck of the boat, grinning at them. Molly clambered aboard behind him, followed by Ella. Haydon scrambled away from Ashley, who drew a nearby towel across her.

'Would you like us to swim again?' he asked. 'So you can be alone?'

Cheeky little sod, Ashley thought. But she could deal with Bastien. It was Molly's reaction she was worried about. Ella's too, when it came to it. If Bastien had kept his mouth shut, perhaps they wouldn't have been any the wiser, because she didn't think they'd seen anything, but it wouldn't take either girl long to figure out what he meant by his mischievous comments.

'Mum…' Molly said, and a second later her frown turned into a grin too. 'I knew it!' She turned to Ella. 'Didn't we guess?'

Ella nodded enthusiastically.

'You're OK with it?' Haydon asked, glancing uncertainly between them.

'Yeah, of course!' Ella said. 'I wanted you to get a nice girlfriend, and if you get married me and Molly get to be sisters!'

Ella could have had no idea just how close she was to the actual truth of her relationship with Molly, and the thought of it twisted Ashley's gut. She'd barely come to terms with telling Haydon, and she still wasn't sure she even wanted to, but she couldn't say anything to Molly or Ella until he knew. She felt like she was being sucked into a sinkhole where the further down she went with the lie, the harder it was to climb back out, and yet she was already so far down that the only way to go was to continue with it. Would it be such a big deal if nobody ever knew? Would it be so wrong if it meant that everyone lived in blissful ignorance? Ashley would carry the deception alone and everyone else could get on with the business of forming new bonds.

Her plan might have been the perfect solution but for one tiny but significant detail. Ashley couldn't carry the deception alone because this kind of deception wasn't one you could carry for long. And besides all that, on a practical level, her mother knew everything.

'That would be insane!' Molly squeaked, grasping Ella's hand. 'Would we all live together? Maybe me and Mum would have to come and live near you… or maybe you'd come to York…?'

'Whoa!' Haydon held his hands up. 'We haven't even got past the end of the holiday yet.'

'Wait until I tell Mum!' Ella said. 'She'll be so happy.'

'Relieved, more likely,' Haydon said with a half-smile.

'There's nothing to tell anyone yet,' Ashley cut in.

'Why?' Molly clamped her hands on her hips, exactly the way Sue often did.

'Because we're only just working it out ourselves,' Ashley replied. 'If you'd only had one date with a boy would you be telling me straight away? Because I'm pretty sure you'd wait until you knew you liked him before you brought him home to meet me.'

'It's not the same,' Molly began to argue, throwing the tiniest glance at Bastien that made Ashley do a double take. Was this the stirrings of another holiday romance? On another day, perhaps she'd have quizzed Molly about it, even indulged in some gentle ribbing, but there was so much else going on today she couldn't think about that right now.

'It's exactly the same. Haydon and I will tell people when something needs to be told.'

'So Bastien didn't just see something going on?'

'It's none of your business if he did or didn't!' Ashley fired back.

'But we already know,' Molly insisted, unperturbed by Ashley's denials, 'so what's the difference? Who else needs to know more than we do?'

Ashley's mouth opened and then closed again. She didn't have an answer for that, because Molly had a point. Nobody else was more important than the kids.

'*I'll* tell people,' she said finally. 'Not you – me.'

'When?'

'When I'm ready.'

'Why do you think people will be so bothered?' Molly asked. 'Is it because of when you knew Haydon before? It's not the same now, though, is it?'

Ashley's mouth fell open. Ella's wasn't far behind while Haydon looked vaguely embarrassed and Bastien looked as if he was about to fetch popcorn and get comfy.

'How did you know about—'

'Gran told me,' Molly said.'

'And what else did she say?'

Molly shrugged. 'Some other stuff. I don't remember it all now.'

It was obvious that Molly did remember the other stuff and that none of it had been complimentary, so Ashley thought better of pushing the matter here and now. Trust her mother to give more away than she should – she was little better than a teenager herself at times. Ashley could only assume that Molly's carefree demeanour meant that Sue hadn't spilt the most important details about her and Haydon's previous meeting, which she supposed was something to be thankful for.

Perhaps Haydon could sense a stand-off, because he intervened now. He gestured at the leftovers still spread on the picnic blanket.

'Let's get this lot cleared up. We've got to return the boat before we worry about anything else.'

Ashley sighed as she got up. She didn't have the answers either.

Chapter Fourteen

They'd cleared the deck and set a course back to Saint-Raphaël, Ashley quiet and thoughtful and Haydon probably wondering whether he'd blown it as he threw her the odd, anxious glance. He hadn't, not exactly, or if anything was blown then it had been a joint effort. Ashley wanted to communicate this to him but she didn't have the words, so she said nothing at all.

As they walked back to their villas the teenagers chatted and laughed as if nothing had happened. Once or twice Molly or Ella would look back to check what Ashley and Haydon were doing and sometimes there would be an encouraging smile. Once Haydon had tried to reach for her hand but she'd moved it subtly out of range, even though she wanted nothing more than to feel his skin on hers. There was no telling who was out and about to see it, and she couldn't risk this getting back to her mother before she'd had time to explain.

As for the other things she'd needed to air, the right opportunity was looking less likely to appear by the day, and the guilt over continually deceiving Haydon about the biggest and most important secret she could keep from him wasn't helping her feel any more comfortable with his shows of affection. Even though it hadn't been entirely her fault (and even she had to admit that), she knew she should have told him – before he'd told her how he felt, before that first kiss, before the kids had found out. She should have told him long before any of this, back when she'd first seen him again on the beach. Now it looked more hopeless than ever.

'Will I still see you later?' he asked in a low voice as Molly and Ella said their goodbyes at the field where their paths separated.

'I need to do some things first,' she said. 'I don't know.'

'You're unhappy? I've done something wrong? I'm sorry it got out of hand on the boat—'

'It wasn't your fault.'

'But the kids finding out…'

'If the kids hadn't worked it out today they would have at some point.'

She gazed up into his eyes, searching for an answer in their depths. 'I can trust you, can't I? Please don't break my heart again.'

He gave a thin smile. 'So I broke your heart before?'

'Didn't you wonder why I was so shocked to see you again?'

'Yes, but…' He let out a dry chuckle.

'What? How is this funny?'

He shook his head. 'It's not. I felt the same, that's what's funny. All these years I'd thought you weren't interested in me beyond that one night… isn't that crazy?'

She gave a small smile. 'I suppose it is.'

'Maybe now we can pick it up again? Maybe this is our opportunity? A few years late, I'll admit, but there's no reason why not, is there?'

'I just need some time to get to grips with it. Is that OK?'

'God, yes!' he said, blowing out a long breath. 'Anything you want!'

'Thanks. I'll text you later.' Ashley called to Molly, 'Finished there?'

Molly nodded and turned to walk towards her.

As Haydon and Ella left them, Sue emerged from the house. It was immaculate timing, and Ashley couldn't help wondering if she'd been watching for them to return.

'How was your day?' she asked as they closed the gates to the garden behind them.

'Amazing!' Molly said. 'The boat was *so* cool.'

Sue wrinkled her nose. 'I thought cool wasn't a cool thing to say any more...' She raised her eyebrows. 'At least that's what you said when you told me to stop saying it.'

'I can say it because it's ironic when I say it.' Molly grinned. 'I'll tell you about it later – just got to get changed...' She turned and jogged after Bastien, who was already on the veranda waiting for her.

'I think there might be a little holiday romance starting there,' Ashley said in a low voice, tilting her head in their direction as Molly giggled at something Bastien had said.

'Just as long as that's the only one I need to know about,' Sue said.

'What does that mean?'

'She's not exactly distressed. I take it she still doesn't know about Haydon?'

'Of course not.'

'But you were going to tell him today?'

'Yes, but...'

'You would have told her after.'

'Not necessarily. It wasn't exactly the time or place.'

'I would have expected Haydon to say something then, considering he'd have a lot of making up to do.'

'He's not that reckless.'

'How is it reckless for her to know that her dad has been sitting right in front of her all week?'

'There's a way to do these things, Mum...' Ashley skirted around her and headed for the veranda. But then Sue's voice halted her on the path.

'You still haven't told him, have you? Why not?'

'Because the right moment just hasn't presented itself.'

'There's never going to be a right moment. Is there something you're not telling me? I have eyes, Ashley. Are you falling for him? Is that what's going on here? Because if you are…'

Ashley turned to face her. 'Would it matter?'

'You are?' Sue asked, her eyes wide.

'That's not what I said. I just want to know what difference it would make. I mean, surely it would be a good thing…'

'He left you flat! Pregnant!'

'He didn't know.'

'That's because he disappeared.'

Ashley sighed. 'It wasn't his fault, Mum. The phone number he gave me was wrong. And I never gave him mine.'

Sue folded her arms. 'The phone number was wrong? That was handy, wasn't it? The fact remains that he used you, and you suffered the consequences of that.'

'He didn't use me – it wasn't like that. *He's* not like that…'

'Dear God, you have fallen for him, haven't you! Ashley—'

'I'll tell him,' Ashley snapped. This was a conversation she didn't need to have right now. She might have known her mother would work it out – she always did. 'I'll tell him and he'll be so angry he'll dump me – is that what you want?'

'Don't be so pathetic. Did I really raise you to be so needy? If he dumps you then he was never worth your affection.'

'Maybe not, but I want it. If you think that's needy then I'm sorry, but that's just the way it is.'

Sue stepped forward and pulled her into an embrace. 'I'm sorry. I just don't want to see you hurt again. Can you blame me for not trusting his motives? Are you quite sure he doesn't just see an opportunity for an action replay of your holiday in Ibiza?'

Ashley pulled back and dragged a hand across her eyes. 'We've both got kids in tow and mortgages we'll have until we die – it's hardly an action replay.'

'You know what I mean. Be careful, that's all I ask.'

'I am, and I will be. And you're right about everything – and I will tell him.'

'It gives me no pleasure to be right about this and I know I can't tell you what to do any more, but this is something that won't just go away if you ignore it.'

'I know.'

There was a pause. 'Do you think Molly suspects anything?' Sue asked.

Ashley shook her head. 'Why would she?'

'Because she's a bright young girl who might well be doing the maths as we speak.'

'How can she do any maths when she…' Ashley frowned. 'I know you told her that I knew Haydon from a previous holiday. What else did you tell her?'

'Just that. But clearly she knows that you haven't been on holiday without her and that you were just shy of nineteen when she was born, and she'll have worked out that it was unlikely you would have gone abroad without me before you were eighteen, and she'll know that a woman is pregnant for nine months and—'

Ashley held up a hand to stop her mum. 'OK, I get your point. I just don't think she's considered it all that deeply.'

'I wouldn't bank on it, though – that's all I'm saying.'

'Please don't tell her.'

'It's not my place. But I think you ought to give it some serious thought before she works it out herself. I wouldn't like to be on the receiving end of that temper tantrum if she does and she figures out you knew all along.'

'She won't, and I will tell her. When I've told him.'

'You've got two more days until you go home and tomorrow is going to be taken up with Violette's party.'

'I know,' Ashley said, trying to curb the irritation in her voice. It wasn't aimed at her mum, but at the situation as a whole. 'You don't have to tell me this because I bloody well know…'

'So when are you going to do it?'

Ashley chewed on her lip, her gaze trained on the horizon where the sun was beginning to sink, burnishing the fields.

'Tonight,' she said. 'For better or worse I'll tell him tonight.'

Ashley looked at her phone. She could text Haydon right now and tell him everything, and then it would be done. Perhaps it was a cruel way to hear it but a damn sight easier for her. The bedroom was cool and the sheets smelt like fresh air as she lay on them, gazing up at the pits and divots of Madame Dupont's old ceiling as the evening shadows moved across it, a soft breeze bringing the scent of jasmine through the open window. She'd claimed a headache and escaped a family dinner that was too noisy and hectic. She could hear Molly now, laughing, and Bastien's voice raised as he spoke in English above the rabble of everyone else's French. There was definitely something starting between those two; maybe it had even started already. But what could Ashley do about it? She'd had the birds and bees talk with Molly a couple of years before and, given her own current predicament, there was an undeniable irony in trying to lecture Molly on the dangers of teenage sex. Besides, Molly had always been blessed with a good deal more common sense than Ashley ever had and she'd be careful if she did anything. Plus, at least they knew where to find Bastien if the worst came to the worst, though Ashley tried not to dwell on the possibility of such an outcome.

Just as she'd dismissed the idea of a text to Haydon as pretty much the worst one she'd ever had, her phone bleeped. It was him – of course it was.

I had a great time today. Will I see you tonight?
It might be tricky.
Tricky how?
Everyone's here and they might want to know where I'm going.
You definitely can't sneak off? Not even for an hour?

Ashley rested the phone on her chest and stared up at the ceiling again. It wouldn't be impossible to get away if she really wanted to. Her mother would have said she was simply delaying the inevitable, and she'd be right. Seeing him tonight was simultaneously the thing she wanted most and yet least in the world right now and she'd never been more confused and conflicted. Her phone bleeped again.

OK, I came on a bit heavy. I understand it's not easy, and I know
we should take it slow. I'm sorry I keep hassling you.
It's not that. It's just hectic here.
I can wait. Whatever time you can get away I'll be up.

Ashley let out a sigh. For better or for worse, she'd promised Sue. For better or for worse she'd come clean. But now that she was faced with the task, it didn't seem quite so easy.

A light tap at the door made her sit up.

'You can come in – I'm decent.'

Maurice poked his head around the door with a concerned smile. 'How do you feel?'

'I'm alright.'

'Too much sun perhaps? Out at sea?'

Ashley nodded.

'May I come in?'

'Of course. I'm really OK, though, so you needn't worry.'

'I am not sure that's true.'

'Nothing the aspirin I just took won't fix.'

'Sometimes,' he began, taking a seat on the end of her bed, 'it's easier to talk to someone who isn't so close to you that their judgement can be clouded by their feelings.'

'What do you mean?'

'I can't help thinking that something is troubling you, and I wonder if you want to talk about it. My ears exist for your use if you need them.'

'Thanks,' Ashley said, and she couldn't help a smile at his turn of phrase. He'd always had a lovely, quirky way with words. Perhaps it was because English wasn't his first language and so he didn't get caught up in all the clichés that native speakers dropped into so easily.

'I know that sometimes your mother cares too much and it can be hard to tell her things,' he continued.

'You know her well enough alright. It's not her fault.'

'It's not. So, can I be of service?'

Ashley paused. It was a nice thought, unburdening some of this on Maurice, who would listen without judging and who she'd always got on with because they were weirdly similar in so many ways. And if she asked him for discretion it would be guaranteed. But it would put him in an awkward position when it came to her mother and to Molly and she wouldn't wish that on him.

'There's really nothing to tell,' she said. 'But I appreciate the offer.'

He nodded. 'Perhaps you will join us for a little wine?'

'Maybe later. In fact…' She swung her legs over the side of the bed. 'I might go for a walk first – get some air and a little peace and quiet. Will it be OK if Molly stays here with you? In fact, could you cover for me and not mention to anyone I've gone off? I could do with being alone.'

If Maurice was surprised by her request he didn't show it. 'If it will help with this problem that doesn't exist,' he said, inclining his head with a wry smile, 'then I will play my part.'

'Thanks, Maurice, you're one in a million.'

'You will go now?'

'If I go now I can be back before anyone misses me.'

'We will always miss you when you're not there,' he said, getting up and turning for the door.

'Charmer.' Ashley smiled. 'No wonder Mum fell for you.'

He threw her a last grin before leaving her to pull her shoes on.

*

'I'm definitely sunburnt.' Ella pulled the sleeve of her T-shirt up to reveal red shoulders. 'It stings.'

'I'm sure it does,' Haydon said, pursing his lips and frowning. 'You topped up your sun cream like I said?'

'You saw me,' Ella pouted. 'Well, you would have done if you weren't making eyes at Ashley all day.'

'I wasn't making eyes at Ashley! Anyway, how old are you – ninety? Nobody makes eyes at people any more. I thought I was the old codger here.'

'Kevin says it.'

'Figures.'

'You don't like Kevin at all, do you?'

'Of course I do. It's just…'

'Mum would like Ashley and it's just the same.'

'How do you know?'

'Because she wants you to have a girlfriend.'

To lessen her guilt for walking out on him, perhaps, but Haydon knew better than to say it in front of Ella. Instead, he looked at his phone. Ashley had said she would come over, but he didn't know when. Ella should have been in bed by now, and on any other night she would have been. But for some reason tonight she just wouldn't settle and kept sneaking out of her room to join him on the veranda.

'That doesn't mean she'd automatically like my choice of girlfriend. Do you like everyone in your class?'

'No.'

'It's just the same. There's no reason you don't like some of them, but you don't anyway.'

'I know that. It's not the same. Mum would like Ashley because… I can just tell.'

'Well that's great, but don't you think we ought to continue this conversation in the morning? It's your last full day here tomorrow and you don't want to spend it rotting in bed because you had a late night.'

'You're still up. Besides, I can get up if I need to.'

'I'm up because I will be able to get up if I need to. You say you can but then you're like a dead dog and lie in until noon.'

'I don't.'

'Do.'

'Daaaaaaddddd…'

'You know I'm right.'

'I can't sleep yet.'

'Why not?'

She shrugged. 'I feel weird.'

'You are weird.'

'Not like that.'

'What then?'

'I don't know… funny.'

'You're sick?'

'I don't think so.'

'Sad then? Worried about something?'

Ella sighed. 'I just don't know. I can't explain it.'

Haydon patted his lap. 'Come here and give your dad a cuddle.' As she crossed over and snuggled into his knee, he rested his chin on her shoulder. 'I used to be able to rest my chin on the top of your head. You're too tall now – can you please stop growing?'

'I can't help it. I wish I could fit on your knee like I used to.'

'You feel like everything is changing too fast?' he asked. 'You feel like your life is moving quicker than you can keep up with and nothing looks the same as it used to? Mum's got Kevin and I'm starting to date again, you might move to London, and you can't fit on my lap the way you used to. Let me tell you, kiddo – those feelings don't ever go away, even when you're a grown-up. But you do learn that they're a normal part of life and that no matter how odd and new everything seems at first it usually has a way of settling down – for a while at least. It's been like that for me too and at first I hated it, but I think I can see the end in sight and it looks pretty good.'

'You mean with Ashley?'

'I mean with everyone. You're going to London and life will be amazing for you there. At first I hated the idea, but I see now that things will be weird and maybe more difficult for a while but I have to let you go.'

'Even if it's with Kevin?'

'Even with Kevin. He seems like a good bloke and as long as he treats you and your mum well I can hardly complain. Just don't forget me.'

'As if! I suppose if you marry Ashley you'll have Molly when I'm in London.'

'Blimey, nobody's mentioned weddings yet! And Molly is great but she isn't you.'

'She'd be your daughter,' Ella said, and Haydon couldn't help but detect a hint of reproach in her voice. Was she struggling with the idea? A development like that was a world away right now, yet her uncertainty was plain. She liked Molly now, but he supposed seeing Molly take her place in his affections – or at least it *seeming* that way – might quickly sour that friendship.

'*You* are my daughter, no matter who or what else happens. Always.'

Ella wrapped her arms around his neck and kissed his cheek. 'And you're my dad, no matter how many presents Kevin buys for me.'

Haydon grinned. 'We'll put that to the test when he gets you a MacBook.'

'He could buy me ten MacBooks and I wouldn't care.'

'Who even needs ten MacBooks?'

'You know what I mean,' Ella said, laughing.

'I do. And it makes me happier than I can tell you.'

Ella was silent for a moment. Then: 'Everything was changing so fast it was making you feel scared and weird. That's why you hated Kevin and you didn't want me to move to London? That's how come you knew exactly what was wrong with me today?'

'You must get your wisdom from your mum, because yes, you're right, and I hadn't really figured it out myself until just now.'

'It's going to be OK, Dad.'

'I know that now. But thanks for saying it.' He glanced at his watch, and then to the phone sitting on the table beside them, its screen dark. 'Are you sure you don't want to get to bed now?'

'Will you come to bed soon?'

'I'm only going to be just out here.'

'I know, but I feel better if you're in the room next to me.'

'In case the bogic bogeyman comes out?'

Ella rolled her eyes. 'Don't make fun of me…'

'I'm not, I'm sorry. I'm just not tired yet.'

'Can I stay up with you out here then? Just a little longer?'

Haydon bit back a sigh of frustration. Of course he wanted Ella to feel secure and happy but he'd also been bursting with anticipation at the thought of a few hours alone with Ashley.

'A little longer,' he said. 'That's fine.'

'Because we probably won't do this ever again,' she said. 'Next year we might not be able to go on holiday, just you and me.'

'And you definitely won't fit on my lap next year. I'll probably have to sit on yours.'

'But we won't. Will we?'

'You don't know that.'

'I know, I just feel it. Everything is going to change and it won't ever be like this again.'

'Even if we don't go on holiday again we'll always have this one, won't we? And it's been pretty amazing.'

'Yeah,' she said, nuzzling into his shoulder. 'The best.'

*

Ashley was walking across the field that separated the two villas when her phone bleeped to tell her she had a text message.

I'm really sorry but I can't see you tonight after all.

Ashley frowned as she read it again. Seriously? This afternoon he was all over her and now he couldn't see her?

What's wrong?
Ella needs me. She's in a weird place and I think she needs some reassurance so I don't want to leave her alone. Sorry. Maybe we can catch up tomorrow if you have time? I do want to see you more than I can say and I wouldn't put you off unless I really had to.

Ashley let out a sigh. What could she say to that? It was what any perfectly decent dad would do and yet the idea made her bristle. And she couldn't fight off the nagging suspicion that he was lying to her to cover up an assignation with that other woman he'd been seeing… Audrey or whatever her name was. She tried to shake the notion. Surely he wouldn't be that blatant and cruel? But right now she needed to see him, and she needed to get the secret off her chest that became heavier with each day she held it there.

I don't know how much time I'll have tomorrow with the party.
Anything you can spare.
Won't you be out with Ella?
Maybe. I can try to figure something out.

She tapped her phone on the palm of her hand for a moment. Perhaps she could get Ella invited to the party? As Molly's guest? That would leave Haydon free for her to talk to.

Leave it to me – I think I can fix it. I'll text you tomorrow morning and let you know.
OK. I'm missing you already.

Letting out a sigh she sent back a single kiss. She was missing him too and she wanted nothing more than to lie in his arms and feel his lips on hers, but there was this thing, this huge thing between them, and it had to be dealt with before she could even think about any of that. And that was assuming he'd be OK with it. He'd be shocked, that was for sure, and they'd have to do a lot of talking.

She tapped the phone on her hand again. The idea of texting him and telling him the truth about Molly was more appealing by the second. At least she wouldn't be sleeping with it for another night. But it was a terrible way to break news like that and she needed to be there when he heard it. Quickly she decided to stick with her original plan. Somehow, she'd have to get Ella invited to the party and catch Haydon while she was busy.

Chapter Fifteen

'I'm beginning to think you don't want to tell him,' Sue said.

'I do. I mean, I don't because it will be hard but that doesn't mean I don't understand that I need to.'

'It's taken you all week. It's one sentence. *Haydon, Molly is your daughter.* Done. How hard can it be?'

'Mum!' Ashley hissed, glancing at the doors to the house as they stood at the far end of the veranda. The morning was bright and fresh and already, despite the early hour, the house was buzzing with activity for the big event, the thing they were all there for – Aunt Violette's birthday party.

'Oh, for God's sake,' Sue said tartly, 'nobody in there can hear us. There's too much going on for a start.'

'And it isn't as simple as one sentence, is it? There's the fallout – what comes afterwards.'

'About sixteen years of child maintenance should come afterwards.'

'You know what I mean.'

'Nobody's pretending it's going to be easy but that doesn't change the fact that it needs to be done.' Sue rubbed her hands on the apron she was wearing. 'You should have done it when you first clapped eyes on him on the beach. As far as I can tell you've had plenty of time so you're just stalling.'

'Maybe I am, but it's not that simple.'

'You're too kind, sparing his feelings.'

'It's not only his feelings I'm sparing, though. There's Molly, me… Ella, when it comes to it. It's far bigger now than either of us.'

'All this heartache for ten minutes of lust,' Sue said briskly. 'I hope it was worth it.'

Ashley swallowed the retort that burned her mouth. It had been so much more than ten minutes of lust and now that she'd had time to get to know Haydon better she could see how much it could have been if they hadn't been cursed with such shitty luck.

'If we can get Ella out of the way for an hour I can nip over and see him today.'

'That's another thing – all this creeping around his daughter… his *other* one. She's going to find out anyway.'

Ashley frowned. 'Really, Mum? You really want her to find out like that? That's not like you; you're much kinder than that.'

'I'm sick of it is what I am. All this pussyfooting around. She's had the childhood that Molly should have had.'

'You're saying Molly's childhood wasn't good? Just because she didn't have a dad didn't mean she couldn't still be happy. I did my best—'

'I know; that came out wrong. I just mean, they're both going to find out soon enough so why all this secrecy?'

'Because I want them both to find out in the right way and only when Haydon and I have had time to discuss it.'

Nanette came out of the house with an armful of tablecloths. She stopped and stared at them and Ashley felt the heat rush to her face, as if she'd been caught doing something she wasn't meant to be.

'Is all well?' she asked, and from the expression on her face it was clear that she didn't think all was well. Anyone who took more than a second's notice of Ashley and her mum at this moment could tell that all wasn't well – not a bit of it.

'Fine,' Sue replied with a tight smile. 'We were just discussing some arrangements for the party later. Is there anything we can do to help you?'

'Perhaps some assistance with the decorations?' Nanette replied carefully, glancing from Sue to Ashley and back again as if trying to work out what was going on. Ashley couldn't blame her for that.

'Absolutely. No problem. I'll just be a tick.'

'There is no rush,' Nanette said. 'We have plenty of time. Violette has waited a hundred years for this so I think she will be able to wait a few hours more.'

'Yes,' Sue said, though her smile looked as if a gentle shake might crack it. 'I suppose that's true.'

'Nanette…' Ashley called her back as she made for the garden. 'I don't suppose there's any possibility that Molly could have a guest at the party… the girl who's staying at the villa across the fields? They get on so well I thought it might be nice for her to have another girl her own age around.'

'Molly seems happy in Bastien's company,' Nanette said doubtfully.

'Well, yes, she is. But she does like Ella and I think it might be nice for Ella to have some company her own age too.'

'Will her father come?'

'I don't think so – at least I don't think he'd necessarily expect an invite. And I don't imagine Ella will be much trouble – we'll hardly notice her, I bet.'

'I can ask my aunt if you like.'

'That would be great. I'd ask her myself but…'

'That conversation might take a long time,' Nanette said with a wry smile.

'Exactly,' Ashley replied. She glanced at her mum, who simply clamped her mouth shut and looked away. 'So you'll let me know what your aunt says and if it's OK I'll get a message to Ella's dad?'

'Yes, I can do that.'

Nanette left them and Sue turned to Ashley now.

'Ridiculous,' she said. 'All this fuss. Do you know what would be the simplest thing? I go across that field right now and tell him myself.'

'But you won't do that,' Ashley said with a small smile. 'Because you're too nice, and if the boot was on the other foot you'd be doing exactly what I am now.'

'You think so?'

'I know it.'

'Perhaps, but even you must be able to see that this has gone on for too long. Tell me honestly – do you have feelings for him?'

'Yes.'

'Is that what this is all about?'

'Perhaps a little.'

'You think you'll lose him?'

'I already lost him once.'

'If he's a man who deserves you then he'll deal with the news like an adult and it shouldn't be a problem. If he doesn't then he's not that man and you shouldn't be wasting your time on him.'

'I know all this in my head but my heart is scared.'

'Does he have feelings for you too?'

'I think so. He says he does.'

'So you've been able to discuss all this with the kids around but not the other thing?'

'Mum…'

'I'm just saying.'

'And we're going round in circles. Anyway, we didn't exactly discuss it with the kids around—'

'No, you just demonstrated it.'

'What?'

'Molly told me they caught you kissing.'

Ashley frowned. 'We didn't—'

'That's not what Molly says.'

Ashley let out a sigh. It was a huge thing for Molly, she supposed, especially when you considered that this was the first time a man had been introduced into their lives – at least in a romantic capacity – since her last disastrous, three-timing rat of a boyfriend. She probably felt as uncertain about it all as Ashley herself did and it was only natural she'd want to offload on someone. The grandmother she'd always been close to was the perfect candidate. For Ashley, however, it just complicated her problems in ways she didn't need.

'If you like him as much as it seems then it's more important than ever you come clean with him.'

Ashley nodded. 'Today, as soon as Ella arrives here, I'll go across and see him.'

Cousins, aunts and uncles, brothers and sisters and mums and dads all arrived at Violette Dupont's house throughout the morning and pretty soon Ashley wondered whether the entire population of France was somehow related to her because it felt as if most of them were here. Each new arrival brought gifts carefully wrapped, balloons, streamers, flowers or food. They brought laughter and gossip too, and soon the villa was alive with chatter. Ashley tried to make herself agreeable, though her heart wasn't entirely in it, and she wished she could shake

the feeling of dread that the thought of seeing Haydon later brought
with it. She'd been so looking forward to the party of this incredible
little lady who'd welcomed her and Molly into her home as if they were
her blood relatives and she felt that anything less than a cheery smile
would ruin the day – if only the smile didn't feel as if it needed the
surgical placement of a coat hanger to keep it in position.

Relatives jostled for space in the kitchen as they prepared food,
bickered with a gentle humour about the state of each other's attempts
at house decoration and argued rather more enthusiastically about which
wines they were going to bring up from Violette's cellar. In between
all this Maurice dusted off an old accordion he'd found in an unused
reception room behind Violette's equally unused piano and wandered
around the house like a troubadour, amusing and irritating everyone
in equal measure and finding it all hilarious as he played not-entirely-
in-tune tunes. Sue asked him whether he'd already started drinking and
he answered with a mischievous tap to the side of his nose, which just
about confirmed that she was right. There wasn't a lot she could do
about this but throw her hands up in the air and declare him impossible,
which only made him laugh more.

Towards noon Ashley took a moment to breathe while everyone
agreed that, although there was enough food being prepared for the
evening to feed Saint-Raphaël in its entirety, they needed to prepare
more for lunch in the interim, and realised she hadn't seen Molly for
some time.

'Do you know where Molly is?' she asked Maurice.

He shrugged. 'Perhaps she is with Bastien – I have not seen him
for some time either.'

Ashley frowned. She had enough on her plate without having to
search for her daughter and possibly break up some ill-advised teenage

tryst. Marching out to the veranda, now decked with bunting and lights and tables set with crockery, she scanned the garden for them. Apart from more tables and more chairs almost covering the lawns, there was no sign of life. Then came the sound of giggling from the summer house.

'Bloody hell,' she muttered, making a beeline for the source of the sound. Opening the door she discovered Molly and Bastien engaged in what could only be described as snogging. And this was in the most literal, behind-the-bike-sheds way. It was hard to tell where one face ended and the other began, but they leapt apart as they realised they'd been rumbled.

'There's a time and a place,' Ashley said, looking from one to another. 'And this isn't it.'

Without another word, she turned and left them both looking – to their credit – suitably shamefaced. Of all the days Molly could have chosen to go full-on hormonal, it had to be this one. It wasn't that Ashley had any delusions about her daughter and she was quite sure it wasn't the first time she'd sucked the face off a boy, but it was lucky that another member of the family hadn't caught them and Ashley just wasn't in the mood to deal with it. Oh, how she longed for this day to be over, but that seemed like a long way off right now.

*

Haydon stared at his phone again. The screen was unlocked and his finger poised to type out a message, but then he locked it once more and put it back into his pocket. Nothing from Ashley that morning and after blowing her off last night he wondered whether he'd offended her. Three or four times he'd wanted to text but then decided against it. He hadn't dated someone for a long time but he couldn't recall it being this full of endless uncertainties. And yet, he was so desperate for things to work with Ashley that he was almost paralysed with fear, constantly second-guessing each action until he didn't dare take any action at all.

Ella padded into the kitchen where he sat at the table with a coffee, taking refuge from the mid-morning sun for a while. She dripped at the doorway, a towel pulled around her.

'I thought you were going to swim in the pool with me.'

'I am. Just as soon as I finish this coffee.'

'You said that last time I came in.'

'Maybe that's because last time you came in was only about five minutes ago and I can't drink it that fast.'

'It's boring on my own.'

'You're missing Molly?'

'She's stuck at that party. I wouldn't miss her if you were swimming with me.'

'I'll be out in a minute – promise.'

Ella let out a sigh and turned to leave.

'You've got sun cream on today?' Haydon asked.

She turned back with a withering look. 'I'm not five.'

'No, but yesterday you got burnt,' he replied with more patience than his churning stomach would suggest. 'I'm only trying to look out for you.'

'You can look out for me in the pool outside.'

He paused, and then couldn't help a grin. 'Always ready with a smart answer, aren't you?' Downing the last of his coffee he pulled out his phone and glanced at it to see there were still no messages. He put it away again and was about to tell Ella that she'd won the battle when they were hailed from the garden.

'HELLO! Are you at home, *Monsieur*?'

Haydon exchanged a puzzled look with Ella before going out to the veranda. Ella followed.

'Good morning,' Nanette called from the gate. 'How are you?'

'We're good,' Haydon replied, jogging down the path to meet her. 'What can I do for you?'

'Do you have plans for today?'

'Well, not exactly…'

'*Bon.* Then my aunt Violette would like you to come to her party.'

'Oh… well, that's very kind of you but—'

'Molly and Bastien will be there,' Ella cut in.

Nanette inclined her head. 'Of course.' She smiled. 'It was Ashley's idea that you should come to spend time with Molly. Naturally my aunt would not hear of your father being left out and so she would like him to come too.'

Haydon considered the invite for a moment. Ashley had instigated Ella's invite but she hadn't asked for him to be invited. That could mean one of two things: either she didn't want to see him, or she *did* want to see him but alone, with Ella busy elsewhere. Quickly, though uncertainly, he decided that the latter was the case. She'd said she'd figure something out. Was this it?

'Perhaps you ought to go without me,' he said to Ella. 'It sounds as if the invite was really only for you.'

'No, no,' Nanette said. 'The invite is for you too. My aunt would not hear of you spending the evening alone in your house when we are all having fun.'

'You have to come, Dad, or Aunt Violette will be upset.' She threw him a sly grin. 'And Ashley will be there.'

He smiled back. He'd really rather Ashley wasn't there but somewhere else with him. Nanette raised her eyebrows but she didn't ask for more information about Ella's statement and Haydon wasn't about to volunteer any. So much for Ashley's plan – if there ever had been a plan. If she'd wanted him to stay away from her it didn't look as if he'd be able to, and if she'd wanted him to wait at the villa for her it didn't look as if she was going to get that either. A text would have been helpful so at least he knew what he was working with here.

'Thank you,' he said finally, turning to Nanette. 'It's very kind of your aunt to invite us and we'd love to come.'

'Wonderful,' Nanette said. 'We will begin at seven.'

Haydon nodded and watched as Nanette let herself out of the gate and walked towards the path that skirted the field. As her figure grew smaller, he turned to Ella with a half-smile.

'Right then. You'd better get dressed because we're going to have to go shopping for a birthday gift. Though God only knows what you buy a hundred-year-old woman for her birthday…'

'Honey,' Ella said airily as she poked her feet into the flip-flops she'd left at the side of the pool. 'Molly says she eats loads of it.'

'Honey?'

'Yup.'

'OK…' Haydon said doubtfully. He didn't think for a moment that was an appropriate present but he didn't have any better ideas. 'I suppose we'd better get down to the market then.' And, he almost added, but thought better of it, we'd better hope we don't run into Audrey down there…

＊

Molly didn't speak to her all through lunch. She glowered across the table at Ashley and barely had two words for anyone else either, apart from Bastien, who sat next to her and whispered in her ear every so often. She was sulking, probably mortified at being caught in a situation she knew was wrong, and Ashley recognised the backlash only too well from her own teenage years – she'd have reacted in just the same way if her own mother had caught her in a summer house in full face-sucking mode with a boy when she was supposed to be helping the adults out.

After lunch Violette took a nap so she'd have plenty of energy to last the evening and the house was quieter in respect of this as the preparation for the party continued.

'You will come to Paris perhaps?' One of Bastien's aunts smoothed a hand over Molly's hair and smiled as they polished wine glasses together. 'We would be happy to see you and we have an empty bedroom. You would love it very much, I think.'

Ashley looked across to see Molly give her a dazzling smile. Typically, Molly was being a perfect angel in the company of a woman who was not related to her but she supposed she had to be thankful for that much. Her daughter had always known instinctively who she needed to work hard to charm and who she could let rip with, and it was a skill that would probably get her far in life.

'I'd love to,' Molly said. 'I've never been to Paris.'

'Never?' Bastien's aunt pretended to swoon with shock. Ashley searched for her name – there were so many to remember. Fleur? It sounded right, though she couldn't be sure. 'Then you have not lived!' she continued.

'I'd love to see a concert at the Philharmonie de Paris,' Molly said, her eyes lighting up as the idea occurred to her.

'You would? But you are so young!'

Molly laughed. 'Not all teenagers like rap, you know.'

'Of course – I remember now that you play the violin.'

'Yes. I'd like to play in a world-famous orchestra one day but for now I have to be happy to watch them. Not that I get much opportunity.'

'Why not?'

'The tickets cost a lot for the big ones and that's when they come to our town, which is not as often as I'd like. Plus all of my friends hate classical music and Mum's always working so it's hard to find someone to take me.'

'Not even Maurice?'

Molly shrugged. 'I don't like to keep asking him.'

'You are sixteen now?'

'Yes.'

'Then you could go alone.'

'I suppose so.'

'But it is no fun?'

'Not so much. I suppose I'll have to get used to it.'

'Does your father like it?'

Ashley froze, waiting for Molly's reply. It wasn't as if Molly had never been asked the question before and she wasn't quite sure why it put her on edge so much this time when she knew Molly would answer it in the same, matter-of-fact way she always did.

'I think Ella listens to classical music,' Ashley called over from where she was cutting flowers for a vase, unable to bear the suspense any longer. 'She's learning pieces for her piano grades but she likes to listen to them regardless of that.'

'Yes, but she's going to live in London and we're in York,' Molly said.

'I'm sure we could go and visit them and see a concert at the same time; there'd be plenty on in London.'

Molly's eyes widened. 'Seriously?'

'Probably. We'd have to check the finances and my work rota first, of course.'

For the first time since their awkward moment in the summer house, Molly broke into a smile that was just for her mother.

Fleur (possibly her name) moved down the table to start on a new batch of glasses and Molly sidled up to Ashley.

'I'm sorry, Mum.'

'Me too,' Ashley said, kissing her lightly. 'I probably overreacted.'

'You didn't. I was supposed to be helping out and I messed up.'

'You've never messed up in your life.' Ashley smiled and folded her arms around her. 'Let's call it a blip and move on.'

'Yeah, OK.'

Ashley went back to her flowers as Molly picked one up and held it to her nose.

'You like Bastien then,' she said.

'I do, Mum. I really like him.'

'It'll be difficult to maintain when you're back home.'

'I know. We're not going out – just messing around. We both know there's no point in going out properly.'

Ashley nodded. 'Probably wise. You won't be too upset to leave him behind tomorrow then?'

'A bit, but that's life, isn't it?'

'I suppose so.'

'What about Haydon? Is it serious with you?'

'I don't think so.'

'But you could see him again, couldn't you?'

'What do you think? Could you cope with him in our lives?'

'I like him; he's OK.'

'Only OK?'

'Well, I hardly know him, do I?'

'I don't suppose so.'

'Does he seem like a good dad to you?'

Molly popped the rose in amongst the flowers Ashley was arranging in the vase. 'He seems OK. It's hard to know because I don't have anything to measure him against. I wouldn't know a good dad if one slapped me.'

Ashley smiled. 'I don't think that would make him particularly good for a start.'

'No,' Molly said. 'But Ella's happy so that's got to be quite a good sign.'

'Do you think he's a good man then?'

Molly narrowed her eyes. 'What's with these questions? You're not going to marry him, are you?'

'God no!' Ashley laughed, a bit too heartily. 'No. I'm just wondering…'

'It's really nothing to do with me as long as you like him,' Molly sniffed.

'Maybe that's the case with other people but not me. I would never be with someone you didn't like.'

'That's just daft. What if you were totally in love and I wasn't keen? You'd give him up?'

'Yes.'

'I'd hate that. I'd feel guilty for the rest of my life.'

'And I'd feel guilty being with someone you didn't approve of.'

'OK, so I approve of Haydon. So now you can date him with my pointless blessing.'

'Thanks.' Ashley smiled. 'You're not just saying that?'

'Mum!'

'OK, OK! Just kidding.'

From the corner of her eye Ashley noticed Nanette come into the kitchen with the old accordion Maurice had been tormenting everyone with stashed under her arm.

'I will push this down my brother's throat if he does not stop playing it!' she growled and Molly giggled.

'It'd be better if he could actually play it.'

'It would still sound like an awful noise,' Nanette grumbled.

'Moll,' Ashley cut in, 'would you just go and check where your grandma wants these flowers?'

Molly nodded and skipped off.

'Nanette…' Ashley continued, turning to Maurice's sister. 'Did you manage to talk to your aunt Violette?'

'Yes. She was happy and I have arranged the invitation.'

'But I thought you were going to let me know so I could arrange it?'

'It was easy for me to walk to the house. You were busy and I have saved you the bother.'

Ashley gnawed on her lip for a moment. It wasn't what they'd agreed but she didn't want to offend Nanette by saying so. It meant that she'd somehow have to make sure Haydon understood that he was supposed to wait at his villa for her to come over.

'Thank you,' she said.

'Of course.'

Before they'd had time to get any further Maurice came in looking sheepish. He held his arms out for the accordion and Nanette scowled.

'Do you want to make us all crazy in the head?'

'I want to fill the house with joy.'

'Then stop playing this and we will all be joyful!'

As Maurice and Nanette's quips continued to ricochet off each other, Ashley took the opportunity of their distraction to type out a message to Haydon.

Can we talk later?

Sure, I'd like that. As long as you can find the time.

I need to find the time. So you'll be around?

Of course.

OK. See you later.

So that was simple enough. As soon as everyone got settled here and the party was in full swing she'd slip out and head across the field. A nice, uncomplicated plan that couldn't possibly go wrong.

Chapter Sixteen

It was just after seven. The family was gathered in the garden, where tables dressed in crisp white cloths, sparkling silverware and vases of flowers arranged by Ashley were lined up. Lanterns were dotted around the grounds hanging from any available hook or nail, though they wouldn't be lit until much later on. Even so, they looked pretty enough now with the sun glinting off their delicate glass surfaces. There was bunting and flags and photos of Violette at various stages of her life looking beautiful and elegant in gowns from days gone by, and ribbons of flowers looped around the pillars of the veranda. Maurice was now tending to a huge flank of pork on a spit, though Ashley had to wonder at the wisdom of this as he'd already been drinking for a good part of the afternoon. Nobody else seemed concerned, though. And in the air, chased by the early evening moths and gnats and the swallows racing to and fro from the eaves, the notes of live music drifted across the meadow from their villa, a call to celebration to anyone who happened to pass and hear it. Maurice and his cousin had constructed a little hardwood platform that acted as a stage-cum-dance floor and was already scuffed by the heels of enthusiastic shoes as they jigged to the sounds of someone from the town who could actually play the accordion. The band also included a violinist and a cellist – a fact that got Molly very excited.

'Do you think they'll let me have a go?' she whispered to Ashley. 'I've missed my violin so much!'

'You've only been parted from it for a week,' Ashley said. 'It's ridiculous. I bet you wouldn't even be this lovelorn if you'd been parted from a boyfriend.'

'I wouldn't.' Molly grinned. 'My violin never does anything stupid to annoy me, but plenty of boys do.'

'Nutter.'

The song ended and everyone put their hands together in an enthusiastic display of approval. Violette nodded graciously and cast her eyes over the huge crowd of guests – many of them descended from her directly – with a sort of pride that Ashley couldn't even begin to imagine. To be responsible for so many of these incredible people was something to be proud of, though, and she could hardly argue with that. In a voice that was as strong of character as it was physically frail, she gave a short speech, which Ashley did her best to follow. From the small amount she could understand, Violette was thanking everyone and expressing huge surprise to be addressing them at the ripe old age of a hundred when she never expected to make it this far (at which everyone laughed and reassured her that they never doubted she'd make it this far and beyond). She then bade them eat and drink and enjoy the party. The little band struck up again and Molly gazed longingly at the violinist, prompting Ashley to nudge her.

'Seriously, you're at a party – on holiday! Snap out of it! Go and mess around in the shed with Bastien or something – do what normal teenagers do.'

Molly grinned. 'You'd hate me if I was a normal teenager.'

'Quite possibly,' Ashley replied with a chuckle. 'Now go and steal some booze or something and shock me for once.'

'Oh, I intend to do that. Though it's not exactly rebelling if everyone is pushing glasses of wine on me every five minutes.'

'That's true.' Ashley laughed. 'They do seem determined to get absolutely everyone steaming drunk by nine, including Violette's cat.'

'It's the French *joie de vivre*.'

'It's drinking wine like it's pop, that's what it is.'

'You are having a nice time?' Nanette asked, making her way across the lawn to them.

'It's different, that's for sure,' Molly said. 'I've never been to a party like this before.'

'What sort of parties have you been to?'

'They're not usually in a gorgeous garden for a start. More likely to be in some dingy community centre or a pub.'

'Since when did we go to parties in pubs?' Ashley asked, raising her eyebrows at her daughter.

'Since we went to your cousin's wedding reception.' Molly pretended to shiver. 'Honestly, Mum, every time I think about that pub I feel like I need to go and take a shower.'

'Fair point!' Ashley laughed. 'It was a bit of a dive, I suppose.' She turned to Nanette. 'The garden looks beautiful, doesn't it? Team Violette did a great job here.'

'We are very grateful for the help.'

'I suppose it's the least we could do considering we get to share all this wonderful food.'

Nanette gave a gentle laugh. Every sound Nanette made seemed to be gentle, from her voice to the way she sneezed. But then her gaze travelled to the garden gates and her face lit up in a bright smile.

'Ah!' she exclaimed. 'Here is your friend!'

Ashley turned, expecting to see Ella as arranged. But her stomach dropped as she saw that Haydon was with her. It dropped, and then when she saw how handsome he looked in black trousers and a black shirt that complimented the tan he'd developed perfectly, sleeves rolled back to his elbows, it soared. It dropped and soared and couldn't seem to make its mind up what it was doing. But while her heart was procrastinating, her loins approved of the sight, and her head was trying to shout over it all, telling her that this might just signal the ruin of her plans yet again. Why hadn't he stayed at the villa as she'd told him? And then it all became clear. Nanette had invited him to the party too. What else was the poor guy supposed to do if he'd been asked to come with Ella and Ashley now realised she probably hadn't made any plans to the contrary all that clear in her brief texts.

'Hi,' he said as he approached, and he almost sounded shy. He gave Nanette and Molly both a warm smile and then racked it up to sizzling as he turned to Ashley. 'Sorry we're a little late but...'

'Fashionably late,' Nanette said with a chuckle. 'Nobody wants to be the first person at the party – no?'

'Not that. We... um... well I couldn't lay my hands on the keys to our place. Turns out they'd somehow fallen into one of my shoes.' He gave an adorable shrug that made Ashley's heart begin its argument with her brain anew.

'You look lovely,' Nanette said, turning to Ella who seemed to have forgotten how her mouth worked. Perhaps the sight of so many strangers was a bit overwhelming and Ashley couldn't blame her for that.

'You do,' Molly agreed. 'I love that dress... Topshop, I bet.'

At this Ella finally broke into a smile of her own. 'How did you know?'

'You can always tell... at least I can. One of my less valuable talents.'

'You look amazing too,' Ella said, eyeing Molly's floral maxi dress.

'Oh, this?' Molly said, flapping the skirt about. 'I never get a chance to wear it so I thought why not. Probably be freezing when we get back home and it will sit in the wardrobe until next time it's hot. Which will probably be never.' She nodded across the garden to where Bastien had apparently spotted Ella's arrival and was beckoning them both over. 'Come on,' she said. 'Looks like we're wanted.'

As Molly led her away, Ashley turned to Haydon and Nanette. There was an awkward silence, until Nanette smiled briskly and made her excuses to leave. Perhaps she felt the awkwardness between them, or perhaps she sensed something altogether different. Either way, it seemed she'd decided they needed to be alone together.

'I didn't know you were coming,' Ashley said as Nanette walked off.

'But I was invited. I thought… Oh…'

'Not that I mind, of course.'

'You didn't want me here?'

'It's not that, it's just… well, I wasn't expecting you.'

'But they invited Ella and I thought…'

'Of course you did.'

Haydon's gaze went to the floor, his voice now dull. 'I should go then. I mean, if it's going to make you uncomfortable having me here then…'

'Don't be daft.' Ashley forced a smile. 'I didn't mean that at all. I was just surprised. To tell the truth' – she took a deep breath – 'I was hoping Ella would come without you so I could get a moment alone with you at your place.'

'Oh.' His face lit up again and immediately Ashley regretted her choice of words.

'Sorry, but I needed you alone to talk. I mean, it's not that I wouldn't have loved the other thing too, but…'

'So… what did you want to talk about?' he asked. 'Is it about us? Because I know this is all pretty fast but—'

'About us, but not in the way you think.'

'Then you don't regret what's happened this week? You don't regret our time together?'

'Of course not.'

'And you want to carry on, right? When we get back to England can I see you again?'

'Absolutely. We'll make arrangements. I think the girls would like that too.'

'They do seem to get on really well,' Haydon said, glancing across at the trio of teenagers, heads close as they laughed at something on Molly's phone. 'We couldn't have asked for that to work out better really. Especially if—' He paused, and Ashley read the uncertainty on his face. 'Especially if we get more serious.'

Ashley knew she was supposed to reassure him at this stage, to tell him that was what she wanted too and that he was right to hope for more. But how could she when she had this huge secret that could bust them apart, still unspoken?

'Ella's sweet,' Ashley said. 'I don't see how anyone could dislike her so it's no wonder she's getting on with Moll. You've done a good job with her.'

'Molly too,' Haydon said. 'I didn't like to ask but… you've brought her up alone? Always? What about her dad?'

'He…' She glanced around at the other guests, laughing, joking, drinking, dancing… Was this the moment? Could she make this work? Perhaps nobody would notice if they slipped away somewhere quiet for a while to talk things over. 'He doesn't know about her…'

'Oh…' He paused, looking confused and uncertain, and Ashley steeled herself. Was he about to work it out? 'I know it sounds crazy but I can't help but wonder if I'm—'

'Haydon!' Maurice roared from across the garden. Abandoning his pig-spit station he began to stride across the grass towards them and

Ashley held in a groan. She turned her eyes heavenwards and uttered a silent curse. It was like somebody up there was determined the truth was never coming out.

'It is good to see you!' Maurice said, clapping Haydon on the back.

'Thanks for inviting me,' Haydon replied, shooting Ashley a look that was almost apologetic.

'You are most welcome,' Maurice said. 'Where is your drink?' he added with a disapproving click of his tongue. 'You have no drink at a Dupont party! That will never do!'

Grabbing Haydon clumsily by the hand, Maurice dragged him away to the kitchen, presumably to equip him with the necessary alcohol befitting a guest at a Dupont party. Ashley let out a sigh. At this rate she'd have to resort to a singing telegram to send Haydon her news because she was fast running out of other options.

Ashley didn't see Haydon for a good hour after his arrival. Later, she discovered that Maurice – who seemed to have taken a huge liking to him – was showing him Violette's wine cellar. Ashley had no idea how much Haydon knew about wine, but, as it was one of Maurice's favourite subjects, it was actually surprising that he'd only been missing for that long. Once, she'd been given a lecture by Maurice on the difference between European and New World wines that had lasted almost an entire evening. Not that she remembered a bit of it, because as she'd nodded politely her thoughts had been mostly concerned with Molly's sandwiches and whether she'd ironed her school uniform for the following day.

But then Haydon turned up again and, to her consternation, he looked as if he was already on his way to a state of advanced tipsiness. Not only had Maurice been showing him the wine cellar, it seemed he'd been persuading him to sample a good deal of it too. As Ashley looked across at the tiny wooden stage, Haydon was being nudged towards it, laughing, by Molly. Then, after a brief exchange with the band members, Haydon took the cello from its owner and Molly borrowed the violin and they began to play.

They'd obviously agreed on a piece they both knew well at some point beforehand because they were perfectly in synch, the mellow tones of the cello adding warmth to the sweet, soaring strings of Molly's violin. Ashley vaguely recognised it as a classical piece Molly had spent a lot of time learning, though she'd have struggled to name it. Despite the circumstances, Ashley was filled with pride to see her talented daughter play so beautifully, but it was a bittersweet thing. There she was, playing with her father in a way that suggested they were connected on a level that was almost telepathic, and yet neither of them had a clue just how connected they really were. The irony of the fact they'd both been attracted to string instruments was not lost on Ashley. They even wore the same expression of concentration as they played.

She glanced away, hastily wiping a tear from the corner of her eye, to see her own mother looking pointedly at her. It wasn't hard to guess what Sue was thinking. Ashley looked quickly away, back to where Haydon and Molly played together, and she wondered if the fact that they looked like father and daughter was registering with anyone else at the party. Then her gaze wandered down the line and fell on Ella. Haydon's other daughter played piano, didn't she? Ashley had never heard her play, of course, but she was sure it had been mentioned at some point. Perhaps she was feeling left out that there wasn't a piano at hand for her to play along (apart from the old dusty one in the house that was far too big to transport out to the garden). Whatever it was, Haydon's younger daughter looked strangely forlorn and lost as she watched the performance. Ashley moved along the line of people gathered to listen and sidled up to her.

'Perhaps we can get you on the piano inside later,' she whispered. 'So you can show us what you can do. Your dad says you're really good.'

Ella shrugged, never moving her eyes from Haydon and Molly. It was uncanny, the way she looked at them, and for a startling moment Ashley wondered whether she'd somehow figured out the truth where all the adults around her had failed. But that was ridiculous – surely there was no way she could have done.

'You want a drink?' Ashley asked.

'No thanks.'

'You're OK? There's nothing you want to talk about? Only…'

'I'm fine. Thank you.'

Before Ashley managed to get another question out, Ella moved away to stand next to Bastien. She appeared to brighten a little as he whispered something in her ear, but she still looked far from the happy-go-lucky girl she had always appeared to be – at least from what Ashley had seen of her this week.

'What's the matter with her?' Sue asked, moving into the space next to Ashley that Ella had just had vacated.

'Don't know.'

'She looks like someone just took her winning lottery ticket away.'

'She does a bit. Poor thing.'

Sue turned her gaze onto Haydon and Molly. 'I presume this friendly little performance means you still haven't told him or Molly.'

'When would I have had a chance? I didn't expect him to be turning up here today.'

Sue clicked her tongue against the roof of her mouth but said nothing.

'I *am* trying, Mum.'

'Yes, you're that.'

'It's not easy. It's alright for you to judge because you haven't got to do it.'

'I did offer.'

'Don't be ridiculous. I couldn't think of a worse way to break the news to Haydon, or to Molly for that matter. They need to hear it from me – both of them.'

Sue was silent for a moment, her attention back on the performance. 'It's funny,' she said finally.

'What is?'

'How they play together – how similar they are. Funny how they both ended up with the same interests.'

'I was just thinking the same thing.'

'You never said her dad was musical.'

'I didn't know. We didn't exactly discuss it the first night we met.'

Sue threw her a sideways look. 'I don't think you discussed very much at all the night you first met.'

At this Ashley couldn't help a small smile. 'I don't suppose we did. Certainly not accurate phone numbers for a start.' She let out a sigh. 'All those years we missed for the sake of some dodgy digits.'

'If he was telling the truth about that.'

Ashley turned to see Sue regarding her in a measured gaze. She shook her head.

'He wouldn't. I might have thought so too, once upon a time, but now I know him better… No, I don't believe he'd have done that.'

'Age mellows us all. Perhaps he feels guilty about it now. Perhaps he does want a relationship and you look pretty good now he's on the scrapheap, so he'd tell you whatever you wanted to hear.'

'No.' Ashley shook her head more forcefully this time. 'You're wrong. Neither of us are on the scrapheap either. It's not our fault we're both single.'

'It's absolutely your fault that *you* are. It's not like there's been a shortage of interest from men over the years.'

'I was too busy with Molly – you know that. And then when I tried to have a relationship look what happened.'

'Perhaps you ought to be more picky,' Sue replied.

'Is that a dig at my current interest?'

'Make of it whatever you will.'

Ashley folded her arms tight across her chest and stared at the stage.

'Sulking isn't going to change anything.'

'I'm not sulking and I'm not trying to change anything.'

'Yes you are, and yes you wish you could.'

Ashley turned to her. 'Isn't there a bottle of wine somewhere waiting for you?'

'I'm only trying to help,' Sue sniffed.

'I know, but you're not. I'll deal with this in my own time. Molly has managed this long without a dad so a few more hours isn't going to make any difference now.'

Sue shrugged. 'You get on with it then. You're right – you don't need my input at all considering what an amazing job you've done of sorting things out so far.'

'Mum!' Ashley hissed, but Sue just held her hands up in a gesture of surrender.

'I'll go and see if Maurice needs any help roasting that pig. In fact, I'll chat to the pig because I'll get more sense out of it than you.'

Ashley scowled as Sue left her and crossed the garden to the spit where Maurice was nodding along to the music as he brushed more oil on the huge slab of pork. Her mother was right about it all, of course, but just being right hardly helped matters. Ashley didn't need any assistance recognising what was right and wrong here, she just needed the moment and the courage to address it.

The guests began to clap and cheer and she realised that Haydon and Molly's impromptu performance had come to an end. There were calls for an encore but Haydon simply nodded and gestured to the musicians who were supposed to be playing.

'Far be it for me to deprive a fellow cellist of his instrument,' he said with a laugh. He was flushed and clearly thrilled to have such an appreciative audience. And then he exchanged such a tender, exhilarated look with Molly that Ashley could barely keep herself from bursting into tears. For a moment she could almost imagine what it would have been like had they always lived together as father and daughter and she wanted to weep for all the times like this that they'd already missed.

'What did you think?' Molly asked as they came across to her. 'We weren't bad, were we?'

'Very nice,' Ashley said. 'I've always loved to hear you play.'

'You were incredible,' Haydon said, beaming at Molly. 'No wonder the conservatoires are queuing up to get you in.'

Molly laughed. 'Not exactly.'

'You've got real talent,' Haydon insisted. 'In fact, I'd go so far as to say that you're the most talented musician of your age I've ever come across.'

Molly blushed, a broad grin splitting her face. 'You think?'

'Absolutely. And with your mum's permission I'd love to try to help you get a music-school place somewhere. There's a real shortage of young people wanting to follow the classical route and anyone who

shows an interest needs to be encouraged and their talent nurtured.'
He turned to Ashley. 'Don't you agree?'

'Of course,' Ashley said. 'It's just that…'

Before Ashley had time to finish, Haydon turned to Ella as she
tugged at his arm. 'Hey you, how are you enjoying the party?'

'Yeah, it's good,' Ella said, though Ashley could see the look again
that told her Ella wasn't being entirely truthful with her answer.

'Did you see Molly play?' he asked. 'Wasn't she amazing?'

'Yeah,' Ella said, shooting a dull glance at Molly. 'You were both
really good.'

'You want to come and get some food with me?'

'Um, sure, OK.'

Haydon turned to Ashley. He made a slight move towards her,
and then seemed to realise his mistake as he pulled away again with a
suddenly awkward smile.

'Can we get you anything from the food tables? Or a drink, maybe?'

'I'm fine. You two go ahead and we'll catch up with you later.'

'OK.'

As Ashley watched him walk away with Ella, Molly spoke.

'You know when you asked me before about whether I approve? I've
decided I do. He's really cool, Mum. If you have to have a boyfriend
then I'm glad it's him.'

Ashley gave her a tight smile. When Molly finally learned the truth,
would she still feel the same way?

*

It wasn't hard to overfill a plate with all the amazing food on offer.
Ella had been a little more reserved as she chose from the buffet tables
but Haydon hadn't been able to resist trying a bit of everything and

now he probably had too much – though he was doing his best to get through it.

'Isn't this the most amazing stuff you've ever eaten?' he asked Ella, who was sitting next to him in a shady corner of the garden. He could see Ashley and her mother deep in conversation across the lawns. From time to time one or the other threw a guarded glance in his direction and he couldn't help the feeling that he was the topic of their animated discussion, though he tried not to dwell on that possibility or what it might mean if they were. He'd got the distinct feeling throughout the evening that Ashley's mum didn't like him. He could only guess that Ashley had told her some of their past and he supposed that it might look bad to a parent. If he'd felt a boy had abandoned Ella in that way he'd probably be furious about it no matter whether it had been done deliberately or not. Still, the idea that he had to win over Ashley's entire family at the same time as getting Ashley herself to trust him again wasn't one that filled him with positivity. At least Maurice's family seemed to like him and he quickly decided to make the most of their gracious invite.

Getting no answer from his daughter, he looked to see she was staring in the direction of Molly, who was sitting close to Bastien as they dangled their feet in the swimming pool. She hadn't touched any of the food on her plate.

'Everyone likes Molly better than me – even you.'

Haydon paused, a forkful of sauce-smothered pork halfway to his lips. He stared at Ella.

'What?'

'She's so good at everything. And she's pretty. Everyone likes her better than me.'

'No they don't.'

'You got so excited playing your cello with her. And you're always saying how you wished I'd play a string instrument.'

'Only because I'd know more about it. Ella… what's all this about? You've never cared about that before and honestly I love that you made your own choice instead of following me.'

Ella didn't reply. Instead her eyes began to water. Haydon dropped the fork onto his plate and hastily put it to one side so he could gather her into his arms.

'You're my daughter – you will always be the most important person in the world to me.'

'What if Molly was your daughter? She'd be your favourite, I bet.'

'Ella… what's happened? I thought you liked Molly? Is this about me and Ashley dating? Are you scared of what it might mean for us as a family? Because if it is—'

'No.' Ella gave her head a forceful shake. 'I do like her.'

'Then what?'

'Bastien likes Molly. They're going out – they told me today.'

'But what…' Haydon frowned. Then the gears slid into place and suddenly everything was clear. 'Oh, Ella…' He pulled her closer. 'You like him?'

'I thought he liked me too. I should have guessed it would be Molly – she's older and prettier and says smarter things. She even knows a little French and sometimes they speak in French so I can't tell what they're saying.'

'Well, that's rude. I ought to have a word with them about that.'

'*No*, Dad! That would make it even worse!'

'But if it's bothering you this much—'

'Please… no. I'm begging you – don't. I wish I'd never told you now.'

'I'm glad you did and if it's going to upset you more then I won't say anything, even though I think I ought to. If someone is doing something that upsets you it's far easier for them to stop if they know. They probably haven't even realised they're doing anything wrong and how are they going to if we don't tell them?'

'You can't tell them! They already think I'm an annoying hanger-on without thinking I'm a snitch too!'

'Annoying hanger-on? What the hell?'

'Because I'm younger.'

'And have they said this to you?'

'Of course not. But I know they think it. I don't even know why I thought Bastien might like me because he's sixteen and I'm not even fourteen yet.'

'I know. Age gaps can seem massive right now but I promise you in a few years it won't matter a bit if he's ten years older than you.'

'He would have fancied Molly anyway.'

'How do you know?'

'Just do.'

Haydon gazed down at her and wiped a tear away. 'This is not my Ella. What's happened to that smiley face and optimism that I love so much?'

'Sorry, Dad.'

'I'm not saying it so you can be sorry! I'm saying it because it makes me sad to see you sad, that's all. You don't need to apologise for the way you feel.'

'But you won't talk to Molly and Bastien about it?'

'Not if you don't want me to.'

Ella nodded. 'OK.'

As if summoned by the mention of their names, Molly appeared, flanked by Bastien. Ella looked up as their shadows fell across her, alarm etched in her features, but if Molly had overheard any of their conversation then she didn't show any signs of being concerned by it. She smiled broadly at them both.

'Did you see us play?' she asked Ella. 'I had no idea your dad was so good!'

Haydon gave her a tight smile. While he wanted to gush about Molly's talent, he sensed that it might be a little insensitive in light of his recent discussion with Ella. She had to learn not to be oversensitive, of course, and that in life there was always going to be someone better-looking, more talented, more successful, and that you had to strive for your own perfection and disregard the negative thoughts that might distract you from your own success, but perhaps now wasn't the time for that lesson.

'You were brilliant together,' Ella said, and Haydon was instantly proud of the grace she showed, shrugging off the doubts of a few moments earlier. 'It made me wish I'd taken up the violin instead of the piano.'

'There's a piano inside!' Molly said. 'Show me how to play?'

'I wouldn't be as good as you are on your violin.'

'You're younger – I bet you will be when you're sixteen. Please, show me. I've never had a go before.'

Haydon raised his eyebrows. 'Never plonked about on an old keyboard in the school music room? I thought everyone had done that at one time or another.'

'Only music nerds like you,' Ella said. And Haydon was glad to see that she seemed brighter now.

'OK, I hold my hands up. There was a time when I'd plonk about on any instrument I could get my hands on until I settled on the cello. Now I teach it I hardly have time to look at other instruments, let alone play them.'

'Maybe I'll take up the cello too,' Molly said, beaming at Haydon. 'You could teach me.'

'I'd have a long way to come for your lessons.'

'Maybe when…' She looked coy for a moment and Haydon had to laugh.

'Let's not get ahead of ourselves,' he said. 'Though I'd be honoured to teach someone who is as much of a natural as you. I bet it would be a doddle.'

Molly dipped her head and blushed again, but she was clearly flattered by Haydon's words.

'Come,' Bastien said, grabbing Ella by the hand. 'Let us find the piano and you can teach us how to play.'

Haydon watched, feeling helpless as Ella followed him and Molly inside. He could only imagine how difficult it was for her and he could remember vividly how difficult unrequited love was when he was that age. Thank goodness those days were over, although sometimes when he reflected on his current love life he wondered if they were actually easier after all.

He was reminded forcibly of this when he looked for Ashley and found her making her way across the lawns to him. But she didn't look happy or relaxed, and she didn't look as if she wanted to slow dance to the lazy tunes now being played by the little band from the village.

'I need to talk to you,' she said.

'Actually, I need to talk to you too,' he replied.

Ashley paused, her mouth open, but the words that were meant to follow her first greeting now seemed forgotten. Perhaps his tone had seemed a little brusque but he needed to get this off his chest.

'I wouldn't mention it like this normally,' he continued. 'It's just that Ella is really upset and I thought you might be able to have a quiet word with Molly about it.'

'What's it got to do with Molly?'

'Everything really. It's this business with Bastien. You see, Ella likes him…'

'And?'

'It can't have escaped your attention that Molly does too. I think there's something going on there actually—'

'If there is that's none of your business. Just what are you trying to say?'

Haydon's eyes widened. 'I'm not trying to tell you how to raise your daughter,' he said. 'I only wanted to request that she perhaps respect the feelings of mine. Ella's younger and more impressionable and she's very sensitive – easily upset. She thinks that… well, she'd hoped that Bastien would like her the way she likes him, and clearly that's not the case. All I ask is that Molly and Bastien don't rub her nose in it like they're doing right now.'

'What!'

'I don't think it's an unreasonable thing to ask. They do seem to be flaunting it a bit and it's making Ella miserable. Probably teenagers showing off – you know how they do with younger kids – but perhaps you could talk to them? This holiday is so important for me and Ella and—'

'Why don't you talk to them if it's affecting your precious flower so much?'

'Ashley, why are you being so awkward? I don't understand—'

'Don't understand? Do you have any idea how patronising this sounds?'

'I only wanted you to have a word where I can't. I'm not trying to patronise anyone.'

'*You* do it.'

'She's your daughter.'

To his amazement, Ashley started to laugh.

'Oh, the sodding irony,' she said.

'Ashley?'

'Forget it,' she said. 'I'll talk to Molly later but don't bother talking to me again tonight. It's obvious that you and me moving forward was nothing but a silly dream. It was nice for a while, but it's never going to work.'

'What are you saying? That we can't be together because of the kids? That's crazy! It'll take work but other families do it.'

'Not these ones. Sorry.'

Ashley turned to walk away but he grabbed for her arm and spun her back to face him. 'Please... don't end things like this.'

'You're making a scene,' she said, lowering her voice and glancing around the garden. 'And I see now you've had too much to drink to talk any sense.'

'I'm not drunk. You seem to be the drunk one to me. You're really going to throw what we have away because of something I said about Molly? Which wasn't even bad anyway?'

'We don't *have* anything. We tried to pick up where we left off in Ibiza and it was nice until reality bit. There's no picking up from there, not ever, and we were both just fooling ourselves.'

'Why not?'

'You really want to know?'

'Yes.'

Ashley stared at him. It was intense, like she was trying to see his soul. But then she just shook her head.

'What's the point? Why not let sleeping dogs lie?'

'What the hell are you talking about? Ashley… there's something about Molly—'

'Go and find Ella,' Ashley cut across him, turning to walk away again. 'Go and make sure your daughter is OK.'

'Ashley! What have I done?'

By now some of the party guests had noticed that all was not well with two of their number and Haydon was suddenly aware of curious eyes upon him. But if keeping the peace meant losing Ashley then he didn't care too much for shutting up. Ditching his plate of food, he strode after her.

'You don't get to call this without an explanation,' he said. 'Don't I at least deserve that?'

She spun to face him. 'Maybe. But it's too complicated and I've just realised that maybe it's just too hard to deal with.'

'What is? Whatever it is I can help you!'

She shook her head, her eyes awash with a sadness so vast and deep he almost felt it would swallow him too.

'Please… just let me try,' he said, his voice low and urgent. 'I won't lose you – not now.'

'You say that but when you find out the woman I really am you might not be so keen.'

'Nothing you can tell me will change the way I feel.'

'You're certain? You know your mind so well that you're sure nothing could change it?'

'At least try me.'

'That's not the answer I wanted. That means maybe you doubt yourself after all. You're wondering whether there is something that would put you off, and you're scared your feelings are not as strong as you thought they were.'

'This is crazy.' He lunged forward and pulled her into him, planting a kiss on her lips that she didn't refuse but didn't return.

'I'm sorry,' she whispered.

'You have nothing to be sorry for.'

'Haydon…' She paused. 'We really need to talk.'

His reply was cut short by the arrival of Maurice and Sue.

'Is everything alright?' Maurice asked. 'We did not want to listen but…'

'You weren't exactly being discreet,' Sue added, glaring at Haydon.

He stood for a moment, while a woman he barely knew seemed to scrutinise every little detail of his being. Was Ashley's sudden change of heart something to do with her mother? Did Sue really have that much of an influence?

'We're trying to sort things out; that's all,' Ashley said.

'So you've told him?' Sue replied.

'Told me?' Haydon looked at Ashley and then back at her mother again. 'Look… Mrs—'

'Dupont,' Sue cut in. 'At least get my name right if you can't get anything else right.'

'Mrs Dupont,' he replied, doing his best to rise above the jibe. 'I know that you probably don't think much of me and I can understand why, but what happened in Ibiza… it was a mistake. Nothing more and nothing less. A mistake that anyone could have made.'

'What!' Sue cried. 'A mistake? Is that what you call it? I call it bloody irresponsible! I call it cowardly and low! Leaving a poor girl high and dry – what sort of a man does that?'

'I'm not that sort of a man!' Haydon said. 'I really liked Ashley. I never would have left the wrong phone number on purpose!'

'Phone number!' Sue stared at Ashley, who gave her head a tiny shake.

'What else are we talking about?' Haydon asked, looking between the two women.

'Hell's bells!' Sue cried, swinging her arms so wide that an arc of wine sloshed from the glass she was holding. 'Molly's an intelligent girl but she clearly doesn't get it from her father!'

Haydon looked from her to Ashley, confusion written all over his features.

'And yet he still doesn't have a clue,' Sue continued. 'What does it take to get the penny to drop?'

'Mum!' Ashley warned, firing Sue a look that begged for her to stop before things went too far.

'Come on, Einstein!' Sue rolled her eyes at Haydon.

'Mum,' Ashley repeated. 'Please, this is not the time—'

'It's the time, alright!'

'But I…' Haydon turned to Ashley now, his eyes wide. And then he seemed to stop breathing and he uttered a single word. 'Molly…'

'Finally,' Sue said, turning to stagger away. She beckoned Maurice to follow, with a look that said her work was done. 'Finally he gets it.'

Ashley shook her head slowly, tears burning her eyes. 'I'm so sorry you had to find out like this.'

He knew the truth now for sure, but it didn't seem possible that the conclusion he'd slowly been coming to could be the right one. And even as he said it he couldn't quite believe it.

'Molly's my daughter?'

Chapter Seventeen

To humiliate Haydon like this in front of everyone wasn't what Ashley had wanted at all. It wasn't fair and nobody deserved that, not even the man her mother considered public enemy number one. Later, when the dust had settled, Ashley would have a stern word with Sue but for now she had more pressing things to deal with.

Staggering back, Haydon fell into a seat. 'Why didn't you say anything?'

'Believe me, I've been trying to.'

He buried his face in his hands and doubled over in the chair. 'Shit.'

'Pretty much what I said when I saw the pregnancy test. I'm sorry, it wasn't supposed to come out like this.'

He looked up. 'You're sure?'

Ashley's expression hardened. 'Do you think we'd be having this conversation now if I wasn't? You think I don't know who the father is because I slept with so many men in Ibiza that week?'

'No, I… Oh God, Ashley. I feel like the biggest bastard on the planet.' He got up from his seat and staggered across to the trees at the far side of the garden, by now deep in shade. 'I need a minute… I wondered, but I never imagined… need to take this in…'

Ashley followed him across the lawns. As they reached the trees she tugged at his arm and pulled him to face her.

'I'm sorry. I've honestly been trying to tell you all week.'

'And you pick today? Here?'

'My mother picked today. You sort of forced her hand too.'

'She's known all along? All those times we've spoken this week and she knew? What must she have thought of me? Who else knew? Does everyone here know about it? Does Molly know?'

'Just my mum. I told her after I saw you down at the beach that first time. I never told a soul up until that point, not even Molly.'

'Didn't she ever ask about her dad?'

'Sometimes. But we agreed that as I didn't know where you were it would do no good to dwell on it. And we were happy, just me and her together.'

'She'll hate me,' he said, his face sinking into his hands again.

'She might not. She doesn't hate you as a person so it's only fair we give her a chance to get to know you as a dad.'

'You thought I didn't want to be with you. So did Molly think that too?'

'I hadn't really talked to her about it in that much detail.'

'But she thought her dad was an uncaring git.'

'She didn't have an opinion either way. You just weren't there and it's all she's ever known.'

'She'll never forgive me. How can *you* even forgive me?'

Ashley shook her head. 'I already have. Surely what we've said and done this week tells you that much.'

'So this is why you wanted to end it?'

'Just then, when we'd had that conversation about how Molly and Ella weren't getting on, it suddenly seemed hopeless.'

'I never meant that they weren't getting along.'

'I know, but it just showed me what we were up against.'

'Of course,' he replied, looking up and taking a deep breath. 'There's no argument over that at all. You must have been going mad keeping it all in.'

'A little. But I didn't want to blurt it out. Turns out that's exactly how it went.'

'That's my fault as much as yours – I should have figured it out myself. It's not as if the clues weren't there and I wondered so many times, but I just figured you'd have told me…'

'I wish you had worked it out. Life would have been a lot easier for me.'

'I'm an idiot. But now I know I'll do anything you need… Maintenance payments and other stuff… I can check that with the solicitor who acted for me when Janine and I…' He faltered. 'What am I going to tell Ella?'

'We'll tell her together.'

'Oh God, she's going to hate me too.'

'Don't be daft, Haydon. How could you have known? We lost touch so there's no way you could be responsible for any of this.'

'I could have been responsible sixteen years ago.'

'Don't you dare! There's Molly, our beautiful, talented, intelligent daughter, and I wouldn't have her gone from my life, not for a second! Don't you dare wish her away!'

'I didn't mean that… sorry. Forgive me; I don't know what I'm saying.'

'You're in shock and I get that. But I don't want you wishing the past to be different, not ever. Even if I'd known back then what would happen, I wouldn't change a thing. I'd always choose Molly over any other future I could have had.'

'I just need… I need time to wrap my head around this.'

'I know.'

'I mean, this is huge.'

'I know that too.'

'What the hell do we do?'

'We just work it out, I suppose. I hadn't really thought any further than actually telling you.'

'I suppose you wouldn't.'

They were silent for a moment. Then Ashley spoke again.

'I know I said there was no reason to doubt Molly is yours. But do you believe me?'

'You've said it.'

'A lot of men wouldn't trust my word alone. Is there a bit of you that wants to know for certain? A bit of doubt?'

'If it had been anyone else I might have wondered. But it's you.'

'And that's enough?'

'Yes. And seeing Molly is enough. I can't explain why I feel like this, but it makes sense. Seeing her now I just know it's right. Other people might say I'm an idiot but I don't care.'

'You don't feel like you want to do… you know… tests or anything?'

'Put Molly and you through that?' He shook his head forcefully. 'No.'

'Wow…' Ashley let out a breath. 'I almost wish you would. Just so we'd be straight about it all. As it is I feel as if some day later on, when you've got over the shock, you might look at Moll and wonder.'

'I would never…'

'But if you did you could talk to me about it, right? It's better for you to feel sure.'

'I already feel sure.'

'I'm just saying. Promise you'll tell me if it happens.'

'OK.'

'Promise!'

He gave an uncertain laugh that bordered on hysteria. 'I've got another daughter. Bloody hell!'

'You've always had another daughter,' Ashley said, unable to hold back a small smile. 'She hasn't suddenly appeared.'

'I know, but... Jesus, this is so weird. And Molly... Well, she's incredible!'

'She is that,' Ashley said.

He looked up. '*You're* incredible. Making her into the girl she is all by yourself.'

'I was never by myself and I think Molly might have had a hand in that.'

Taking a seat on the lawn and leaning against the trunk of a tree, he was silent for a moment, gazing out at the party. It seemed their altercation had soon been forgotten and everyone was getting stuck into the revelling as if nothing had happened. Somewhere, Ashley supposed, her mother and Maurice were discussing the developments. She could only hope that Maurice would have enough sense to persuade Sue to stay out of Molly and Ella's way until Ashley and Haydon had the chance to break the news to them both. She couldn't be certain of that at all, but right now Haydon needed her and she couldn't just leave him. She took a seat on the grass beside him.

'What about us?' he asked.

'You still want there to be an us?'

He took her hand and kissed it. 'God, yes! Now more than ever! We can be a family, like we were always supposed to be.'

'You have another family, don't forget. I don't think it's going to be quite that simple.'

'Janine will be on our side.'

'What about Ella? Didn't you just say she's got issues with Molly?'

'That's not exactly what I was saying.'

'Sounded that way to me.'

'I'm sorry if it did. Even if there was a problem the girls will want to put differences behind them when we tell them – I'm sure of it.'

'I wish I could feel as optimistic about it as you do.'

'We can make this work – I know we can.'

Ashley wiped away a tear and sniffed hard. All that he promised was like a dream and yet it felt so unreachable right now, despite the fact he'd taken the news about Molly so well. Their families were going to be a bigger obstacle than he seemed to imagine and she couldn't take any happy ending for granted. Perhaps she was so used to waiting for one that she didn't know how to stop, even when it was there for the taking.

'We also live about two hundred miles apart,' she said.

'I've got a car and endless patience.'

Ashley leaned into him and he folded an arm around her. 'You might well need it,' she said.

He was silent. The sweetness of freshly cut grass filled her nostrils while his heart beat steadily in the ear she had pressed against his chest. Everything was different, and yet it was still the same. He hadn't disowned her and now, as she sat in his embrace, she wondered how she could have been so scared. She looked up to tell him so and saw that in the moments they'd sat quietly together he'd been crying.

'Ignore me,' he said, hastily wiping a hand across his eyes.

Taking his face in her hands she kissed him tenderly. 'I'm sorry.'

'It's me who should be sorry.'

'I don't want you to think that. You have nothing to be sorry for.'

'But this is all my fault. If I hadn't been such an idiot that night in Ibiza and left you the wrong phone number—'

'Stop that. I believe one hundred per cent that you're a good man who made a tiny mistake with his pen and a drunken brain and you don't need to say anything else about it. We've both made mistakes and throwing around blame won't change any of that.'

'But all those years we missed…'

Ashley smiled. 'You wouldn't have met Janine and you wouldn't have Ella. Everything happens for a reason.'

'When are we going to tell the kids?'

'Perhaps we should pull them out of the party now? Go for a walk somewhere quiet so we can discuss it properly?'

He nodded. 'Sounds like a sensible plan. They'll know something's up as soon as we suggest leaving, though.'

'Probably, but they'll think it's something to do with us dating. And I don't suppose it really matters that they guess something's up or not as we'll be telling them soon enough anyway.'

He grabbed her hand again. 'I'll admit to being nervous as hell.'

'Me too.'

Together they stood up. Ashley brushed grass from her skirt and gave Haydon an awkward smile. He'd taken this news so well – better than she could ever have imagined. But while he appeared calm on the outside, was that really how he felt? Was this a delayed reaction, the calm before the storm? Would he go back to his villa later and the truth suddenly fall on him, crushing all reason? Would he see his new reality for what it was and freak out? The fear of losing him returned – sharper, colder, stealing her breath – and her smile, as uncertain as it had been, faded.

'It'll be OK,' he said.

Ashley nodded, her mouth dry and a reply deserting her. Looking out from the secluded shade of their tree, she now saw her mother walking across the lawn towards them. She glanced at Haydon and there was no mistaking his reaction, even though he quickly wiped it away. Ashley guessed his thoughts were along the same lines as her own – how much more trouble could her mother stir up? Hadn't she already done enough damage? Whatever she was on her way to say or do, Ashley needed to nip it in the bud before she made things even more difficult. She stepped out from the shade of the tree, Haydon at her side, and went to meet Sue halfway.

'Mum…' she began, but Sue got in first.

'I'm sorry, love,' she said.

Ashley blinked.

'I was out of order back then,' Sue continued. 'I didn't mean to blurt everything out like that – it wasn't my place to interfere and I should have trusted that you were going about things in the way you thought best.'

'The worst thing was the scene, Mum,' Ashley said. 'Everybody else didn't need to know what was going on.'

'They don't,' Sue said. 'Nobody has realised exactly what it's about so don't worry about that.'

'Maurice knows.'

'I think we would have had to tell him sooner or later, love.'

Ashley pursed her lips, determined not to agree with her mother even though she would have to later.

'I feel like such an idiot. Everyone was looking at us. Haydon feels like that too.'

'I'm sorry,' Sue said. 'What more can I say than that?'

'Your mum was just looking out for you,' Haydon cut in. 'It's only what we'd do for our daughters.'

'Speaking of which,' Ashley said, turning to Sue again. 'I suppose you've spilt the beans to Molly too?'

'Of course not!' Sue squeaked.

'She probably overheard us anyway, the whole business was shouted so loud.'

'Nobody heard us,' Sue insisted. 'I'm quite sure nobody's any the wiser – they were all far too busy enjoying the party to listen to what we were going on about and half of them don't speak English anyway.'

Before Ashley could answer, Haydon's phone began to ring from his pocket. Pulling it out he frowned at the name on the screen.

'Janine...' he murmured before declining the call. But a second later it rang again. He gave Ashley and Sue an apologetic look. 'She doesn't normally call again like this unless it's something really important. It might be some emergency back home...'

As if they didn't already have an emergency of their own here. But Ashley could do nothing other than nod.

'It's OK, I know you wouldn't say you needed to take the call unless you really had to,' she said.

He clicked to unlock the phone and, after a brief greeting, he walked away to a secluded corner of Madame Dupont's grounds, a deep frown creasing his brow as he went. Ashley was distracted for a moment as she watched him. Whatever that phone call was about, she already knew it wasn't good just by the look on his face. It seemed about par for the course considering the sort of day they were having, but she just hoped it wasn't something so awful that it would take him away from her before they'd had time to talk through all their new issues properly.

'I'd better round up the kids,' Ashley said. 'I expect they're still messing around on the old piano in the house,' she added, shielding her eyes and scanning the garden to see that only the adults were out there, chatting in small groups or watching the band play as they sipped glasses of wine.

'What for? Surely you're not going to tell them now?' Sue asked.

'Better now coming from us than later from someone else.'

'I told you nobody overheard anything.'

'I don't even want to take the risk. The way Haydon found out was bad enough but it would be ten times worse for the kids to—'

She stopped, mid-sentence, and exchanged a look of alarm with her mum. From across the grounds, out of their eyeline, there was shouting, followed by a loud scream and a splash. And then all hell broke loose.

Chapter Eighteen

'She said what?'

Haydon's frown deepened as he let himself out of the gate that separated the main gardens of the house from the overgrown orchard beyond. It looked as if Madame Dupont had struggled to tend this over the years and if she had a gardener they certainly didn't see to this bit. But it had its own sort of beauty in its wildness as the low sun blazed through the verdant space beneath the twisted branches and the long grass that whispered with the calls of crickets rustled around Haydon's legs. At another time, perhaps he would have been in a better mood to appreciate his surroundings. But for now, Janine's call had his brain tied in knots.

'How the hell…? There's no way she could know this!'

'So it's true?' Janine asked, and there was no mistaking the sharpness in her tone.

'It's more complicated than that.'

'How? It's either true or it's not.'

'Well, yes, but—'

'Yes?' Janine cried. 'I don't believe I'm hearing this!'

'Just let me explain—'

'Yes, please,' Janine cut in, 'please do explain because my head feels as if the top is about to blow off! Please explain how this can be possible because I really, *really* want to hear it.'

'You're angry?'

'What do you think?'

'It was before I met you.'

'That makes it worse! Did you know? How could you keep this from me all the time we were married?'

'I didn't keep anything from you because I didn't know.'

'But you never even mentioned this girl! Not once. If you can keep this a secret, God knows what else you've hidden from me.'

'It's not like that – calm down, Jannie, please.'

'Don't you *dare* call me *Jannie*! If ever there's a time to drop that nickname it's now. How could you do this to us? Not only have you kept this from me for fifteen years, but then you're careless enough to let it slip so that I have a distraught Ella on the phone who doesn't know what the hell to think! I am *never* letting you take her anywhere again! Are you getting that? Never!'

'Please, just give me a minute and I'll explain.'

'Right. One minute, and it had better be good. Then I'm getting on the next flight to Nice and I'm taking Ella back with me.'

'What's the point in that?' Haydon replied, his own temper flaring now. 'We're coming home tomorrow anyway. Calm down for pity's sake and listen. God knows you've never bothered to listen to me in the past so it'll be a novel experience.'

'You think this is a time for jokes?'

'Nobody's joking here, Janine.'

There was a heartbeat of a pause. 'OK. Tell me what's going on.'

'First off, I've only just discovered this myself – literally this evening. As far as I knew Molly didn't even know—'

'Molly?'

'My…' Haydon winced, aware of how this was going to sound to the mother of what they both had thought was his only child. 'My daughter,' he said. 'The daughter I have with Ashley.'

'So this girl you knew before me… Ashley. She's told you Molly is yours? Tonight?'

'Yes.'

'Don't you think that's an odd thing to do?'

'Not really.'

He heard a barely restrained sigh from Janine's end of the line. 'She's been in Saint-Raphaël all week?'

'Yes.'

'And you've been friendly with her and her daughter all week?'

'Yes.'

'But she only just thought to tell you this news now – the night before you're all due to go home? I think that's an odd thing to do even if you don't.'

'What are you trying to say?'

'Come on, Haydon, you're not that naïve, surely?'

'You think she's lying? Why?'

'Because she can get a daddy for her child, that's why. All these years she's never looked for you to tell you about this but suddenly, when she meets you on holiday, she tells you something this important?'

'She doesn't need to trap me if that's what you're getting at. We're already seeing each other and we plan to see more of each other when we get back to England.'

'Yes, but there's no certainty in that. There's no money in that.'

'You think she's telling me this for *money*?'

'It's the only reason that makes any sense of it.'

Haydon shook his head. 'You're wrong. Molly is mine – *that's* what makes sense in all of this.'

The long, impatient sigh Janine had been holding back escaped now. 'Believe what you want – at the end of the day it's none of my business now. But when it upsets Ella it *is* my business. So if you're saying Molly didn't know, how come she's telling Ella about it?'

'I don't know. Ashley says she's never told Molly. She's never told anyone who Molly's father is until this week when she told…'

'Who?'

'Her mum. Who's staying here at the villa with them. But she said… Bloody hell. Sue promised she hadn't told Molly about it.'

'Looks like the mother's as big a liar as her daughter.'

'Janine! Why are you being such a bitch about it?'

'Why are you being such an idiot about it? Contrary to what you might believe, I still care about what happens to you and I can't stand by and watch some freeloading tart turn you into her own personal bank account without saying something. And when it involves Ella as well then I'm doubly invested. If I have to fly over to that place myself and give her a good talking-to then I bloody well will!'

'You won't need to – I'll sort it.'

'Your record so far isn't very impressive.'

'I've only just found out! What do you want me to do? I'm still in shock and it's not that easy to think it through when everyone else is shouting at me too!' He pushed a hand through his hair and stared out towards the gardens. 'I'd better find Ella,' he said.

'I meant what I said about flying over,' Janine said. 'I can't have this messing Ella up, not after she's come through our divorce so well.'

'You keep saying that but I don't think you really know what's going on in her head. I think the reason you say that is more about guilt than what you really think. She hasn't come through our divorce well at all and I wish you'd stop pretending.'

'So all this is my fault now?'

'No, but I'm sick of you being right about everything and me being the villain. You wanted the divorce and you put Ella through it.'

'Well you're making it worse,' Janine fired back, the bitterness of her tone unmistakable. Had he hit a nerve? Maybe, but he was finally sick of trying to keep the peace, of trying to be reasonable and understanding, of taking responsibility for everyone's mistakes and of everything being about what Janine wanted. She was wrong about Ashley and she had no right to lash out. He was Molly's father and he knew it for sure, even if he couldn't explain to Janine how. Now he had to be father to Molly and to Ella equally. Even if he hadn't fallen for her, he would still have a duty to Ashley, who had struggled for so many years without him. He simply ground his teeth, unable and unwilling to respond to Janine's accusations in a way that wouldn't escalate into something they'd be unable to move past when it was over. But she was right about one thing – he needed to find Ella and put things right with her and he needed to do that before anything else.

'I'll get Ella to call you when I've had a chance to talk to her so at least you'll know everything is sorted,' he said.

'Don't screw this up.'

'You mean don't screw yet another thing up?'

'I didn't say that.'

'I know. You didn't have to.'

He wasn't looking for another argument, despite his words, and it seemed Janine felt the same. She ended the call without acknowledging them. Haydon shoved his phone back in his pocket and faced the gate that separated the orchard from the garden, where the party was still in full swing. But then he realised something that hadn't occurred to him before. The music had stopped. Not that it was particularly shocking, but the chat and laughter seemed to have stopped too. With a frown he started to pick his way through the grasses towards the gate. As his hand went towards it, Ashley appeared, her expression tense.

'I don't know how but Ella's found out about Molly.'

'I already know,' he said. 'She phoned Janine and Janine has just phoned me to give me a roasting,' he added in answer to her silent question. 'She says Molly told her. How did she know? Was it your mum?'

'There's no time for that now,' Ashley said, opening the gate and beckoning him through. 'Ella's done a runner.'

'What!'

'I'll have to tell you about it while we look for her.'

Haydon paused. 'She'll be upset. She'll have run back to our villa.'

'Bastien has already been to look and she's not there.'

Hayden got his phone out but Ashley shook her head.

'I doubt she'll answer that either because she's not answering to anyone else.'

'She'll pick up if it's me,' he said, dialling the number. But after a few moments it rang out and he had to admit defeat, along with a vague sense of building panic. 'She can't have got that far,' he said uncertainly.

'Maybe not. Maurice and my mum are out now and I told them to phone me if they find her. Bastien's with Molly. She's… well, let's just say she's not taking it very well. She feels just terrible about what happened.'

'And what exactly did happen?' he asked, striding around to the entrance of the house while Ashley jogged after him. 'I thought your mum said she hadn't told anyone.'

'I think Bastien overheard us and went to Molly.'

'Little shit!' Haydon hissed.

'You can hardly blame him,' Ashley said. 'He's sixteen and he gets hold of a piece of news like that, what else is he going to do? If it makes you feel better he got his comeuppance.'

'What does that mean?'

'Ella pushed him into the swimming pool.'

'Sounds like Ella,' Haydon replied, his expression grim despite the humour in his comment. 'She seems like an innocent little princess but you cross her at your peril. Gets that particular personality trait from her mother. She's going to take some talking down from this now.'

'Where do you think she might have gone?'

'Not a clue. Best to check back at the villa first, just in case she was hiding from Bastien. Where did you say your mum was looking?'

'Not sure where they are. Maurice mentioned going down the beach – said it was a suitably moody location for a teenager to have a crisis.'

'Funny. Has anyone ever told him he's not a comedian?'

'I don't think he meant anything by it – he's as worried as everyone else but he's just trying not to freak people out. Remember there's still a birthday celebration going on and most of these guests don't know you from Adam so we don't want to get them all involved in our little drama – do we? Making a big fuss about it will do that so Maurice is just trying to play it cool.'

Haydon nodded as they made their way into the front gardens of the house.

'Mum!'

They both turned to see Molly racing after them. Bastien followed, a towel pulled around his shoulders but otherwise dripping wet and looking as shamefaced as Haydon felt he ought to. Later, the boy who'd caused so much trouble was going to get a piece of his mind, but for now, he just wanted to make sure Ella was safe.

'We want to help you look,' Molly cried.

'There's no point in you wandering around the place,' Ashley said. 'It'll be just what we need if you get lost too.'

'I wouldn't get lost because I have Bastien with me.'

Ashley glanced at him and shook her head. 'I'm not risking it. Stay here. Hopefully we won't be long.'

'It's better with more people,' Molly insisted.

'Your mum's right,' Haydon said, and now Molly looked at him as if she'd only just seen him for the first time. They had a lot to talk through too, and he knew she must have been feeling as confused as he was. But now wasn't the time and he was grateful to see she understood that perfectly.

'Is it true?' was all she asked. And when he nodded she gave a small smile.

Ashley stepped forward and kissed her on the forehead. 'We can talk about this later. Now, please… the best thing you can do to help is to stay here where we know you're safe. OK?'

'OK,' Molly said, though the reluctance in her voice was obvious.

'Come on,' Ashley said, turning to Haydon now. 'Let's get across to your place and check it over.'

She cast a glance at the sky and Haydon understood what she was thinking because he'd been thinking it too. It was still bright, but the sun was slipping down towards the horizon and they had perhaps an hour before dark. Hopefully they'd find Ella sulking in her bedroom at the villa and all would be well. But if it came to scouring the surrounding countryside for her, he didn't fancy their chances – or hers. This wasn't an alien planet, but for all Ella knew about the countryside of Southern

France it might as well have been. Then again, that probably went for all of them. Undoubtedly the rest of the party guests would have to get involved if it got to that point and the idea of things escalating even further didn't bear thinking about. So he tried not to and instead he faced forward as they stepped out onto the path and headed for Bastide de la Mer.

Haydon continued to try Ella's phone as they walked, but there was no reply. Either she didn't want to talk to him or there was another, more worrying explanation for the phone silence. It didn't matter what the reason was, the lack of contact was ramping up his stress levels exponentially with every second that passed.

'I'm sorry,' Ashley kept saying, and though he reassured her every time that he didn't blame her, a small part of him did. It wasn't something he would have admitted and it wasn't a feeling he welcomed, but he was angry. Not about Molly, but about the fact that Ashley had kept it from him for so long. He could understand why, but if she'd come clean earlier it might have happened in a less dramatic fashion and they might not be faced with this mess now.

At the house a quick search revealed it to be empty. It didn't look as if Ella had been back there at all. So where was she?

'I'll call my mum,' Ashley said. 'See if they've found her.'

It was pointless and they both knew it. If Sue had found Ella she would have called them already to tell them so. But he let Ashley make the call anyway because he didn't know what else to do and doing something was better than doing nothing. So he listened, feeling increasingly helpless and anxious as she spoke to her mum. It was obvious from the half of the brief conversation he could hear that Sue and Maurice hadn't found any sign of Ella either.

Having confirmed his suspicions, Haydon tried Ella's phone again but now it went straight to voicemail. He could only assume she'd switched it off, not wanting to talk to him. Perhaps she thought that he might persuade her to come back to the villa – if that was the case then she was throwing one hell of a sulk, the likes of which he'd never known her to have. But then she'd never found out that she wasn't his only child before. As revelations went, it was kind of a biggie.

It was tempting to try Janine to see if Ella had called her mother again since he'd last spoken to her and given a clue of her whereabouts, but doing that would mean admitting to Janine that he'd lost Ella. She'd already threatened to jump on a plane to take Ella home – if this incident came to light Haydon was quite sure that Janine would see him in court to stop him having any access at all.

As he rubbed a hand through his hair and gazed out over fields that were rapidly fading into twilight, a feeling of increasing helplessness washed over him. He couldn't help but reflect ruefully that the events leading to this moment had been set in motion on a sultry night in Ibiza after one too many sangrias. Ashley could tell him that she wouldn't have changed a thing but he wondered whether a little sobriety that night might have meant they weren't in this mess right now.

'What shall we do?' Ashley asked, breaking into his thoughts. He looked at her, his frustration tinged with guilt. She'd suffered too. 'She'll be OK,' Ashley added. 'She won't have got far and there's no real danger hereabouts. She's probably having a cry under a tree somewhere.'

Haydon nodded, but he wished he could feel encouragement from Ashley's words. He didn't really think Ashley believed them herself, though she was trying to be brave and optimistic.

'Is it worth rechecking Madame Dupont's house?' he asked.

'I'll ask Nanette to do it,' Ashley said, dialling the number.

'We might have to tell people what's going on so we can organise the other guests into a search party,' Haydon continued. 'We didn't really want to involve every Tom, Dick and Harry in this but the alternative is to have Ella missing after dark and I don't fancy that.'

'Sure,' Ashley said as she waited for Nanette to pick up. 'I understand.' After a moment she ended the call. 'Nanette's not answering. I could ask Molly to look. She wanted to help, after all.'

'OK.'

But Ashley's call to Molly went unanswered too.

'For God's sake,' she muttered as she locked her phone.

'Do you have a number for Bastien?' Haydon asked.

Ashley shook her head. 'Never imagined I'd need one. What now?'

'We'll have to walk back. I'm hoping that Ella's got over whatever tantrum she's having and has had the sense to head back there if she's not here at our house. And if she's not there then…'

'The police?' Ashley asked.

'Let's see what the rest of Maurice's family have to say about it. We're out in the middle of nowhere and I don't imagine the police will be here quick. We might find her faster ourselves if we all pitch in.'

They started to stride in the direction of the Dupont home. Ashley had to jog to keep up but Haydon didn't dare slow down for her. With every minute that Ella was missing his sense of panic rose and he just wanted to find her, to explain everything, to tell her that no matter what he was still her dad. He didn't dare imagine what was going through her mind right now but the guilt was crushing. She was never going to be second best, but she must have felt like it, and the revelation couldn't have come at a worse moment – just when she was already feeling vulnerable and inferior to Molly, this had happened to reinforce her fears.

As they got through the gates of Madame Dupont's home they were greeted with sombre faces and a distinct lack of a party. Someone had spilled the beans already, perhaps, but maybe that was to be expected in the circumstances. Perhaps it didn't matter because if they didn't find Ella soon they were going to need all the help they could get and that would mean coming clean anyway.

'No Ella?' Ashley asked Nanette.

'No.'

'What about Maurice and my mum? Are they back?'

'They're still looking. They're on their way to the beach.'

'I don't honestly think Ella has got that far already,' Haydon said. 'It's a fair walk.'

'We must look everywhere,' Nanette said. 'My cousins are going to try the vineyards and farms nearby. Aunt Violette will telephone everyone she knows to look.'

Haydon glanced at Ashley. Was that really necessary? But then he thought about how desperately he wanted Ella back and quickly decided it didn't matter any more who knew.

'I'm going to have a word with Molly,' Ashley said. 'Find out exactly what happened. It may help give us a clue.'

'There is another problem,' Nanette said, twisting her skirt in between a thumb and forefinger. 'Molly and Bastien have gone too.'

Chapter Nineteen

'Christ, I told her to stay put!' Ashley cried. 'Sorry,' she added, seeing that her reaction had distressed Nanette. 'How long has she been missing?'

'I do not know,' Nanette said. 'I have only just realised because we wanted to ask her and Bastien what happened to make Ella so upset.'

'Then how do you know about…' Haydon began, but Ashley gave a wry smile.

'Maurice told you?' she asked Nanette, who nodded.

'Does that mean we have to look for them too?' Haydon asked. Ashley was sure it wasn't meant as heartlessly as it sounded. Ella was out on her own and Molly was with Bastien – not to mention that she was also two years older. Haydon wouldn't have wanted to say it, but Ella had to be their priority.

'They'll be out looking for Ella like us,' she said. 'Chances are we'll find them together. It explains why she didn't answer her phone when I called earlier.'

'Does it?'

'She knew I would have told her to get back here if I'd managed to get hold of her.'

While Aunt Violette continued to phone everyone she knew, Ashley, Nanette and Haydon organised the search parties into groups and between them everyone decided what ground they should cover.

There was only really Violette who knew the countryside well and she was too old to go out, but she'd given a good indication of the places where she thought Ella could be hiding, so everyone took responsibility for one and headed out.

Ashley tried to phone Molly once more and, getting no answer yet again, was finding it difficult to keep her irritation in check. She should have known Molly wouldn't have been content with leaving the search to everyone else but now Ashley had even more to worry about. She couldn't say it to Haydon, who was clearly out of his mind with worry over Ella, but she was concerned for Molly too. Molly might have been with Bastien and she might have been older, but that didn't mean she couldn't get into trouble. The wrong set of rocks at the beach, a creaky old barn with a paper-thin roof, the gathering darkness, a less than friendly stranger… the possibilities were endless and Ashley tried not to think of them. She should have let Molly come with her and Haydon when they went to check out Haydon's place but she tried not to dwell on that either. She seemed to be an expert at making mistakes these days.

The sun was almost gone but at least it was still light as they headed out again. After a brief chat with Maurice to find out where he'd already covered with Ashley's mum, she and Haydon headed for the old town. Haydon had suggested going in his car to get there faster but Ashley had pointed out that if Ella was on the road somewhere on the way, speeding past in their car wasn't going to be very helpful, not to mention how much they'd both had to drink, so they'd decided against it. One party was searching the nearby farms and fields, one was on the way to the old town and two had decided to cover the long harbour – one at end each.

It certainly wasn't the centenary celebration anyone had envisaged for the marvellous Violette Dupont, and for that Ashley was truly sorry, but she was also grateful for the help all her guests had been only too happy to offer. Violette was going to call the police now that she'd finished checking with people she knew, though nobody was sure how long someone had to be missing for it to be considered a matter for the police and so nobody was sure how much help that would be. Meanwhile Maurice and Sue had now taken to knocking on doors to see if they could check out local outbuildings, though none of these strategies filled Ashley with hope.

She glanced at Haydon as he strode beside her, muscles twitching in a tight jaw, eyes trained on the road ahead. If he hadn't been angry with her over the way the news of Molly had been broken, he had to be angry now. He hadn't once blamed her, though, or Molly, and in some ways this was worse. What was going on in his head? When all this was over where would it leave them? It wasn't the time to ask and so she walked by his side, silent save for the remarks that they shared pertinent to the search for Ella.

'She'll be OK,' Ashley said into another long silence. She couldn't be certain of that at all, but what else could she say? Sorry for the tenth time?

'I just wish she'd answer her bloody phone,' he replied. 'Doesn't she realise this is torture?'

'She's fourteen, so probably not.'

'Not even fourteen yet,' Haydon said. 'Christ, Ashley… what am I going to tell her mum?'

'We might not need to tell her anything yet.'

'It's my fault.'

'It's not your fault.'

'I should have talked to her the minute you told me about Molly.'

'You were in shock yourself and we couldn't have seen what would happen. If you want to blame someone, blame Bastien.'

'I can't. You're right – he's a sixteen-year-old boy – what else was he going to do but tell the girls what he'd heard? He probably thought he was doing a good thing.' He rubbed a hand over his face and let out a sigh. 'Shit. This is a disaster.'

'It's a stumbling block.'

His jaw tightened again but he didn't reply. Ashley could have guessed what that reply might have been had he been the type of man to air it, and he'd have been right. She was worried about where Molly was right now but it was nothing like the fear he must have been feeling over Ella, who was alone, hardly spoke enough French for a useful conversation and had now been missing for over an hour. She wanted to reach for his hand, to let him know that she was there for him and they'd work this out together, but it was like there was an emotional force field around him, one that she couldn't get past, one that she didn't dare to push past for fear of what she might find beyond it.

For the fifth, maybe sixth time in as many minutes, she tried to call Molly. If she could just reach her, get a clue, find out what the hell was going on… But, like all the times before, the phone went to voicemail.

'For God's sake, Moll, stop pissing around and pick this up!' she hissed, immediately regretting her outburst as the message was saved to Molly's phone. Losing her temper probably wasn't the best way to persuade an already emotionally unstable teen to answer her calls. She had to keep reminding herself that Molly was in a weird place too right now. She'd just found out about Haydon and the fact that she'd taken it upon herself to assume responsibility for Ella's disappearance and do something about it even though she knew that would incur Ashley's wrath was testament to her selflessness. When her own world had been blown apart, she was still trying to fix everyone else's. At any other time, Ashley might have sat on a wall and sobbed for the mess of it all. But she couldn't, because Haydon needed her. Molly needed her and Ella needed her, and she had to keep it together for all of them.

'Molly has enough sense to head back when it gets too dark to search,' Haydon said.

'You don't think Ella does?'

'Normally I'd say yes.'

'You think the news has affected her that badly?'

'Put it this way – Molly has always known that she had a dad out there somewhere. For her the news is, or will be eventually, a positive thing. At least I hope so. But for Ella, who has grown up thinking her dad belongs to her and nobody else, it's like something's been taken away from her life, not added. For her it poses questions while for Molly it gives answers. They've both had a shock but it's not the same at all.'

'Nobody's taking you away from Ella.'

'That's not how she's going to see it.'

'You don't know that for sure.'

'No, I don't suppose I do. It's just things she said to me tonight… It doesn't matter now. What matters is finding her.'

'I'm sorry.'

He looked at her now. 'You don't need to keep saying that.'

'But I am. You think this is all my fault, even if you don't say it.'

'Now's not the time to lay blame. We can talk about all that after we find Ella.'

'So you do?'

'I don't have the energy to get into it, Ashley. I can't even think about it until I have my daughter safely back with me.'

My proper daughter was what Ashley felt like he meant when he said that. But maybe she was just feeling hypersensitive about the whole thing. Another apology itched at her lips but with a huge effort she stopped it from coming out. She wanted to keep saying sorry until she was hoarse but what good would it do? Being sorry wasn't going to get Ella back, and part of her didn't even know why she felt she had to take all the blame, but she couldn't help it. Just so she wouldn't have to think about apologising again, she dialled Molly's number and listened forlornly as it rang and rang until it went to voicemail.

They'd been in just about every café in the old town of Saint-Raphaël and every shop that was still open, though the lateness of the hour meant there weren't many of those. Nobody had seen Ella, Molly or Bastien. As each visit led to another dead end Ashley dared to glance at Haydon's darkening expression. She couldn't tell whether he was set to cry or explode with rage and frustration and she didn't know how she'd cope with any of those scenarios. For now he seemed to be holding it together, despite the increasing tension on his face.

Ashley made another brief call to her mum, who informed her that nobody there had managed to turn anything up either, though the consensus was that Molly was probably OK with Bastien as long as they hadn't encountered any physical dangers. Nobody dared dwell on the fact that Ella was not in such a fortunate position.

'She could be halfway to Dover for all we know.' Haydon stared towards the harbour while Ashley ended the call.

'We'll find her,' Ashley replied, though she wished her conviction could carry the same weight as her words. 'She can't have got that far.'

'Everyone keeps saying that but if she hasn't got far then why haven't we found her? Half of Saint-Raphaël is out looking now and nobody's found so much as a flip-flop. What if she's got into trouble somewhere? What if she's injured or stranded?'

Ashley chewed her lip. 'Do you think it would be worth phoning your ex? I know you don't want her to know about this but it might be that Ella has been in touch with her since she went off—'

'Janine would have phoned me if that was the case. She'd have taken great pleasure in telling me just what a useless dad I am, and she'd be right.'

'You've been dealt a tough hand, that's all.'

'Perhaps I don't deserve to be dealt any hand at all. Two daughters and I haven't done right by either of them.'

'Don't say that.'

'It's true.'

'You're doing your best. It's all any of us can do in the end.'

Ashley reached for his hand but he recoiled and the action sent a spike of regret and shame to her heart. She only wanted to reassure him in his hour of need, to offer some comfort, but his rejection showed that he was not in a place to forgive her for the events that had led to this moment. Perhaps he never would be now.

She fought the tears burning her eyes and tipped her face to the sky. If anyone was looking down right now, they had to hear her prayer, surely? She'd never asked for anything, had always strived to give of herself and never take, but she was asking now – begging – for one favour. Please let Ella be OK. Her mum was right – Molly had Bastien and together they'd stay safe. At least she had to believe that. But Ella…

She dragged a hand across her eyes and pulled herself up to her full height. For Haydon's sake, she would be strong – strong enough for both of them.

'I know Violette was going to phone them, but let's go and find the police station,' she said. 'We won't leave until somebody agrees to do something, regardless of what the official rules are. We're tourists and they'll want to help when they find out how young Ella is.'

'Do you know where it is?'

'No, but I'm sure it will come up on Google Maps. Give me a minute and I'll figure it out.'

'Thank you, Ashley. And I mean that.'

She looked up from her phone and gave him a wan smile. The sentiment was welcome but she didn't think he meant it at all. Right now he was desperate and glad of help, regardless of the form it took. Right now he'd be showering his worst enemy with presents if he thought it would get Ella back, and she knew that because she'd have been doing the same if it had been Molly lost and alone.

'Right,' she said. 'There seems to be more than one but I'm guessing one is like the coastguard because it mentions "maritime" in the name. Maybe this… the *Police Municipale*… maybe that's the one.'

'If it isn't I'm sure they'll direct us to the right place,' Haydon replied in a flat voice. 'I just hope someone speaks English when we get there.'

'Of course they will,' Ashley said, though she wasn't so sure either. 'If not we'll get Maurice to come down.'

'Perhaps we should get him to come down anyway? It makes sense.'

'I suppose it does,' Ashley said. 'He's had too much to drink to drive but we can call him and get him to walk down and meet us there.'

'OK,' Haydon said.

'Will you try Janine?'

'Maybe. Not until I absolutely have to.'

'She's going to find out about it sooner or later.'

'I know, but I'd rather it be later. Preferably when Ella is back with me so it won't seem like such a big deal as it does now.'

Ashley didn't comment on the fact that she thought Haydon owed Janine the full picture as soon as possible – as a mother herself she'd hate to think something like this was going on without her knowledge. But it wasn't her place to put him right and it certainly wasn't the time. Instead she dialled Maurice's number and briefly told him their plan, to which he readily agreed, telling her he was leaving the house even as she ended the call. She glanced at Haydon as he strode beside her, his face turned to the road ahead and his jaw set and resolute. He looked like someone with purpose, with a plan, but she knew that was all show. If he didn't force himself to look like that he might just collapse sobbing on the roadside. She knew it because she felt exactly the same and it didn't matter that Ella wasn't her daughter.

'Was Molly back at the villa when you phoned?' Haydon asked, never moving his eyes from the horizon.

'No.'

'You're worried about her?'

'I'd be lying if I said I wasn't, but it doesn't seem right to say so. Like everyone says – she has Bastien with her.'

'If you're worried then you're worried. It's only natural – you're her mum.'

'I know, but…'

'I'm sorry. That wasn't what I meant. It's hard for me to remember… I don't really know her. You understand?'

'You don't feel like her dad?'

'I don't know what I feel, only that I don't really know who she is. It's going to take time.'

'For all of us, I expect. Ella too.'

'Perhaps Ella will need the most help dealing with it. She never asked for any of this.'

'Neither did Molly.'

There was a pause. But Ashley never got to hear what his answer would be because her phone began to ring and, seeing it was her mum, she stabbed at the screen to take the call.

'You have news?'

'You'd better get back here,' Sue said. 'The police have just arrived.'

Chapter Twenty

Ashley was clutching her side as they arrived back at Madame Dupont's villa, stitch stabbing at her as she fought for breath. She couldn't remember the last time she'd run that fast or that far and as she looked over to Haydon she was almost irked that he showed no signs of fatigue at all. The police car was parked a few feet away in a little passing place on the road but it was empty, the occupants presumably inside the house.

As he yanked open the gate and strode up the path to the veranda and the main door, she followed, wiping sweat from her brow. Maurice and Nanette came out to greet them.

'She's OK?' Haydon asked, bristling with tension that was almost palpable. No matter how he'd been reassured that physically Ella was fine, it was clear he wouldn't be happy until he'd seen for himself.

'She's a little shaken,' Nanette said. 'But she is unharmed.'

'And Molly…?' Ashley hardly dared ask but she had to know.

Nanette shook her head. 'I'm sorry, but she and Bastien have not returned yet.'

'They're probably still looking for Ella,' Haydon said, taking the steps up to the veranda two at a time.

Ashley threw a look at the darkening sky before she followed Haydon inside. She'd make sure everything was OK with Ella and then she was going to have to turn her attention to looking for Molly regardless of whether Bastien was with her or not. In fact, she was surprised that Bastien's family weren't making more of a fuss about his absence, but none of them had seemed too concerned so far.

Two *gendarmes* were sitting at Aunt Violette's dining table. Each had a glass of wine in front of them and were chatting casually to some of her guests as if they were party guests themselves. Ella was sitting next to Sue, who had a protective arm around her shoulder, and she was letting out that peculiar hiccoughing sound that only comes when someone has been sobbing so uncontrollably that their diaphragm seems to go into overdrive. It pained Ashley to see Haydon's youngest daughter so distressed and to know that a great deal of it was down to her. As her father entered the room Ella looked up and for a moment both froze, uncertainty written into their features. But then Haydon took the room in less than three strides and Ella threw herself into his arms and started to cry again.

'I'm sorry, Dad,' she wept. 'I'm sorry I made you so worried.'

'You have nothing to be sorry for,' he said, kissing her head. 'Nothing at all. If anyone's sorry it should be me and I am, more than I can say.' He pulled back and gave her a critical once-over. 'You're alright? You're not hurt?'

'She was lucky.' One of the *gendarmes* cut in, not a bit fazed by the emotion of the scene unfolding before him. 'If the driver had not been looking she would have been under the lorry.'

'A lorry!' Haydon glanced from one policeman to the other. 'Nobody said anything about a lorry! I thought…' He looked at Maurice and Sue. 'When you said a road accident I thought…'

'We thought it was a car too,' Sue said. 'It doesn't matter now – the main thing is the driver managed to avoid her and she's safe.'

Haydon pulled Ella into his arms again and held her tight. 'Jesus, Ella… don't ever do that to me again – I don't think my heart could stand the strain.'

'I'm sorry,' Ella sobbed.

'Don't be – just promise me that when something upsets you in the future you'll come and talk it over with me instead of reacting blindly to it. OK?'

She nodded, sniffing and spluttering uncontrollably. 'I will; I promise.'

'Perhaps you two need some time alone?' Sue asked, and Ashley's heart went out to her mum, who looked about as mortified and guilt-plagued as she'd ever seen her. 'I suppose you've got things to talk about.'

'Come on… let's go for a walk,' he said, gently leading Ella to the doorway. Ashley watched them go and fresh tears filled her own eyes. She'd lost him now, she was sure of it.

'You're bearing up?' Sue asked, and Ashley turned in response to the gentle hand her mother laid on her arm.

'Yes,' Ashley said, sniffing hard. Madame Dupont poured some wine into a glass and held it out to Ashley, and she didn't know whether to laugh or cry at the kind but ultimately misguided gesture. The last thing she wanted right now was a glass of wine. But she forced a smile and took it.

'I'll go with Maurice and find Molly and Bastien,' Sue said.

Ashley glanced at the two policemen who were listening to the conversation with interest but didn't seem overly concerned that two teenagers were still missing. In fact, they looked as if they were about ready to join the party. But then one of them seemed to realise that Ashley's pleading look meant they were probably supposed to offer some sort of assistance.

'We will alert our colleagues and we will soon find them,' he said.

'Thank you,' Sue said.

'We will need some details,' he continued. 'If you could assist…'

'Of course,' Sue said, going over with her phone and clicking onto her camera roll to give them photos of the two teens while Ashley watched, feeling all at sea and wondering how the hell she'd got here.

*

The sky was indigo-washed as Haydon stepped out onto the road that led back to the villa he'd shared with Ella for the past week. Ella walked quietly by his side. She looked delicate, as if the wrong word might break her, and he was suddenly terrified that he might utter it.

'Is it true?' she asked in a small voice. 'I thought… I thought Molly and Bastien might have been playing a trick on me.'

'Yes, it's true.'

'But you never told anyone…'

'I didn't know, Ella, I swear. I found out literally ten minutes before you did.'

'But you liked her so much. When you played your cello with her and you looked so happy, and then when Bastien said, I thought…'

'That I must have known all along? God, no, Ella. I would never keep something so huge from you, and it doesn't matter how much it looked as if I liked her, she will never come between you and me. Nobody will ever do that.'

'But she's your first kid.'

'That doesn't matter. You're my daughter and I love you more than life itself. Molly will come to mean a great deal to me in time, I'm sure, but what we have will never change, even when that happens.'

'You don't love Molly more than me?'

'How could you even think that for one second? I've been going out of my mind tonight when I thought I might never see you again!'

'Molly's lost too.'

'She went out to look for you but Bastien is with her and I'm sure Ashley is sorting that out now. I don't want you to worry about it.'

'It's my fault.'

'The only person who isn't at fault in all this is you. Sweetheart, you've done absolutely nothing wrong.'

They lapsed into silence. Perhaps Ella was computing it all, and Haydon grasped for the right thing to say, something that would be an instant fix. But the fact was, such a thing didn't exist and, if it did, it was certainly way out of his reach.

'I suppose I always wanted a sister,' Ella said quietly into the gap.

He gave a half-smile, relief welling up in him. Ella was resilient; she'd had to be over the past couple of years, and perhaps she'd cope with this new shock better than he'd feared once they could move past it.

'Was Mum really mad at you when she called?' she continued.

'You could say that. But I've put up with worse.'

'Really?'

'No, not really,' he said with a laugh. 'But it's OK.'

'Will Molly and Ashley move in with you?'

'It's too soon to think about things like that yet.'

'But will they one day?'

'Would it make you sad if they did? You like living with your mum and Kevin, don't you?'

'I suppose.'

'And there'd be plenty of visits any time you liked.'

'But they'd be with you all the time and I wouldn't.'

'It wouldn't make me love Molly more than you if that's what you're thinking.'

'I know,' she said. But Haydon had to wonder if she really did know. He had a feeling that was something she'd take a long time to come to terms with.

'That's something that may or may not be in the future and I don't want you to worry about it now.'

'But you love Ashley?'

Haydon fell to silence again as his gaze turned to the glow of the setting sun. Right now he didn't know how he felt about Ashley. Part of him wanted to hate her for the secrets she'd kept and the trouble they'd caused, and part of him felt desperately sorry and sick with guilt for all the years she'd coped alone and all the years they could have had together. But of course, she was right about a lot of things and one of those was that if they hadn't been forced apart by circumstances then he wouldn't have met Janine and he wouldn't have Ella.

Did he love Ashley? The question had occurred to him earlier that night as he got ready for the party, his stomach flipping at the idea of spending time with her. He'd almost convinced himself that he'd always loved her, right from that first drink in Ibiza. But that was crazy, right? That didn't happen in real life. He didn't know what to think or say to Ella in reply to her question; he only knew that the thought of Ashley disappearing from his life now pained him more than he could comprehend. If that was love then yes, perhaps he did love her.

'You can say it – I won't freak out this time,' Ella said.

'I know.' He looped an arm around her. 'I just don't know what to say. Love is… well it's not often as straightforward as we'd like it to be. And being in love with someone doesn't automatically mean you can be with them.'

'Why not?'

'Loads of reasons. Sometimes being in love with someone doesn't even mean that being with them is the best thing for everyone involved.'

'Like when you split up with Mum?'

'Yeah, I guess so.'

He looked down at Ella. So young and yet already so wise that she could see what he and Janine had both denied – they'd been in love even as they'd signed the divorce papers but they'd never been right for each other and ultimately their love couldn't overcome that. Whatever happened, he knew that he and Janine would always care for each other even though they couldn't be together. Was Ashley any different? If Janine had loved him and yet he'd still lost her, who was to say he wouldn't lose Ashley too in the end, even if they decided to give it a go? When he thought about it now, what did he actually know about her? They'd become so close so quickly and yet he didn't really know her at all.

'Will you have to give Molly money?' Ella asked, breaking into his thoughts.

'Straight for the practical considerations, eh? I would even if I didn't have to. Remember she's had no dad for sixteen years so it's the least I can do.'

'But it wasn't your fault?'

'It wasn't really anyone's fault – it just happened that way. I met Ashley on holiday and I didn't know how to contact her when we both went back home. She didn't know how to contact me either, so when she found out she was expecting Molly she couldn't tell me. It's only a crazy coincidence that means I know now. If we'd never come here perhaps I'd never have known. Weird, eh?'

Ella let out a long breath and Haydon couldn't help but detect a note of disapproval in it. Even he had to see the irony of that coming from his nearly fourteen-year-old.

'It was all a bit stupid,' he agreed with a wry smile. 'There was no Facebook or Snapchat or anything back then, though, so it was easier to lose people than you might think.'

'Did you miss her?'

'Sometimes. But then I met your mum so I didn't think about her so much after that.'

'Do you wish you'd married Ashley instead of my mum?'

'Never. I wouldn't have you then, would I?'

'But you wouldn't have known that.'

'I know it now. I'm not interested in what might have been, only what I've got now and the most important bit of that is you.'

'Do you want to go back and see if they've found Molly?'

'Do you?'

Ella shrugged. 'I'd feel bad if she was in trouble.'

'I don't think she'd be in trouble for long. I do need to talk to her at some point. You understand that, don't you? I need to talk to her because we haven't even discussed the fact that I'm her dad yet, and I don't know how she's feeling about it.'

'Will you have to do a test?'

'What sort of test?'

'You know, like to test whether you're her dad for real?'

'I don't know – I haven't really thought about it yet. So you want to head back now to see if she's back yet?'

'Yeah, I suppose so.'

'OK.'

There was a brief silence as they turned to retrace their steps. Then Ella spoke again. 'Dad… please don't be angry…'

Haydon frowned. As if there hadn't been enough drama, apparently there was something even worse coming.

'What?' he asked, a note of new trepidation in his voice.

'When I saw the truck coming at me I dropped my phone.'

Haydon blinked.

'The screen smashed and now it doesn't work,' she continued, and as he looked at her he could see fresh tears in her eyes.

'Oh my God!' he cried, relief flooding through him as he pulled her into a hug. 'If that's the worst thing to come out of tonight then I'll be very happy to buy you a hundred new phones!'

*

As soon as Haydon had left with Ella, Ashley's veneer of strength finally cracked. As she collapsed, sobbing into her mother's arms, Maurice tipped her chin up and smiled down at her.

'Don't worry – we will find Molly. All will be well and we will be partying again by the end of the night.'

'It's all such a mess – and it's my fault!'

He shrugged. 'It is only life. Sometimes it's good and sometimes not so good, but you will always find a way through.'

One of the *gendarmes* spoke rapidly into his radio as Maurice began to organise another search party. Bastien's uncle did a fair amount of what could have been swearing in his native language and Ashley was only glad that Bastien's parents had been unable to make the trip down to Saint-Raphaël because she wouldn't have wished the trauma she and Haydon had been through tonight on another parent.

Then her thoughts turned back to Haydon. He'd been reunited with Ella and, of course, she was happy about that, but she couldn't help reflecting on the fact that Molly was still missing and he wasn't here. Didn't he care? Was this a huge signpost to what their future relationship – if there was even going to be one – would look like? She understood that it was hard for him to take in the news that Molly was his daughter but surely he must have been vaguely interested in where she was now? Would Ella always mean more to him? She supposed she could understand that too, but the fierce mother tiger inside her didn't have to like it. Molly was their daughter and his firstborn, and that had to mean something. He'd said he was going to talk briefly to Ella, so why hadn't he come back to help find Molly?

'We will leave now to make the most of the last daylight,' Maurice said, leaning in to kiss Sue.

Ashley stood up. 'I'm ready when you are.'

'Stay here,' Maurice said. 'You have been searching for hours and you are exhausted. We will find her, don't fear.'

'I can't just sit here and wait.'

'That's exactly what you can do,' Sue said. 'Maurice is right – they all know the area better than us and they'll get around much quicker…'

'Without a hysterical mother?' Ashley finished for her.

'It wasn't quite how I was going to put it. Besides, someone has to be here in case Molly comes back of her own accord.'

'Aunt Violette will be here.'

'It's hardly fair to expect her to deal with it on her own if they do come back to find only her here, is it?'

'I can't just sit around and wait.'

'You can because I say it's right.'

'I'm thirty-four, Mum.'

'You're also in a state. Please… arguing is only delaying everyone else's departure and it's getting darker by the minute. I'll get you a cognac and we'll do some phoning around while the others are out.'

Just as she was about to nod reluctant agreement, Haydon appeared at the kitchen door with Ella.

'Still no sign of them?' he asked.

'Not yet. We're going out for another look,' Maurice said.

'I'll come with you,' Haydon replied. He threw a pleading look at Ella and she nodded with a small smile.

'Sure,' she said. 'Should I stay here?' she added uncertainly.

'You can sit with us if you like,' Sue said. 'I'm staying behind with Ashley and Madame Dupont in case they come back of their own accord.'

Without another word Ella took a seat. The policemen, who had been murmuring amongst themselves in between making calls, now stood up and took their leave while the rest of the search party headed for the door.

'Bring her back,' Ashley said.

Maurice gave her an encouraging smile. 'Before night falls they'll be here.'

Ashley nodded, though it wasn't Maurice she'd been addressing. But Haydon didn't say a word; he just kissed Ella on the head and told her not to worry, and then they were gone.

It didn't matter how often Ashley tried Molly's phone, it kept on ringing out. Ella tentatively offered the idea that perhaps Molly's phone had somehow come to a sticky end, just as her own had, but nobody really thought this was the case. More likely Molly was stubbornly sticking to the notion that she somehow had responsibility for finding Ella herself. Ashley had texted her to say that Ella was back safe with them at Villa Marguerite and all she could do was hope that at some point Molly would check her phone and see the message.

Ella sat on the swing seat on the veranda now, staring out into the dusk. She'd been out there for twenty minutes as Ashley paced up and down the kitchen and Sue conversed with Aunt Violette in her best French about the events of the evening. Every so often Ashley would look out of the window to see Ella in exactly the same spot, silent and still. Looking out for the search party that contained her dad, Ashley supposed. She'd wanted to go and talk to her, but what was she supposed to say? There was this huge thing now, a barbed-wire fence between them full of snags and sharp edges. Did the news about Molly now make Ashley the enemy? If there was to be any kind of future between her and Haydon then she needed to get Ella on side, but any friendship with her seemed like a distant dream now.

Folding her arms, she turned back to Sue, who was reading a text from Maurice.

'Any news?' Ashley asked.

Sue looked up from her phone and shook her head. 'God knows where they could have got to.'

'I wish she'd just give it up and come back. She must know she can't do much more now.'

'Stubborn. Who does that remind you of?'

Ashley gave a wan smile, but a squeal from outside halted her reply, and both she and Sue raced to the window.

'Thank God!' Ashley cried as she bolted out to the garden.

Ella had beaten her to it and was now hugging a tearful Molly.

'I couldn't find you!' Molly sniffed, while Bastien stood a foot or so away and ran a hand through his hair, looking relieved that the ordeal was over.

'I'm sorry,' Ella said, and now she was crying too.

Then Molly looked over her shoulder and Ella, realising why, relinquished her grip, turning to Bastien to continue her apologies while Ashley ran to Molly and pulled her close.

'You can be so bloody infuriating!' Ashley said, holding her tightly.
'I told you not to go out when everyone else had it under control!'

'I'm sorry, Mum.'

'Fat lot of good sorry is. Tell it to the new grey hairs I've developed
over the last few hours!'

'I didn't mean to.'

'Oh yes you did. But it doesn't matter – I'm just glad you're back now.'

'I'll let Maurice know to send everyone back,' Sue said from
behind them.

'Everyone's out looking for you,' Ashley said in answer to Molly's
silent question. 'Well, almost everyone.'

Molly's eyes widened.

'Don't look so terrified,' Ashley said. 'You could hardly expect us
to sit around waiting for you. I just hope the police aren't going to be
too mad that we've wasted their time.'

'The police?' Molly's face seemed to lose three shades.

'What else were we going to do? Three teenagers missing and not
the foggiest where to start looking…'

'Sorry,' Ella said again.

'Where the hell were you for all this time?' Ashley said to Molly.

'We just walked around… We didn't know where to look so we
went everywhere.'

'And I suppose you didn't stop to consider that while you were just
walking around everyone else was just walking around trying to find you?'

'Sorry,' Molly said.

'Sorry,' Ella repeated.

Ashley waved away the apologies. 'Let's not dwell on it now – none
of us. What's done is done and everyone is safe and sound again. Just
as soon as your dad gets back I think we might need to talk. Is that

OK with you two?' she asked, looking at Molly and Ella in turn, who both nodded.

Which, after all that had happened that night, would be fine – as long as Haydon was in the mood to talk. Ashley couldn't be sure of anything where he was concerned.

Chapter Twenty-One

By the time the search party arrived back at Madame Dupont's house every member of it knew about Ashley and Haydon and their secret. Nobody said so, but Ashley could see it in the way they looked at her and in the way everyone carefully avoided any sort of conversation that might bring it out into the open for general discussion. It was obvious, really, that somebody would have asked what the hell was going on and Maurice or Haydon would have had to put them straight.

So on their return there were words of relief and words of reprimand for the teens and even talk of restarting the celebrations that had gone so badly awry, but no words on the girl who stood before them now and who knew for the first time in her life who her father was. Or the other girl who stood before them, suddenly robbed of the privileges of being an only daughter and faced with a new, uncertain relationship with the father she'd wrongly thought she'd known completely. And certainly no words on Ashley, who had expected judgement at the very least but was served with none. Throughout her stay with Madame Dupont she had experienced nothing but kindness and tonight, despite the drama and revelations, that didn't change. It was a relief, but if it had been any different she could have borne it knowing that Haydon was OK with her. But she didn't think he was. The fact was she still didn't know where she stood, despite him calling them all together to talk in a secluded corner of the garden as festivities got underway again elsewhere.

Lanterns swung in a gentle breeze from the trees that they sat beneath, flickering shadows dancing on the lawns and the strains of music as the little band struck up again reaching their ears. Whenever she recalled this moment in a future that she couldn't yet see, Ashley would always remember the sweet smell of the grass, layered with lavender and rosemary and wildflowers from Violette's unruly gardens. The breeze would rise and fall, bringing the fragrances to meet her senses in waves. Right now, as Molly and Ella fired questions at the adults, which they did their best to answer as honestly and delicately as they could, Ashley couldn't think of the scents of an evening garden at all, only of how on earth they were ever going to move on from this day.

Haydon would pause at every new question directed at him and he would glance at Ashley, as if trying to telegraph what his answer was going to be in the hope of her approval. But of course, she couldn't know for sure what he was going to say – she could only trust that he'd make it the right thing. The girls nodded in the appropriate places. Sometimes they were quiet, and sometimes they talked over one another, words tumbling out as quickly as the thoughts that formed them. There were so many questions, sometimes just the same ones asked in different ways, but they amounted to one huge fear that all four of them were, in their own way, trying to articulate. What did the future hold for them now that they were a family?

Haydon was giving nothing away, his attention wholly dedicated to his daughters, who each wanted and needed his approval, to know that they were each as important as the other. If Ashley had been a more selfish woman she would have wanted this bit to be over so she could talk to him alone and find out what the future held for them as a couple, but that wouldn't be right or fair. Their priority had to be the girls, but it was increasingly hard to remember that when all she could do was look at him and desperately wish for a sign that his feelings towards her hadn't changed in light of all that had happened.

'Is it weird?' Molly asked. 'That I sort of knew?'

'Really?' Ashley raised her eyebrows and exchanged a glance with Haydon.

'I didn't know, of course. But when Bastien told me I sort of wasn't really surprised.'

'Why?' Haydon asked.

'Just the way Mum looked at you sometimes. And all that whispering between her and my grandma in the garden away from everyone. And the fact that grandma always looked like someone had shoved a wedge of lemon in her mouth whenever she saw you.'

Haydon let out a low chuckle. 'She did that, but I'm not surprised, all things considered.'

'If she hadn't given the game away would you have told me?' Molly asked, directing a frank gaze at Ashley that made her want to squirm.

'I wanted to from the start but… the time never seemed right.'

'So you were going to tell me?'

'Of course I was.'

Ashley glanced away to find Haydon looking at her in the same way. Was he thinking that too? Was he wondering if she had ever planned to tell him? And if he was, did that mean he couldn't trust her now?

'It was just difficult,' Ashley continued. 'With everything else going on. I was always going to tell you both… And I would have talked to you afterwards, Ella,' she added, seeing that Ella's gaze had gone to the floor. It wasn't difficult to see that this was just another way in which

Ella felt left out, as if she was surplus to her dad's new life. 'To make sure you were OK with it.' She paused. 'Are you OK with it?'

Ella shrugged. 'I guess.' She looked at Molly, who smiled.

'I've got a sister. That's so weird.'

'I know,' Ella replied, a small smile of her own now breaking free.

Haydon was about to reply when his phone bleeped. He frowned as he read the message.

'Your mum,' he said, glancing up at Ella. 'I'd better phone her or she'll be on the next flight out here.'

As he got up Ashley opened her mouth to speak. She wanted to ask him if that was the end of their talk. She wanted to ask him whether he had words for her, what his thoughts were, what he wanted for them, because in the whole time they'd been discussing this with Molly and Ella he hadn't mentioned their relationship once. But her courage failed her again, and she let him go without a word.

In the end the party took over. Maurice came to fetch the girls to join in again and insisted that Ashley return to the celebrations rather than sitting alone waiting for Haydon to finish what might turn out to be a lengthy phone call. Aware that she'd already put a significant dent in any goodwill her hostess and the other guests might have had towards her by managing to pretty much single-handedly set off the chain of events that had almost ruined the party, she realised that the best thing she could do now was to go back to the celebration, explain and apologise.

It promised to be awkward but was far from it. The attitude of earlier as they'd all returned from searching for Molly and Bastien, the collective, unconscious decision not to judge, was still in evidence and it took Ashley by surprise. She'd expected some disapproval, some raised eyebrows or whispering behind hands, but every single person she spoke to had nothing but genuine pleasure at how things had turned out. It was a miracle, some said, and a marvel, others decided, that a father and daughter should be reunited after all these years when it had once looked so hopeless, and that Ashley and Haydon should rediscover their long-lost love. She wasn't quite sure about that last bit, but she smiled and gracefully accepted the good wishes and wondered where Haydon had got to every time she had a spare moment to check her watch. By now he'd been gone for over an hour and surely he couldn't still be talking to his ex-wife?

Frequently her gaze went to Ella and Molly, who seemed to be getting fussed over at every opportunity by any guest who could get their hands on them. After all the drama, they both seemed to be dealing with things well – even giggling together at times – and neither seemed too concerned that their dad was now missing instead. There was real hope that they would one day become as close as sisters who'd grown up together, of that Ashley was certain. At least it was one thing to feel positive about.

When she could stand it no more, she sent a quick text to him.

Are you OK? I'm worried.

Nothing. Not that she expected a lightning-fast response, but as she stared at the phone, willing him to reply, she couldn't help but be disappointed that he wasn't, perhaps, waiting for her to send him a message.

Seeking out her mum and finding her washing dishes with Nanette, the pair of them chatting and laughing as they did their best to keep Aunt Violette's house as orderly as possible, Ashley beckoned her over.

'Haydon hasn't come back yet,' she said quietly.

'He's gone out?' Sue asked, frowning.

'He went to phone Ella's mum.'

'But that was ages ago.'

'Exactly. I'm worried he's freaking out somewhere.'

Sue looked as if she was about to deliver some scathing comment, but then her features softened again.

'Shall I ask Maurice to do a little recce to see if he can find him? He's getting a lot of practice at that these days so he ought to be an expert,' she added with a wry smile.

Ashley shook her head. 'Just keep an eye on the girls for me? I'm going to have a walk around outside, see if I can find him. He's probably just gone somewhere for an hour by himself and that's fine – I know exactly how he feels – but I want to make sure he's OK.'

'Right.' Sue leaned forward and kissed her lightly on the cheek. 'Be careful, won't you?'

'I'm always careful these days,' Ashley said. 'But maybe that's part of the problem.'

As Ashley stepped off the veranda of Madame Dupont's house her phone pinged the arrival of a text message. She whipped it from her pocket, relief flooding through her as she saw that it was Haydon.

I'm OK, no need to worry. Just need time to think.
Where are you?
Not far out. I'm OK, don't worry.
Can we talk?
Not sure I'm up to it yet.
I think it's important that we do. We've discussed the girls but we haven't discussed us.

There was no reply. Ashley left it for a moment as she walked in the direction of his villa. The lights were out so she guessed that he wasn't there, but in the absence of any other good ideas, she was heading over to check anyway. As she walked she sent another text.

I'll only spend the whole evening looking for you and I won't stop until I find you and we talk this through so you might as well tell me where you are.

Another pause. She was about to tap out another message when his reply finally came through.

I'm at the beach. Our bit.
OK. Wait there, I'm on my way.

Ashley put away her phone, changed direction and picked up the pace.

∗

Twenty minutes later she found him. He was sitting on a rock at the edge of the sand, staring out to sea where the silver orb of the moon left trails of diamond dust scattered over the gentle waves. The shadow of a single boat bobbed on the horizon, strings of lights around the mast and boom reflecting onto the black ocean it danced upon, the faintest sounds of music from that direction echoing across the bay. Perhaps there was some sort of party going on aboard, but it was only the vaguest thought running through her head as he turned at the sound of her footsteps.

'Mind if I join you?' she asked.

'Would it make a difference if I said yes?'

Ashley baulked. She'd expected him to be confused and she'd been prepared for rejection, but she hadn't expected hostility.

'Sorry, I'll—'

'I'm sorry. I shouldn't have said that. Of course I don't mind.'

'You don't really mean that, though.'

'I don't know what I mean. I don't know if I even recognise my life any more, let alone how to say the right things to people.'

'But you handled it so well… back there with Molly and Ella…'

'That's my job, though, isn't it? I could hardly freak out. I'm their dad, and if they can't rely on me then who can they rely on?'

'But I thought…'

'That I was OK? So did I at first.'

Ashley perched next to him. The rocks were sharp and cold and she wriggled to get comfortable.

'Would you rather have never known?'

'Ignorance is bliss they say, which would be fine, but I can't go back to being ignorant now, so I can't say whether I'd rather not know because I do know. You know?'

'Yes.' Ashley followed his gaze out to sea with a small smile. 'I'm not expecting anything from you. That's not why I told you.'

'You might not be but the fact remains that I am morally obliged to offer… well, things. All sorts of stuff.'

'No you're not. Molly and me have got by just fine this far.'

'Which is the first and biggest injustice. You're hardly making me feel better about all this by saying that. I should have been there for her – for you.'

'It wasn't your fault.'

'It wasn't yours either.'

'True. We can't change that now; we can only go forward.'

'Which means?'

'You're doing it now. You're thinking about it and you recognise that you have new priorities, which is the only way you can start.'

'And then what?'

Ashley paused. 'I don't know. I suppose we'll just have to take it one day at a time.'

'But what am I supposed to do with all those days? What's expected of me? I can't be a part of Molly's life and Ella's life in the way I should because there's just no way I can split myself fairly. Who do I prioritise? Molly, who's owed so much lost time, or Ella, who will feel rejected and overlooked if she thinks I'm giving too much time to Molly?'

'I don't know the answer to that either. I suppose eventually things will just work.'

'And if there's… if there's us,' he said slowly. 'If *we* happen, if we end up living together… I don't know if Ella will be able to deal with that. She'll feel more pushed out than ever because it will mean that Molly has me there all the time and all she's got is the occasional weekend. Not even that when she moves to London with her mum and Kevin. I've been so scared of losing Ella and the irony is she might be losing me.'

'That's not your fault and she'll understand that.'

'But will she?'

Ashley wanted to ask if that meant there was still a chance for them, but as she framed the words his next sentence left them forgotten again.

'Janine's expecting.'

'What?'

He nodded. 'Ella already knew before we came on holiday but Janine had sworn her to secrecy until she'd worked out how to tell me herself. Poor Ella – it must have been so hard for her not to say anything. I can't believe Janine would do that to her. But it explains why the news about

Molly hit her so hard. She must feel like she's being pushed out in all directions – first a new baby for her mum and Kevin, and then Molly.'

'So when did you find out about Janine? Did Ella tell you?'

'No. She'd never do that if her mum had asked her not to. Janine just told me when I phoned her. She said seeing how we were sharing secret kids she ought to tell me. I think she was trying to have a pop at me, truth be told, but once it was out I think she regretted the way it happened. But it's out now so…'

'God. I don't know what to say.'

'It's been one hell of a night, that's for sure.'

'How do you feel about it?'

'Numb. My brain tells me I ought to be able to feel something but I can't seem to make sense of anything. Like there's so much to take in that it's all a big jumble and I can't focus on any of it.'

Instinctively, she reached to lay a hand on his. 'If you want to talk, I've got all the time in the world.'

He looked at her, the moonlight casting shadows on his face. There was pain in his eyes and she wished she could take it from him.

'I don't know that I want to talk,' he said. 'I've done so much talking already I'm sick of it.'

'What can I do to help then? Name it.'

He said nothing. Reaching across, he took her face in his hands and planted a soft kiss on her lips. Then another, and another, until they were kissing like they might never kiss again. He pulled her close, his scent and the smell of the ocean mingling, and as fireworks erupted from the boat out on the glittering sea, they fell to the sand together.

Chapter Twenty-Two

Ashley woke as the sun burned through the cotton curtains of her room. Prising her eyes open she took a moment to wake properly before a slow smile crept across her face. On the other bed beside her Molly still slept, exhausted from the party that hadn't broken up until the early hours. Ashley couldn't recall now exactly what time, but she could remember wondering how on earth the hundred-year-old Violette Dupont was managing to stay awake.

Haydon had been there, by her side, and hardly a moment passed when he wasn't touching her or reaching for her hand or sneaking a surreptitious kiss. When they'd made love on the beach it was like they'd both opened the gates to their hearts. From now there would be no secrets, no doubt, only a growing conviction that they were meant to be. They'd walked back up to Villa Marguerite hand in hand in silence, but they didn't need words. At the house nobody asked them where they'd been or why they'd taken so long to come back but there'd been plenty of knowing smiles. Even Molly and Ella knew better than to ask. It had been simultaneously the worst and the best night of Ashley's life and this morning as she woke she could barely believe any of it had actually happened.

Her phone bleeped a message and she rolled over to retrieve it from the bedside cabinet. It was from Haydon, and yes, it meant that the previous night had definitely happened.

Hey gorgeous. Are you awake?
Hey yourself. How are you feeling?
Like I need to see you. What time are you planning to leave today?

Ashley had been so happy when they returned to the house the previous night that she'd tried to forget the next day would see them parted as they returned to their own distant parts of England. It didn't seem fair that they'd only just found each other to lose one another so soon afterwards.

Maurice wants to have lunch and then set off. How about you?
We have to go earlier. Got to get the car back to the hire place and then catch our flight.
Bugger.
Last night was incredible. Not all of it, obviously. You know which bit I mean. I can't stop thinking about you.
Me too. You want me to come over to your place?
Now?
I'm awake and so are you. We might not get many opportunities to see each other in the next few months.
I'm getting dressed now. Come when you want but I can't guarantee that Ella will be asleep.
It's OK. I just want to see you.

It wasn't particularly early but the Dupont house was strangely silent compared to every other morning she'd spent there. It was no wonder when Ashley considered how late everyone had stayed up partying. She'd left the place looking as if someone had loaded food, crockery and cutlery into a giant party popper and set it off, and that was despite sporadic efforts to clean as they went along. If she'd ever wondered just how debauched a centenarian could be she had her answer now. But there was no time to worry about the mess, because she wanted to get to Haydon before the rest of the world woke and demanded her attention. Silently slipping from the house, she strode across to his, the morning shiny and bright and new.

He was waiting at the gates, taking her into his arms before they'd spoken even a word and kissing her with such fire it left her breathless.

'You smell amazing,' he said.

'It's called a shower.' Ashley raised her eyebrows and he laughed again.

'Come and sit on the veranda for a while.' He pulled her by the hand towards the house. 'You want a coffee?'

'I'm good. I don't want to let you out of my sight, even to make coffee.'

On the love seat overlooking gardens painted yellow by the climbing sun, he pulled her close and she nestled into him.

'I've been thinking,' he said. 'And I don't want you to say no this time because I'm Molly's dad so I get a say officially now.'

'OK.'

'I want to help her get into music school.'

'But we talked about the one where your friend worked and—'

'The one she wants. In York. I want to pay the fees.'

Ashley sat up to face him. 'But you can't! They're astronomical! And you have Ella to support already!'

'Did you think I wasn't going to offer financial support to Molly too now that I know?'

'That wasn't the reason I told you – we've managed fine for all these years.'

'I know it wasn't, but what kind of bastard would I be if I didn't? Besides, she has incredible talent and we mustn't let her waste that.'

'You really think so?'

'Of course I do! Don't you?'

'Well yes, but… I'm her mum, aren't I? We always think our kids are the best.'

'Let me tell you that even when I didn't know Molly was my daughter I was blown away seeing her play. She's fantastic, Ash, and she needs the best place to nurture that. So I was thinking… maybe you wouldn't mind so much if I came up to York to take a look around the school and help you get her enrolled?'

Ashley raked her teeth over her lip as she gazed at him. She was in no doubt that he meant every word of what he said and it would make all Molly's dreams come true. But it was a huge ask and she was so used to refusing help from others that it was hard to shake the notion that she ought to refuse it now. Stubborn, Sue had called her, and perhaps she had a point.

'You know it makes sense,' he said, seeming to read the conflict in her head.

'What about Ella?'

'When the time comes for Ella to choose I'll work something out with Janine for her, just like I'm doing with Molly now. Besides, Janine's got that loaded numpty of a boyfriend who's determined to move them to some luxury flat in London. If he's serious about being a part of her life as he keeps saying he is then he'll have no trouble sticking his hand in his very deep pockets too.'

Ashley couldn't help the giggle that escaped her. 'You don't like him much, do you?'

'I'm sure he's a decent bloke. But you know I'm very insecure and how am I supposed to compete with such perfect husband material? Sarcasm and derision are the only weapons I've got to fight back with and I have to keep some semblance of self-respect intact somehow.'

She leaned in and kissed him. 'You have absolutely no reason to feel second best. If it makes you feel any better, I'm glad he's so perfect because it means Janine won't be trying to get you back from me and I get to keep you forever and ever.'

He gave her a crooked smile. 'I don't suppose that would be *so* bad then. Maybe I could like him a bit better after all…'

Wrapping her in his arms, he pulled her in and kissed her again, long and lazy, the smell of him and the taste of his lips driving all other thoughts from her head.

Then a sound from behind had them leaping apart.

'Ella!' Ashley said, heat rushing to her cheeks. She suddenly felt like a teenager caught in her bedroom with the boy she'd snuck in. 'Good morning.'

Ella looked as if she couldn't decide whether to burst out laughing or vomit. She clearly felt as uncomfortable as Ashley for chancing upon her dad in what might have been the first flush of foreplay.

'Hi, Ashley.'

'Everything OK?' Haydon asked, straightening imaginary creases from his clothes.

'Can I use the last of the milk for my cornflakes? I mean, we're going home today anyway, so is it OK?'

'Of course. Go ahead and get your breakfast. Ashley and me will be in to sit with you shortly.'

'Is Molly coming over for breakfast?' Ella asked.

Haydon looked at Ashley. Any romantic assignation had already been scuppered so it seemed like a nice idea to get Molly over and have breakfast as a family. Hopefully it would be the first of many, and what a way to start the tradition as the sun rose over the beautiful Côte d'Azur.

'I'll go and wake her,' Ashley said. 'I think she'd love to come for breakfast.'

*

If he'd have said so to Ella, Haydon suspected that she would have felt like a replacement daughter had taken her spot. But the fact was, Haydon had somehow, over the past couple of days, made peace with the idea that Ella might move away with Janine and Kevin. He was sure that the new baby, while representing a big shock and upheaval for Ella, would settle them as a family even more. There was no getting away from the idea that Kevin was here to stay and that he was now as much a part of Ella's life as Haydon himself was, and as long as Kevin was a good stepdad then Haydon supposed he couldn't really ask for anything more. He'd still be sad about it sometimes, but the world had changed and Haydon knew now that he had to change with it.

And then there was Ashley and Molly. Whenever they came to mind he tried to temper the building excitement that his own happy ending was on the horizon. He'd learned in recent years that life often disappointed but he was quietly hopeful that this time what had become his normal expectation would be confounded. Ashley was special, and the fact that they already had a daughter together brought them closer in a way that other couples at this stage of a new relationship could never be. Whether that would turn out to be a good thing or not was impossible to say right now, but Haydon was optimistic and filled with determination that this time, with Ashley, he'd get it right.

Molly threw him a bright smile as she passed the coffee pot as they breakfasted out on the veranda of his villa, and hope swelled in his breast again.

'I'm so excited to get back home,' she said. 'Not that I won't miss being here with you,' she added quickly. 'But I want to get the application in for my music course.'

'If you need help with any of it just shout.' Haydon poured his second coffee of the morning. 'I've written one or two personal statements in my time so I might be able to give you some pointers. I mean, I'm sure you're capable of writing one but…'

'I'd love that,' Molly said, beaming. 'I may have passed the audition but I still want to get the application just right. This means so much to me and I can't tell you how happy I am that you're helping me to go.'

Haydon smiled warmly. But then his gaze flitted to Ella, who was quietly watching the exchange, and he gave her an encouraging smile too.

'Both of you – whatever you need, remember that you can come to me any time. It's what I'm here for and I want to give you both the best start in life that I possibly can.'

Ella's mouth briefly stretched into a smile of acknowledgement, but Haydon could sense that she was still troubled. He felt pretty sure that not all of it was down to the news that he had another daughter and that he'd have to talk to Janine about her emotional welfare when he got back. Ella had told him that she felt guilty about keeping Janine's pregnancy from him and she couldn't seem to get past that, no matter how many times he'd reassured her that she'd only done as her mother had asked and that he didn't blame her at all. As for Haydon himself, now that he was over the initial shock of Janine's pregnancy and moved on to a whole new level with Ashley, the idea didn't worry him all that much. Janine had a new life to live and so did he, and at least he had a good solid friendship with his ex-wife for them to support each other through the trials that their new lives apart would bring.

Ashley pushed her plate away and gave a contented sigh. The sun filtered through the branches of a vine heavy with deep green leaves and threw dappled shadows on her face. She was dressed simply in a white vest and jeans, her hair gathered in a loose plait, and yet he didn't think she'd ever looked lovelier. When he'd first spotted her in a crowded bar in Ibiza all those years ago the effect she'd had on him had been like a punch to the stomach. Something had clicked and he'd known, crazy as it would have sounded had he said it out loud, that she was the one. He hadn't been able to believe his luck when she'd accepted his offer of that first drink and he'd known without knowing that he'd been falling for her as soon as they'd started to chat. Now, it was like that first night all over again, except this time he was more certain than ever that they had a future – the one he'd been convinced of at the start. He'd had to wait a good deal longer than he'd ever imagined, and the road had been fraught with detours, but it had come at last.

Ashley stretched and glanced at her watch. She frowned.

'I didn't realise it was that late,' she said. 'We're not even packed to leave yet.'

'Do you absolutely have to pack?' Haydon asked. 'Can't you stay here and I'll help you throw your knickers into the boot of Maurice's car later?'

'No.' Ashley giggled. 'But I appreciate the offer. Anyway, don't you have a flight to catch too?'

'I can pack for us,' Molly put in. 'If you wanted to stay here with Haydon' – she blushed – '*Dad* for a while longer.'

'It's OK,' Haydon said. 'Your mum's right, Ella and I have packing of our own to do and a flight to catch.'

'Right,' Molly said. There was a brief pause. 'Can we see you next weekend?'

Haydon's smile would have split his face if it had got any wider. 'I'm sure we can figure something out if that's OK with your mum...'

'It's more than OK with me,' Ashley said. 'I can't believe you even have to ask.'

Haydon turned to Ella. 'What do you think? Reckon your mum will be OK with us going to York next weekend?'

'You want to take me?'

'Of course I do!'

'Only if you want to come,' Molly added. 'I could show you around if your dad doesn't mind me taking you out. There's some really cool shops.'

It was Ella's turn to smile broadly now. She turned to Haydon and he nodded.

'It's OK with me,' he said. 'As long as I get to drop you off in town and you keep me posted where you are I'm sure it'll be fine.'

'I'll ask Mum!' Ella squeaked, and she raced off to get her phone.

'We'd better go,' Ashley said, and he could hear the regret in her voice. It was the same regret settling over him now, but he forced a cheery tone.

'OK. We should be getting sorted now anyway.'

At the garden gates, Molly threw herself into his arms. 'See you next week,' she said.

'You bet,' he replied.

With a quick glance between her mum and dad, she gave a knowing smile and then began to walk ahead.

'Catch me up when you're ready, Mum.'

Ashley turned to Haydon and reached to kiss him.

'You've got my phone number?' he asked.

She nodded. 'You know I have; I've been texting you.'

'But I don't want to take any chances. So you've absolutely, definitely got my phone number this time?'

'Yes.' She smiled. 'I've got it, tattooed on my heart. How's that?'

'Will you be able to put it on speed dial from there?'

'You're funny.'

'Ella doesn't think so.'

'Well she's had more time to get bored of you. I'm looking forward to having enough time to get bored of you myself.'

'I think there's every chance of that happening. The girls will be nagging us to get together at every opportunity for a start.'

'So you need nagging to see me?'

'Of course not…' He pulled her close and kissed her. 'I need nagging to stay away. And even then I'm not listening…'

She smiled. 'You know that thing you said last night?'

'I said a lot of things last night.'

'When you said you loved me. Tell me now. Tell me you love me.'

He smiled down at her, his heart thudding. He'd never imagined he'd get to say it out loud, that he'd ever have the right to say it out loud to her, but here it was. And a more perfect moment, underneath the cornflower skies of Saint-Raphaël, he couldn't imagine.

'I love you,' he said.

'I love you too,' Ashley said. 'Tell me again.'

'I love you,' he repeated, dipping to kiss her.

Her smile was broad and content as they broke apart. 'I don't think I'll ever get sick of hearing that.'

'I've got a good few years to make up for so I'll be saying it a lot.' He frowned. 'Do you think Molly will forgive me? For not being around.'

'It wasn't your fault.'

'I know, but I kind of feel like it was.'

'You worry too much. She likes you. Especially now you're helping out with the music school.'

'Yeah, but she doesn't know me, not like a daughter should know her dad.'

'But she knows enough to see that you could be a good dad and you know what they say about better late than never.'

'I think they were probably talking about arriving at parties and things when they invented that saying.'

'I think they were talking about just this sort of situation. Yes, we've all lost a few years but what's past is past. The important thing now is where we go from here.'

'York?'

'No, silly!' Ashley prodded his chest and he grinned.

'So you think we can be a proper family?'

'I know we can. Just as soon as we can work out the actual logistics of it.'

'Where will we live?'

'I've no idea!' Ashley laughed. 'Talk about forward planning.'

'It's just going to kill me being apart from you all the time.'

'It's going to be hard for me to move south – for the next few years at least.'

'I know, and I wouldn't expect you to make that sacrifice anyway. You have so much up in York with your family and I would never ask you to leave that behind.'

'I would if I had to.'

'I know that. If anyone ought to move it's me, but… I can't leave Ella just yet to come north. Things may change when Janine has her baby and they move to London, but at the moment…'

She reached to kiss him. 'I wouldn't ask you to make that sacrifice either. There's no rush – for now we'll just visit tons until you work it out. I think you'd like York, though.'

'It sounds to me like you've already decided where we're going to live.'

'Just saying,' she replied, aiming a coquettish smile at him. 'It's cool.'

'If all the people there are like you and Molly then I believe that.'

'I can't speak for all of us, but there's a fair few. So for now I get to see you next week?'

'Whether you like it or not.'

She kissed him again. 'I can't wait,' she whispered.

*

She'd never been one for emotional goodbyes, but there had been tears as Ashley kissed a fond farewell to Violette Dupont and Nanette and the rest of the wonderful people she'd met that week. She'd miss waking up with the sun on the walls of her tiny guestroom at Villa Marguerite and having breakfast on the veranda where butterflies played kiss-chase and bees hummed a drowsy tune, lunch at whatever pavement café caught her eye and late suppers in the cool kitchen listening to Aunt Violette's stories, Maurice's translations broken up by his sporadic laughter.

As Maurice now started the engine and the little house with its pink walls and wildflower garden moved slowly away, she spared a moment to reflect that it hadn't all been idyllic plain sailing. But that was OK. If someone had told her to go through meeting Haydon again with all the anxiety and uncertainty that had brought, knowing what waited for her at the end of that rocky road, she still wouldn't hesitate, not for a single heartbeat. During what had simultaneously been the worst and best week of her life, the shape of her future, though still hazy, had changed beyond recognition. Molly's too, because Ashley trusted Haydon completely when he said that he'd do everything in his power to make Molly's dreams come true. Now that Ashley herself had a partner in her struggles to give Molly all that she deserved in life, she was sure that between them they could do just that.

As for Ella, Ashley was sure that having Molly in her life would eventually be a good thing, despite Ella's own uncertainty. In Molly she had a role model, someone to look up to, someone to turn to when life with Janine's new baby got too much, someone more her own age she'd be able to confide in. Haydon had been concerned about their relationship but Ashley didn't think he needed to be.

The countryside flashed by now and she settled back in her seat with a contented sigh. Glancing over to Molly, who sat next to her, Ashley could see that she was texting Ella already, despite the fact they'd only left them an hour before. It just added to her growing confidence in their future as a family. A year down the line, maybe even less, all that was new and strange now would be normal and comfortable and it was a lovely thought. Even lovelier was the idea that she and Haydon might be together, a proper couple living in the same house with their daughter. She smiled as her tummy did somersaults that were nothing to do with the bump in the road Maurice had just taken at speed. It didn't matter that she'd lost sixteen years with Haydon, because they had so much more to come – a future better and brighter for the years they'd had to wait – and she just knew it was going to be amazing.

A Letter From Tilly

Wow, I can't believe I've just released my eighth novel for Bookouture and my eleventh full-length novel overall! The last few years have been a whirlwind and I've loved sharing it with you! I really hope you've enjoyed reading *The Summer Getaway* as much as I enjoyed writing it. If you've loved Ashley and Haydon's story then I'd be hugely grateful if you could spread the word or leave a quick review. The more people who hear about it, the more we can share the love.

If you ever want to catch up with me on social media, you can find me on Twitter @TillyTenWriter or Facebook, but if you don't fancy that, you can sign up to my mailing list and get all the latest news that way. I promise never to hassle you about anything but my books. The link is below:

www.bookouture.com/tilly-tennant

So, thank you for reading my little book – as always I'm so grateful for your support. And please look out for my next book, *The Christmas Wish*, coming out around… well, Christmas!

Love Tilly x

@tillytennant

www.tillytennant.com

Acknowledgements

The list of people who have offered help and encouragement on my writing journey so far must be truly endless, and it would take a novel in itself to mention them all. However, my heartfelt gratitude goes out to each and every one of you, whose involvement, whether small or large, has been invaluable and appreciated more than I can say.

There are a few people that I must mention. Obviously, my family – the people who put up with my whining and self-doubt on a daily basis –are top of the list. My mum and dad, who brought me up to believe that anything is possible if you want it enough, no matter how crazy or unlikely it seems. My ex-colleagues at the Royal Stoke University Hospital, who let me lead a double life for far longer than is acceptable and have given me so many ideas for future books! The lecturers at Staffordshire University English and Creative Writing Department, who saw a talent worth nurturing in me and continue to support me still, long after they finished getting paid for it. They are not only tutors but friends as well. I have to thank the team at Bookouture for their continued support, patience, and amazing publishing flair, particularly Lydia Vassar-Smith, Kim Nash, Noelle Holten, Peta Nightingale, Lauren Finger and Jessie Botterill. Their belief, able assistance and encouragement means the world to me. I truly believe I have the best team an author could ask for.

My friend, Kath Hickton, always gets a mention for putting up with me since primary school. Louise Coquio also gets an honourable mention for getting me through university and suffering me ever since, likewise her lovely family. And thanks go to Storm Constantine for giving me my first break in publishing. I also have to thank Mel Sherratt and Holly Martin, fellow writers and amazing friends who have both been incredibly supportive over the years and have been my shoulders to cry on in the darker moments. Thanks to Tracy Bloom, Emma Davies, Jack Croxall, Renita D'Silva, Angie Marsons, Christie Barlow and Jaimie Admans: not only brilliant authors in their own right but hugely supportive of others. My Bookouture colleagues are all incredible, of course, unfailing and generous in their support of fellow authors – life would be a lot duller without the gang! I have to thank all the brilliant and dedicated book bloggers (there are so many of you, but you know who you are!) and readers, and anyone else who has championed my work, reviewed it, shared it, or simply told me that they liked it. Every one of those actions is priceless and you are all very special people. Some of you I am even proud to call friends now.

Printed in Great Britain
by Amazon

42806058R00185